The Heater and The Hack

The Heater and The Hack

Chronicles of the Dance
RcotD -:- Tome I

Leslie R Waggoner III

The Heater and The Hack

Chronicles of the Dance Series - RCotD -:- Tome I

First Edition

Published in 2025

Copyright © 2025 by Leslie R. Waggoner III

All rights reserved.

ISBN-13: 979-8-218-51463-1

Library of Congress Control Number: 2024919889

Publisher:

Leslie R. Waggoner III

Salina, Kansas, USA
https://www.leswaggoner.com

Cover Layout by Leslie R. Waggoner III

Illustrations by the incomparable Monika Zagrobelna - https://monikazagrobelna.com/

Printed in the United States

First Edition, May 2025

Foreword

This book is foundational.
It is not simply a story—it is the structure upon which the pantheon stands. A mythology begins here. A philosophy begins here. And if you miss that, you miss everything.

If you read to finish, you will finish. You may even enjoy it.
But you will not understand it.

If you read slowly to enjoy—**truly enjoy**—you will uncover a devastation rare in depth, and a kind of uplift you never saw coming. Not in plot, but in pattern. Not in word, but in meaning.

This is not—**simply**—entertainment. This is resonance.
There is no shame in simply enjoying the tale. But should you feel a thread pull tight—follow it.
And if you listen carefully, the Dance will speak.

In Balance, Brilliance.
Leslie R. Waggoner III

A sincere thank you to the following, for inspiring and encouraging:
M.C.Monasmith
D.Allen
M.Zagrobelna

The Heater and The Hack

Dedication

In Memory of Telk

Just as the sky reaches out to touch the horizon, your light has touched all that traveled within your circle of influence. The multitude of hearts and souls you have touched is uncountable. Your sacrifice remains a monumental example of the ability to galvanize and empower those around you.

—RCotD—

The Heater and The Hack

Prelude

As I set ink to parchment, within this tome I carve into the annals of existence the historic context of what has unfolded—a record, immutable and unyielding, for all to see and know. In dreams I am, as a bird upon the wing or a cloud adrift, an observer from heights unattainable, glimpsing that which defies perception, knowing that which yearns for clarity and resolution. Were it not for an extraordinary gift, these stories and these moments—these very words—would dissolve, forgotten in the ceaseless tide of time and the collective experiences that shape us all.

Though you may question the hand that writes, know this: it moves not by the will of its owner, but as the witness of truths beyond itself. It chronicles not its own perceptions, but only that which is—unyielding, unembellished. Bound by edicts that predate the stars, these stories—fleeting instants in time yet timeless in their gravity—are etched into my mind, each a gem whose facets I polish but cannot create, for I am without the power to turn carbon into diamond.

As I wander through the vignettes of existence, the unseen specter of my charge, a great weight presses upon me. An invisible phantom, when chronicling my charge, I am unable to set pen to parchment save for when the truth demands it. I scribe these truths, these visions, into permanence, preserving their essence within the boundless vault of eternity, and I offer them now as a gift of clarity— to deepen and lift the understanding of what has transpired.

These words hold only the basest truths—what was, what is, and what may yet be. They emerge from a struggle… a quest to discern the tangled threads of the journeys herein. In the waking times, I live as fully as I am able, but when I lay my mind to rest, I traverse the lives of those I am destined to follow, their moments entwined with mine yet held apart. In dreams, I am granted vistas beyond comprehension and am privy to knowledge unattainable—sights unseen and whispers too faint for the unaided errancy of mortal ears—each as vivid as the sun and thunderously distinct as the lightening woven amidst the darken clouds, yet still devoid of emotion or care.

The Heater and The Hack

The manuscript presented herein unfolds as greatness itself—its wings spread like a hawk soaring high, its tale unfurling like sails catching the winds of truth, propelling us across seas of wisdom and experience to lands uncharted. Upon the shores of the unforeseen lies the future of all, disembarking burdened by fears and regrets that should long since have passed into oblivion.

I ask only for your understanding and acceptance—that the words within are unbiased, genuine, and balanced only by the hopes, expectations, and dreams of the lives they recount. Within every glyph's curve and script's line drawn upon this parchment, I otherwise immortalize visions not meant to be seen, whispers of truths unspoken, and the enigmatic echoes of events that remain mysteries even to those who lived them.

The truth I offer must come untainted, discovered by oneself, and shared among kindred souls. It is not mine to keep—it is yours to take. Though I am only the alchemist's catalyst, stirring the pot in which change brews, the transformation belongs to the base substance itself, the reader

If you are willing, take this journey of words and truth. Partake as you would of a feast, consuming only what nourishes your spirit and fills your heart, for each of us gathers uniquely, harvesting what sustains us, and no other will taste what we each find in this banquet of discovery. This journey, if you allow it, will transform you, lifting you to soar like a bird and to drift as a cloud carried by the wind toward boundless potential.

The path before you, though inevitably your own fate, is forged by choice. Walk it with intention, for destiny bows to the direction of your heart.

—RCotD—

Prologue

Emanrasu leaned against the wall, his eyes skimming across the carnage wrought.

Bodies strewn about in odd angles, left where they fell amidst the chaos of the battle. The Bren, once milling about, stirred to life as Boldar's orders cut through the morning air.

The acrid, pungent bite of burning flesh lingered, thick in the air, oppressive as a weight pressing down on him, and the shards of light from the rising sun matched the starkness of the cold, crisp morning. The clanking of metal on metal and the creaking of leather against leather became a constant backdrop as the Bren gathered up the fallen brigands, bandits, and colorfully garbed warriors.

As planned, the bodies were stripped and separated from their weapons and the other equipment left strewn about in the aftermath—the equipment destined for the smiths and artisans for repurposing, the bodies for the wolves and carrion.

Emanrasu's sweat-drenched tunic invited the cold to come and lay against his skin. Shuddering from the chill, he drew a breath and, upon releasing it, steeled himself once more against the briskness of the morning. The exertion spent leading up to this moment, entwined with an emotional fatigue that tugged at him as if walking through a deep bog, left him exhausted and hollow.

As Tarlis turned and departed, Emanrasu searched for something to keep himself occupied. The buildings on the compound needed to be investigated and cataloged, but that was for another time. The weight of their victory settled over him—not as crushing as this morning's reality but profound in its own quiet gravity.

The little group, which had started this journey from Erzt, had, with the help of the White, successfully rallied the town, bolstering its spirits, providing hope, and giving them back their pride.

The Heater and The Hack

Looking across the courtyard, he gazed at Serrah, dressed in the bright yellow and red tunic and trousers she had decided upon for her battle dress. The relief at finding her unscathed was immeasurable, and he still felt the remnants of his fear sneaking around the corners of his mind.

The journey from Erzt had endeared her to him, and when he struggled with her possible loss, especially on the heels of Rezua's fall, it was almost more than he could bear.

With abilities that far exceeded her appearance back in Erzt, he grew more and more impressed with her as each day passed.

"Erzt..." The thought flitted, unfocused, shifting like sand.

"...the embarrassment in the bathing room seemed such a long time ago..." A smile crept across his face, which only grew broader as he recalled the stench of her disguise.

Closing his eyes, he imagined her standing next to him as girochih and shehchih danced in waves ahead of the breeze as the night deepened. Vowing to himself to reveal his feelings before this day was out, he scanned the courtyard and stepped over to a group of the Bren as they went about hefting bodies and equipment into carts.

Wandering around, he helped where he could, loading carts with the bodies of the brigands and bandits, along with the occasional body of the colorfully garbed warriors.

The crushing loss of Rezua bore down on him again, forcing his shoulders to sag. The vision returned—over and over, ceaseless. Again, the bolt struck—again, the giant scribe fell. The memory slammed into him, vivid and merciless. Grief twisted in his gut, sharp and unrelenting.

"Grappling with the large man's loss..." he thought as he gathered the weapons close by. "...will never pass."

Prologue

The safety of Serrah and the ultimate success against the occupants of the Zerocha Manor served to soften his grief but not his regret. Trading one for the other felt like an unwinnable choice.

The black buildings held an ominous and unnerving air as he let his sight scan across the courtyard.

The fighters from Bren, or simply the Bren, as Emanrasu came to think of them, were being directed by Boldar as they dispatched the foes still moving and gathered up the dead.

Emanrasu's first command and his guidance of Boldar as his second had turned out well—if success could be measured in survival rather than cost. Rezua's unexpected demise, Eirikr's loss, the blood that had seeped into the dirt beneath them—none of it felt like a price paid, only a debt incurred.

The trading of the town's safety for his friend's life settled like iron in his gut, too steep a cost, too bitter a choice. In the rush of battle, in the frantic press of strategy and instinct, the decision had been made before he even realized he was making it. But now, in the quiet that followed, its weight gnawed at him.

He had always counted the risk in terms of his own life and had imagined death in battle as a solitary fate—his, not theirs. That comfort had been stripped away. Would he have chosen differently if he had known? The answer lay just out of reach, refusing to solidify into anything he could accept.

The town stood. Rezua did not. Eirikr did not.

And in the end, he could not say if the trade had been worth it.

The incessant barking of dogs in the distance brought him from his depressing revelry, only now impressing itself upon his ears, only to be drowned by the gathering crows and other scavenging birds.

The Heater and The Hack

He peered across the courtyard opposite Boldar and spied Tarlis working with Darth and Olaf. Further and beyond them, Freydis and Catlina were intent on tasks Tarlis called out to them.

Serrah helped the Bren lift and pile the bodies into the cart, his eyes following her as the conversation ensued.

She stood up and stretched, and catching his eyes, she smiled broadly, reaching down to lift the next body.

As she reached down, a hand shot up from the prone body of a warrior. Grabbing a fistful of her tunic, the warrior dragged her close, plunging the dagger blade in and out of her chest and torso several times at an almost blinding speed.

For a breath, the world stopped.

Serrah—her body convulsing, blood spilling.

Then Emanrasu was running, the roar ripping from his throat.

SERRAH!

Thundering across the courtyard, he tore off the Heater and the Hack, flinging them to the ground as he ran to her. He barreled toward her, his gaze afixt as she seized the tunic of the multicolored warrior and pulled him close.

Her blade materialized swiftly in her hand, and she plunged it deep into the warrior's skull through the man's soft throat. She twisted the blade violently, and as the warrior shuddered and stopped moving, she slumped over, pulling the now motionless warrior atop her.

Tarlis, the first to reach her, grabbed the back of the multicolored tunic with one hand. In one motion, he lifted the warrior from Serrah, and the sound of cloth tearing ripped through the still silence that followed his roar.

Tarlis effortlessly threw the man's body more than four horse-lengths away, where it crumpled lifeless against the side of a building.

Prologue

Emanrasu reached Serrah, throwing himself to his knees and frantically working through her tunic to evaluate her wounds. Her hands clenched, one around her dagger, the other still clinging to the remnants of the multicolored cloth her hand had ripped from her attacker.

His heart seized.

Rezua. Now Serrah.

The weight of it crushed him—unbearable.

He struggled to staunch the bleeding as others arrived. The gathering of Bren townsfolk and fighters provided for whatever he asked. The silence of the gathering, to him, spoke volumes of their respect, not only for Emanrasu but for the magnitude of support shown to and provided by this remarkable woman over the last moons.

Knowing it was ultimately insufficient, he bound her wounds as best he could; tears filled his eyes, blurring his vision before a swipe of his forearm cleared them once more.

Tarlis placed a hand on Emanrasu's shoulder. As he knelt, his armor glinted in the sunlight, accompanied by the whisper of metal on metal as the scales rippled with each motion.

Serrah's gaze turned to Tarlis, and she managed a weak smile that disappeared into a bloody cough.

"You did well, girl," Tarlis said, his stoic figure belied by the quiver in his voice. Emanrasu knew Tarlis, too, had grown to love this young woman, gradually filling his heart as the daughter he once lost; she had become family.

She coughed, and the tepid spray of blood spattered Emanrasu's face, mixing with the warm tears he struggled to hold back.

"I should have told her!" Shouting in silent anger and desperation, his mind struggled.

The Heater and The Hack

Reaching down, he pulled her to him, lifting her to bind her untenable wounds. His hands and body were almost automatic in their actions as he looked up into the eyes of friends and acquaintances, then back down at the beautiful face of Serrah.

"I am sorry… I should have…"

"Don't…" she whispered as she struggled to form words.

Her raspy, gurgling breath tore at Emanrasu's heart, leaving him empty and filled with guilt and rage.

Shoving the guilt and rage deep into himself, he peered into her face. Her eyes focused on him, her face relaxed a bit, her fists clenched tightly by the pain that seemed to dominate her.

Serrah raised her arm weakly, her grip unrelenting as her fingers still clamped tight around the ragged piece of cloth. She gently coaxed him closer into a hug, the hug he had so desperately wanted before all of this. He held her close, her shallow breathing getting weaker by the moment. He could only say the one thing he had struggled not to say.

"I love you," came the whispered admission. "I don't know why, but from the moment we met in the inn—me, a wandering idiot with a silly quest, and you, working beneath your skills as a maid—since that very day, you have always been in my heart."

She coughed again, the warm spray spattering his face once more.

Her mouth opened, but the gurgling refused to form words.

As she struggled to focus on him, her eyes streamed tears steadily down her face. "I know," she mouthed. Her body relaxed, her eyes ceased to focus as the last breath seeped from her, and she grew still.

Her eyes, once glassy orbs of exquisite beauty, turned dull, now unmoving. Emanrasu stared, unable to look away from the fixed, unblinking gaze of the only love he had ever known. Regret tightened in his chest as he reached up, sliding his fingers over her eyelids, closing them for the last time. He held her body gently in his lap, cupping her head in his hands.

Shrugging off a hand that touched his shoulder, he buried his head into her shoulder, pressing his cheek to hers. Her last rasping breath crept out of her and finally stopped. First Rezua... now her... the pain continued to grow unattended.

People started moving away to leave him to grieve, each offering a light touch on his shoulder, back, or head in support as they did. The chill in the air, once brisk and refreshing, now crushed him, almost callously oppressive. As through a thick pane of frosted glass, his conscious acknowledgment of the people leaving was barely noticeable and without consequence.

"Rezua... and now Serrah..." thoughts swam in uncertain random circles. The exquisitely horrid reek of her transformation into the old hag was now a memory he struggled to hold onto.

He held her, waiting for the chill to take her as he struggled to understand the depths of grief. His wait fully encompassed him as the snow blankets every part of the field. Thick, soft, oppressive cold drained the warmth of his feelings away, leaving behind a cold, barren, lifeless mass of sorrow.

Holding her, his body provided continual contact, keeping her body warm. This kept his mind full of hope with the illusion that she, somehow, had not fallen and fed his hope unreasonably. His fingertips against her throat confirmed there was no pulse.

Leaning over, he kissed her forehead, then picked her up and gently slid her off his lap, back down onto the dirt that so eagerly lapped at her life's blood.

He brushed back a wisp of hair from her face and knelt beside her for a fleeting eternity.

A hand gripped his shoulder, and he looked up. Tarlis nodded as he gazed down at him, whispering, "It is time."

The Heater and The Hack

Emanrasu's heart sank.

Her life had ebbed away from him, much the way each wave of sparks and flames ebbed and flowed across the fire fields. Closing his eyes, his thoughts drifted to the fields of girochih and shehchih she had shown him and the spectacular waves of sparks.

Tarlis helped him to his feet. He shifted unsteadily under the weight of the loss of his friends, his thoughts buried in clouds of grief. He stood for a moment, a hand on Tarlis to steady himself.

Tarlis, after a time, took a deep breath.

"What...?" he whispered, dropping to his knee as he reached out to Serrah.

Her skin continued to redden, the color deepening with each heartbeat. Tarlis reached out—tentative, deliberate—and the instant his fingers brushed her shoulder, his fingertips sizzled and hissed. He snatched back his hand, tendrils of smoke trailing behind it.

"She's burning up," he muttered, half in disbelief, holding out his singed fingers. "Her body... I've never seen the like."

He stared at Emanrasu, jaw slack, eyes wide—sharp and glinting with questions that had no answer. For a breath, time hung suspended between them, held in place by Emanrasu's sorrow and dread.

"What in the Da—"

The explosion tore through the air.

The world convulsed. Emanrasu and Tarlis were hurled across the courtyard like discarded dolls. The earth rose to meet them—and everything went black.

The swirling images of the Dance rushed in and filled the void of his consciousness with the promise of answers but dissolved just as suddenly, returning him to the harsh, biting, crisp cold of the morning.

Prologue

The cosmic representation of balance to which he was tied provided no relief and served only to engender more resentment in his losses.

Emanrasu opened his eyes and struggled to his feet, taking in the scene and aftermath. The deep thundering boom had sent nearby horses into a frenzy—some rearing, others sprinting away as handlers scrambled to catch them.

The incomprehensible force provided nothing to which he could tie it, and the magnitude of it was similar to the full force of a horse's charge.

He briefly hesitated, filling his lungs with the crisp, cool air, clear but tinged with the acrid and pungent odors of burnt flesh wafting about them.

Moments ago, there had been hope. But now—now only he and Tarlis remained.

Of the small group who had departed from Erzt, seeking to protect Serrah from the abuses heaped upon her. Just the two…

The bonds that had formed during the journey, now tattered and torn, seemed to die in the wake of Rezua and Serrah's fall.

The Burden of Legacy: Chapter One

"A journey of discovery and legacy, fraught with danger, is always mitigated by the camaraderie of friendship."

—*RCotD*—

Peering intently down the street, the sun well overhead at apex, Emanrasu smiled as his overly large friend, Rezua, squatted behind Morthen's cart in what appeared to be a poor attempt to hide. Even at night, Rezua's towering height and broad frame would challenge subtlety; in midday sun, concealment was inconceivable. But Rezua had never been known for subtlety.

The street lay deserted, and to Emanrasu, it felt as though the quiet itself was scolding him for arriving too late for his father and leaving too early for the rites. The townsfolk remained occupied with rites hastily begun and nearly concluded without him. His father had joined the Dance the previous night, one final stumble that led into the bakery oven—which was an unfortunate but fittingly ignoble end for a reclusive man whose love of spirits sometimes outweighed reason.

Emanrasu had returned from Tothis with Rezua only to find the ceremonies already underway, proceeding indifferently without a son's presence. Standing amidst the mourners, both genuine and spurious, Emanrasu had kicked at the dirt as he stood awkwardly listening to the stories… his disappointment felt distant… and well… more detached than grief-stricken at the bitter estrangement confirmed by and continued in death.

And then… then there was Morthen, ever callously practical, clearing out the bakery even before the final rites had ended.

Emanrasu shook the thought off, shading his eyes against the glare as he approached his friend with growing levity shown externally only in the wrinkling in the corners of his eyes. "Hiding works better at night, my humongously-large concealment-challenged friend!"

The cart creaked and groaned amidst the aroma of dry grain and yeast that spilled from the open door of the empty bakery as the enormous young man strained to tip it by lifting one side.

Their eyes met, Rezua's gaze sparkling with a mischief Emanrasu knew well— the same look they had always shared when conspiring in mischief. Today, its poignancy, raised against the landlord, Morthen, reflected Emanrasu's own frustration with the miserly man.

Rezua hoisted the side of the cart ever higher, and as the creaking wood protested beneath his strength, his apparent halfhearted attempt at concealment was finally revealed for what it was.

The amusement in his imposing friend's grin contrasted sharply with his own low, hissing attempt to stop the towering scribe. It was concern in tone only— his hands moved to preserve the belongings, but his heart had long since discarded them, just as Morthen had discarded his father's.

"What are you doing?" Emanrasu asked in a low, hissing whisper.

He could hear the shifting items in the cart as they slid against its rough wooden floorboards.

Coaxed and encouraged by the large young man, the cart finally reached the apex of its path. It teetered as Emanrasu tugged and pulled on his best friend's tent-sized tunic.

Rezua let go of the cart and shrugged off Emanrasu's hand. With a quick nod in the direction of the road, Rezua snatched up the pack at his feet and made his way toward the edge of the village. His lumbering gait reflected a speed that was much faster than one would expect.

The Burden of Legacy: Chapter One

Emanrasu watched the cart as it teetered for a moment on two wheels. He reached out and gave it a gentle shove. As the tipping cart gathered momentum, Emanrasu spun and quickly followed his large, lumbering friend.

The crash of Morthen's cart, echoing with the clatter of scattered wares, brought a widening smirk to Emanrasu's face—justice, as only his best friend could deliver.

After attending his father's funerary rites, Emanrasu found the remnants of his father's belongings tossed carelessly into the street by the callous, uncaring landlord. His father's possessions had been piled up and left for any and all to rummage through.

The howl from Morthen signified his return to his cart and that he had found its contents tipped and strewn in the street, much as his father's things had been.

With his father gone, Emanrasu had planned to gather what few items he could and depart this depressing little village, and having found his legacy already tossed out in the muck and mire solidified his intent. The parting offer of solace from his lumbering mountain of a friend added direly needed levity to a day that had not offered much to smile about.

They ran for some time, well into half-set, before Emanrasu had to call out to the tree-trunk-legged man.

"Enough..." he huffed as he slowed to a walk. "...enough of this running... I doubt..." Emanrasu knelt down and leaned over to catch his breath. Taking a deep breath, he stood.

*   *   *

"I doubt he is following..." Emanrasu's grin brightened his face, "...though he just might have a clue as to the culprits! We are halfway to the setting of the sun, and I would rather save the energy for setting up camp."

The Heater and The Hack

Turning, Rezua walked backward for a bit, then halted. Reaching into his pack, he rummaged about and finally extracted a loosely bound collection of parchments. A second rummaging produced a quill and ink skin.

"Ink skin... ink well, ink bottle, but... ink skin?" Emanrasu shook his head as he mused silently, "Rezua is the only person I've ever known to write so much that he needed an ink skin with him."

Thus began Emanrasu's long journey across the lands to find a grandfather he had never met and to understand his own true destiny. The days and nights passed in relative quiet, each much the same as the last, trudging along, frequently in silence, with only the scratching of Rezua's quill on parchment. The two occasionally found themselves debating this or that, then settling back into a comfortable silence.

Once, they even broke into a wrestling match, though Emanrasu's comparatively diminutive size put him at a distinct disadvantage.

As Emanrasu, weary from days of travel, trudged along next to Rezua, he shifted the bulky, heavily laden pack from one shoulder to the other, then watched as Rezua followed suit, readjusting his own comparatively tiny pack.

The immensity of his grandfather's legacy, in the form of the shield and sword, weighed heavily on Emanrasu as they continued on the impromptu planned journey to his ancestral homeland, Rinewood Gulf. From what his father had told him, it was a small village near where his family originated.

As they walked, Emanrasu let his thoughts wander among the memories he and his steadfast friend had gathered since childhood.

Emanrasu let a slight, almost imperceptible smile sneak into his normally stoic and serious demeanor. "When we were small children..." His thoughts screeched to an abrupt halt before continuing.

"Well, when I was a small child..." Emanrasu grinned at his internal correction and the thought of anyone calling Rezua small. Ever!

The Burden of Legacy: Chapter One

When time allowed, the two could always be found together. "I wonder if we would still be friends had it not been that we were the only two our age in the village," Emanrasu mused.

It was a thought he dared not say aloud, as Rezua was a sensitive sort, belying his towering stature and stout girth.

Though Rezua stood head and shoulders above Emanrasu, and he himself, was half a head taller than most, the large man was timid and preferred not to get into altercations. As children in Rintha, the village in which they grew up, Emanrasu had seen Rezua hit a man in the chest. As they were only eleven and ten mains old, respectively, the feat was devastatingly effective.

The man had flown across the dusty wind-blown street and lay on the other side in the weed-filled ditch. Helplessly, he had watched his friend as the large boy alternated between a slack frowning visage and a tight-jawed scowl, his teeth ground as his hands clenched and unclenched in concert with his expressions. Rezua had paced back and forth, retreating as he frowned and advancing as he scowled.

The dank aroma of the road, heavy in the air, and Rezua, alternately cringing in guilt and fuming in anger, he could only say, "He shouldn't have said that about Mother; she was a good woman! May the Dance keep her!"

The impertinent man lived but took two full moons to recover from the devastating blow from the ten-main-old Rezua.

They entered the dense growth of Rosewood Forest and steadily advanced into the deepening shadows; each step measured and sure to carry them onward and away from the only home they had ever known. As they traveled the winding dirt road to the Gulf, Erzt would be their first of several stops.

The sunlight streamed through the canopy, casting patches of dancing light on the forest floor. The damp undergrowth exuded a moldy aroma of decaying plants as they walked.

The Heater and The Hack

As they continued deeper into the forest, Emanrasu could hear the scratching of Rezua's quill on his... journal... map... or whatever he wanted to call the homemade leather-bound pages he was constantly scribbling on. The natural quietness of the woods, a calm that soothes the soul, was only disturbed by Rezua's constant scribbling and the occasional animal that peeped or squeaked as it scurried away.

After a time, Rezua, having fallen behind, hurried to Emanrasu's side. He reached out and took hold of Emanrasu's shoulder, bringing them to a halt. The two stood along the side of the dirt path.

"Listen to this," Rezua grinned. He held his journal before him as he read the words he had scribbled there. "The sky, a bright blue that faded into purples, reds, and yellows, peeked through only in patches amidst the foliage while sunlight struggled to stream through the leaves of the canopy created by the forest. The unending glow of patchwork sunlight fell to the ground and lay there illuminating...

"Wait," he said and scribbled quickly in his journal, then continued, "...lay there silently illuminating the road; sparsely it lay, here and there, the bulk of the road hidden in a ragged cloak of blackest shade. The forlorn trees murmured quietly in the whispering wind as they stretched their boughs eagerly across the furrowed road. The dirt..."

Ahead of them and off to the side of the road, the swishing of leaf on leaf was followed by the sound of the deep rumble of a falling tree.

Rezua froze, then quickly flipped a page, mumbling as he scribbled. "As they... well-deserved respite... distance... ripping and crackling of... hmm... the creaking of... thunderous reverberation... ancient tree stood no more."

He cleared his throat. "As I was saying—

"The dirt, rutted and gouged unevenly, filled with gashes from the wheels of many a cart and wagon. The stark and stoic road, soft as freshly kneaded dough from the recent soft sprinkling of rain, had the musty earthen aroma of life that permeated the stillness of the wild wooded area. The wisps of wind, struggling to pass, were held at bay by the staunch blockade of trees guarding the passage of man."

He looked up, eyes bright. "What do you think, Eman? Pretty awesome, right?"

"Well," Emanrasu replied, "I suppose if that is how you see it, then you should write what you feel. I admire your ability to put things in a flowery manner, but try as I might, I can't. I enjoy your way of describing things; it's just not the way I see things."

A twig snapped somewhere off the road. The two paused and scanned the trees but saw nothing. They looked at each other, and Emanrasu shrugged.

Emanrasu glanced around.

"I'm pretty sure it was a deer," he thought. When no other sounds followed, he let his mind wander elsewhere.

As the two continued, Emanrasu noticed Rezua veering closer to the middle of the road. He reached out and gently guided him back to the side of the road. "The ruts could easily catch a boot and twist an ankle," Emanrasu told him. "Best to stick to the side of the road."

"Ah," said Rezua, and he paused slightly and scribbled something in his papers. "Hmm… wheel-plowed ruts scraped from the road and deposited…"

Rezua stopped walking and jotted down a couple more thoughts before his feet moved his large bulk again. He glanced at Emanrasu and smiled, then turned his focus back to the road.

Emanrasu watched him fall into step again, the journal tucked away for now. He seemed somehow lighter—more present—as though the path itself welcomed his attention.

He gazed at Rezua. "Was there ever a time when you didn't turn tales into legends? Even as a child, when we played fox and hound...

"I had to be the fox—because when I played the hound, I would just walk up behind you and tag you while you stood there, engrossed in some insect or plant."

Rezua's giant face stared back at him—slack, unblinking, and devoid of emotion.

Emanrasu continued, waving off the too-obvious attempt at ignorance. "You remember when I knocked you on the head while you were focused on that berry plant? You fell headlong into the briars."

Smiling, he chuckled. "I must have apologized a score of times before you stopped being mad at me."

Rezua grinned. "Yes, I recall it vividly!

"The berry patch silently lay in wait, whispering to the wind and swaying gently back and forth in anticipation. Eagerly, they scratched and clawed at the boy as he fell headlong into their naked talons, pulling him further in the more he struggled.

"That was a few days before I plowed that insolent ruffian mid of his chest, drove the wind out of him, and broke four of his ribs," Rezua frowned as he recalled. "I still have chills when I think about that! I thought I had killed him! I was so mad, but he had no right to say that about my mother; she was a kind and compassionate soul. May the Dance keep her safe and entertained."

"That was, what, nine mains ago?" inquired Rezua.

"Ten mains, almost eleven," came the reply, "I recall it well, as that was the year the Festival of the Dance was held up the road in Tothis."

Emanrasu mulled over the plans for his life, "Or rather, the lack of them," he mumbled as he walked.

The Burden of Legacy: Chapter One

"Twenty harvestmains, still unwed, with no real direction…" Emanrasu thought, kicking at leaves and dust. "With each passing main, I fear I'll grow old without adventure—just like my father."

"One thing is certain: I don't want to be a baker; they lead such dull and unimportant lives," he scrunched his nose, "and I am eager for more, something, anything more… even a traveling delivery man would be better than the monotonous life my father led."

*　　*　　*

The shield and sword, relics in the stories handed down to him by his father, had the weight of generations. This weight was now seated firmly on his shoulders as they continued their journey.

Until his father had gone to the Dance, he had never thought much of the storied relics—that is, until he found them discarded atop the pile of his father's belongings.

"Uh…" he thought as he trudged beside his towering friend. "Father's entire life tossed outside the lodging he had gotten from Morthen. Until then, I had never even seen these storied items up close."

Emanrasu's thoughts drifted as they walked, and he recalled his sadness at seeing them on top of the tattered remnants of his father's life. The time-encrusted shield and sword appeared to be in deplorable condition, which he imagined was due to his father's disregard for his past and ancestry.

Though his father told the stories of the shield and sword, he seemingly had shunned his ancestry and family for the sweet smell and warm comfort of baked goods.

"A fair baker," he thought, drawing a deep breath as they walked. "Not great, but fair… Safer than his former life, he'd said."

The Heater and The Hack

His father had chosen baking, ostensibly to escape the peril and bloodshed of their lineage—though perhaps more so to spite his grandfather. Thus, the burden of his father and Emanrasu's family lineage fell to him.

Rezua had immediately given them legendary status and come up with dozens of reasons for their poor state and half a dozen on how Emanrasu's father had acquired them. All the stories were fantastical and bigger than life.

"…fantastical and bigger than life…" Emanrasu mused quietly, "But father was neither…"

His introspection was broken by Rezua, stomping his feet heavily as his persona shifted suddenly into the Giant. Watching him now, Emanrasu realized the large man had perfected the role over the mains, an entertaining and somehow imposingly reassuring act.

Rezua stomped his feet as they continued forward, mimicking the aggressive behavior attributed to most huge men.

"So," roared the Giant.

"If you have never met them, why would you want to make the long, tedious trek across Aleon to the Gulf following beside the grand flow of the Algiotze? All that way to find a family who never visited you…? Just to introduce yourself? And next—I suppose we shall travel land and sea to the far side of Alaeon itself to see the other side of the world!" Rezua bellowed the questions in the rumbling voice he reserved for his monstrous and heroic alter ego.

"And if you do… decide to voyage to the far side—you can count me out… unless, of course—you ask me to go."

Rezua let go of his Giant persona, but not his line of questions. "We could have sold the shield and sword and lived grand lives for a few moons, maybe even a main, well… maybe not a main."

The Burden of Legacy: Chapter One

Suddenly halting, Emanrasu wheeled about and fixed his gaze on the wide uneven eyes of one intent only and exclusively on quick wealth and worth.

For long moments, the pair stood staring, locked, unblinking—until, eventually, they broke into a laughter that shook the birds from branch and bough, chirping loudly as they scattered aloft.

Not just laughter—a specific laughter, one that stitched their friendship together across the mains.

Returning to the road, Emanrasu gave it some thought.

"Curiosity, I guess," he said. "The shield and sword, it seems, must have some history. Not the history or stories—you—come up with, but Father was always telling tales, and I guess it would be nice to know if Grandfather was as great and as crazy as he said."

Their discussion wound deftly around the places and people they might meet, while the road to Rintha stretched ever longer behind them.

As the eve slowly descended upon them, Emanrasu reached out to the sun, aligning his fist with the horizon, placing one hand atop the other to judge the time.

"Barely a hand and a half until set," he told Rezua.

Rezua did the same—reached out his arm to the sun, aligned his fist with the horizon—and staunchly declared, "Well, sire, I see barely three knuckles until the rise is upon us," he teased, a smile sneaking stealthily onto his otherwise immobile face.

"Ah—and there it is… If I had melons for fists like yours, perhaps I'd judge a full day as four knuckles as well. But one of us here—my friend—has fists larger than the village average. So, with that in mind,—sire—, you may now cease your jest and start looking for a good place to bed for the night," he said, winking at his towering friend as they stepped in and out of the shadowy, underbrush-laden rows of trees, searching for a suitable clearing.

"Another night… and darkness fast approaching," Emanrasu realized.

The thought made him consider just how lengthy this journey would be. Fourteen days on the road and still two and a half—maybe three—days from Erzt. Rinewood Gulf might be two thousand tweflight, according to Rezua, and at best they were doing twenty a day.

He shrugged, stretching his shoulders, trying to shake loose the knotted pain of carrying the unfamiliar weight of pack and gear. Seeking a spot a fair distance from the road, they continued scouring the trees. Rezua appeared unaffected by the travels, seeming as spry as ever.

"Well," Emanrasu thought, "as spry as a man his size could be." He grinned wryly.

Rezua spied a small clearing and called out. The area was flat and open, with a large rock outcropping off to one side. The top of the rock was twice Rezua's height and barely wider than Emanrasu was tall.

The clearing and surrounding area had little wildlife, mirroring the lack of travelers on the road. Searching, they found a suitable spot near the rock and began making camp for the night.

Exhausted, Emanrasu let the pack slide from his back to the ground with an audible thump. The searing pain in his back forced a grunt from him as he muffled his cry of pain. Slowly, he knelt down, enduring the fiery pain in his legs and the stiff pangs in his back.

Rolling his neck, he felt it loosen the muscles. He looked up and surveyed the area, noticing that Rezua was not within view. "Ho!" Emanrasu called out. "Where did you go, my tiny little giant?"

The Burden of Legacy: Chapter One

"I be here, on the other side of the rock, engaged in the creation of a magnificent bed. Rearranging the castle and the not-insubstantial and varied items I have carted in. The accommodations are well suited to a knight such as I," Rezua let the words flow from his mouth.

"You should take up a musical instrument," Emanrasu yelled back, grinning, "You have a way with words as good as any bard or minstrel I have ever seen. Which, to tell the truth, is only two.

"Sire, we shall need a fire hot and ready," Emanrasu continued. "So in all your knighthood, do you think you can deem it not beneath you to start one?

"If you don't, then thrice I shall slap you on the belly while you rest!"

Rezua remarked in a humorous tone that reverberated throughout the little clearing.

"You, sire, by the grunts and groans of recent, have shown you are in resplendently little shape to be making such threats, and should you be of want, you can, to yon bushes, accompany and assist me in relieving my bladder and bowels to water and fertilize the lands. But should you be of a mind, you will need to up and make haste!"

"Well, go then; I shall attempt to off-load my own pack to match the great and fanciful abode that you have made," Emanrasu retorted.

Chuckling, Rezua winked, "You're getting better. We shall make you a wordsmith yet. Someday, perhaps, but certainly not today!"

Emanrasu heard the crumpling of leaves and twigs, indicating that Rezua was indeed off to the bush. Emanrasu stretched and succeeded in slightly loosening the muscle in his back.

"My back hurts from the journey almost as much as my brain does from trying to think up words to satisfy the big man's desire to mold me in his verbal image," thought Emanrasu.

The Heater and The Hack

The memory of the many times Rezua had accosted him with verbal sparring ran through his mind. From a young age, the mountain of a man had spun words like... like... well, like a weaver on a weaver's loom.

Emanrasu unpacked his bedroll, within which the sword had been wrapped securely, scabbard and all. He was anxious to learn more about this mysterious sword and the enigmatic shield his father had hidden away for so long.

"Had I been a heavy sleeper, I may never even know he had them."

Seeing as his father only brought them out in the still of the night, there must be something interesting about them! Emanrasu took hold of the hilt and drew the sword from the scabbard; the excitement as he did was fresh and seemed to renew him with thoughts of family and legacy. The pains and aches subsided as his focus on the ancient artifacts grew, along with the joy of what they might bring, or for that matter, what they might mean.

As he held the sword and examined it, Emanrasu felt a sense of unease. His stomach twisted with foreboding as he looked around intently. The surroundings, muffled in a blanket of silence, held no surprises but did not assuage his feelings.

"Rezua," he hissed, trying to garner his friend's attention. He waited, but no response came.

"Rezua!" He called, raising his voice but trying to keep the sound from carrying too far.

There was still no response. Concerned, Emanrasu started in the last direction he saw his friend go, "Rezua!" He yelled, now uncaring if he was heard.

Rezua's flowery retort came floating back, "I would, in some far-off future, hope that one could walk into the Dance's green woods for a modicum of privacy and have that modestly requested privacy respected."

Emanrasu slowly exhaled, letting his angst go in a long, drawn-out sigh, shaking his head.

The Burden of Legacy: Chapter One

Shrugging off his previous feelings of unease, he swung the sword to get the feel of it. It felt unwieldy and unbalanced in his hands.

"It seems to take its own direction," he grinned. "Someday, perhaps, I'll learn to wield a sword like this—maybe even a finer one—to…"

His brow unfurrowed slowly, his lips pulling upward from the depths of concern into a faint smile.

"Someday," he muttered softly, continuing his thoughts, "…a sword like this, to… save the weak, and um… punish the… um… strong?"

He reached down and spun the pack around to access the lashes on the shield. Loosening it from the pack, he slipped his hand through the straps and felt the heft of it. Holding the shield, he swung the sword, attacking an imaginary foe before him.

His poor skill betrayed his imagination, and as he flourished the blade, it meandered wildly, seemingly with a mind of its own.

These antics nearly cost him an ear, though he was able to jerk his head to the side at the last moment. Luckily, his ear remained intact as the blade flew by so close the rush of the air caused his heart to race.

"This poor, tarnished, unappreciated weapon seems awkward and useless," he thought. He continued swinging, albeit much slower now.

"Mostly useless… at least, useless in my inexperienced hands for sure," Emanrasu mused. He kept swinging and moving much like he had seen the performers do at a festival he had attended mains ago.

He slowed, then paused. A cold, icy feeling crept up his back, much like the climb up the face of a treacherous cliff. It climbed steadily until, finally, sitting at the base of his neck, he shuddered as if a frigid wind had swept up his spine, though the motionless air was still warm.

The Heater and The Hack

Upon scanning the camp and seeing nothing, he shook off the feeling of unease and focused his attention on the shield and sword.

*   *   *

He wasn't sure what the shield and sword truly meant—but knowing his grandfather had once wielded them gave the moment weight. A thread of connection, however thin.

"Your grandfather, Aeraun, was a towering, unbending, selfish man! He thought only of himself, his little band of men, and whatever random task they were on. He cared not about my rightful..." his father's tale had trailed off. His subsequent refusals to explain made Emanrasu think there was more to his story.

As he grew older, Emanrasu could sense his father's unfettered emotions rise to the surface on more than a few occasions, and this description might not hold the whole truth. Emanrasu painted a picture of his own towering and righteous grandfather, which he held onto as he grew.

Emanrasu felt excited, almost renewed and energized, as he held the shield and sword. Feeling as if he could take on the world, he imagined he could become the stoic, towering legend that his father had described his grandfather to be. "The Bleak, or Blek," Father had called him.

"Hmmm... doesn't seem like much of a name to strike terror into the hearts of one's enemies." He grinned at the absurd thought.

"It is not the words that you use, but the deeds behind them that make a name a legend," Emanrasu muttered under his breath.

The pain and weariness of the journey had all but been forgotten as he mused and played with his father's legacy. He slowly and methodically went through imagined motions and stances.

Guard, block, strike, guard, push.

The Burden of Legacy: Chapter One

The shield and sword felt wieldy, at least more than when he first picked them up. He continued swinging the sword and shifting the shield into various positions. As he worked with the shield and sword, they seemed less awkward in his hands.

He paused and studied the artifacts his father had left him. When he had retrieved them from the pile outside the bakery, they had appeared dull and tarnished, with an encrustation that defied his meager attempts to remove it.

Now they seemed a bit less drab and dreary—but perhaps his appreciation was changing his perspective... and at least he felt they held promise.

"I should find someone to clean them properly," he mumbled.

The crunching of leaves and snapping of twigs announced the return of Rezua. Emanrasu raised his head and spied his large friend as he stepped into the clearing.

His large friend froze, and his enormous eyes opened wide as Emanrasu heard the twig crack—not from Rezua—but from behind him.

His shield extended wildly as he abruptly whirled about, throwing his shield arm out. Amid the swirl of rainbow-hued confusion from the attacker's garments, the axe glanced off the shield's edge, narrowly missing Emanrasu's ear.

As he spun uncontrolled, his wildly swinging shield slammed edge-first into the wrist of the attacker's knife hand, which followed behind the axe blow. The dagger flew to the ground and clattered across the rocks as the attacker's hand drooped in response to the shield strike.

Without a moment to contemplate, he frantically jerked his arm, and the shield again landed in the path of the axe, changing its direction, but not enough to save the layer of skin it shaved from Emanrasu's arm.

He whipped around to run, but his body, laden with the unfamiliar weight of the shield and sword, felt cumbersome. Twisting a bit too far, he lost his balance and landed on one knee as the backswing of the axe once again whistled past, tugging at the bits of hair trailing his spiraling twist.

His knee slammed into the rocky ground just as the axe tore past, and the jolt wrenched the sword from his grip—flinging it wide as his body twisted out of control.

He barely kept from falling by slamming the shield's edge into the earth to steady himself. The long arc of his sword continued unabated past the attacker, as it cut a wide swath and kept traveling as his body twisted.

His glance flitted to the axeman's face—his expression melting from a snarling grin to wide-eyed disbelief.

Emanrasu froze, caught in the strange stillness that lives between action and understanding. The man halted mid-stride and dropped his axe. Only then did the truth land: he was trying in vain to press his insides back in.

A river of viscera spilled through the gash in his midsection.

As the scene unfolded, Emanrasu's senses cracked open. The sun had dipped beneath the trees, its final rays retreating into the dark. The forest, suddenly ancient, filled with the damp weight of moss and peat. Somewhere distant, an owl hooted—a hollow, bone-deep sound that seemed to echo off the unseen.

Leaves crunched behind him. A heavy weight landed on his shoulder. He couldn't turn, couldn't raise the shield. His body hadn't caught up to his thoughts.

Then—relief. Rezua's massive hand closed around his shoulder, steadying him.

Before him, the axeman stared down, eyes fixed on the ruin that bisected his belly. He dropped to his knees, blood streaming between trembling fingers. The strength drained from him visibly, like water from a broken barrel, until he slumped into a still, slack pile of what could have been.

The illusion of glory shattered.

The Burden of Legacy: Chapter One

"Not the outcome one imagines," Emanrasu thought, swallowing hard, the taste of breakfast rising unwelcome in his throat.

As he gazed down at the now lifeless body, his sight blurred, his face flushed, and his head pounded rhythmically with the realization of how close he had come to being at the end of his journey instead of the start. He glanced at Rezua and slumped to his knees as the gravity of the attack set in.

Emanrasu took a deep breath and settled himself. Scanning their little camp with renewed vigor and awareness that comes in the aftermath of all heart-pulsing events, he braced himself.

"Be wary," he whispered softly to Rezua. His large friend produced a rock almost as large as Emanrasu's head and stood at the ready.

Emanrasu and Rezua slowly crept to the edge of their little glade and followed it around, the darkening sky swallowing any hope they had to see; they paused every few steps and listened intently.

As they made their round in silence, Emanrasu heard the chirps and skittering of small creatures slowly returning; he realized that the silence earlier might have been due to the attacker's presence.

Though they discovered nothing to indicate other intruders, they found a pack off in the direction from whence the man had come. This they brought back to the rock to investigate further.

"We probably should make a fire," Rezua whispered.

"Make it quick, my large friend. A fire will at least keep away some of the beasts. And while you do that, I will drag the man far enough away that the smell of death will not draw unwanted guests."

With a nod, Rezua went to his pack and rummaged through it.

The Heater and The Hack

Sheathing his sword, Emanrasu decided keeping the shield strapped on would be wise. He turned to the task of disposing of the attacker's body, but as he began, he realized that the man was in no shape to easily be transported alone.

Stripping the gloves from the dead man's hands, Emanrasu laid out the cloak and carefully dragged the body onto it, attempting to minimize further gore. He quickly packed blood-soaked leaves around the corpse and tightly wrapped the cloak, securing it with firm knots. Emanrasu hoped this would hold him together until they could, at least, move him away from the camp.

A quick search produced a handful of hidden knives, daggers, and other nasty-looking items, as well as some various coins, unidentifiable in the failing light.

"Eman," Rezua said softly. "I can't find my shehchih. I have plenty of girochih, but…"

"Yes, I have some."

Emanrasu promptly rummaged through his pack and produced two pouches, a mortar and pestle. Handing them to Rezua, the big man returned his partial kit to his pack and poured a small portion of shehchih plant from one pouch and then a matching portion of girochih from the other. As the two plants touched, their oils caused them to lightly sparkle.

Emanrasu helped gather the rest of the wood for the fire as Rezua stripped down bits of bark to use as tinder. Once the fire was laid, Rezua used the pestle to crush the plants together. The small blue flame that resulted burned bright, and the heat from it was only tempered by the unique design and makeup of the small mortars.

"Who in all the land would figure out you could make a little bowl that could contain the heat of the little blue flame, Eman? Tell me, who?"

Dumping the burning plants into the tinder, the fire spread quickly.

Within moments, the fire was lighting up the glen, pushing back the shadows all the way to the edge.

The Burden of Legacy: Chapter One

"I will need to have your help moving him. The gash is wanting to allow everything inside to spill out."

Rezua returned the chih and fire kit to Emanrasu, who then tossed it into his pack.

"Most likely a thief or bandit," Emanrasu said as he peered down on the lifeless body.

"Yes, he was from the south, out of the mountains, I think. The bear tattoo on his neck and the wolf one on his hand are from a large band down that direction. At least that is what I was told by someone coming up from Elund."

"I just hope he was alone," Emanrasu said, pointing at the lashing across the man's torso, "I bound him up a bit, and I am hoping it is enough to get him far enough away. You grab his legs, and I will grab him under his arms. This should kind of fold him and help keep things together."

A quick prayer to the Dragon, the Phoenix, and the Dance settled the two men somewhat.

Together, the pair carried the bandit out of the glade and at least far enough away to discourage animals that might be interested in the unattended meat from making their way into camp. On the way out, the bindings on the cape failed, and the man spilled out. While Rezua stepped away to retch, Emanrasu re-secured the body, tying the bindings tighter than before.

Rezua had to step away once more, claiming, "It's the utterly repugnant mix of acrid odors and pungency filling the air with a ghostly presence that continues to twist my insides."

They placed the body on the edge of a ravine, and as a parting gift, Emanrasu placed a boot on the body and shoved him over. Though they could not see it through the fading light and thick vegetation, they heard the body as it rolled and thumped into various things until it was silent.

The Heater and The Hack

Retracing their steps, the two men focused on their surroundings. Detecting nothing, they relaxed.

The only thing that broke the natural silence was Rezua's constant mumbling to himself, "…a swift swing of the blade… slid down…"

Emanrasu shook his head in the darkness and grinned. "I feel he's going to have fun with this one," he thought.

Once back at their little camp, they took one last circuit around the glen. Finding nothing amiss, they returned to their bedrolls.

Emanrasu unstrapped the sword and set it within reach. Kneeling, he felt the weight of the day settle over him, exhaustion pressing deep into his bones. He removed the shield and propped it against the rock face, letting out a slow breath as fatigue finally washed over him.

For a time, he simply sat, his body weary, his mind emptied of thought save for one: the blind luck that had carried him through this night.

Nearby, Rezua shifted, dragging his bedroll closer to where Emanrasu sat. By the fading light, he scribbled notes in his book, scratching out the last of the day's record before darkness made further writing impossible.

The world felt unrelenting and dangerous as the final usable light slipped beneath the horizon, leaving all bleak and still. Emanrasu reached out and laid his hand upon the shield and sword, his fingers tracing their contours. There was an odd comfort in their proximity. And with it, he drifted off to sleep.

The misty dream of cosmic powers flowed round and round within him as he slept, in a dance of unimaginable proportions, encompassing the beginning and the end of all, engulfing him in the eternity of life.

Hurried Preparedness: Chapter Two

"One's worth is not measured in possessions or abilities; rather, it is measured in friendship and resourcefulness; as you journey through life, never lose yourself in deference to an imagined ideal."

—RCotD—

As Emanrasu woke, his hand still on the shield, he felt invigorated to live another day, especially after the excitement of the previous eve. With the first light of the rise, he stretched and glanced around. His eyes settled on the tiny giant, Rezua, who was already up and had built a radiant fire to warm them from the night's chill.

Thick billows of smoke drifted from the fire, hanging heavy in the cool forest air. The aroma of the damp, leaf-laden forest floor, subtly masked by the thick smokiness of the fire, left a chill mix of forest and burnt wood.

Producing a small package of rations from his pack, Emanrasu reviewed it and mentally calculated what remained. "Enough for about three or four more days of travel," he said to Rezua.

"I hope it will get us there," said the wonderfully eloquent mountain-with-boots.

He divided out the morning meal. It was not much, but it would sustain them until they were able to gain work in Erzt.

"Hey, Rez, have you seen that pouch the bandit was carrying?" Emanrasu asked as he dug through his belongings.

"Ah... here it is," he said, pulling it free.

He emptied its contents onto his bedroll and spread them: twelve copper, six silver, and a gold coin. A pendant was also present, which Emanrasu picked up and inspected.

The Heater and The Hack

Its delicate intricacies belied sturdy craftsmanship; unexpectedly heavy, its polished oak gleamed smooth, stained faintly in blue and green. Carved symbols of gold adorned its surface in each corner: a sun blazing opposite a fiery phoenix above, mirrored below by a delicately scaled dragon across from an exquisite tree of life.

The etchings and metalwork were subtly reminiscent of the Dance. Each corner symbolized the elements of the Dance as they embraced the green and blue tinted fields.

The piece was a marvel to behold, and as Emanrasu turned it over, he found a small but simple engraving of a shield and sword in its center. Around them, ten groupings of symbols formed a pattern.

"I wonder what the inscription means… have you seen this before?" he asked Rezua.

Rezua peeked over Emanrasu's shoulder. "Zubava bana zufova pensam. Something about writing in the past and understanding in the future, I think…" he mused. "Looks like a better version of the talisman Aiesa had."

"Aiesa?" Emanrasu questioned. "Who?"

"You know, the village elder, Aiesa. He had one like this, but… do you mind if I look at it?" Rezua asked, reaching out his hand.

Confused, Emanrasu gave the pendant to Rezua, who inspected it and turned it over and over. "Yes, it is similar, though much more intricate and, I dare say, more expensive. Aiesa said his pendant was a talisman of luck, so I suspect this one is as well. Though I am certainly no expert!"

"Aiesa… Aiesa… Oh, Aiesa? Aiesa went to the Dance, what… almost fourteen mains ago. Leave it to you to remember a pendant you saw once when you were six or seven mains old—or even only two or three mains! Your memory still astounds me," Emanrasu said, shaking his head at Rezua's uncanny recollection.

Rezua grinned as he held out the pendant for Emanrasu to take.

"Keep it," Emanrasu told him. "At least until we can determine its worth. I imagine it would fetch at least a couple of gold coins—but then again, I'm certainly no expert either!" He chuckled.

They both chuckled at their less-than-expert evaluations and vowed to have someone in Erzt examine the pendant—if someone with sufficient skill and knowledge was available.

Emanrasu repacked the pouch as Rezua attempted to hang the pendant around his thick, muscular neck. He struggled for a bit, then, after adding an additional length to the string, got it over his head. As a finishing touch, he reached up with his large, meaty hand and, engulfing the pendant, tucked it into his tunic.

As rise broke and the soft glow of light parted the leaves, pushing at the shadows, Emanrasu and Rezua sat and placed the bandit's pack between them.

The contents provided a storied history of the dead man's life—things he felt compelled to carry with him. A history of secrecy hid within the creases and crevices of the worn pack. Tucks within plackets hidden in pockets—crannies so deeply hidden—hinted at a mind both devious and untrusting.

"A pack this complex might suggest hidden treasures within," Emanrasu thought as they sifted through the progressively smaller compartments.

"Pay close attention to any odd lumps and shapes, or hardened areas that seem more reinforced than normal. I have a feeling this man carried more than he was willing to entrust to normal pockets," Emanrasu suggested to his small-dragon-sized friend.

Rezua nodded in agreement, his fingers playing on the pendant. "If I were writing the story for him, I would check for a false bottom," he divulged.

"Ah... devious—and most would never check beyond what's tucked in the myriad pockets," Emanrasu said as he glanced sidelong at his childhood friend with new respect.

"Your storytelling—your colorfully detailed way of describing things—might have finally found a practical use in the real world! Not to mention it shows how ingenious you can be... when you're of a mind," he added with a teasing grin.

"I would never have guessed," he murmured, shaking his head. "I suppose that— even between us, after all these mains—surprise is still a possibility."

Emanrasu started digging through the pack, each pocket a trove of small, curious treasures. As Rezua would say: a veritable life's work in a single complex, compartmented bag.

Emanrasu smiled at the thought but said nothing.

First out were the food items—easily found and retrieved—suggesting the man was built to move fast and travel light—something deeper, more deliberate, than a mere bandit. The amount of dried meat, nuts, and grains they pulled from the pack was astonishing.

"A week's worth of rations—enough for three days, maybe four if we stretched it," he said, looking up at Rezua, who froze mid-chew and hastily hid his hand. Rezua winked, grinned, and resumed munching.

"I guess that makes it three days then."

Emanrasu shook his head with a grin and returned to digging in the pack.

"What is this... a hook?"

Emanrasu splayed the hook open and latched it, felt its heft and practicality, then unlatched it and folded it back up.

The hook folded cleanly with a faint metallic click.

Hurried Preparedness: Chapter Two

The scrollwork that flowed on every surface—engraved, and in places inlaid with gold—too finely made for a bandit's tool. The lines curled with purpose, possibly a blessing or prayer. It felt mythic for something so mundane.

He ran his fingers over the markings, waiting for meaning to emerge.

Just a hook, he thought. Probably.

He set the hook aside, along with the length of rope attached to it.

Reaching back into the pack, he pulled out a worn leather-bound case with little strips of steel and wire. "Probably lockpicks," Rezua offered as he happily chewed away.

Emanrasu glanced up at him, impressed, then resumed his quest through the bag. Slowly, they pulled out dozens of items: herbs and spices—some of which Rezua quietly noted might be poisonous—two sets of rainbow garb, a waterskin, a bladder of wine, and six daggers in total: four for throwing, two for fighting.

They dug deeper and discovered a black wig, then another, this one dark brown. "The man had yellow hair, so maybe these are for disguises? Oh, and here... here are various jars and bottles of makeup. I guess disguises are the most likely suspect for those," he grinned.

Rezua took one of the wigs and fitted it upon his head. He stood and curtsied in an imaginary dress. Emanrasu forced the grin from his face.

"Please, never do that again," he pleaded softly.

They both laughed as Rezua tossed the wig back to Emanrasu.

"Unless that is, you want to be like the smithy back home, who snuck out on an occasional night to make himself up as a woman, in full dress and makeup, no less."

The large man cowered and stared in mock horror.

The Heater and The Hack

"Oh, dear! I forgot all about that! And I heard that Aiesa actually took him home one night. Oh, to be a mouse in the corner for that surprise!" Rezua laughed.

He continued, pulling out some parchment, several quills, and a metal bottle containing a black liquid—presumably, ink.

Lastly, they removed a flint and steel, along with several candles.

"Is that really flint and steel?" asked Rezua, his jaw hanging open. "That would be great to have if we run out of chih!"

Emanrasu regarded him with uncertainty. "What is a flint and steel?" he asked.

Rezua reached out and gathered them up, holding one in each hand, he struck the steel with the flint.

Nothing happened.

Rezua tried several times in various ways until he could, at last, produce a spark. A couple of tries later, he was getting a consistent and usable spark each time.

"Interesting. Chih is easier," Emanrasu commented as he picked up the bag.

Emanrasu took the bag and shook it a bit. "Can you hear that, Rezua?" he asked. And as he shook it again, the distinct clink of "coin on coin" was heard.

Meticulously, the two friends started going through the pack again and found two secret compartments. The first carried loose coins and a cloth that wrapped up various pieces of jewelry. The second was a manuscript or journal of sorts. "It appears to be gibberish," Emanrasu said, handing it to Rezua.

Rezua flipped through the pages. "Alongside the other items, a book of gibberish would be out of place. Coupled with the fact that it was in a hidden compartment, it might suggest it is not just gibberish but might be written in some code."

Rezua stuffed the book in his own pack to puzzle over later.

*   *   *

Hurried Preparedness: Chapter Two

Emanrasu refilled the pack with most of the items, retaining the coins for himself and handing the jewelry to Rezua. "While you are out checking for libraries or schools of learning, see if you can get these appraised and maybe even sold," Emanrasu said to Rezua. "If any are recognized, just relate the story, without embellishment, mind you, and let them have the items. We do not want to cause a scene that we may not be able to extract ourselves from."

Emanrasu counted the coins: ten silver and fifteen gold coins. "We shall be able to travel somewhat comfortably with this," Emanrasu thought.

He separated out five copper, two silver, and three gold coins and deposited them in his own pouch, then filled the brigand's coin pouch with the rest and placed it carefully at the bottom of his pack.

Rezua, having already packed, was scribbling in his own book. Occasionally, he raised his head and scanned the camp, then returned to writing as Emanrasu began gathering and stowing gear in his own pack, burying the coin pouch under the rest of his belongings.

As he rolled up the sword in his bedroll, he paused. "We might be safer if I keep the sword handy," Emanrasu said.

"I think we would be safer if they were not tied down or buried inside my bedroll," he told Rezua.

"Mmmm... hmmm..." came the absent-minded response.

"I shot a rabbit with my fishing pole, and then he turned into a bear. Thanks for helping me get away," Emanrasu said with a smirk.

"Mmm... hmm... uh... What was that?" asked Rezua, not really paying attention.

"I said... uh... never mind..." Emanrasu replied, shaking his head.

The Heater and The Hack

He finished packing, then turned his attention to the sword. He struggled to fasten the scabbard around his waist. Several strings hung from the scabbard, but he had no idea what they were for.

Ultimately, he tied the strings to the back of his belt despite the thought they might possibly attach to his leg.

Once the scabbard was in place, he fumbled awkwardly with the sword. He struggled to align the blade's tip with the scabbard's opening, the proper angle elusive. Finally, after more than a few tries, the tip found the slit, and as the blade entered, it seemed almost to pull itself inward until it was fully inserted. Snugly nestled, it remained immobile and silent.

Emanrasu straightened, turning first sharply, then more slowly, getting a feel for how the weapon rested against him.

The scabbard flopped awkwardly, at least more than he felt it should; its movements seemed unpredictable to him. It swung more freely than expected, shifting wildly with each motion. His abrupt pivots felt the delayed weight tug at him before it settled back against him.

He untied the tethers from the back of his belt and secured them around his leg instead, knotting them tightly to keep the scabbard in place. Cautiously, he shifted through several movements—side steps, short lunges, and a half-turn—to see how it responded. The difference was pronounced.

Though the scabbard still had some give, it was not erratically swinging as it had before.

Satisfied, he grabbed the hilt and attempted to draw the blade; feeling the resistance as he tugged, the scabbard shifted. The process felt awkward and unwieldy. His jaw clenched and brow furrowed as he tried again, still lacking the fluidity he expected.

Emanrasu paused, forced his body to relax, and took a deep cleansing breath; this time, changing tactics, he adjusted his grip, grasping the scabbard itself to hold it steady as he pulled the blade free. The draw, though not effortless, was cleaner and workable.

"Not as simple as I had hoped, but this should do for now," Emanrasu thought until he realized he would have to unsheathe with a shield on his arm. "Rise!"

Grabbing the shield, he slid it over his arm and tightened the straps. He practiced drawing the blade several times until he was satisfied with his ability, though his attempt to draw quickly was rewarded with an awkward fall.

"If you stick to fending off old men and women, you might be quick enough," Rezua said, chuckling as he returned to scribbling in his journal. Despite feeling that he was still awkward and a bit inept, he felt more confident while wearing them, which, in turn, seemed to energize him.

"Hey, tiny!" Emanrasu called over to Rezua. "Get up and get your pack on; we are ready to travel. Oh, and you also get to carry the brigand's pack."

Emanrasu smiled at slipping that last part in, though he was surprised when there was no resistance. Rezua just shrugged his acceptance and finished getting ready.

Emanrasu set the shield down and, with a practiced hand, deftly slung his burden to his back, promptly tightening and adjusting the pack. He smiled and thought, "Now, that is the speed I need while donning the shield and sword. I just need to use smooth, measured movements and understand where each strap goes and how it gets there."

While practicing, he noticed that both the shield and sword had been nicked during the fight. The marks had chipped away at the timeless incrustations that had built up.

Here and there, the sword's surface caught the light where patches of the encrusted layer had flaked away. The shield, too, showed faint streaks of green and blue where it had been scraped clean.

The Heater and The Hack

"The hands of scrubbing and scraping," he recalled. "Many hands over many mains, my father had struggled to clean them."

"I suppose hammering away at them—metal clashing against metal—in the dead of night while his son was meant to be asleep," he mused with a grin, "wasn't exactly the best time to test armor."

Though he had never seen the shield and sword up close, not in the way that mattered, he had watched his father toil over them almost nightly—scouring, tending, shaping. The ritual had been relentless, unwavering, carried out with a fervor that now seemed almost presumptuous.

"Rise… the man obsessed over them. Who am I kidding?"

Yet, for all his father's attentiveness, he had never spoken of them—not in sooth. Whenever Emanrasu had asked about them, the answers had always been curt, dismissive, as if their significance amounted to nothing more than decorative things. His constant care was simply to keep the metal intact, fending off rust, and ensuring the weight of time did not settle too heavily upon them.

"I would have been happy to help," Emanrasu thought. The weight of that realization pressed into him.

Why did he pretend it was just maintenance? The answer, whatever it was, would never come—at least, not from his father.

As he looked at them now, he could see the shield and sword bore eons upon them—caked in time and layered in neglect—but here and there, where the encrusted surface had chipped away, a shimmer of blue and green peeked through. The sight stirred something deep within Emanrasu, offering a quiet reassurance.

Seeing the blue and green peeking through filled him with a kind of joy he could not name. He didn't know why—but having the shield and sword at the ready gave him a sense of comfort. Of courage.

Hurried Preparedness: Chapter Two

He chuckled lightly as he thought, "Knowing we are that much safer gives me a little pep and energy as well."

Again, he and Rezua set foot to the path and continued the journey.

As Emanrasu stepped over yet another gnarled root, his mind drifted through the swirling dream and its complexities. The Phoenix and the Dragon were constants in this area, as were the Sky, Earth, Tree, and Sun—all revered throughout Aleon.

He ducked to avoid an outstretched tree branch just as it smacked Rezua square in the chest. The big man, absorbed in his writings, barely reacted beyond a grunt. Emanrasu grinned—his hulking friend had always been like this, forever getting a limb in the face or twisting an ankle in a rut. Left to his own devices, Rezua would probably walk straight into a ravine as large as the one they had cast the attacker into.

"The attacker..." The garb had been unusual. The colors, echoing those in his dream, stood out fresh in his memory.

"Perhaps he was from across the Tubata Mountains..." The Dance lost its hold beyond the mountains, where the Surge and the Hold warred unchecked.

With this leg of the journey almost behind them, Emanrasu realized that the Dance had always comforted him, as it did now. While his father had never been one for philosophical or religious constructs, he had also never denigrated them.

*   *   *

Thus, they traveled for hands, making good time. His spirits seemed to lift and free him from the usual weariness that had plagued him in days prior. However, the reverse seemed to afflict Rezua—he constantly lagged behind, complaining of exhaustion and pleading with Emanrasu to slow down.

To accommodate the big man by heeding the request, Emanrasu eased his pace, though they were still making far better time than he had expected. Yet, somehow, he felt more ready than ever to continue.

"We are making excellent time, little-giant," he called over his shoulder to the lagging mountain-with-feet.

Rezua grabbed Emanrasu's shoulder and tugged him slightly. Upon looking at the big man, he saw the man's eyes narrow, and his brow wrinkled.

"I have never seen you this way; you have never been able to outwalk me. Outrun, yes, but I have the stamina of an ox, and still, you seem to be wearing me out today," Rezua complained.

"How about we take a breather and sit for our midday meal and relax a bit?"

His pleading eyes, more convincing than his words, melted Emanrasu's—and so he agreed.

Shortly thereafter, they came upon a fallen log a short distance from the side of the road, and it was there they took their midday. Emanrasu portioned out two helpings of food, but before he could claim his own, Rezua's hand had scooped up both portions.

"Hungry?" Emanrasu asked the big man.

"Practically starving from the pace you have going today," Rezua said as he snuck the muffled reply around a mouthful of food.

They relaxed and recharged, allowing Emanrasu time to bandy about with the sword. It was heavy, but he seemed to be getting the hang of it, making it lighter or at least worth the effort to bear the burden.

"Hey, listen to this," Rezua said with a twinge of pride and excitement quivering his voice. "The faithful scribe entered the clearing, scanning it deliberately. His eyes fell upon Emanrasu, sleeping soundly in his roll. His weapons were close at hand, as always, the steel and tinctures glinting in the gathering dusk. A slight movement beyond the sleeping warrior caught the scribe's eye, but before he could utter a word, Emanrasu was up and at the ready, shield in defense, sword at the ready.

Hurried Preparedness: Chapter Two

"Emanrasu deftly dodged the skilled axe man, intent on relieving our hero of his life and limb. Emanrasu smacked the man on his backside, showing his skill was unmatched by any, and certainly not by this lone assassin.

"The assassin was shocked and swung another precisely placed blow that should have cleaved Emanrasu in two. However, Emanrasu Bakerson was faster than the sunlight today and again dodged the deadly blow as if the assassin were a mere child in training.

"It was in this manner that the assassin attempted several times to finish the job, but each showed the superior skill and dexterity of the future emperor.

"Two more assassins stepped from the shadows, and with a knowing nod, they synchronized their attacks. For an ordinary man, this would have been the death of him. However, our hero was no mere man; the Dance itself came when he beckoned, and as the three became five, Emanrasu silently prayed to the Dance.

"The glow of his aura and the shine on his weapons were the Dance's answer. His blade flicked in and out as his shield became a veritable castle wall against the ineffective attempts from the master assassins sent against him.

"In the span of three heartbeats, the sword quit flicking, and the shield dropped to a resting position. The five assassins lay at his feet, the last of their life's blood seeping into the soaked earth beneath them."

"Uh... I... I am not sure," Emanrasu said, but Rezua promptly held up a thick sausage finger, abruptly cutting off any further comment.

"Without a second thought, Emanrasu placed down his shield and sword and called over to his trusty scribe, the lone witness to the destructive power of our hero and the Dance. 'Get some rest, my dear scribe,' he ordered. 'We have a journey to finish on the morrow.' And with that, Emanrasu laid down and rolled over, almost instantly sleeping without worry.

"Well, what do you think, Eman? I was going to make it a dozen assassins, but I didn't want to draw out the narrative," Rezua explained.

The Heater and The Hack

Emanrasu stood and stared at Rezua for a moment, trying to get a handle on what the big man had just done.

"I am not sure we want that version to become known. We both know that is not the way it happened.

"You saw... had I not had luck on my side that night, we might both be lying on the blood-soaked ground," Emanrasu said, correcting the tall tree-with-a-quill.

"It's called poetic privilege, Eman, you know that—at least that is what I have told you. And anyway, I swear I saw an aura about you that night. It wasn't blinding, but I swear to you... it was there," Rezua insisted.

"Look, Rezua, if you're going to insist on including me, at least try to make it grounded in reality. A fanciful tale like that—insisting I have a mystical connection in some way—would be the death of us. Or, at the very least... loss of limb.

"People from all over might come to try and test us just to find out how good we are. I would much rather be the simple lucky traveler with a whole lot of good fortune and determination," Emanrasu said, attempting to set the big man's expectations appropriately.

"Fine," replied the gentle giant. The pretend quiver in his lips and his cowering demeanor were not enough to convince Emanrasu to change his mind.

After Rezua rested and his things had been stowed, they once more set foot-to-road and continued on.

They passed the occasional traveler, and everyone seemed to give them a wider berth now. Perhaps it was the shield and sword.

As the sun dropped below the treetops, they started to see more traffic, even a cart or two. It seemed their progress was bringing them closer to Erzt than Emanrasu had expected.

"I thought Erzt was farther," he said.

Hurried Preparedness: Chapter Two

"Or maybe... maybe... You have driven me on like a dog does a cow. Pushing me continuously forward without care and..." replied the giant ball of complaining.

"Of that, I am sure I would have fallen by the way by now had it truly been that far," said Emanrasu.

"Perhaps my distances were wrong... or the man gave me the incorrect information," Emanrasu thought.

He stopped a passerby who confirmed it was indeed Erzt.

As they approached the bustling town, they saw that many of the patrol guards stepped back from them, whispering and prodding one another.

"Not much of one..." he overheard one of the guards say.

"Right, or his gear would be better kept," another replied.

Though it made Emanrasu a bit uncomfortable, he did not change the way he presented himself, as protection was his paramount concern.

"Just ignore them, Rezua," Emanrasu said to the large, lumbering, trunk-legged man as he attempted to cheer him up. "Ignore who?" came Rezua's query.

"The guards..." Emanrasu started to explain but let it trail off as Rezua was again standing motionless in the middle of the street, his quill flying like a hawk on the hunt.

Emanrasu reached out, grabbed a handful of the man's tunic, and gently coaxed him into a steady shuffle. Rezua's scribbles never stopped, as they continued slowly down the street. Each slow plodding step a victory of monumental effort.

As he walked, Emanrasu asked many to direct them to an appropriate inn, whereupon they were steered to the Bucket and Nail by almost all those they questioned. By most accounts, it was the most reliable—notwithstanding the one passerby who, rather emphatically, informed them that the Whorestep was a far better choice if one only intended to stay a hand or two.

They reached the Bucket and Nail, a quaint little inn and tavern, well-kept from what Emanrasu could tell and without the usual rank ale and vomitous stench he would have expected.

They entered, and Emanrasu approached the bar, behind which stood what appeared to be the barkeep—or perhaps the innkeeper. He queried the man about the availability of a room, two beds, and a hot bath.

As his gaze fell upon the gold coin Emanrasu had laid down, the keep confirmed they could easily provide the requested comforts. Flagging down a serving wench, he relayed the requirements with succinct efficiency.

Quietly pleased with their timing and choices, Emanrasu guided Rezua to the back of the inn and up the stairs, toward what might be their room for the week.

"We might as well see the town sights while we are here—and you'll need to find a jeweler to get those trinkets appraised," Emanrasu said.

Rezua mumbled something unintelligible, then paused as understanding settled across his face.

"Yes," he replied, "and I need to see if there are any libraries or scholarly establishments. I'd like to see what books they have."

He exhaled, rubbing a hand over his face before adding, with a moisture-less desert dryness: "And yes... I will take —my precious time— and spend it on getting your trinkets appraised."

*   *   *

The short hall at the top of the stairs led to five rooms—two on each side and one at the end. The air hung thick and musky, a clear sign that many paybys had slipped upstairs for discreet entertainment. The floor was worn smooth, polished by the many varied feet that had traveled its length over countless nights.

Hurried Preparedness: Chapter Two

Their room was the lone, ornate one at the end of the hall. The door swung wide as a maid hurried in and about, putting the final touches on what had been deemed "considered" guests' quarters—rooms offered to those who might well be of means but preferred not to advertise it.

As Emanrasu approached, Rezua trailed behind, furiously jotting notes. The maid glanced at Emanrasu, offered a small smile, and then quickly returned to her duties as he stepped inside.

The newly made bunks could have passed for military quarters, given the taut pull of the covers and, to his surprise, the pillowed sacks provided for their heads. The room was utilitarian but not sparse—a desk and chair stood against one wall, a table with two chairs beside it. At the foot of each bed sat a sturdy chest, and matching equipment stands awaited various weapons and tools. Everything bore the marks of extensive use, yet none of it was in disrepair, the careful upkeep evident in every detail.

Rezua immediately commandeered the desk, a choice Emanrasu did not contest. It was, after all, much more his domain. However, the chair at the desk proved woefully inadequate for Rezua's massive frame, prompting him to gesture to the maid with an inquiring glance. She met his eyes, nodded in agreement, and disappeared briefly. From the hallway, her voice carried as she conferred with someone downstairs. When she returned, she informed Rezua that a more suitable chair would be provided shortly before resuming her task of touching up the room.

A moment later, Emanrasu caught her sneaking glances in his direction. He held his gaze on her until she noticed, at which point she flushed crimson, immediately looking away as she busied herself with her work.

He slung his pack onto the chest at the foot of his bed, then retrieved the brigand's pack from Rezua, setting it beside his own. Carefully, he disarmed, hanging both shield and sword onto the equipment rack before finally acknowledging the exhaustion creeping into his body. The long trek had worn him down, his legs throbbing, his back tight from the relentless travel. He reached down, kneading his thighs, then sat in one of the chairs to rub life back into his calves and feet.

He felt the maid's gaze again but pretended not to notice. This time, her glances lingered, not out of curiosity, he felt, but as if passing judgment. The thought sat uneasily in his mind, prompting him to consider the image he and Rezua must present, roaming the roads and streets together.

Emanrasu was lanky, his long, thick black hair invariably tied in a tight half-tail—though, with some small vanity, he often let it drape over his shoulders despite it lying limp against his back now. Though lean, he was not weak. Mains of toting grain and flour, along with the trudging march of the grinding wheel, had kept him in a respectable state of fitness. His skin, though rough, bore no scars—a rarity for a man of his age and station, let alone for one who carried the weapons he now laid aside.

Rezua, by contrast, towered over most men, ducking through doorways not built to accommodate his uncommon height. His muscular frame carried a strength that could knock a man clear across the street.

Emanrasu glanced toward the equipment rack, his thoughts lingering on the previous night's events. A slight twinge of pride settled in him—he was still amongst the living. That pride, however, colored his perception of the shield and sword, their surfaces now catching the sun's glow as it streamed through the lone window, striking them at just the right angle. As he sat, marveling at the protection those marvelous devices had afforded him, glints of metal and tinctures shone through the layers of time-encrusted muck, mire, dust, and grime that had clung to them for ages. He chuckled lightly at the thought of his father, laboring night after night in his futile attempts to scrub them clean. Why not simply beat the filth from them? The battle had already begun the process, flaking it away quite nicely.

An enormous chair was brought up from the sitting area downstairs, and the inadequate chair was removed. Almost immediately, Rezua shifted from the bed where he had been sitting to the desk. Snatching up the lantern sitting there, he lit it and adjusted the lighting, allowing him to continue. Ignoring the outside world, Rezua delved deeply back into furiously chronicling.

Emanrasu glanced up and caught the maid's eye again.

This time, she had no luxury of pretending disinterest. Their gazes locked; crimson surged into her cheeks a heartbeat later. She dropped her eyes, finished her task with renewed urgency, and hurriedly made for the door. At the threshold, she hesitated. Turning back, she gave a quick, almost nervous curtsey, then spun, reaching for the door to make a hasty retreat.

Before she could slip away, Emanrasu called out.

"Wench. Come hither."

The words rang out, sharper than was his intent, stopping her in her tracks.

The large man's incessant scribbling and scratching paused. Immediately, Emanrasu's eyes flitted toward his friend before returning to Serrah.

Rezua's hand hovered above his parchment, quill poised. Emanrasu watched him raise his head; Rezua's eyes darted from the girl to Emanrasu and back, his eyebrows raised in delighted surprise, announced by the corners of his mouth curling into a broad, expectant grin. He twisted in his seat to take in the unfolding scene, his amusement barely contained.

The maid turned hesitantly, clearly debating whether to flee outright. Emanrasu produced a coin from his pouch and extended it toward her.

Puzzlement flickered across her face before deepening into something else—a flush of ruby red, either from anger or mortification.

The realization struck him a breath too late... and Rezua took the majesty's seat in the theater of Emanrasu's embarrassment.

The Heater and The Hack

Rezua, already seeing the misunderstanding unfold, had scooted his chair further around with a scraping noise against the wooden floor, ensuring he had an unobstructed view. He caught the girl's eye, then pointed a meaty finger at her before gesturing toward the coin in Emanrasu's hand.

"Go on!" he urged with exaggerated encouragement, his eyes alight with mirth. The only indication he wasn't entirely serious was the slight arch of his brow.

The girl tensed, her body shifting as if she might bolt.

…and in a slow finality, Emanrasu's understanding finally clicked—she thought he was propositioning her.

"Wait! No!" he blurted, his grin collapsing as horror rushed in. He lifted his hands slightly, palms outward—an instinctive gesture of reassurance.

"No, no… Dance, no! This is just in appreciation for a job well done… and… um… I'm not saying you're not pretty, but… this was encouragement. Just encouragement. In the hope that you'll take good care—of the room—going forward as well..."

She hesitated, scanning his face for deception. Cautiously, she stepped forward and reached out, her hand poised to withdraw at the first sign of trickery.

"Thank you, kind sir. You are most gracious," she murmured, her voice clear yet soft, belying the shyness that had colored their interaction.

She snatched the coin and, with a speed that suggested she meant to forestall any further advances, hurried out of the room. The door closed behind her, but the expected sound of retreating footsteps did not follow immediately.

Rezua pressed a finger to his lips and grinned as he caught Emanrasu's eye. Then, with exaggerated stealth, he took two steps toward the door.

A flurry of footsteps resumed outside—swift and fading, as the girl fled.

Hurried Preparedness: Chapter Two

Rezua erupted into laughter, a deep, rumbling sound that filled the room. "You practically frightened the girl to death!" he bellowed. "I am so proud of you!"

He wiped away an imaginary tear from one eye, then the other, still chortling.

Emanrasu sighed in resignation. He stepped over to the bed, grabbed a pillow, and flung it at Rezua, who barely ducked in time. He swung his legs up and lay down without further ceremony, exhaling deeply.

The bed was, without a doubt, the most comfortable he had ever had the pleasure of lying upon. Then again, that wasn't saying much—he had only ever slept in one other, and that had been little more than slats between two boards.

He closed his eyes, ignoring Rezua's muffled snickers. Soon, the rhythmic scratching of quill on parchment resumed—soft and steady, a strangely soothing sound.

As dusk deepened, Emanrasu surrendered to sleep—deep, dreamless, and mercifully free of further embarrassment.

He had naught for dreams.

In Disappointment: Chapter Three

*"Unpredictable is life—be prepared, seek knowledge, acknowledge our possessions'
limitations, and revel in both camaraderie and companionship."*

—RCotD—

L ight streamed through the shuttered window of the inn room as Emanrasu
woke. The clattering of pans and clinking of dishes mingled and merged
with the succulent aroma of roast and eggs, setting his stomach growling. Though
his sleep had been deep, an unsettling emptiness lingered, pushed aside by his
stomach's insistent demands.

His midsection growled incessantly as he glanced over at Rezua, who was
slumped over the desk, snoring lightly, his head nested in the crook of his arm.

Grinning, Emanrasu delivered a swift, decisive kick to the chair. Rezua, startled,
jerked awake, tumbling from his perch. He caught himself on one knee in front
of the desk while the chair crashed behind him as papers—scribbled upon deep
into the night—scattered across the wooden surface, several taking flight to settle
like autumn leaves upon the floor.

Measured and purposeful, he climbed to his feet, each slow, intentional
movement thunderous as only a man of his massive frame could make it.
Sweeping a hand across the floor, he snatched up the scattered sheets. Still
clutching papers in one gentle hand, he turned, singling Emanrasu with his thick,
massive, meaty finger.

Rezua placed the papers gently on the desk before turning to Emanrasu. The floor
groaned beneath his weight as he stepped forward. Leaning in, his towering frame
loomed over the not-so-small Emanrasu, his face alight with swirling expressions
of humor and delight.

Emanrasu, familiar with this ritual, threw his arms up in a half-hearted defensive
stance.

The Heater and The Hack

"You!" Rezua boomed, his brow furrowed in feigned anger and mock concern. "You!" he repeated, the mock fury crumbling into a burst of tremendous laughter, rolling through the room like breaking thunder.

Fighting to regain his stern demeanor, he jabbed a finger forward. "You, my little man," he declared before his stern tone melted into a grin, "owe me some breakfast!"

Emanrasu couldn't help but smile, shaking his head slightly—only Rezua, with his giant frame, would dare to call him "little."

"Oh, little, is it? And I owe—you—breakfast? Fine, my enormous friend..." Emanrasu said, grinning at the hulking figure, "... let's tally our debts! I wager you'd come up short in that counting!"

"Well then, holder of the coin, pass me some so that I might repay my burdensome debt."

Emanrasu tossed Rezua a silver as they began preparing for their departure.

"The sneaky aroma creeping up from below, now assaulting my nose, is a tragedy," Rezua said with a deep, exaggerated sniff. "If someone doesn't take hold of the offending food and show it who's boss, it would be a tragedy twofold!"

"Ensure you bring the jewelry and the pendant," Emanrasu reminded his gargantuan companion. "We need to assess their value, which may serve to replenish our coffer."

Rezua peered at him from under a single raised brow. "It's not like we don't have plenty of coin..."

The enormous man grinned. "We could keep it..."

"Or we can measure its worth..." Emanrasu responded with a wink. "To task, your majestic mountainness."

In Disappointment: Chapter Three

The two worked methodically, filling the chests at the foot of their beds and securing them with the ornate keys provided by the innkeeper.

Peering at Rezua, Emanrasu chuckled as the robust scribe attempted to loop his key around his neck. Though Rezua managed to get it over his head, it snagged against his brows and ears, dangling awkwardly between his eyes like an ornately dangled headband.

Rezua muttered something under his breath as he slid the key free and tucked it into his pouch. Emanrasu grinned but continued into the hall as Rezua secured the last of his gear.

Emanrasu's gaze fell upon a man exiting a room and heading toward the stairs. The soldier's leathers were plain, but his weapons gleamed—a polished contrast to Emanrasu's own, dulled and battle-scarred.

Embarrassment flickered through him—not for the weapons themselves, which had repeatedly proven their worth, but for the neglect they bore despite his father's meticulous rituals. "A tragedy twofold," he muttered, a wry smile playing at his lips as he echoed Rezua's phrase.

Rezua's footsteps followed closely behind as Emanrasu stepped into the hallway. He had barely adjusted to the dimmer light when a maid emerged abruptly from a chamber to his right, gasping softly as she nearly collided with him. She hesitated, her cheeks brightening as she glanced up at him. "Are you seeking a wash?"

The question caught him off guard, heat prickling his face until he noticed the steam curling from the doorway beyond her shoulder. A half-filled tub gleamed in the dim light, its rising wisps explaining her flush—it was the warmth of her duties, not the awkwardness he'd imagined.

Emanrasu stammered a reply and shifted uneasily as Rezua's elbow nudged his shoulder. "Uh... maybe, uh... later."

The Heater and The Hack

"Apologies, my practically wordless friend," Rezua said, his grin laden with mischief.

"Could... could you have the garments on the bed cleaned and returned?" Emanrasu queried, grasping at any words that might save him from embarrassment. "Yes, sir," she said, stepping back into the bathroom to let them pass.

They had taken only a few steps when Emanrasu stopped and turned, trying to catch another glimpse of the maid. Rezua's broad frame blocked his view—at first, perhaps by chance, though Emanrasu soon suspected otherwise as each attempt to peer around his companion met with another shift of the bigger man's position. After a few futile attempts, Emanrasu grasped Rezua's tunic and guided him firmly aside.

"What is your name, girl?" he asked. "Or would you rather I just call out 'Hey, you!' when we have need?"

The girl reddened, obviously struggling not to read anything more into it than the question stated. "Serrah, sir. You may call me Serrah," Serrah replied.

"Ha!" Emanrasu thought with satisfaction. "She definitely flushed that time."

Hiding the grin, Emanrasu let go of Rezua and turned around, descending the stairs.

The pair descended into the Great Room, where the long table was set with food. Most of it was simple fare, but it looked to be well-prepared.

Emanrasu spotted an empty seat at the community table and sat. With his sword hanging at his side, he struggled to find a comfortable resting place, and Emanrasu adjusted it several times before waving Rezua to a table next to the stairs. Emanrasu followed, adhering to the sword's subtle insistence to find a more comfortable and suitable place to eat.

In Disappointment: Chapter Three

There were pegs on the wall next to the table, and upon glancing around, he saw that many of the tables against the walls were populated by soldiers and warriors of one kind or another. Upon the pegs close by the tables, the nearby soldiers had already hung weapons and other gear, keeping them at hand but out of the way. Following their lead, Emanrasu unstrapped his sword, hung the shield, and scabbarded the sword on the pegs. At once, he felt more comfortable and more nakedly vulnerable.

*   *   *

Emanrasu sighed heavily, then grinned as Rezua found a short bench, which he pulled over to their table, scraping and clawing at the floor. He placed the... to him, ...tiny little chair in the spot vacated by the bench.

Rezua sat opposite Emanrasu, and shortly, a server brought meats, bread, and various other morsels, including roots and leafy plants. The savory air was thick and inviting, but the yeasty aroma tugged at Emanrasu's memories of the bakery.

Rezua dove right in, grabbing great handfuls of meat and bread.

"The only time the man is quiet," grinned Emanrasu, "is when he has stuffed food in his gaping maw."

Immediately, he was proven wrong, as Rezua, mouth full, jested with him, "I think she likes you," he said with a mouthful of a grin. His cheeks puffed out as the food within tried to resist his grinning attempt at humor.

"Just shut up," Emanrasu said. "...And eat so that we may get on with our day!"

The pair ate their fill, though each time Emanrasu regarded Rezua, the big man grinned knowingly.

Upon finishing, Emanrasu stood and, turning away from the crowded room, fumbled quietly as he buckled his scabbard back in place. When he finally got this done and retrieved the shield, he led Rezua toward the door.

"We need to find a jeweler, a reliquarist..." Emanrasu started.

The Heater and The Hack

"A brothel," bellowed the big voice behind him as Emanrasu's eyes locked with Serrah's.

"And a smith!" Emanrasu insisted meekly.

Face flushed with rising heat, he glanced away, raising his voice to drown out the human mountain with no brain.

"And a broth…" Rezua stopped as Emanrasu wheeled suddenly and glared at him.

Rezua laughed a hearty laugh. Emanrasu turned around to lead them toward the door, and Rezua clapped him on the back in a friendly gesture of understanding. The timing of the gesture was perfect, or in Emanrasu's case, the worst possible timing. In mid-turn, Rezua clapped him on the back, causing him to lose balance and stumble before balance ultimately failed him, and a firm, steady hand reached out and kept him upright.

Grateful, Emanrasu turned to thank the man but came face to face with Serrah; her steady hand and firm grip on him righted him, then let go.

Serrah grinned hugely. Emanrasu covered the stumble with a quick thank you, querying, "Can you hasp our door until we return this evening?"

"Yes, sir," she said, producing a lock and heading toward the stairs.

"Thanks," Emanrasu said again, barely a whisper as she was out of earshot unless he wished to yell it.

Emanrasu lowered his head, still embarrassed by his earlier clumsiness. He stepped through the door and out into the street. The inn had been relatively quiet and dim, so the busy, bright street felt sharply different and helped distract him from his thoughts.

The street was busy with activity as carts and wagons made their way up and down, their wheels clattering on the cobblestones, pulling Emanrasu's attention away from his embarrassment and back to the world around him.

In Disappointment: Chapter Three

A girl with a stick batted at rocks as she walked, bringing a slight smile to his face, reminiscing about his upbringing, where toys were what he could find in the wild and not the intricate carvings that the upper class might have. He turned and followed a cart down the street, occasionally inquiring about the whereabouts of a jewelsmith or a charmonger.

Having no luck with his questioning, he spied a woman off to the side of the street.

The woman was sweeping a stoop while a black and brown cat vied for her attention and was shooed away with the broom. The woman continued cleaning, but the undeterred cat returned repeatedly, only to be shooed away again.

Emanrasu called out to the woman as they walked up, "My pardon, miss, where might one find the artisan sections? I am in need of some specialty advice. A reliquarist, a jeweler, and…"

"A smith, by the look of those," the old woman finished for him, nodding to his shield and sword.

"Take the street up in that direction," she motioned. "When it forks, the right will take you to the jewelers and the smiths, and the left will take you to the less reputable shops and trades. You should be able to find a reliquarist there."

"Thank you," Emanrasu replied, glad for the short answer, allowing him to escape this overly blunt individual.

He turned to Rezua… "Where in the world…" he thought, looking around, not seeing the big man anywhere.

Emanrasu returned the few steps to the inn and went inside. Rezua stood there with his journal in hand, furiously scribbling as he observed the inn's interior. Emanrasu clapped him on the back to get his attention. "Let us depart; you shall have plenty of time to sit and write once our tasks are complete."

The Heater and The Hack

They quietly walked past many street carts touting wares, tidbits, and morsels for consumption, taking in the sights, sounds, and various aromas that bombarded them as they stepped to and fro, avoiding the various bustling folk. Emanrasu wove through the crowd while Rezua walked unhindered as the crowd parted before him.

The trek through the town was excruciatingly slow for Emanrasu. He started out at a good clip but always seemed to leave Rezua behind, standing in the middle of the street, whereupon he had to return and guide the one-man roadblock, urging him to at least step off to the side if not actually make progress toward their goal. At one point, he had lost Rezua entirely and, as he backtracked, found the mountain of a man exiting a binder's hut with two small books in his hand, which he tucked into his tunic.

"What do you have there, my very large, slow, and disappearing friend?"

"A couple of small primers on Tubatonona, my little impatient man," replied Rezua. "A Study of the Tubata Tablet, and The Dragon Cliffs in Light of the Tubata Tablet."

His large, expansive tunic swallowed the little books as Rezua tucked them away.

The journey continued until the road eventually split, and the two took the right and found several smiths clustered in a row. Emanrasu walked down the row, looking at the various wares and the quality they might have. After reaching the end, he backtracked to approach the smith he thought would be the best at his task and gather up Rezua once again.

The pair approached the smith, who was busy heating up a metal strip in his forge.

"What can I do for you, young man?" asked the man. As Emanrasu approached, the smith seemed to regard him and his shield and sword but said no more.

"I am in need of someone talented enough to return these to their former glory," Emanrasu told the man. "My father had no knowledge of such maintenance and allowed them to fall into disrepair. I decided it was time to have someone competent complete the job he never could."

The man stopped pumping on the bellows and approached Emanrasu. "Let me have a look," he said, holding his hand for the shield.

Emanrasu handed the shield over, and the smith rubbed at the time-encrusted covering. He examined the colors and metals of the parts that seemed to be peeking through. "It may take some time. I would say give me a week, as I have many tasks ahead of you that need to be addressed," the smith said.

"How much would it take to move to the front of your list of tasks?" Emanrasu queried.

"More than the likes of you have, boy," the smith laughed, "I would have to compensate my current regular clients, as they would be the ones to take the brunt of the delays."

"Well, how much time do you think it will take once you begin?" Emanrasu inquired.

"It should not take more than a couple of hands, but again, it will perhaps be a week before I can fit you in."

* * *

Emanrasu dug into his pouch and fished out one of the gold coins. "What would it take to get it done today?" asked Emanrasu, holding the coin in plain view.

The effect of the gold on the smith was striking; his eyes grew wide, and his eyebrows pushed high on his forehead. He grinned and appeared to scrutinize Emanrasu more meticulously.

"Not quite that much, boy, but if you have three silver on you, I can finish in a couple of hands and compensate the rest of my patrons by finishing their stuff at no charge."

The Heater and The Hack

His fingers fumbled with the knots, which were decidedly more problematic to undo under the watchful eyes of someone who knew what they were doing. At last untethered, he gave the smith an awkward smile as he handed him his sword belt.

"Boy, you have never worn a sword or carried a shield before, have you?"

"Well, no…"

"Come here. You see this and this… they loop around here like this," said the smith. The smith placed the shield in Emanrasu's hand and adjusted the straps. "Hold it firm, but don't grip too tight," he said, demonstrating the motion.

He then did the same with the scabbard, showing him the proper way to draw the sword without struggling. Throwing in a couple of defensive stances, when the smith was done, Emanrasu could at least look the part and unsheathe it with only one hand.

"I have been around a lot of warriors in my time, and boy, I hope you are not aspiring, not at your age anyway," the smith said.

Emanrasu forced a grin, trying to ignore the knot tightening in his stomach. "Aspiring?" he thought. "I would settle for not embarrassing myself."

Emanrasu dug into the pouch and gave the smith four silver, after which the smith gave him a questioning look. "For the advice," Emanrasu said. "And thank you."

Emanrasu stepped out, scanned the street, and located Rezua.

He laid a hand on the big man's shoulder. After a moment, Rezua stopped scribbling and looked at Emanrasu.

"It is truly time to put those away, my mountain-sized assistant. You need to find a jeweler while I take the pendant and find someone who can give us an idea of its worth."

In Disappointment: Chapter Three

Rezua grabbed the pendant through his shirt and mustered the most enormous puppy dog eyes he could. The subtle, understated whine came from deep within Rezua and subsequently rumbled out, startling several passers-by.

"Alright, alright."

Emanrasu agreed to the request without Rezua vocalizing it. "If the pendant is not worth anything, I will not sell it, and you can have it back."

"Thanks, Eman, I knew you would cave in."

Rezua reluctantly removed the pendant, handing it to Emanrasu with a wink and a grin.

"Put your papers away; I don't want to have to find that I will need to see the jeweler as well," said Emanrasu.

The colossal scribe tucked the papers into his tunic, along with his quill tube and his ink skin.

"I promise, no more writing until I have had the appraisals done."

The two parted ways, agreeing to meet back at the Bucket and Nail no later than dusk, Rezua to find the jeweler and Emanrasu to find a reliquary.

Emanrasu backtracked through the artisans, glancing at all the various wares and gear in the shops. Some were master-crafted, while others might as well have been plucked off the battlefield and thrown on display. One piece even had what Emanrasu suspected to be blood in the crevices and seams.

As he approached the edge of the little conclave of artisans, he spied a tailor with brightly colored cloth, and Emanrasu stopped to look through the wares. The craftsmanship on the pieces could have been worn by royalty, save the simplicity of the garments. "I should get something for Rezua. His massive frame was always hard on the tailor in Rintha, as there was rarely enough of one cloth to fit his frame properly. Even as a boy, he always wore more patchwork clothing than anyone else," mused Emanrasu.

The Heater and The Hack

The tailor was well-dressed in bright blues and greens. The garments, though plain, appeared ideally suited for her profession, with little pockets here and there for pins and thimbles, bits of cloth, and buttons. "Or is it tailoress?" he thought. He stood there briefly, looking through the well-crafted wares and waving to the woman to garner her attention. "Tailor, a moment if you will."

"Seamstress would be more apt," she grinned as she approached. She held out an arm. "Brinia, at your service. Seamstress extraordinaire," she said, smiling, her eyes bright and lively.

The woman was matronly, full-figured, and round in the face. Her hands touched the various fabrics as she approached, the colors and textures of each bringing a slight change in expression, knitting her brow on some, relaxing her brow on others, her eyes smiling, and her lips frowning as she touched one, then the other. Her ease of movement through the crowded little area was reminiscent of his childhood, weaving in and out of people at the Festival of the Dance, which suggested to him that she might have had a large family at one time.

The woman had a look about her of one who had transitioned from making clothes for a large family into this profession. The gray in her hair belied the smooth features of her face. She smiled, and the wrinkles around her eyes concurred with the gray in her hair, but only a little.

"Apologies, seamstress. I have a large friend that..." Emanrasu began.

"Yes!" the seamstress raised her hand high above her head and then spread her arms as wide as she could reach. "You do indeed!"

"Then you noticed him as we passed by?"

She laughed, "My boy, I am not sure you realize how enormous he is. That is, if you have to ask if someone noticed him walking by. I would have to be blind or, perhaps, in the far back corner of my shop, where I cannot see the street."

She smiled again, a genuine smile not typically used in this business-like setting, "The boy most likely would need a tentmaker to find enough cloth, but you're in

72

In Disappointment: Chapter Three

luck because I carry a large stock of many different materials, though I don't have the silks that some of the other shops might. I have linens and wools of many colors if you are interested." She winked and continued, "Assuming, of course, you're looking to make a garment that looks like it was made for him, not something patched together. I suppose I should have clarified your intent before I made my assumptions."

"No, no," Emanrasu replied, grinning at the realization that no one ever misses his little giant. "Very hard to hide a frame like that!" he thought.

"You are correct. I am looking to buy him a garment or two, something simple with lots of pockets," Emanrasu gestured to the little pockets on her garb. "Similar to what you have there, though they should have a large pocket, suitable for a manuscript or book about this big," Emanrasu reached out and indicated the length and width of his friend's leather-bound journal, "and about this thick," he indicated.

"I can supply his garb, though it will not be cheap. It will be appropriate for his size, and the complexity to which you wish does not make it any cheaper. You look like you could use something a little less threadbare yourself," the seamstress commented. "I can have both done by the morrow morn if you are agreeable."

*   *   *

He was shoved from behind at this moment and swiftly turned to find it was a horse being led by a boy and a girl. Emanrasu checked his pouch and found it was still intact, though the little mishap had caught him unaware. The two children were already leading the horse away, back to the middle of the road. "No need to say something now since they seem to understand what they are doing," Emanrasu mused as he turned back to the seamstress.

"Yes, please make me two outfits as well, and if you could also locate or suggest a good cobbler, I would like to have a new pair of boots for my friend and me as well, though I am afraid I do not know the size of his feet, maybe about this big," Emanrasu held up his hands about shoulder-width apart.

The wise old seamstress smiled and grabbed Emanrasu by the tunic. "Come," she said and walked directly to the middle of the street. She positioned herself in front of Emanrasu and eyeballed him. "Are you sure you don't know his size?" she queried as she let her eyes drop to the ground.

Emanrasu followed her gaze, and there in the dust and dirt was the unmistakable bootprint of his tremendously colossal friend.

He grinned, and she took out a small measuring strip and expertly measured the print.

"Luckily, my cobbler friend has been down on his luck of late, so he will be happy for the work," Brinia informed him. "If he has the material, he should be able to finish on the morrow rise, as well."

They returned to her shop, and after Emanrasu provided the coin to purchase the garments and boots, he thanked the woman profusely. He took his leave, happy, amused, and proud of himself for doing something nice for his constant companion.

He worked his way back to the fork in the road, and the old cat lady had not steered him wrong; the reliquaries were easily found.

He wandered through the few shops that seemed to be available and selected one. He entered the dark abode and stepped to the side, allowing his eyes to adjust to the dimly lit space.

A man was sitting at a desk at the far side of the shop, incessantly tapping on something in front of him on a desk strewn with various bits and bobs. Looking around, he saw random items hanging from the ceiling as if to form a maze for anyone taller than seven hands. But Emanrasu deftly ducked and weaved his way across the small room to stand in front of the table, waiting for the man to finish his task and notice him.

In Disappointment: Chapter Three

The man never looked up.

A slight breeze ran through the shop, causing the hanging knickknacks to sway. Occasionally, they would greet one another with a soft tinkling sound and then return to silence.

"Well?" the man raised his voice slightly as he glanced up from his task. "Out with it already! Or are you just going to stand there looking gangly?"

Reaching into his pouch, Emanrasu retrieved the pendant and handed it to the man.

"What might this be worth?" Emanrasu shook his hand a bit so the old man would take notice as he held out the pendant.

"To me, or you? Worth is subjective, if you must know. What is your intent?"

"To sell, if it is worth selling," shrugged Emanrasu.

The man finally focused on Emanrasu, reached out to take the pendant, and produced a looking glass to examine it. His brows went high, and he took the glass from his eye, held the pendant out, and examined it again, turning it over and over in his hand. Then he brought it in for a closer inspection, albeit without the glass. He shrugged and offered the pendant back to Emanrasu, who took it and stood there waiting for a verdict.

"Exquisite," the man mumbled softly, barely a whisper.

"Well, I can tell you two things about it. First, it is the work of a reliquatorian out of Dohnata named Aniast, who, as it turns out, is dead this past score of mains, and as he was known to deal with unsavory characters, it is no surprise he was found belly-up in a pool of his own blood."

"Second," he continued, "In my experience, it is mostly worthless to nearly everyone. This pendant was created for a particular reason: to give luck to someone deserving, which one rarely ever finds in our line of work; thus, to me, it's worth nary a copper. It is worth noting that it might be powerful should it find one deserving enough. Here, hand it back," the man said.

He outstretched his hand expectantly.

Emanrasu handed the pendant back to him. The man picked up a lantern, hooded but for a sliver, allowing just enough light to work but not enough to illuminate the shop very well.

The man unhooded the lantern fully, and the illumination filled the place as Emanrasu studied the various hanging items. He saw claws and beads, paws and teeth of all manner of wild beasts. Some were etched; others appeared freshly removed from the now-dead carcass of the animal.

The smell of lighting oil reached his nostrils, and he unexpectedly sneezed. The reliquarist just gazed at him, lips very slightly pursed, which Emanrasu interpreted as him being annoyed.

Under the added light, the furrowed visage of the old man was illuminated, his eyes gleaming as he shared his knowledge. "I wonder if he uses his trinkets to enhance his longevity," came the fleeting thought. Emanrasu's eyes flicked from one to the other of the many pendants and talismans the old man wore on his wrists and about his neck, the complex shapes and designs steeped in colors unique to each.

The man held the pendant under the light and then turned it so the light shone across its surface. He flipped it over to the back and held it up to the light again, letting the light flow, not down upon, but across the back face of the trinket.

"There," he said, indicating the faint circles on the pendant with a pointy metal device. "Do you see the three interlocked rings behind the shield and sword?" he queried.

"That indicates a life bond. Once the pendant has bonded with someone deserving, it is bonded unto the death of the individual. The inscription talks about past writings and future knowledge, but beyond that, only Aniast would have known what the intent was."

Emanrasu's gaze drifted to the hanging trinkets, the intricate details of the different items setting his imagination to work, his fingers gliding over the smooth surfaces of some. In contrast, others were rough and seemingly unfinished. He fiddled with a couple of trinkets hanging nearby, and his gaze drifted to the next and then the next as he silently examined each.

The old man cleared his throat and shifted the position of the pendant slightly so Emanrasu could have a better look. "That is another reason the trinket is worthless to me," he explained a bit louder, which garnered Emanrasu's full attention. "If the trinket is bonded, then even if it is taken from the one with whom it is bonded, the owner, master—we call them wardens—the pendant will not realign to a new warden until the previous warden has expired. Until then, the warden is the only person who can benefit.

"Aniast... he was not a smart man, as far as foresight goes, but he was skilled and greedy. Two traits that work well for a time but invariably end badly," the reliquarist said, his eyes drifting in thought as his furrowed forehead deepened into a thoughtful crevasse, much like Rezua's when he loses his train of thought in the middle of writing; only the old man's wrinkled face started out that way and just got more pronounced.

"Most likely, he was dispatched by his own client for either the bits and bobs he had or the inability to create one. It could even be this one, which would not surprise me, as a piece like this, commissioned by one of his clients, would never have worked for the person who commissioned it since it is for someone deserving luck, not just wanting it."

As the old man finished his brief speech, he shut the lantern back to a mere slit and, as though Emanrasu had never been there at all, returned to his work. Emanrasu cast a curious glance around, taking in the myriad pendants dangling from every nook and cranny of the dim, musty shop. Then, without another word to the reliquarist, he stepped out of the hovel.

Stumbles, Mistakes, and Mentors: Chapter Four

"Accept that ignorance and limitations in one's life can be a catalyst for finding resources to correct the mistakes and always seek growth and knowledge."

—RCotD—

O n the street in front of the reliquary, Emanrasu stopped, squinting at the bright light of the day. His shoulders drooped as he thought of the pendant, almost chuckling. "Of course, it was worthless, probably stolen from some unsuspecting person or other. Besides, there's little chance it was protecting the bandit."

He let his eyes adjust and surveyed the street, unsure of his next step. "Back to the inn? Or shall we see more of the town?"

Slightly disappointed, he dropped the exquisitely worthless trinket back into his pouch and decided to wander about, seeing the sights since there were still hands before sundown.

As he meandered through the streets, taking in the various wonders unfound in the handful of streets and backways of Rintha, the tantalizing smell of food assaulted his senses. He followed his insistent nose and growling stomach to an area filled with purveyors of food and produce. Within this little market, there were various cooks and vendors.

"Slaving away, creating rare and delectable delights designed for designated drifters and dalliers as they deviated from their designed destinations, drawn by the devouring desires of their downright undeterred appetites," Emanrasu's eyebrows climbed at the spontaneous thought.

"I wish Rezua were here—he'd be so proud... and probably pretend to wipe away a tear."

The Heater and The Hack

He grinned, shaking his head softly.

"I'll likely never be able to recall the moment, let alone the string of words that slipped so easily through my mind. The big man's gift for absurd description must be infectious."

The food at the inn had been marvelous, and this promised more of the same if the aromas were any indication. Emanrasu followed his nose and stepped up to the first of many stalls he planned to sample. The clang and clatter of pans and pots filled the air as the aroma drifted about, toying with his anticipation.

The cooks, the cookeries, the vendors, and the purveyors all dwindled as he sampled each. Emanrasu frowned in disappointment at the quality of the food.

"The taste never approached the quality of the aroma," Emanrasu kicked at the dust and dirt, glad he could return to the tasty fare he had eaten at the inn.

He strolled through the various sections of town, encountering a variety of sights and sounds. The laughter, broken by heated discussions or outright arguments, permeated the air. As he wandered, he helped a man shove a barrel into a cart. The man thanked him profusely, and the two chatted for a time.

Letting his feet take him where they would, he marveled at the friendly manner in which the local townsfolk seemed to regard each other.

As he wandered, familiar shops came into view, and he realized he had returned to the artisan's quarter—where he and Rezua had once sought out a smith to clean the shield and sword.

Looking at the sun, he realized it had been more than the allotted couple of hands the smith had indicated, so he set his feet to purpose. He followed the sounds of metal hammering metal, and the smell of emberstone and embershard swept him into a barely remembered memory.

*　　　*　　　*

Stumbles, Mistakes, and Mentors: Chapter Four

Emanrasu felt a sharp pang of homesickness, recalling the many mornings back home during his deliveries, the sweet smell of yeasty sourdough mingling with the acrid odor of emberstone.

Once, as a boy, at the end of his round of deliveries, he slipped into the smithy and watched Maris pound away, shaping hot metal into various implements and utensils. The piles of black rock in bins around the room filled his nostrils with an almost dirt-like smell mixed with the unique aroma of the aftermath of a lightning storm.

"Don't touch that," Maris had told him as he investigated the curious rocks the smith fed into the forge.

Emanrasu had snatched his hand back from the bin, having been a bit taken aback.

"Here," Maris said, tossing him a black rock.

Catching the rock, the black dust had instantly marred the clean surface of his hands. It had felt almost crumbly, like the blackened char left from burnt wood.

"This one is emberstone. See how dull it is compared to the stones you were looking at over there? This is much more common than the smooth, shiny embershards in that other bin. The shards are rare and much more costly, but they burn quite a bit hotter. I reserve the shards for only the most difficult and important pieces of work," Maris had told him.

Emanrasu let the errant thought go and eventually made his way to the smith, where he had left the shield and sword.

The man was hunched over his work, intently filing and scraping, a frown on his face and brow furrowed. He spied Emanrasu's approach and heaved a weighty sigh, then relaxed the intense demeanor he had previously worn.

He reached out, offering an arm, which Emanrasu clasped to his own.

"I am eager to see the results," Emanrasu proffered excitedly.

The Heater and The Hack

The man's brow furrowed, and he frowned again as before. "Well, that is the thing, then, isn't it?" Heaving another sigh, the man guided Emanrasu over to the piece he had been toiling over. "The good and bad of it; the metal is of quality composition, and the forges it would take to effectively work this quality of steel only exist in the larger areas."

Picking up the sword, the man ran his fingers over it gently as if stroking a cat or the hair of a beautiful woman. "Feasibly Krelish, where the mountain men are from, or perhaps there is a chance you might find someone that could properly work them in Erald."

He shifted his gaze up from the shield and sword, then continued—his voice proud and confident. "The bad of it lies in my inability to remove the encrustation encasing them. I do not know what has adhered to your shield and sword, but it defies my attempts at removing it. I have tried everything, including throwing it in the forge, but the metal never softens, and the encrustation remains."

"Erald, you say?" Emanrasu asked. He wanted to return these legacies to their rightful state and, even if unable to pass them off to his family in the Gulf, at least be able to put them on display in a future abode when he ultimately settled down with family and kids.

"Isn't that up past the Gulf?"

"Yes, past Rinewood Gulf a bit, maybe a half day's ride," the smith said as he gathered the shield and sword. "I have accomplished nothing and, in doing so, have set back my schedule without compensation. There will be no charge."

"Nonsense!" Emanrasu reached into his pouch and produced a coin to compensate the man. "I am currently able, and the attempt you have made, as well as the information gained, is worth something.

"I would be willing to split your loss, paying half the agreed-upon price. The understanding between us was that your current customers were to be delayed in addressing the cleaning as best you could. In my mind, you have done your utmost in good faith."

The smith opened his mouth and paused as his face wrinkled slightly. "Were I not in quite such a predicament, I would never agree to such a thing." He waved a hand at the table behind him, filled with various items, from horseshoes to wagon wheels and broken hinges, impressing upon Emanrasu the smith's plight.

"However, the situation being what it is, I would be grateful for the offer." The man sighed slightly, the tension flowing from his face. The smith's toothy grin encompassed the man's face, cheek to cheek. "You shall always be welcomed here, and if you are in need, I shall do my utmost to assist in any form I can muster." He returned the shield and sword to Emanrasu and waited for him to ready himself.

The smith grinned as Emanrasu donned them in the manner instructed earlier in the day. "I see you are a quick study as well." The smith offered his arm again. "My name is Chander. But my friends call me Snort." Emanrasu accepted the arm again, and the smith squeezed the grip firmly. "Your generosity and compassion are fast placing you among my friends, so you may call me Snort."

Chander chuckled, ending with a snort—punctuating the most apparent reason for his nickname. Emanrasu thanked him and promised to call on him again, were there ever a need.

Emanrasu wove his way through the tables, the acrid smell of burnt ember filling the air. As he wove in and amongst the finished and unfinished, he smiled—his shield and sword once again situated on his person. He stood taller and walked with a confidence he hadn't realized he'd lost.

He departed the smithy, and Snort, delayed though he was, returned to his work with furious energy.

The Heater and The Hack

Emanrasu, not completely unhappy with the outcome, was "a little sad at the continued state of the shield and sword," he admitted to himself—the hope of sporting well-cared-for equipment dashed, at least for now.

As he wandered, he happened upon a narrow alley where several men were harassing an old man. The ruffians jeered and pushed him as the frail old man continually retreated, his hands and arms raised in defense against the incessant attacks. The man dropped his cane, and as he stooped to retrieve it, one of the men shoved the old man into a wall and, from there, into a corner. Emanrasu's jaw clenched in anger at this behavior, and he resolutely entered the alley, demanding the ruffians stop accosting the man.

Two of the ruffians turned to face Emanrasu, drawing hidden blades. They grinned wider as Emanrasu struggled to pull his blade; even with practice, Emanrasu realized in the heat of the moment that it was not so easy.

As they approached, the two men snickered and jeered at the state of his shield and sword. Emanrasu was not overly concerned, as he was secure in the belief that the length of his blade would trump the short blades they had produced. The ruffians feinted several times, prompting Emanrasu to overreact and overextend; the jerky motions of his blade provided cause for merriment to the attackers.

Emanrasu advanced toward the ruffians, sword at the ready, shield still on his back. The ruffians lunged at him just as he stepped into a pothole in the street, causing him to twist and flail, but as luck would have it, the first knife struck the shield dead center and knocked it from his hand. The knife fell to the cobblestone with an epically resounding tink.

Emanrasu fell awkwardly, landing turtle-like with the knife hand of the second ruffian above him. He swung at it, but the sword slipped, twisting in its path, and smacked the man's hand with the flat of the blade, causing the fingers to go limp. Another knife clattered to the ground, and even though he had been upended, the ruffians—realizing the old man had, to their surprise, resoundingly beaten their companions—backed off, deciding there was nothing more to gain.

Stumbles, Mistakes, and Mentors: Chapter Four

Emanrasu struggled to slip out of the shield's straps and, like a turtle, rocked from side to side; though he could at last slip out, it was a most embarrassing predicament. Climbing to his feet and retrieving the prone shield, he turned toward the old man. Emanrasu was promptly greeted with a crack and instant pain as the old man hit his leg with his cane.

"I will teach you to mind your own business," the old man said. "At the very least, query the besotted to verify if they need or even want your help!"

The man struck the other leg, but the next blow was turned away at the last minute as Emanrasu flailed wildly to dodge; however, the next two hit his arms. Both arms...but he thought...I have a shield on this one...

Emanrasu just barely dodged the next one, but as he turned his attention to the old man, all he saw was the cane as it came down upon his head, then blackness.

*   *   *

The swirling figures, balanced on a backdrop of blue and green, swam in and out of focus; a phoenix and dragon hovered in the air as if two long-lost friends had once again discovered each other and were desperate to catch up and relay all that had happened since last they had met. Upon a deep blue expanse, dotted by the radiant sun, while upon the green, the tree of life stood staunch against time itself. Calmness and understanding abound in this arena; the cosmic answers to life lie before him in the tree nest, four blue jays and two green swallows. Somehow, the answer to the meaning of life is almost at the tip of his tongue, but it escapes him as the dull throb slices through the dreamscape, pulling him back to... the alley. The man stood over him, examining Emanrasu's head.

"You'll be just fine," the old man said.

"Mighty fine gear you let waste away in disrepair," he continued, nodding toward the shield and sword. "You mightn't want to bring those out if you can't use them; it could get you killed."

Emanrasu reached up and rubbed the knot on his head. Luckily, his long hair would cover the knot, sparing him awkward questions.

"Why did you hit me?" he asked the old man. "I was saving you from those ruffians!"

"You twit; you were doing nothing of the sort. What you did… is save them from a well-deserved beating… that is what you did. I led them here to ensure no one else got hurt while I instructed them on why their behavior should change!

"They call me Tarlis," the old man said as he reached out and helped Emanrasu to his feet.

"I have been training since long before you were born, boy. And though I am still better than most, were it not for the failing strength in these arms, I would still be a force to be reckoned with.

"So, trust me, if you are going to walk around with those, you should probably seek some real training. You are clumsy and slow, and the fact you did not get sliced into small pieces is—not—a testament to your skills; it was sheer dumb luck that kept you from getting skewered."

"But why did you attack me?" Emanrasu queried Tarlis. "I was only trying to help!"

"Because you needed to know that jumping into situations of which you know nothing, can not only get you hurt, but can get you killed. A slight bump on your noggin is fair payment for such a lesson, don't you think?" replied Tarlis.

"Besides, you deprived me of a bit of fun with the ruffians back there, and I have not had such fun in ages!"

"Why were you so interested in them in particular?" Emanrasu held up his hands in mock defense. "That is, if you don't mind me asking. One bump is quite sufficient for a half-set, and I dare say the evening as well!" He rubbed the still-tender lump.

Stumbles, Mistakes, and Mentors: Chapter Four

"I have been watching them harass and, at times, rob random folks, not sure if the folks are local or if they are just passing through, as I have only been here a few days myself, and I tend to drift where the wind blows."

Tarlis reached down and lifted the shield and sword from where they had fallen. He examined both, rubbed at the encrustation on the sword, and handed it to Emanrasu.

"This could be very handy if it were in the right hands."

He turned it over and scraped encrusted and tarnished surface with a thumbnail, without success. He tapped the shield a time or two in different locations, listening intently as he did, then handed it back to Emanrasu.

"I am unsure what you have been dipping these in, or if you have not, then where you might have stored them, but I have never seen such a covering layered over good steel. It almost appears to be bonded to the metal, though you can see where it seems to have flaked off during the fight. You see, here and here, and even here," the old man indicated spots on the shield and sword that had flaked off during the brief incident.

"I used to train fighters in all manner of weapons, but circumstances being what they were, I took my leave. Having little else, I wandered, finding odd jobs, cleaning this and that, making deliveries… I no longer do the heavy lifting type stuff, but I used to."

Tarlis smiled hugely and gave Emanrasu a wink. "Now I keep my battle skills sharp—well, relatively sharp—by teaching lessons. As you saw, it takes a bit of acting to lure them in, and since there were only six of them, it would have been a fair workout. I am called Tarlis, and what might I call you?"

"Only six? Only six? Either you're a madman or a master swordsman of world renown—and I, for one, have never heard of you!"

The Heater and The Hack

"I believe that your not knowing who I am is actually more telling for —you— than it is for me. It shows that you have not adequately trained with anyone of note.

"This means you're either self-taught, in which case a fine instructor might be able to make a fair fighter of you. Not a great one, mind you, but fair." Tarlis's eyes twinkled.

"The other option is that you —were— trained by someone, in which case, you were robbed.

"Your style is slow and predictable to anyone with any knowledge. I anticipated the movements by the positioning of your body and the twitching of your muscles." He held out his arm. "When you make a strike, this muscle and this one will tense, and the swing will be advertised by your core, stomach, and back, that is."

"My movements were swift because my visual cues are minimized and left for the last moment." Tarlis's hand barely moved, but the air that swooshed by Emanrasu's forehead was enough to emphasize the old man's point.

Emanrasu mulled the idea over as Tarlis talked about this weapon or that, discussing how to defend against each and the little things to watch for. Emanrasu came to a decision and posed two questions to the old man.

"You said you taught lessons, and yes… I know it was a little more of a humorous comment than an actual job description." Emanrasu studied the old man and decided he liked him, which made the next part easier. "I have come into a bit of money recently, well, me and my hulking friend."

Tarlis grinned. "Yes, I saw him… not sure anyone —could— miss him!"

"Be that as it may," Emanrasu continued, ignoring the old man's comment. "Would you be willing to travel with me to the Gulf and teach me along the way? I am actually taking these back to what family I might have left in the Gulf, though I have never met them.

"My father has passed these past few moons, and the shield and sword were his, but I would like to restore them to anyone in the family who might actually have a use for them."

Meanwhile, Emanrasu had dug into his pouch and now held out two silver coins to the old man. "In exchange for training and teaching me the basics, well, potentially before the basics…"

"Oh, and my name is Emanrasu."

Tarlis reached out and took the silvers, knitted his brow, paused, and tossed one of them back to Emanrasu. "I agree to accompany you and teach you what I can, though a single silver will suffice for the trip as long as you pick up the food and board along the way."

"Agreed," Emanrasu pouched the silver coin, proceeded to sheath the sword, and slung the shield to his back.

A wave of energy and relief rushed in. "I feel as though I could take on the world at this point, though now I know," Emanrasu smiled to himself, "I am woefully inadequate to do so. If I am to take on the world, I suppose I will have to learn and develop some skills."

"Heater," said Tarlis.

"What?"

"The shield is a heater; you know, the design, the style is called a heater."

"Oh," Emanrasu said. "We should definitely start before the basics."

Balance and Burden: Chapter Five

"In life, one's expectations and hopes must be balanced by realities and the unexpectedness found. Actively seek to control what you can and mitigate what you cannot control."

—*RCotD*—

N othing in Emanrasu's life had prepared him for someone like this old man—the depth of his knowledge, the ease with which he carried it, and the unusual way he chose to impart it.

"Well then, let's make our way back to the inn, and I will introduce you to Rezua," Emanrasu said as they started walking. "I've known him practically all my life."

Emanrasu grinned at the thought of his tree-trunk-legged friend.

"When I decided to make the journey to the Gulf, he was packed and ready before I was. I hadn't even told him I was going yet, and there he stood, bags slung over his shoulder, as if it had already been decided."

A brief, amused breath escaped him.

"I suppose he just expected to come along. I never told him no, and in truth, I was glad for the company."

Tarlis gave a scant nod, then adjusted his stance. "I need to gather my equipment before we head to the inn."

Emanrasu nodded and fell into step beside him.

The two made their way through twisted streets and alleyways. Tarlis wasted no time discussing various aspects of fighting—different styles, techniques, and assorted weapons.

"Balance..." the old man said suddenly, "...the most essential aspect of anything... is balance, and it is no different in fighting and battle."

The Heater and The Hack

Emanrasu watched a tiny ball of a furious kitten, spitting and hissing as it chased, or perhaps followed, a stocky, unconcerned dog around the corner of one of the buildings as they approached.

He glanced back at Tarlis with a raised eyebrow. "What do you mean?"

"Balance permeates our lives. If you do not have balance, you fall."

Tarlis halted mid-stride and stood silently, looking down at the cobbles. Suddenly lifting his eyes, he looked around, finding and settling on a spot. With deliberate care, he set his cane before him, its tip resting upon the cobblestones, his weathered hand wrapped firmly around the polished handle.

"In life, when balance fails—take hope, for instance," Tarlis's eyes settled piercingly on Emanrasu. "Too much hope leaves you vulnerable. The smallest setback shatters expectations, breeds frustration, then despair, and finally leads to anger."

The old man continued, "Hope on the other hand, is what holds this cane upright when I release it." His fingers loosened their grip. The cane stood for a heartbeat, as if defying the very stones beneath it, before tilting slowly and clattering against the street.

"If you moderate hope—understand it for what it truly is: a construct, an illusion that forestalls action—you will see its nature clearly. Hope serves those content to sit and wait, for it demands nothing from them."

With practiced grace, he retrieved his cane and scanned the ground, quickly found, and picked up a rock.

He took Emanrasu's pack and set it down, leaning the cane against the pack, then wedging the rock against the cane to create a stable base.

Meeting Emanrasu's gaze, Tarlis slowly withdrew his hand. "Hope requires nothing from you. Any fool can hope, but hope alone did not keep my cane from falling. I expected it to stand, so I took steps to ensure it would. Expectations demand action. Without action, you have only hope."

"I imagine you hope I can train you well. I expect to train you effectively, but I can only do so if you 'expect' to learn. Your progress rests in your hands.

"My methods will not fail you, but I control only what I can control. The rest lies with you." He pointed at his cane.

"Hope costs nothing and delivers as much; expectation demands everything and delivers results."

With swift precision, Tarlis kicked the rock aside and snatched the falling cane from the air. He lifted Emanrasu's pack and, returning it, they resumed their walk.

After some thought, Emanrasu ventured, "Isn't that just playing with words?"

A smile spread across Tarlis's face. "The way you speak shapes how you think and act. If you settle for hope, you'll never set true expectations, not for yourself, and certainly not for others.

"Master your expectations and ensure they're met, or resign yourself to mere hope. Your viewpoint frames your life's balance, and with balance, all things become possible. Consider laughter—one who laughs without knowing tears cannot comprehend true joy. They lack the frame of reference that gives meaning to either.

"In short, yes, it is a matter of semantics, and it is not the words that hold the import... it is the concepts that allow you to remember. You will soon not forget the falling cane or the way in which I stabilized it. Ultimately, actions are crucial to driving change, but balance helps you to do it correctly."

As they continued to the inn, Emanrasu turned his head and glanced down the alley where the chase had ensued moments ago. The dog sat, nosing around a pile of garbage; the kitten evidently was not finished with the dog and continued to spit and hiss at it.

The Heater and The Hack

Mulling it over, Emanrasu realized, "I want to do what needs to be done, even if it doesn't seem possible, even if the outcome is not what I expect."

As he finished the thought, the kitten suddenly leaped at the dog. The startled dog jumped and, in doing so, lost its balance for a moment and fell unexpectedly. It righted itself and turned to look at the tiny ball of bristling fur.

He smiled, surprised at the certainty of the thought.

"I want to be the kitten."

As they made their way to retrieve the old man's equipment, the discussion turned to the basics: sword styles and shield types, which people use with particular weapons as a generality, and some of the advantages and disadvantages of each type.

"It's like sitting at the dinner table; you have specific tools for specific jobs. You can't eat soup with a knife, and the reverse is true as well; you can't eat meat with a spoon, at least not without a knife to cut it into manageable chunks, or you could make a stew of some sort, but then you would still need the knife." Tarlis grinned, "I suppose that just proves there are always exceptions to every rule. Keep that in mind."

In time, they arrived at Tarlis's current abode.

"Well, maybe abode is too strong a word; 'hole' would be more precise," thought Emanrasu as he studied the hollow.

The place was, unexpectedly, a shallow hole near the wall of one of the shops. Covered by brush and cleverly hidden from view, one would never suspect there was anything or anyone tucked away under the debris. Tarlis adeptly slid in, with a dexterity that defied his age, and began hurling things onto the street where Emanrasu was standing.

"How in the world does one hide a full set of scale armor under such rubble, and have it come out looking as if it had been newly smithed?" Emanrasu wondered.

Balance and Burden: Chapter Five

It was pristine at first glance, but as more things were tossed out from the hole, Emanrasu examined the armor closely.

It was not new, but it was exceptionally well cared for. Nicks and dents from battles had been carefully straightened and repaired; the whole of it was as clean as a newly plucked goose, save for the dust stirred up by the gear flying out of the hole.

Looking down, Emanrasu evaluated his own equipment. His face flushed with the realization that he entertained little thought of laboring over it as his father once had. The shield and sword seemed to present themselves better than when he started his journey. However, this was only in spots where the time-encrusted filth had flaked off during battle.

The shield's unidentifiable coating allowed it to escape encounters without blemishes, and the areas where the shield had taken blows showed no signs of damage.

He reached down, drew a small rag from his pouch, and wet it with his tongue. Then, with determined fury, he scrubbed at the encrustation. Making no progress, he finally acquiesced, folding the cloth deftly in defeat. He finally accepted that his own efforts were as effective as his father's were—which is to say—not at all.

Emanrasu tucked the cloth away as he watched Tarlis emerge from his small shelter, unwilling to reveal that he had only now realized the care he should have been taking with his weapons.

"You'll get there, boy," the old man said, apparently aware of what had just transpired.

*   *   *

Tarlis began bundling his equipment with practiced ease—each part and piece, every knickknack and bauble—fell precisely into place as he assembled his pack.

The Heater and The Hack

Ducking his head into the burrow, while he waited, Emanrasu started at the sight. He glanced at Tarlis, then back into the rut the old man had stayed in, then, once again at the pile of gear that Tarlis was intent on lashing together.

Looking back into the narrow shelter, Emanrasu mused, "It's barely big enough for the old man himself, let alone the trove of gear he's thrown out of it."

Yet, as Tarlis finished binding everything into a single, compact pack, Emanrasu realized he was witnessing a magician without magic. The pack was slighter than Tarlis himself, yet it contained all he needed; securing the final knot in the makeshift bundle, Tarlis turned and gave Emanrasu a nod.

"I'll carry your pack and gear to the inn, but I'll need you to carry mine."

Tarlis's eyes twinkled, the corners of his mouth hinting at a hidden smile.

"He's enjoying this too much," Emanrasu thought.

Without further thought, he agreed and handed over his pack, as well as his shield and sword. He then lifted the old man's pack onto his shoulders—or rather, quite the reverse—he attempted and failed, unprepared for its surprising weight. This time, with his expectations set, he braced himself and slung the pack onto his shoulders.

The pack, laden with eons of martial experience that the old man must have endured, was borne without an audible complaint. Emanrasu guessed that Tarlis had stowed it away one piece at a time; indeed, the total weight was more than the fragile old man could handle in his aged state. As spry and nimble as the man might still be, the strength of his youth had most likely departed, and the days when he could easily heft such a burden were long since passed.

In time, Emanrasu focused and trudged under the weight, with Tarlis keeping pace beside him. The old man meticulously examined the shield and sword, tapping lightly on them and listening intently.

"What are you doing?" Emanrasu asked, startled.

Balance and Burden: Chapter Five

"Checking for telltale signs of cracks or weaknesses."

"Amazingly enough, your weapons, though in a sorry state of upkeep, are in sound condition."

"You can tell that just by tapping them?"

"Yes. It doesn't ring true if the metal has a break or weakness." Tarlis shifted from the sword to the shield, and his face scrunched slightly, brow furrowed in concentration.

"What is it?" Emanrasu asked.

"Nothing... well, only the colors showing through on your shield reminded me of an old and dear friend. His shield bore much the same colors, though I have not seen him for many mains. Just a bit of reminiscing."

The old man ran his hand over the metal expanse of the shield and tapped it lightly with his finger, producing a bright, clear 'ting' that echoed in the air.

After some time, they approached the inn; the sun was well past apex, and dusk would soon follow. Without delay, they stepped inside.

The innkeeper stood behind the bar, and Emanrasu, still burdened with the pack, approached and indicated that the old man would be sharing their room. He settled on a couple of extra coppers, which the innkeeper took with a knowing grin, his eyes bright with implication.

It struck Emanrasu that the innkeeper thought he was with the old man—not just with him... but—with—him. Flustered, he instantly clarified that Tarlis was a traveling companion and would be training him.

The innkeeper nodded, though his eyes gleamed with unspoken amusement, and a faint smirk lingered. "Yes, a travel companion. Someone to show you the ropes, I understand."

The Heater and The Hack

Satisfied that he'd set things straight, Emanrasu turned to the stairs and led the old man to their room.

Finally able to unshoulder the burden, he let the pack slide to the floor. His shoulders ached, and his back twinged a bit from the strain, but the task was done, and he could relax. He forced himself to relax and stretch. Tarlis returned the shield and the sword after Emanrasu had relaxed and stretched. He felt, once again, renewed and invigorated.

Another puzzled look flashed across Tarlis's face and promptly disappeared again.

"I wonder what that old man thinks," Emanrasu thought as he adjusted the shield and sword.

"Doubt I will need these in the room," he grinned and laid them both on the bed.

Emanrasu knelt in front of the locked chest at the foot of his bed, adroitly divesting it of his meager belongings, and made way for the invaluable gear the old man possessed.

After verifying that Tarlis needed nothing else from the pack, Emanrasu placed it entirely inside the chest, locked it, and respectfully handed the key to the old man for safekeeping.

"You can have my bed," Emanrasu said as he moved to gather his gear and belongings.

Tarlis's eyes twinkled, and a slow smile tugged at the corners of his mouth.

I haven't slept in a proper bed for probably fifteen mains," the old man said. "The last time was just to humor my wife." Tarlis's face turned suddenly somber as he extracted his bedroll and rolled it out with the foot directly beneath the window.

The door opened, and Tarlis was at the man's throat in an instant, the tip of his cane applying firm and consistent pressure to Rezua's throat.

Balance and Burden: Chapter Five

"Uh, um… Eman? Who is the old man?" Rezua motioned to the old man with his eyes.

Emanrasu tried not to laugh and kept a straight face a moment longer.

"Eman?" came the insistent query.

Tarlis looked at Emanrasu, and Emanrasu grinned and waved the old man away.

"He is my weapons master and has agreed to teach me how to use the shield and sword." The grin faded from Emanrasu's face, though not easily.

"He what?" Rezua's eyebrow raised, and his brow furrowed as the question was posed.

"I have agreed to train him in the martial arts. Specifically, the shield and sword he now carries. To his death—I'd wager—if he doesn't learn to wield," Tarlis said succinctly, interjecting himself into the conversation.

Rezua shifted his gaze to Tarlis, then back to Emanrasu, then back to Tarlis again. Rezua shrugged and, with two strides, stood in front of Tarlis, his meaty hand outstretched, offering his arm in greeting. "I am called Rezua the Great," he grinned. "Rezua the Scribe, to some. Just Rezua to others."

Tarlis hesitated briefly, then locked forearms with Rezua. "I am pleased to meet you, Just Rezua."

Rezua chuckled, obviously enjoying the witty response. "Rezua would be fine, and you are?"

"Tarlis, if you must call me anything, Tarlis will do."

"Well, I needn't call you—anything—but I will still call you Tarlis," Rezua said and grinned.

Tarlis let amusement tug at the corners of his mouth, lifted by the twinkle in his eyes. "I suppose you shall."

The Heater and The Hack

The trio settled in, and Emanrasu recounted the events of the day. He reached into the pouch, produced the pendant, and held it out to Rezua, but Tarlis was quicker and snagged it from the outstretched hand.

"A Pendant of the Dance," Tarlis mused aloud. "I have not seen another of these since I left the White, and very nice craftsmanship, I will say." Tarlis turned the pendant over in his hands, studying it.

Rezua held his palm out, obviously waiting for Tarlis to return the pendant. "It's supposed to give good luck," Tarlis said, returning it to Rezua.

Tarlis covered his mouth with the back of his hand and yawned. "I believe that is all for me, and the rise comes earlier than one might expect."

The old man grabbed a chair from the table and barred the door by wedging it firmly beneath the handle. He retreated to his makeshift bed under the window.

Emanrasu dragged the equipment stand closer to his bed to avoid being in Tarlis's way in the morning. He settled the gear upon the stand; its straps and buckles hung where they might. He swung his tired, heavy legs onto the bed and lay back, where he promptly drifted to sleep.

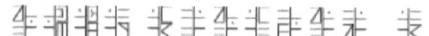

Of Despair and Decisions: Chapter Six

"The interplay of duty, compassion, and prudence when facing unexpected challenges requires caution and awareness, but within these moments of adversity, compassion and adaptability remain essential as we weigh our decisions."

—RCotD—

Colors swirled and coalesced into a green pasture under a thoughtfully expansive blue sky.

A luminous sun stood in constant vigilance high in the sky, its radiance almost blinding in its brilliance. Off in the pasture, some distance away, a tree resided. It was massive and ancient, and from the beginning of time, it had stood eternally. It clawed its way ever upward and outward, striving to remain one with the cosmos. In tandem, the sun erupted, and the tree burst. Emanrasu awoke.

Emanrasu jerked awake, his whole being ripped out from within the void between reality and sleep, and with his eyes still closed, he froze as the tip of the blade touched his throat. His hand lay upon the shield as it had the night through. Struggling to understand what was happening, he felt the cold metal tip pressed lightly under his chin.

With all the speed he could muster, Emanrasu closed his hand on the shield's edge and brought it to bear against the sword in one swift motion. The sword went clattering and clanging across the room, where it skidded to a stop under Rezua's bed. The sound of the blade on the floor was deafening, and Rezua, fast asleep, jerked awake, rolling and scampering away from the sound, a look of confusion on his face.

Emanrasu scrambled frantically backward, bringing the shield to bear defensively between himself and his attacker.

The Heater and The Hack

The room was empty save for the three of them: Emanrasu with his shield in hand, Rezua sitting on the floor, his eyes alight with confusion, and Tarlis sitting at a table, the magnitude of his grin almost spanning the distance to Bren.

As Tarlis started to laugh, Emanrasu realized there was no attacker.

"What…? I… What just happened?" Emanrasu looked from one to the other quizzically.

Rezua struggled to his feet, his legs still caught in the blankets that wound around them like a fish in a net, causing him to teeter. He grabbed the bed, barely keeping his massive frame upright.

Confused, Emanrasu watched as Tarlis chuckled, struggling to control his amusement. After a moment, he was able to speak again.

"You sleep like a fallen tree in a forest without woodsmen—immobile and without fear," he declared as he stood and gracefully retrieved the sword from under Rezua's bed, his movements measured and deliberate.

Handing the sword back to Emanrasu, Tarlis's grin disappeared. "It was simple enough to take your sword from your sleeping hand, place it on your chest, and catch you completely unaware." His furrowed brow and piercing gaze aimed at Emanrasu helped drive home the importance.

Leaning forward, Tarlis's voice became insistent, "To sleep… without conscious awareness of your surroundings will be the death of you. If your desire is to become a passable soldier or warrior, you must learn to sleep lightly, waking at the slightest movement in your surroundings but able to drift back to sleep just as readily. Sleep is critical, but your life is even more so." Tarlis grinned again and chuckled as he returned to the table.

Emanrasu nodded, acknowledging the old man's wisdom; an awkward grin tugged at his lips. "Clever, old man," he thought. "Always a lesson."

Of Despair and Decisions: Chapter Six

"Sleep lighter," Emanrasu said, rubbing his chin where the sword's point was pressed against it. "Your point is well made."

The excitement had waned, but Emanrasu already imagined many more mornings might lie ahead, each likely to bring other unforeseen challenges. Emanrasu glanced over at the chuckling Rezua, who was now perched on the edge of the bed, absorbed in his pages and the steady scratching of his quill.

"No doubt I'll be front and center of this little tidbit," Emanrasu thought, his eyes darting around for something to hurl at the gargantuan scribe. Finding nothing within reach, he settled instead on clearing his throat. "Ahem," he began, waiting for a response. When none came, he bellowed, "AHEM!" Finally, Rezua peeked up.

"You can stop your scribbling any time now," Emanrasu said, glaring at the mountainous tome-writer.

Rezua met his gaze with a broad grin, said nothing, and promptly returned to his incessant penning.

A soft tap at the door interrupted their mild revelry. Tarlis, seated nearby, rested a hand casually on his cane—a gesture as innocuous as any elderly man might make. Yet Emanrasu knew better: nothing Tarlis did was without purpose. The act only underscored the lesson Tarlis had imparted many times before—that any man, no matter how unassuming, could be a wary and vigilant force without looking the part.

"Enter," Emanrasu called.

Serrah eased the door open, her eyes downcast. She hesitated, scanning the room as though bracing for something unexpected. Her gaze landed on the old man seated at the table, and whatever she'd been about to say dissolved on her lips.

"I'm sorry, sir," she stammered, cheeks flushing a deep and vivid crimson. "I didn't realize your companion was still here."

Emanrasu blinked, glancing at Tarlis, then back at her, confused. "Sorry, but why would you think that?"

"Well... usually companions leave before the other guests are awake, and since, well... you know..." Her voice faltered, and the blush deepened as she fidgeted with her apron. "There's been... talk around the inn."

Upon hearing this, Rezua perked up, arching a single brow. A grin slowly spread across his visage, his eyes twinkling.

"Wait, what?" Emanrasu stammered, the words tumbling out as realization surfaced. "I don't think I underst... oh. Oh! No, no, no! Dance, no! It's not like that!" His hands flailed in exasperation. "He's a traveling companion, nothing more! He agreed to mentor me in swor..."

"—Should—I be so inclined," the old man interrupted, his tone dripping with sarcasm. "I would never choose a young man as gangly and awkward as he...

"I very much prefer my partners lithe and petite," Tarlis said, grinning at the young lady. The sly wink at the girl and nod of his head, coupled with his suggestive tone, left no doubt as to his true penchants.

"And why not me?" Rezua interjected, feigning a pout. The exaggerated expression barely concealed the laughter dancing in his eyes. "Why should the old man be a gentleman of the night and not me? Am I not dainty enough for such rumors?"

Emanrasu's glaring eyes shushed Tarlis, returning to Serrah as he waved Rezua to silence his line of questioning. "With that issue clarified—and let me assure you, it is most definitively clarified—what might I help you with, Serrah?"

"I didn't mean to interrupt," she began, her voice barely above a whisper, "but even amidst our misunderstandings, you've been kind to me, while most men, well... they're just not." Her gaze fell to the floor before continuing. "I heard you might be leaving soon. I don't know where, and honestly, it doesn't matter to me as long as it is away from here."

Of Despair and Decisions: Chapter Six

She hesitated, her gaze darting at each of the men in turn, before returning to Emanrasu. "I'm a good cook, skilled at foraging herbs and spices on the road, and I can hunt and trap small game. I could provide and prepare your meals if you'd let me come with you. I must leave—anywhere but here would suffice, as long as it's quickly."

Tears welled in her eyes, sliding down her cheeks one by one.

The room fell into uneasy silence. Emanrasu glanced at Rezua, who shrugged, then turned to Tarlis. "I thi—"

Tarlis abruptly stood, his posture rigid, his hand gripping his staff as though bracing for battle. "No!" he barked. "Absolutely NOT!"

"Women traveling on the road do naught but invite trouble, and I suggest you consider her company carefully before allowing her to accompany us. I foresee no good from her inclusion."

Serrah turned to the older man. "Please, kind sir, I beg of you, at least let me accompany you to the next town. If you find you do not value my skills, I will take my leave there, but the Dance as my witness, I must depart without delay!" she stammered, her gaze slowly drifting to the floor, as her shoulders drooped.

Her bearing seemed to shift as if she had lost hope. "I fear I am in dire sorts if I do not leave."

Emanrasu glanced at Rezua again, who shrugged and nodded.

Emanrasu turned to Tarlis, who shook his head in opposition. Emanrasu shrugged at Tarlis and ignored his glare. "We will give it our utmost consideration, though we will not be leaving for several days in any case."

Her eyes widened, and she stepped back as if to leave, the tears streaming down her face in a waterfall of receding hope. She promptly composed herself and wiped the tears from her eyes and face with a clean spot on her apron.

"Thank you, sir, but I am desperate and must leave more immediately. I am sorry to have bothered you."

She paused at the door, half-turning back, her voice trembling. "Please, do not tell the keep. I must continue to work until I leave, and he is not the fairest when it comes to keeping staff." Her eyes pleaded as much as her words. "If he finds out…" She hesitated, her gaze dropping. "Please, just don't let anyone know my intentions."

As she turned to go, the short sleeve of her blouse shifted slightly, revealing bruises on her upper arm, faint but unmistakable.

"Hold!" Emanrasu abruptly called out.

She froze, uncertain, as Emanrasu strode toward her. At first, she flinched away from his outstretched hand, but he persisted, gently lifting the cuff of her blouse. Dark marks encircled her arm—bruises, clearly the imprint of a man's hand. His fingers traced the outline of the violence, his face darkening.

"Who did this to you?" His voice was low, dangerous.

"A man who claims to be my suitor," she whispered, barely able to meet his gaze. "I have never accepted his advances, but he will not leave me be. I don't want to cause trouble, but…"

Her voice broke, trembling. "I am afraid he will do… worse."

She swallowed hard, then continued, her words spilling out in a rush. "He's a member of the city guard, so he patrols constantly, and I feel there's nowhere in this city where I'll be safe from him."

"Tell me who he is and—"

"No!" Tarlis's voice cracked like a whip, leaving no room for reply.

"No! Do NOT!" Tarlis hissed, his voice low but commanding. "Rather, we should depart with the young lady now than what you are hinting at.

Of Despair and Decisions: Chapter Six

"You—are not—prepared to face someone of skill, and you won't be anytime soon," Tarlis sighed deeply, his aged brow creased with his emphatic response.

"As for myself, I'm no longer as capable as I once was. Confronting an opponent on his own territory..." He trailed off, his fingers thumping insistently on the table, emphasizing the gravity of his warning. Emanrasu listened to the old man, knowing his own impulsiveness might not be the best way, but unwilling to retract his offer to help.

After some thought, Tarlis continued. "Instead of challenging a warrior in his stronghold, it would be best to flee with her now rather than follow the path you're considering. At least on the road, away from his territory, we might have a fighting chance. Staying to take on a trained swordsman—and a guardsman at that? You'd need the Dance's favor just to survive."

"Then we're agreed," Emanrasu said, meeting Tarlis's wary gaze. "She will join us, and we will depart at apex, putting as much distance as possible between us and the town before set."

Tarlis sank back into his chair, the tension visibly draining from him as he slumped, looking suddenly older and wearier. "Yes," he murmured, his voice heavy with resignation.

Emanrasu glanced at his towering companion, who met his gaze with a solemn nod.

*   *   *

"We will depart before the sun peaks in the sky," he told Serrah. "Make ready and make haste."

Serrah brightened considerably, and she even produced a genuine smile. She grabbed Emanrasu's hands in hers. "Thank you," she said, "thank you, thank you, thank you! You will not regret this!"

Turning to Tarlis, she emphasized, "I swear you will not regret this!!"

The Heater and The Hack

She turned to Rezua, nodded thanks, and immediately slipped out the door.

As the door closed, Tarlis stated, "We will certainly regret this..." He trailed off.

"Or we might not!" emphasized Rezua. "Few know aught of the future and what it might hold, and I, for one, can say that I do not," he jerked a thumb toward Emanrasu, "certainly not him! Considering the thought carefully, I believe you to be as ignorant of the future as the two of us!"

"Very well, I can see your minds are made, and we must make quick preparations." Tarlis turned to Emanrasu and held out his hand. "Give me two silver."

"Wha... What? You have done naught thus far to deserve it!" exclaimed Emanrasu.

"What in the dan..." Rezua started.

"Not for me, you twit! It is for the cart and ox we will need to buy in order to get her out of town, unbeknownst to the guard. If she were to leave with us on foot, then word would get back to her supposed suitor, and we would have no end of trouble upon our trail. And in any case, I saw you struggle with my pack, and believe me, on foot, we would barely be to the edge of the city before all of the guard were upon us."

Tarlis poked a finger into his own head. "Think, boy, think!" Tarlis chastised him.

He jerked a thumb in Rezua's direction. "I am sure even he knows when to follow and when to lead!"

Emanrasu reached into the pouch, produced two silver coins, and held them out to Tarlis, who tucked them into his waistband, retrieved his cane, and, with nothing further, exited.

As the gravity of the situation was fully realized, Emanrasu and Rezua started preparing their gear and equipment.

Of Despair and Decisions: Chapter Six

They repacked all the minor items they needed from their packs during the brief stay.

Emanrasu paused momentarily to think. "What else...?"

Mulling it over briefly, he realized that his other garments had been taken by Serrah to be cleaned but had never been returned. The thought of his clothes being cleaned brought the seamstress to the forefront of his mind. "Rise!" he thought.

"I need to retrieve some items. I shall return as quickly as I can," Emanrasu blurted rapidly. "If you will finish packing, then all that will be left is to await Serrah and the old man."

Rezua nodded. "Go. I will finish gathering our belongings."

Emanrasu placed a hand on the big man's shoulder in silent thanks, then hurriedly exited. As the door closed behind him, he forced himself to pause and slow down. He sauntered down the hall, trying to appear nonchalant.

Slowly, he descended the stairway to the main room and traversed it without losing focus on the door.

Exiting into the street, Emanrasu surveyed it and then let his gaze dart back into the inn as the door closed. "Good, no one seems to be following me," he thought as he stepped off the stoop and into the lane, setting his course to Brinia's shop. Once out of sight of the inn, he sprinted.

The shop was not far, and he arrived in good time. Though it was currently shuttered and locked, Brinia was nowhere to be found. He sat on the bench beside the shop's door to catch his breath.

A hand passed, and he thought, "If I had known she wouldn't be available this early, I might have walked." He frowned slightly and gauged the time again. "Plenty of time before apex, so I probably shouldn't worry so much."

The Heater and The Hack

He was glad they were helping the young maid, Serrah. "…though the trouble that comes with her might not be as pleasant as she is." Her auburn hair and striking green eyes burned into his thoughts as he sat there.

After a short while, Emanrasu noticed Brinia coming down the street from the market, carrying more sacks and bags than most would have thought possible.

Emanrasu calmly rose and strode down the street to meet her.

"Would you mind if I helped?" he asked as he reached out.

"If you please," she gave him three bags and two sacks, allowing her to shift the remaining sack and bags to a more comfortable position.

"You are an early riser, I see. Kids these days don't seem to appreciate the mornings anymore, so I expected you later today." She winked at Emanrasu and continued, "So, it is a good thing I did not wait until the last moment, eh?"

"So, are you saying they are ready?" Emanrasu queried, filled with hope and dread. Remembering the old man's discussion about hope and expectations, he smiled.

"Yes, quite finished, and the cobbler finished last eve before dusk." She placed one bag on the bench, then unlocked the hasp on the door. "Seems we have to be more and more careful these days, what with the younger generation feeling they are owed and should not have to pay."

Brinia retrieved the bags, and, entering the shop, she indicated a spot for him to set the bags down. She did the same, then headed toward the back of the shop.

"Follow me, sir. We will give a quick check for fit before we let you take them," she said over her shoulder.

"It really isn't necessary; as long as they are not too small, we should be fine."

"Nonsense," she explained as they walked into a moderately open area in one room. Emanrasu let his eyes wander around, in and amongst all manner of fabrics and fasteners. The room was cozy but not cramped. A long bench stood to one side, and half-finished garments were set in nice little stacks on top of the table. Across the room from the table was an oversized padded chair.

Emanrasu's eyebrows rose as he spied this. "There is no need to be uncomfortable while I work," she said, noticing the puzzled look on his face.

"Oh, my late husband was a large man. Bigger than your friend even. I keep the chair as a remembrance and because it is, oh, so comfortable," she grinned.

"Stand on here," she said, kicking a sizable wooden box on the floor.

Emanrasu stepped onto the box. She walked over to the workbench and went through one of the more extensive piles, bringing back a tunic and a pair of breeches. "Turn around," she requested. He turned and faced away from her and shortly felt her holding the garments up to his body, checking for fit, he assumed.

"Okay, you can step down," she said. She went over and started filling a sack with the garments. "If you or your friend need to have them adjusted, bring them back, and I will make alterations." She was quiet for a moment, her brows furrowed in thought. "I will give you the length of a moon to check and make sure they are suitable. After that time, I will need to charge you for any alterations you have me do."

"I feel that is more than fair, Brinia. Thank you for getting these done so quickly," Emanrasu thought a moment, "My companions and I have had a change in plans, and we will be going… uh… to Aris, to… uh… visit a friend," he continued.

"Excellent, I have friends in Aris, too. A smith and his wife, Olath and Enid. Good people. If you happen to have a need while you are there, you just let them know Brinia sent you with her recommendations," Brinia finished packing the sack and handed it to Emanrasu. "Thank you for your patronage," she curtseyed.

She led him back through the shop to the door, and Emanrasu thanked her again before stepping out into the street.

Though he could not let go of his anxiety entirely, he pushed it back into the recesses of his mind as he walked back to the inn, taking his time. "Several hands before apex, and no need to feed the anxiety by rushing around," he thought.

As he neared the inn, a distant crier announced an upcoming festival—and warned townsfolk that wolves had been seen venturing closer to the town than usual. He called for hunters, gamers, and anyone willing to help rid the city of this unpredictable threat. There was something else about bandits and Bren, but it was lost in the murmur of the growing patronage of the area.

Emanrasu noticed a bookbinder as he made his way back. He stopped and briefly bargained for some books bound with blank pages. Taking his leave of the binder, he made the rest of the journey without incident.

Emanrasu paused at the inn's door, took a deep breath, slowly let it out, and entered the lively room. The morning meal was still underway, and Serrah was busy serving and cleaning. Looking around for Rezua but not seeing him, he assumed the huge feather wielder was still in the room.

Overt Obscurity: Chapter Seven

"In all things, find, guide, and hold onto the humor and humanness. The intricacy, urgency, and uncontrollability of life cannot destroy that which they cannot control."

—RCotD—

Emanrasu's eyes fell on the innkeep standing behind the counter, and a thought suddenly crossed his mind. With Rezua's package of new clothes under his arm, he feigned a chipper demeanor as he crossed the room to approach the innkeep. With each step and breath, he forced his anxiety down.

The innkeep leaned against the bar, cleaning tankards and plates, directing maids, servers, and various boys to one duty or another.

"My good sir," Emanrasu said to the innkeep. "My companions and I will be away for a day or two. We are traveling to Aris to visit a friend, but we will return, and rather than relinquishing the room, we will use it to store our belongings so that we may travel light. I believe I purchased the room for five more days; is that correct? Five, or is it six?"

"Five more," the innkeep answered almost too quickly. "We have plenty of rooms at present, so keeping the room secure for a day or three should not be a problem."

"Ah, that is good," Emanrasu said.

He considered requesting Serrah's presence at apex under one guise or another, but doing so would place them directly under suspicion once her absence was discovered.

"If there is anything else you will be needing for your journey, please let me know," the innkeep said.

"Now that you mentioned it, can you have someone bring up a sack of provisions?" Emanrasu asked, reaching into his pouch and fishing out two copper coins for the supplies.

"Certainly," the innkeep replied, reaching out and taking the coppers.

"Serrah!" The man hollered. "Come here, girl!"

"Ay!" came the reply from Serrah.

Emanrasu scanned the room, his gaze fixed on Serrah as she finished clearing one of the tables. Stacking the plates and tankards, she hurried back to the bar with them. She set them on the table and gracefully curtsied to the innkeep and Emanrasu.

"Gather a sack of provisions for this gentleman and his companions. They will be away for a few days and will need sustenance for the road," the innkeep told her.

"Quite good," she answered him. "Would there be anything else?"

The innkeep shook his head in response.

Serrah glanced up at Emanrasu as she departed, but her emotionless gaze revealed nothing of her intents.

"Thank you, my good man," Emanrasu said, heading to the stairs and nimbly taking them two at a time. Upon returning to the room, he glanced around. Rezua was sitting at the desk, ever scribbling in his journal. He had neatly stowed the equipment and gear in the packs and placed them on the beds. As Emanrasu let his gaze wander across the gear, he noticed even Tarlis's pack was present.

"I thought Tarlis had the key to his chest?" Emanrasu inquired.

Rezua let his shoulders droop slightly. "Uh… yes… I assume he has the key. So, I erred on the side of caution and made do."

Emanrasu let his eyes drop down to the chest. Rezua had ripped the hasp from the chest, and it was now sitting on top of the chest, patiently waiting for someone to repair it.

Emanrasu grinned. "You couldn't wait, huh?"

Overt Obscurity: Chapter Seven

"No," came the sheepish reply.

Emanrasu dumped the sack he had brought back onto the bed and started separating the items. Gathering Rezua's new items, he called out, "Hey, look here!"

As Rezua turned to look, Emanrasu launched the items all at once in Rezua's direction. The big man jerked up an arm to protect himself from the unexpected pummeling of random apparel. He reached down and snagged a tunic from the floor, holding it out by the shoulders.

"It's about time you spent some of that bandit coin on me!" he exclaimed, winking at his little friend.

Emanrasu gestured around the room. "And what have I been doing? Seems to me you're not sleeping in a stable these last couple of nights! And by the look of that plate there on the desk, you seem to be eating well, too!"

Rezua grinned and, for once, seemed to have nothing more to add to the conversation.

"I thought so," Emanrasu said, making sure Rezua understood that silence on his part was effectively giving in.

Rezua stooped and scooped up a boot, placing it against his foot to judge the size.

"How did you... I never thought... It heartens my very soul," Rezua said, his grandiose gestures as exaggerated as his tone. With a dramatic flourish, he hung his head and clutched the boot desperately to his chest. He stayed that way briefly without looking up. Then he raised an eyebrow, glancing in Emanrasu's direction to ensure his emotional display had not gone unnoticed.

"You're welcome, and since we have time, there is a bathing room down the hall. I suggest we use it while we can."

Emanrasu swiftly gathered a tunic and breeches and headed down the hall to the bathing room. He opened the door cautiously and peeked inside. Finding it empty but for the tub filled with water, he entered and placed his new clothes on a nearby dressing table.

He dipped his hand into the water in the tub. The water was warm, and he promptly stripped and stepped into the tub. The door opened, and the gargantuan figure of his friend slipped through, closing it behind him. Stepping off to one side, he sat on one of the benches which lined the walls.

"Never have I experienced anything so extravagant. Would that I had the time to stay here all day. I certainly would," Emanrasu mused.

"That only says you need to get out more," Rezua said as he waited his turn, impatiently drumming his fingers on the wooden bench.

Emanrasu, having not bathed in longer than he wanted to admit, took the hint and meticulously scrubbed himself using the soap left on the table near the tub. He submerged himself completely to rinse off the residual soap and, having done so, stood and stepped out of the tub.

He vigorously dried off and was awkwardly in the middle of dressing, with a single leg lifted, when Serrah entered while Emanrasu was fully displayed.

"Well, the Dance!" He wheeled around, his cheeks burning—and promptly solved the predicament by falling into the tub.

Serrah erupted into laughter—her eyes still averted, though the scene clearly needed no witness to understand what had just occurred. Rezua's booming laughter from behind the door startled her—and deepened her blush into something nearly scarlet.

Recovering her composure, she stifled her laughter and glanced fleetingly toward Emanrasu, then quickly peeked behind the door where Rezua was still engaged in booming laughter.

Overt Obscurity: Chapter Seven

"The provisions and your freshly cleaned garments are on your bed," she said with a grin, hastily retreating, her soft chuckle lingering even as the door shut behind her.

"That went well," Emanrasu said.

"For a shy, embarrassed youth with no experience with females, it went superbly!" came Rezua's reply, which rapidly devolved into resounding laughter.

Emanrasu picked up a drying cloth and chucked it across the room at the big, burly barrel of laughter. "I shall send her back in when you are dangling bits all over the place!"

Rezua laughed even louder.

Emanrasu sighed and dressed rapidly as Rezua, still chuckling, made ready for his cleansing.

"I will see you in the room," Emanrasu stated as he opened the washroom door; he let his gaze flit up and down the hall. "Good," he thought. "Facing her again so soon would be the death of me. Well… it could have been worse. I wasn't exactly standing tall, now was I?"

He quietly slid from the bathing room to his own, all the while maintaining a watchful eye back down the hall lest she suddenly return. Reaching the room, he unlatched the door and promptly ran into the stuck door.

"I feel like a teen again, with all the awkwardness that implies," he fumed quietly.

*   *   *

Without further incident, he wrenched the door open and silently entered the room in one movement, closing the door and leaning against it, his head on his arm in relief. The embarrassment he felt was perhaps the worst he had ever felt, though seen in his altogether more than once. It had always been adult women or girls from the village he had grown up with. It had never affected him in this way.

The Heater and The Hack

"Not exactly the way to impress a beautiful woman," Emanrasu thought. "Especially with Rezua's laughter still echoing behind the door."

"Thank the Dance, it's done and over," he thought.

As he allowed himself to relax a bit after the embarrassment, his hand slowly sank along with the dirty clothes he grasped, and the emotions drained from him. Only to return in full force as someone gently took the soaked garb from his now limp hand.

He knew before he turned, but steeled himself and, as Emanrasu knew he must, slowly turned to see Serrah veritably dancing with joy across the room to the table. She wrung out his garments and laid them out to dry, moving with an almost celebratory grace. But when she looked back at him, her eyes flush with humor and joy, all but drained as her spark faltered—as though she glimpsed something in his bearing—something that betrayed the depth of his trepidation, the weight of his embarrassment now manifested.

She artfully stifled her enjoyment and broke the silence in an attempt to console him somewhat. "I truly saw nothing, sir," she said as she made her way toward him. "And I do apologize for such laughter and finding humor in your embarrassment. It was not my intent to cause you more, so please forgive me."

Emanrasu felt the angst slip from him under the light touch of her soft solace.

"I wasn't… wasn't embarrassed," Emanrasu stammered. And for the first time in his life, he was at a complete loss for words as he struggled to make light of his embarrassment.

He straightened his back, squared his shoulders, and sighed heavily.

"You are right," he admitted, "I was horrified and embarrassed. Why, I know not, as this is not the first time a fair maiden has had the luck to see me without my clothes."

Overt Obscurity: Chapter Seven

He felt the embarrassment subside as he relaxed and forced the thoughts out of his head and into the verbal light of her conversational sun.

Seemingly, she could not help the enormous grin as she said, with what he hoped was mock surprise, "Oh, luck was it. You think they were lucky to see your, well, parts?"

Emanrasu was again shocked and floored by her quick wit and impossibly accurate evaluations of the interaction.

He took a deep breath, again straightened, and squared his shoulders, took another, and replied, "Why, yes, of course they were lucky. Wouldn't you think so? Having the earlier feast for your eyes must have satiated them to no end!"

The humorous interaction successfully replaced the embarrassment, and he fully relaxed, allowing himself to be comparatively okay with the embarrassing happenstances that had just taken place.

She folded her hands behind her and, again, practically bounced as she steadily walked toward him.

"Luck, was it?" she asked again, her eyes waltzing across his visage like a starving kitten eyeing a bowl of milk. Her tongue lightly touched her lips as she approached.

Tarlis swept through the door, and the light-hearted interaction halted as Serrah abruptly veered from her former course, making it appear she had been doing anything but teasing Emanrasu.

She excused herself and slipped out of the room, encountering Rezua as he returned.

Having dressed in the bathing room, Rezua ducked back inside, quietly shutting the door behind him.

Emanrasu strode over to the window and peered out; the sun was approaching its apex, and the time for departure drew near.

"Where is the cart?" he asked, glancing at Tarlis, who had just taken a seat at the table.

Tarlis set the packages down and replied, "Currently, it's out in front of the inn. I'll be procuring some provisions from the innkeep shortly—I wanted to be ready to load them."

"I have already taken care of some of the provisions," Emanrasu said, proceeding to give Tarlis a rundown of what he had previously gathered.

"Good job thinking ahead, my boy," Tarlis smiled and nodded.

Rezua turned around and asked, "What do you need of me? I have been fairly useless to this point. Unless, that is, you count my documentation of the whole ongoing ordeal."

"The ale should be ready by now from the innkeep, so I could use your help loading it."

"We need to get the provisions loaded and somehow get Serrah up here under one ruse or another. I think the window would be crucial in spiriting her away," Tarlis explained, nodding toward the window.

Emanrasu interrupted, "She will be back at apex. I thought it might be good to have a reason for her to be here."

Tarlis nodded as he retrieved his pack from the bed and rummaged through it. He produced a significant length of rope and placed it on the table next to the packages he had brought in.

"What is in the wrappings?" Rezua asked, seeing them now for the first time.

"Items to assist in Serrah's disguise so that she may not be recognized as we depart. Now, Rezua. If you don't mind, take Emanrasu and get the provisions and the drink loaded, then bring the cart around and place it under the window as close to the inn wall as you can."

Overt Obscurity: Chapter Seven

Rezua nodded.

Emanrasu headed toward the door, closely followed by Rezua, who was carrying the provisions Serrah had brought. Without speaking, they descended the stairs to the Great Room and across to the bar.

The innkeep noticed Emanrasu and, without a word, pointed to the two barrels that sat at the end of the bar.

"You get the bigger one, my tremendous friend," Emanrasu said, a grin spreading across his face.

Rezua shifted the provisions from one arm to the other and nimbly lifted the larger barrel to his shoulder. Emanrasu gathered up the other barrel, and they headed across the room and out the door.

True to his word, Tarlis had previously situated the cart outside the front door. Rezua placed the sack of provisions into the cart, slung the barrel off his shoulder, and gently set it next to the provisions. Emanrasu hefted his barrel into the cart next to Rezua's and climbed up onto the driver's bench. He took the reins, clicked his tongue, and snapped the reins.

When they were done positioning the cart, they returned to wait for Serrah.

"I have been mentioning we are traveling to Aris to anyone who will listen. I wanted to make sure you were aware. I had previously made no secret that I was going to Rinewood Gulf, and I thought that going in the opposite direction might throw anyone trying to track us down off our trail," Emanrasu said, looking at Tarlis.

Tarlis cracked a big grin. "My boy, it turns out we have a bit of luck in this after all; I have been telling everyone the exact same thing!"

Shortly, there was a soft knock on the door, and Rezua swiftly rose and opened it. Serrah stepped through. Emanrasu was glad to see her again, but she appeared stouter than before. He put the thought out of his mind to focus on the task at hand.

Tarlis clasped Serrah's shoulder, guiding her to the chair next to the table. He plunked down a foul-smelling package on the table and promptly unwrapped it.

Emanrasu and Rezua intently watched as Tarlis laid out the items within.

He produced a makeshift horsehair wig of sorts, woven together to form a fair covering for her head.

Rezua jumped up and went over, rummaged around in the bandit's pack, and produced the two wigs they had uncovered when they first inspected the contents.

"Tarlis, would this be of use to you?" he held up the two wigs.

"I am not sure where you got those from, but yes, I think they might. Hand me the dark one," Tarlis said, reaching his hand out. He effortlessly fitted the wig to her, and the wig affected a fair change in her appearance, from the dreamy light auburn hair to a coarse black.

In addition to the discarded wig was a pair of threadbare boots and a small vial of some foul-smelling, greasy substance. Tarlis started applying the substance to Serrah's face and then rubbed it off with the cloak that had previously wrapped the items.

"Oh, my!" she exclaimed, her nose wrinkling at the odor. "What is it?"

Rezua dug into the pack a second time and located the makeup kit the bandit had been carrying as well.

"How about this?" he said, holding up the makeup kit.

Tarlis held out his hand, and Rezua stepped over and gave it to him. Tarlis inspected it, sniffed it, and then handed it back to Rezua. "Not quite everything this sort of makeup is intended to do."

Overt Obscurity: Chapter Seven

Answering Serrah's question, Tarlis said, "If you must know, it is a varied bit of substances gathered along the way. A bit of cat piss and dirt I was lucky enough to come across at the most opportune time, some ox dung, a bit of wood ash, and some rancid lard from out back of the inn. Exquisite, don't you think?" Tarlis grinned.

Rezua walked over, picked up the makeup that Tarlis was applying to Serrah, and sniffed it.

"The Dance!" he said, wrinkling his nose as Serrah had.

Emanrasu smiled as, in typical Rezua fashion, the big man lifted it to his nose a second time and sniffed again. The second inhalation of the putrid mixture caused him to gag a bit and wrestle with his morning meal. Rezua put down the greasy substance, and Emanrasu chuckled as he watched him take deep cleansing breaths to quell the food in his stomach and keep it there.

"It is rather exquisite," Tarlis grinned at Rezua's reactions. "It is not only to hide her features; the smell is to keep anyone from getting close to her." He continued to darken her skin and stepped back occasionally to evaluate his work. Meticulously, he worked until she appeared as if she had not washed in months. He handed her the rock, a flat, smooth, large pebble, which he bade her to put in her mouth between her cheek and gums to subtly alter the shape of her face.

"When you speak, speak as a man, low as if you are just getting over a cough."

"Like this, my good man?" she said in a mock attempt at imitating a man's voice.

"No," Tarlis said. "Feel it come from your belly, more of a rumbling voice."

Serrah continued saying, "Like this," in various attempts to imitate a man's voice.

*　　*　　*

Like a charaund smearing its grubs in pungent resin, Tarlis coated her exposed limbs with foul-smelling grease, working with brisk precision. Threadbare boots and a stained cloak completed the illusion. He tugged the back hem of her skirt into her waistband, then cinched the cloak tight, sealing in the cleaner garb beneath. His nose wrinkled involuntarily at the stench.

He stepped back and gave a single nod.

A charaund's grub, sealed in its foul cocoon to molt unseen—Serrah's change was no less complete. Had he not known the truth, he would have passed her in the street with a wide berth.

Tarlis picked up the rope and looped it around the leg of the bed. He stepped to the window as he unfurled it.

He cracked the shutters and glanced up and down the street, then at the cart below, which had been placed just beneath the window. Satisfied that there were no prying eyes, he tied his pack to one end of the rope and lowered it out the window, swinging it out when it got close to the cart, and letting it thud delightfully into the bed of the cart.

Tarlis turned to Serrah and, to her surprise, reached down and deftly looped the other end of the rope through her legs and around her buttocks, creating a sort of cradle. So zealous and unexpected was this that she did naught, nor had time to, though she did bellow out a "Hey! Watch it!"

Emanrasu repressed the urge to grin and could see Rezua was struggling with it himself. As he turned his back to Serrah and Tarlis, he let a grin spread across his face.

Tarlis paused and stared at her briefly. "That's the tone you need to have, that right there!" he said. "Do not speak much, as even trained actors can have a hard time with such a drastic change without practice.

"Should anyone query you, you are heading to Elund. You heard we were heading to Aris, which is along the same route, and you begged us to allow you to accompany us. You are heading to Elund to be with your sister and her daughter, who are there waiting for you. You can make up the details along the way if needed. You will sit at the rear of the cart and, unless directly addressed, remain quiet," he explained.

Tarlis hastily glanced out the window again, peering up and down the street. "We will lower you down, and when you get to the cart, untie the pack and pull the length until it falls in its entirety. Then, roll it up and stow it under the cart's bench.

"Got it?"

"Yeah, I got it," came the gravelly response.

Tarlis took one last glance up and down the street and then helped Serrah out the window. The three of them lowered her hurriedly to the street below.

Apparently satisfied that Serrah was settled in the cart and her disguise complete, Tarlis motioned the young men toward the door and followed them out as they traversed the hallway and down the stairs.

From out of nowhere, Tarlis clasped Emanrasu's shoulder and shook him slightly, bellowing out laughter as he said, "...and were it not for the pig, the chicken would never have revealed the deception!"

Taken slightly aback, Emanrasu hesitated, but Rezua seemed to be right on track with Tarlis. "So, they ate it?"

"Yes, my boy, the pig—and the chicken—were eaten that day!" he grinned, and Rezua shook the room with the depth of his laughter.

Emanrasu studied them, his eyebrows drawn together. "I don't get it..."

"I suppose we shall have to start at the beginning again," Tarlis sighed.

Lagging a step behind the others, Emanrasu realized the quick misdirection from Tarlis a beat too late. Tarlis and Rezua broke into a belly laugh, this time Emanrasu realized it was for an entirely different reason.

The Heater and The Hack

As they headed toward the door, Tarlis caught the innkeep's eye, and with a sly smile, a nod, and a wink, they exited the inn.

Out of sight of prying eyes, they hurried around the building to the waiting cart, where an old hag sat with her feet dangling off the edge.

Emanrasu marveled at the transformation. Serrah.

He tossed his packs into the cart and mounted the driver's bench beside Tarlis. In the back, Rezua climbed in, carefully positioning himself as far away from Serrah's marvelous stench as possible.

With a click of his tongue and a snap of the reins, the cart jolted forward.

He sat stiffly beside Tarlis, his sword comfortably strapped on, his shield leaning against his leg on the footboard. His fingers drummed absently on the wooden bench as his stomach twisted itself in knots. He drew in a slow, measured breath and let it out. Then another. By the third, the tension in his gut began to unravel.

Without a word, he tugged at Tarlis's tunic, tilting his head in the opposite direction. Tarlis barely glanced at him before shaking his head slightly and continuing forward.

Nearing the edge of the city, Tarlis guided the cart past a group of city guards lounging near a wall, their dice clattering against the stone as they played. He drove just beyond them, then, as if struck by an afterthought, pulled the cart to a stop.

Turning in his seat, he called over his shoulder, "Is this the road to Aris?"

One of the guards sauntered over, giving the foul-smelling old woman a wide berth, wrinkling his nose as he passed her. He jerked his thumb toward Serrah.

"What's with the hag?"

"She's seeking passage to Elund, and we were going to Aris," Tarlis replied.

The soldier squinted at them, then shrugged. "Yeah, this is the way to Aris, but watch yourselves, there has been talk of bandits in the woods." He tapped the dice in his palm and pointed toward the road. "Don't travel through at night. Best to pass through in the daylight—at least then you might see the bandits coming."

Satisfied that their story held, Tarlis flicked the reins. The cart lurched forward.

Behind them, the guards grew small, then vanished.

Like the dwindling peak of a mountain, left behind as a charaund falls, the city shrank in their wake. Each clatter of the wheels pulled them further from its shadow, until its spires were no more than a memory of shape on the horizon.

Knowledge Passed is Present: Chapter Eight

"Cunning deception and strategy, sometimes required as a catalyst for renewal and rebirth, can transform through adversity to start anew the journey of one's life."

—*RCotD*—

The cart was slow, bouncing and jolting for much of the journey. Emanrasu let his eyes wander as he gazed around at the farms and random mills. He watched the breeze softly push at the tops of the grain stalks, causing them to move in unison like a wave on the open lake. As they traveled, the way eventually smoothed out, and the cart jostled slightly less.

During a brief respite from the cart's jostling, Rezua pulled out his journal and began furiously scribbling.

Reaching the crossroads—instead of going straight through, which would lead them to Aris and Elund—Tarlis guided the cart frostwise, heading away from the forest, river, and mountains beyond. The tree-field scenery gave way to flat lands, interspersed with the occasional farms and random copses of trees.

After they had traveled some time, Tarlis pulled the cart off the well-worn trail, headed deep into a field, and stopped next to a small pond surrounded by trees. They were out of sight of the road, and the privacy it afforded them allowed a break from the hardwood seats of the cart.

The cart halted a short distance from the small copse of trees, offering them and the pond protection from prying eyes. It felt safe and secure, affording a moment of ease and relaxation after the tense moments of their departure. The woods surrounded the pond on three sides, the wind gently pushing the lapping water up to the edge of the golden grasses and reeds of the field.

Small animals skittered through the underbrush while the hum of insects filled the air, accompanied by the occasional splash of a fish snapping at the surface—a rhythm of nature Emanrasu had not realized he missed.

The Heater and The Hack

The heavy aroma of mud wafted up from the water's edge, complemented by the musky scent of death and decay. It was pleasant after the town's striking odors, which had attacked the nostrils at every turn. Here, the cool breeze married well with the scent and sound of nature—of life, death, and renewal.

The area was quiet, and a slight breeze drifted through, the grasses swaying lightly and rippling across the meadows.

Emanrasu hopped down, leaned briefly against the cart, and breathed deeply of the fresh air. "This reminds me more of home, doesn't it for you too, tiny?" Emanrasu said to Rezua, clasping the gargantuan scribe on the back as he passed.

Emanrasu watched the ease with which Tarlis shifted into giving guidance—though others might simply call it issuing orders.

"Emanrasu and I will head back the way we came and eliminate traces as best we can. Serrah, you can clean up here if you have a mind, and if you don't... do it anyway," he said.

"Rezua, would you mind tending the ox?" Rezua nodded his head and climbed out of the cart, reaching out and offering a hand to Serrah.

Serrah took Rezua's offered hand, "I definitely want to."

Rezua winked at her, as he tapped the side of his nose. "We appreciate you taking pity on us."

She chuckled, jumped from the cart, and reached back to snatch up the small sack she had brought. She removed the foul cloak, letting it drop to the ground.

Emanrasu spun away as she began removing her layers—only to come face-to-face with Rezua whose gaze lacked even the courtesy of discretion.

Emanrasu reached up and thumped the big man in the forehead.

"What was that for?"

"For not being a gentleman," came the reply.

Knowledge Passed is Present: Chapter Eight

From behind Emanrasu came a bright, tinkling laughter as Serrah immediately chuckled. "I am only removing layers, but not all of them," she said.

Rezua grabbed Emanrasu's head in his dragon-sized hand and slowly turned it to face Serrah, who was in the midst of removing perhaps the third or fourth layer of clothing.

"That's why you looked... well... heavier—you smuggled extra clothes by wearing them."

Serrah smiled at Emanrasu. Reaching down, she picked up the cloak, draped it over her arm, and headed promptly toward the pond.

Emanrasu left his shield and sword behind in the cart and followed Tarlis back the way they had come. "What are we doing? This does not appear to make any sense to me. We are well out of sight of the road," he queried the old man.

Tarlis glanced over his shoulder at Emanrasu, "Tell me why you think we did what we did. Why did you decide Aris?" The old man walked briskly through the tall reeds and grasses and followed the trail left by the cart's wheels.

Emanrasu thought about their actions after leaving the inn.

"We turned toward Aris because previously I had made no secret of going to Rinewood Gulf..." he started, then trailed off.

They walked, the grasses and reeds parted in their passing, closing up in their wake, removing all but the slightest hint they were ever here. As they walked, Emanrasu mulled over this morning's actions. Occasionally, his face would light up briefly, and he would nod silently to himself. He raised a finger several times and opened his mouth to speak, but each time, he thought the better of it. The soft earth gave slightly under their feet, and the old dried grasses crumpled and crackled as they walked.

"If any suspect Serrah had left with me, and they suspected we were trying to evade them..." Emanrasu mused out loud, "then going to Rinewood Gulf would be the logical choice, since we told everyone we were heading to Aris. They might assume it was a ruse to throw them off our trail."

Emanrasu squinted an eye and cocked his head in confusion, "But why did we talk to the guards?"

Emanrasu suddenly stopped and straightened up; his eyes opened wide as understanding lit them up. "You needed them to see Serrah, perhaps to judge the effectiveness of your ministrations? That... That is why you stopped to talk to the guard! But you drove the cart past them and stopped so that they would see the woman as they approached, and failing to recognize her, they could say, with certainty, it was not Serrah and could relay as much to anyone that asked. Brilliant!"

In his excitement over having pieced the deception together, he barely felt the ground as it reached out and caught his boot. Emanrasu stumbled forward and narrowly missed Tarlis as he tumbled to the ground.

As Emanrasu lay there, the world was quiet save for little creatures that scurried through the wisps of grain and reed. "I should probably work on my footwork," he thought, grinning as he lay there.

Tarlis reached out, offering a hand to Emanrasu, and with a strength Emanrasu had never suspected—or in truth, had discounted—helped him to his feet.

"It sounds as though you're catching on," Tarlis admitted.

Reaching the road, Tarlis motioned Emanrasu to follow him out onto the road. "Turn around and look. Can you tell where we turned off?" he asked as he waved his hand, indicating the side of the road.

The location where they had turned off was evident from the bent and broken vegetation crushed beneath the cart's wheels. "I am starting to understand. We have to remove all traces of us exiting the road so that even if they were to, somehow, make it this far, they would continue on past."

Knowledge Passed is Present: Chapter Eight

Tarlis touched the side of his head with a finger, then pointed at Emanrasu. "You're much smarter than you are a swordsman," he said with a grin. "I think we shall work to change that. And you are already catching on to core concepts. I believe you might make a passable fighter in a couple of mains, though I wouldn't want you to face anyone with more than average skills."

Tarlis walked back to the field. "You see this?" he said, indicating a bent reed. He reached down and massaged the reed back into an upright position. "It's not perfect, but unless someone knows to look closely at it, it will fool the casual observer."

The two started working their way back to the cart, straightening grasses and righting the reeds; Tarlis showed him the different plants and how damaged they were during the passing, some broken beyond the ability to bend back into place.

"Here, gather a handful of the dried weeds and vegetation and prop up the ones that will not stand on their own." Tarlis demonstrated this by scraping a handful of dried leaves and grasses. He then used them to support the broken plants in the areas where it was critical to hide their path.

The two worked methodically back toward the cart, righting and propping as needed to hide the damage done by the cart. As the two worked, Emanrasu still thought about the deception.

"I kind of understand now," Emanrasu said. "Each turn was intended as a deception, making the logical conclusions all wrong."

"Boy, you have a sharp mind. You've shown humility when faced with the truth, compassion in adversity, and trust when faced with the inexplicable. In truth," Tarlis continued. "Though I had seen something in you that urged me to agree to train you, it is only now that I am truly committing to train and mentor you. Your actions and abilities, to take action when required but follow when needed, have shown you can be trained by a weapons master and properly trained at that."

The Heater and The Hack

Tarlis leaned back, stretching his muscles. "I have seen many a young lad desire to be a great legend only to fail when the sword hit the shield. Since most were of noble backgrounds, they demanded preferential treatment, had no compassion for the less fortunate, and some could not simply think through complex strategies. You, my boy, have been spot on with all but the why we were walking back to the road," Tarlis stopped and locked eyes with Emanrasu, then held out his forearm. "From this day to my last, I pledge to train you and teach you all that I know until my last breath."

*　　*　　*

Emanrasu hesitated briefly before stepping in and clasping his hand around Tarlis's forearm even as Tarlis grasped his.

Somehow, Emanrasu understood what this meant to the old man. No fanfare, no tremendous fiery display—just a simple offered arm. A slow smile spread across Emanrasu's face. His respect for Tarlis grew markedly, and he vowed to learn everything he possibly could from the man.

Tarlis released his grasp on Emanrasu's forearm and turned to continue walking.

"Wait," said Emanrasu, "What is our next step? I do not see a clear choice between anything we might do next, though the logical choice would be to continue forward; the opposite of that is to go back where we came from, which doesn't sound logical to me."

The old man peered over his shoulder and grinned, "Our deception is as foolproof as we can engender on such a moment's notice."

Looking back toward the road, Emanrasu saw that he and the old man had virtually erased all signs of their passage up to this point. The outcome seemed to have quite pleased Tarlis, "I have seen seasoned military men do a poorer job than you have done, and you are a mere backwoods villager for all intents and purposes, no offense intended."

"None was taken," grinned Emanrasu.

Knowledge Passed is Present: Chapter Eight

Working quickly and quietly, the pair reached the location where they had left the cart and their companions.

Serrah had cleansed herself, the cloak that she had worn, and cleaned what gear she found needed it.

She had also foraged in the vicinity for edibles, which she had gathered and combined with a few herbs and honey stolen from a beehive. Serrah had made a proper repair of sorts on the threadbare boots Tarlis had provided for her disguise to make them useful should they be needed again.

She hummed to herself as they approached, and her eyes lit up her face as she saw them.

Rezua, on the other hand, was not looking as pleased. His face and hands were covered with red welts. He rubbed the welts vigorously with a chalky liquid. "The Dance curse bees!" Rezua exclaimed under his breath. "Thank the Dance Serrah knows a little about remedies, though it is not taking away the itching completely; at least the salve is moderating the irritation."

"What happ..." started Emanrasu.

Rezua interrupted with a wag of his finger, "Not a word from you, little man, or you shall feel such the wrath as you have never felt!" Rezua gathered himself up and took the pose of Rezua, the Giant, but immediately devolved into vigorously scratching again.

"Rezua was gracious enough to gather some honey for me," Serrah said, stifling a grin. She turned to Rezua, "Thank you, kind sir," she said and curtsied politely.

Rezua paused briefly from his incessant scratching and bowed to Serrah, "You are more than welcome, m'lady."

Tarlis played a light curl about his lips, though the furrow in his brow remained.

"Jesting and humor aside," he said, the smile fading.

The Heater and The Hack

"We've covered our tracks as best we could," he added, glancing at the others. "There's always a chance they won't fall for the ruse.

"The sun is getting low in the sky, it is best that we make camp around the other side of the pond, well out of sight of the road. We will begin our journey to Rinewood Gulf in the morning."

Rezua, upon hearing this, pocketed his journal, re-stowed the gear they had unpacked while they waited, and climbed into the cart. Serrah handed each a bit of the honeyed mixture she had improvised, then climbed into the cart as well. "I will attempt to provide better fare as opportunities arise in the upcoming days. For now, this is all I found."

Emanrasu tentatively tasted it, then devoured the rest in earnest—quietly impressed by her abilities.

As he mounted the driver's bench alongside Tarlis, he marveled again at the crafty old man's ability to evaluate the possible consequences of each decision they had made, determining the action most likely at each turn to be chosen by the fleeing trio—and selecting the opposite.

He admitted to himself he would never have been able to follow such a convoluted trail had he not been prompted to consider and understand each alternative.

"It will be at least a day before they suspect I ran away... two days, if we're lucky," Serrah mused aloud.

"Well, let's not count on luck just yet, though we have done our best to make sure they have a tough time following us. Not an impossible task, given its impromptuness. It will definitely not make it easy on them." Tarlis grinned and winked at Emanrasu.

Tarlis flicked the ox with the reins, the cart jerked forward, and they bounced rhythmically, once again, from side to side as the cart crossed the uneven ground.

Knowledge Passed is Present: Chapter Eight

The jostling of the cart was uneven and jarring when they first veered off the traffic-worn paths of the known roads. Serrah gracefully swayed with the cart, while Rezua rocked more erratically in the back, frequently losing his place as he studied his language book—often recovering with the judicious use of a massive finger to mark the lines as he read, reread, and scribbled notes in the margins.

The jostling eventually evened out and settled into a slow wobble, prompting Emanrasu to set to work, trying to scrub off the encrustations on his shield and sword. Without much luck, he vowed that he would spend at least a small amount of time doing his best each day.

Mindlessly, he continued to scrub until a flash caught his eye. He glanced up and saw that Serrah had produced a small tube from her pack. As he watched, she gazed into one end and twisted the tube several times, seeming to get enjoyment from the simple act.

"What is that?" Emanrasu asked. "If you don't mind my curiosity."

"This..." Serrah replied—clipped by Rezua, who, still flipping through his language book, interrupted without looking up.

"...a Kaliopdic. They have a couple every Harvestmain Festival in Tothis. It's interesting—but... it doesn't really do anything practical."

"That does not stop me from enjoying it," Serrah said, giving him a gentle push with her foot and a wink before returning the unusual device to her pack without another word.

Rezua looked up and caught Emanrasu's eyes, shrugged, and returned to his reading and scribbling.

Then he reached out suddenly and grabbed Emanrasu's arm. "Tu zoofoti aeno."

"What...?" Emanrasu furrowed his brow. "What does that mean?"

"I'm fairly certain it means 'we will eat in a little while,' but I have a long way to go if I wish to be fluent."

"Fluent in what?"

"The Tubatonona language," Rezua replied. He pulled out the pendant and showed him the back. "Remember the words going around the engraving? When we were in Erzt, I found those books in the bookbinder's shop. It's kind of interesting, you know—they seemed to place a high degree of importance on objects.

"Kind of like you with your shield and sword," he grinned, then feigned to duck as Emanrasu drew back his hand in mock intent to backhand the immense mountain of man.

"I'm just saying… maybe your Tubatononan…"

Glancing at Serrah, Emanrasu shook his head and returned to scrubbing.

Serrah watched the interaction with a smile, then produced a knife from somewhere under her tunic. As they bounced from side to side, Emanrasu watched as she retrieved a bundle of wood she had gathered during their absence.

She selected the longest sapling and tested its flexibility, shaving thin layers off the belly of the bend to ensure an even curve along its length. Flipping it end for end, she did this several times until she seemed satisfied with the bend. She whittled notches in the ends about three fingers from the tip. As she extracted a series of small cords from the hem of her tunic, she looped and strung her makeshift bow, testing the draw. She pulled back and released, then shrugged, unstringing the bow so as not to compromise the bend as it dried.

She selected a thin, straight shaft from the bundle, and as she shaped it, Emanrasu queried her. She explained that she had learned to make a bow and arrow from her father.

Knowledge Passed is Present: Chapter Eight

"He had been the gamer for Ilia, the village where I grew up, and provided fish, fowl, and other game for them in the form of rabbits and other small game, as well as the occasional deer. Once, he even happened to produce a large brown bear that had somehow found itself within range of his bow," she revealed. "He taught me how to make a passable bow and reliable arrows, and occasionally, he took me with him as he hunted.

"He was a good trapper as well, and he taught me various ways to set traps. He was constantly testing my skills with a bow when we went out together, and I became the primary gamer for any small game we came across.

"I really didn't want to be a gamer all of my life, and I told him as much, but he seemed to ignore me on that account.

"So one night, when he was away on one of his frequent trips, I bade my friend and guardian Ansid farewell and departed in search of my destiny."

She grinned, her eyes sparkling like polished crystals.

Serrah also demonstrated a knowledge of foraging that contrasted with her position as a maid, and Emanrasu caught himself thinking, "I would have never expected a maid to have such knowledge of roots and tubers, let alone be proficient at gaming."

Emanrasu, impressed with her knowledge and abilities, considered his own youth, which was entirely different from hers. He had been schooled on the grinding of grain into flour and the mixing of various leavens to produce a variety of breads. Other than that, he spent his early mains in menial manual labor, most of which was associated with the activities surrounding milling and baking.

"Not a very impressive childhood," he realized. "…and there is very little I could do without the millstones and ovens I had been instructed on."

He continued watching her as she finished one arrow after the other, fletching each with thread from her hem and pine needles she had foraged earlier. As he watched, he noticed a fold in her vestment, from which she produced various small tools, including the knife she had been using and several sizes of bone needles, replacing them carefully as she completed each task.

Emanrasu gazed around at his companions, each with distinctive skills that contributed to their survival, save for only him, a baker without flour or an oven.

He marveled at his luck in being grouped with such a resourceful group as his companions were, and he felt inadequate in comparison.

Emanrasu thought, "What do I really have to offer besides baking, of course? I suppose I best put those thoughts out of my mind, or I might dwell on it for eternity."

Tarlis guided the ox around the pond to a secluded area surrounded by trees. There, they set up camp and settled in for the night.

Tarlis created a small fire as Emanrasu, Rezua, and Serrah foraged for something to help stretch the meager stores they had brought with them. Serrah made a stew of dried meat and roots found in the surrounding field.

After they ate, Emanrasu felt the efforts throughout the day weigh on him, and as the night thickened, he said his good nights and laid down, the shield and the sword close at hand.

He slept fitfully through the night, waking several times without cause.

Each time he awoke, he checked on the shield and sword. Eventually, he brought them close and laid his hand upon the shield. He felt better upon doing so and drifted off to a restful sleep.

The dream of swirling colors made no sense to him as he dreamed. Though it caused no concern, he felt there was more to it. He woke before he made sense of it, and the dream quickly faded in the rising of the sun.

Tarlis had already risen and had stowed his gear in the cart, so Emanrasu gathered his gear as well. Serrah and Rezua began to stir as well, and they, too, started preparations for departure.

Knowledge Passed is Present: Chapter Eight

The day was little more than traveling the open fields, mainly on foot, though they occasionally rotated riding in the cart. The ox, ever slow and steady, did not seem to mind the added weight and made no effort to hasten its gait.

After a time, they entered a forest, though the trees were distanced well enough to allow them easy passage. Thus, the day passed quickly and quietly, each lost in their thoughts as the cart swayed and jolted through the wooded area.

In Dreams and Dance: Chapter Nine

"The journey to mastery is a blend of discipline and adaptability, where the rigor of training is balanced by the ability to find humor and learning in unexpected moments."

—*RCotD*—

As the eve snuck by and dusk hurried toward them, Tarlis began talking about the thing he knew best: battle and warfare.

"I grew up outside of Erald in a small village called Pauris. I was small but wiry, and since my father was a woodsman, I wielded an axe at an early age. Cutting and hauling wood, my father rarely let us rest. Every day, all day long, we would be cutting and hauling wood back out of the forest." Tarlis reminisced. "When I did have the rare break, I would steal away and watch the guards training, imitating their movements with a staff I had acquired on one of my trips into the woods. The guards training would often laugh at me; as small as I was, the stick seemed to be oversized."

"Even though they laughed, I was a very determined youth, and I enjoyed the light activity," he grinned.

"Light activity?" Rezua asked incredulously. "From the soldiering I have seen, it does not seem light to me. But then, I am a writer, not a fighter."

Tarlis grinned broader shaking his head. "These days, you would never find a boy talking about military training as light activity, but my father worked us constantly, so for me. It was easy to do, and I had the stamina to continue long after the trainees had petered out and taken a rest."

"Somewhere, I came across a large solid piece of bark from a fallen tree, I think. I strapped it to my arm and used it as a shield for a long time, maybe two or three mains. It is hard to remember now."

143

The Heater and The Hack

"When my father fell ill and finally passed, I abandoned the woodsman's ways and took to the streets, practicing with my stick and finding work where I could. One day, I happened upon an immense tree on the outskirts of Erald; it was gigantic and caught my attention almost immediately. The tree was massive, though when I first saw it, I thought it was fairly close, but it took me almost three days to make the journey," Tarlis recalled.

"I used to go there as a boy, probably around the time I was thirteen or fourteen mains, I not sure exactly, now," he continued, looking off into the distance as if he could picture it in front of him.

"That is where I met the man who would change my life. He suggested I join him, and from that point forward, I found myself fully immersed in becoming a soldier. The weeks dragged into months and the months into harvestmains. Time had proven I had a skill and a mind for strategies, from individual tactics to large companies of armies."

Tarlis sighed heavily. "Anyhow, we can talk more about me some other time," he abruptly said, looking over his shoulder back at Serrah. "We shall make camp soon, and you will need to provide a meal in the morning. Rezua, gather wood and start a fire when we stop."

Serrah took his curt order as she had taken all of the events of the day and nodded. She glanced at Emanrasu but never hinted at what she might be thinking when she did.

Emanrasu looked over at Rezua, who had returned to his own little world and was again deeply engrossed in his little language book. Emanrasu reached over and poked his arm. Rezua lifted his gaze after a moment. "Gather wood and make a fire when we camp for the night, please, and thank you," Emanrasu said.

Rezua nodded and went back to studying the little manuscript.

In Dreams and Dance: Chapter Nine

Tarlis turned to Emanrasu, "We shall begin your training tonight. Though you have the build for a fighter, you are weak and inexperienced, so we will train every moment we can. I haven't long..." he trailed off.

Suddenly, as if an afterthought, he added, "So if you want to be the fighter and soldier we have discussed, you must be willing to put in the work and the effort. Many are the soldiers who put in the work but without the effort. If you put the work in, you will be proficient and have stamina, but if you put in the effort to learn and the effort to train to be better tomorrow than you are today, that is how you excel. That is why there are many soldiers but few leaders, and fewer still that are worth following."

As he finished talking, the forest opened up into a small meadow, and upon finding a suitable place, he pulled up the cart.

Serrah asked, "Are we setting camp for the night here, then?"

Tarlis nodded curtly without further response, and Serrah slid quietly from the cart and veritably glided off to gather food for the morning's breaking of fast.

Rezua pocketed his little book and set about finding wood for the fire, following Serrah off into the woods.

Tarlis waved his hand at the shield and sword. "Bring them," he said, as if there was no chance the young man would not. He walked a moderate way off into the meadow and turned, seeing that Emanrasu had correctly followed behind. "Do you dance?" queried Tarlis.

"What? I..."

"Come, boy, it is a simple question. Do you dance?" he asked again.

Emanrasu was caught off guard by the question. "Well, once..." he started, thinking back to the old man who had swooped him up as a boy, twirling him round and round until he was disoriented and could barely stand.

"That would be a no. Stand here," Tarlis said, indicating a moderately flat area of the ground. "Hold your shield and sword out away from your body, then follow this pattern: step forward, step back, turn, slide your left foot, slide your right foot, then slide back again..."

Tarlis continued until the instructions started over, and then he went through them again, watching as Emanrasu awkwardly followed the instructions.

"Hold them out!" Tarlis snapped as Emanrasu's arms started to dip. Straightening his grip and lifting his arms a bit, Emanrasu continued the dancing, finally getting the hang of it without the old man's incessant instructions, which had tapered off after a while. "Forward, back, side, side, back, forward..." he thought.

Eventually, he noticed that Tarlis was no longer there, having gone off to do who knows what. After a while, Emanrasu lowered his arms slightly as they were starting to ache. Off in the distance across the meadow, a voice bellowed, "LIFT THOSE ARMS!"

He lifted his arms again and thrust out his shield and sword in front of him as he danced. The burn in the muscles of his shoulders and arms only had a match in the instability of his stance as he moved and swayed. Determined now, whether Tarlis was watching or not, he focused on the menial task.

Emanrasu saw out of the corner of his eye that Rezua had lit the fire and found a place to sit. He then opened his journal and busied himself, making notes and scribblings.

Serrah returned, and she must have been watching for a while as she stood still with an expansive and joyful grin on her face. Emanrasu could feel the heat of the blood rushing to his face.

"To have someone see this is embarrassing," he thought as he gave up and dropped his arms.

Crack! The sound of Tarlis's staff on the underside of his arms as they had started to lower. The jolt of the cane shot pain up through them to his shoulders and neck, almost causing him to lose his grip on his weapons. Tarlis, from nowhere, was whispering in his ear, "You will be much more embarrassed if someone cuts off your limb because I was lax in training you."

After some time, Serrah continued with her tasks while Emanrasu continued with his. Tarlis was nowhere to be seen and would appear only when Emanrasu became lackadaisical.

The food was prepared and ready, and still, Emanrasu struggled to hold up the weapons. Finally, from across the way, Tarlis hollered, "Enough! Come clean and stow your gear, then eat!"

By the time Emanrasu was called to finish, Rezua and Serrah had already set to bed, and Tarlis was snuffing the fire.

Emanrasu ate in silence as his arms throbbed and ached. "Tomorrow," he thought, "the real training begins."

Finishing his meal, he bunked down in his bedroll and rested his head on the shield, his sword in hand, drawn close to his body. He drifted off...

Scales and fire... strength and agility... birth, rebirth, life, love, around and around these went amongst a bright blue sky and a vibrant green meadow. The clawed and scaled grip reached out for him and enclosed his chest entirely, slowly crushing him...

As he was jarred awake by the terrifying vision, he opened his eyes wide and saw Tarlis sitting fully upon his chest, legs crossed.

Emanrasu slowly spread a grin across his face.

Tarlis grinned back at him and pretended to struggle to dismount the young man, accidentally placing knees, hands, feet, and elbows strategically, causing Emanrasu to become winded.

"Ooof..." grunted Emanrasu as the precisely placed handholds forced the wind from him.

The Heater and The Hack

Rezua stood, his jaw tightly set as he strode briskly toward them.

Emanrasu surmised Rezua's intent and waved at him to stand down. Smiling at the huge protective mountain of concern, "It appears as though everyone is already awake but me." He winked at Rezua, who just looked at him, seemingly wondering if he should intervene or let the scene play out.

Emanrasu grinned at his friend and, with that, Rezua shrugged, turned, and went back to his journal, scribbling furiously but glancing up frequently at Emanrasu.

Tarlis laughed as he finished dismounting and stood. "You might want to strengthen that core as well," he chuckled.

Emanrasu recovered swiftly and, drawing a breath to refill his deflated lungs, inhaled the wonderful smell of toasted meat and some unknown root vegetable. The exquisite aroma of spices filled the air, and he felt his mouth water in anticipation.

*   *   *

Emanrasu slowly sat up and started gathering and packing his gear until the stout cane of the old man landed on the side of his head. "Ow!" he yelped, ducking quickly to avoid the second swing.

"You should have avoided the first one as well, but we will get you trained. So, quit fiddling with your gear and get up," Tarlis demanded.

Rubbing his ear and the side of his head, Emanrasu rose and turned to face the old man. Furrowing his brow, he asked, "What would you have of me? I thought we would be departing after our meal, so I was packing my gear…"

"Well, we will be eating! You—you will be training!" Tarlis raised an eyebrow mischievously. "Do you have any objections?"

Emanrasu opened his mouth to object but, catching the position of the old man's cane, obviously ready to jump into action at the incorrect response, said, "Why no, old man, I have no objections…at this point." He gestured to the old man's cane and rolled his eyes.

"Well, at least you're observant," Tarlis responded with an openly displayed grin.

Tarlis tossed two palm-sized stones to Emanrasu, both of which bounced off the boy's chest when he reached up to catch them, as he finally noticed the weakness in his shoulders and arms from the lengthy training of the night before.

"Pick them up, son. We will use these as a substitute for your shield and sword this morning. I am not oblivious to the state of your muscles, though I expected them to be a bit more conditioned for a baker's son, seeing as how you would have hefted flour and grain sacks constantly."

Emanrasu reached down and picked up the rocks, each fitting nicely into his hands and being substantially lighter than his shield and sword.

"Back to the dance, boy, and keep the rocks out away from your body, or you will be reminded," Tarlis said, his eyes almost twinkling with delight.

Emanrasu nodded, and, disappointed that his meal had consisted only of the aroma his nose had known briefly, he trudged out to the matted and well-trodden spot of last night's activities. Thrusting his arms out, he began the dance, forward, back, slide…

He progressed through the routine several times before he felt his arms starting to give way, dipping slightly before the rap of the cane stung the bottom of them.

"What?!?" Emanrasu thought as he grimaced slightly. "The old man had been strides away, how…?"

He heard the "thunk" and "tink" of his shield and sword tossed nearby. Emanrasu glanced briefly at them and continued the dance, struggling to hold the rocks out as he did.

"Enough," Tarlis said and nodded at his gear. "Drop the rocks; we will continue with your gear."

The Heater and The Hack

Emanrasu groaned at the thought of lifting the heavier objects and dallied just long enough for the cane to whistle by as he dodged the old man's blow. He wearily trudged over and picked up the shield and sword, returning to the spot where he had been training.

With a massive intake of breath, Emanrasu hefted the shield and sword and held them out in front of him, again beginning the dance. "I will show the old man; I can do this as long as it takes!" he thought. At this point, he steeled himself and continued, his will making the shield and sword much lighter for his determination.

Struggling less than with the rocks, Emanrasu continued to dance. As he did, he noticed the look of confused amazement on Tarlis's face as the old man turned to walk away.

"Ha! I showed him!" Emanrasu shouted to himself with internal laughter, his grin veritably crossing the countryside with its size.

As the morning dragged on, Emanrasu, occupied with the dance, was no longer struggling heavily to keep his arms up, his determination bolstering his physical ability and mental toughness.

Serrah approached with a folded cloth and reached out, handing it to Emanrasu.

"Finally," he thought, letting his arms fall to his sides as he started to reach out, intending to take the food. "Crack!" came the sound from the swift cane, even as the sting of the hit landed on his arms.

"Damn old man," came the instant involuntary thought. His arms steeling again out where they should be.

Tarlis grinned as he walked away, calling over his shoulder, "You train until I decide that you are done and not before. Luckily for you, you are done training," he chuckled gleefully.

In Dreams and Dance: Chapter Nine

Tarlis joyfully bounced back to the camp and started making ready for the group's departure.

Emanrasu glared coldly at the frowning Serrah. "I am sorry, Eman, but he asked me to... I... I was unaware of his intentions." Her look of concern and betrayal touched his soul and raked at his heart, warming his gaze.

As he let his arms down, glancing around to be sure Tarlis was safely out of reach, he leaned the shield and sword against his legs and took the proffered food from Serrah.

"It is fine, Serrah; the old man is always teaching." He laughed. "This lesson was about awareness and disobedience. As he said, I am under his tutelage, of my own will, and if I am to respect his authority, leadership, and mentorship, I must trust in his methods."

Emanrasu ate, his leaden arms struggling to bring the food to his mouth as the strength sapped from them. His hands, arms, and shoulders almost screamed with the ache his training was causing.

Serrah stayed close, and they sat and conversed at length about minor things: the smell of the wooded forest, the spices found in this area, the game available, and surmised the items that they might find as they progressed toward the Gulf. A pleasant conversation, to be sure, as Emanrasu ate. At one point, his strength failing, a morsel dropped from his hand, only to be snagged deftly out of the air by Serrah, who offered it to him again.

The two eased into conversations about their pasts. Emanrasu talked about the constant boredom of his village, broken only by his incessant querying of the town artisans as they went about their day crafting and creating items to be sold or traded for necessities the village lacked.

Serrah delved into her upbringing and the quirks of her father, who, on occasion, hunted with a skin or two of wine or mead to kill the monotonous waiting that sometimes accompanied the tasks.

The Heater and The Hack

"My mother died of the Tonal's cough when I was but a girl," Serrah confided. "I miss her terribly and the warm, welcoming hugs she would give me. I miss just being able to touch her and speak with her. You know, she was the one who taught me how to cook and what spices to use with the different meat. She is the reason that the keep at the inn hired me."

"Why is that?" Emanrasu asked between bites.

"My cooking. Were you not aware that I prepared the meals at the inn?"

Emanrasu thought back to her uncanny ability to procure exquisite meals while traveling together.

"That explains a lot since your ability to make exquisite meals with next to nothing has undoubtedly been demonstrated since we left. I must say, the meal I had at the inn was remarkedly memorable, and now, it makes perfect sense that you were the mastermind of that remarkable meal at the inn."

After a time, Tarlis called out to them, and Serrah stood, offering a firm, strong, but soft hand to Emanrasu to assist in his rising as well.

*   *   *

Emanrasu gathered up the shield and sword, lifting them without too much trouble as the weakness drained from his arms. He carried them, holding them out away from his body as they walked, occasionally performing portions of the dance as they crossed to the camp.

Emanrasu stowed the shield and sword in the cart and gathered his belongings, as Tarlis and Rezua had already packed the bulk of their equipment. Serrah gathered the leftover food and stowed it in a makeshift cloth, tucking it under the driver's bench. She snuffed out the cookfire and coals that were still hot and glowing with a layer of dirt, then tamped it to assure herself there were no exposed coals to endanger the surrounding people and wildlife.

In Dreams and Dance: Chapter Nine

She climbed into the cart as Tarlis and Emanrasu mounted the bench. They set off once again.

*   *   *

Rezua was content with walking beside the cart or riding as the mood would strike, seemingly always with his journal or his language book.

"You know," Rezua had said one day, stopping and stretching as they gathered wood for the fire. "I am learning that Tubatonona words are sprinkled and peppered among our own language.

"Did you know that the names for the fire plants come from the Tubatonona? The girochih plant and the shehchih plant are both Tubatonona in origin. Giro is the Tubatonona word for fire, and chih means plant.

"So, girochih is literally fire plant."

Grinning, he returned to gathering wood. Speaking over his shoulder, he continued.

"When we say girochih plant, we are actually saying fire plant plant. A bit redundant, don't you think?"

"What does shehchih mean, then?" Serrah asked, looking at the monumental mountain of knowledge. "If chih means plant, and girochih means fire-plant, then shehchih must be another something-plant?"

"They think it means something akin to initiate or begin, at least according to my primers. I have come to think of it as a starter. So, starter-plant would be my best guess at interpreting it."

"That means we are calling them fire-plant plant and starter-plant plant," Serrah said, grinning as she walked away.

Rezua grinned with exaggerated disappointment, belied by the humor in his voice. "Exactly my point!" He exclaimed.

"Or at least it would have been," he said, returning to his mock disappointment.

"The expanse of stormy clouds brewing a downpour of knowledge, a bright flash of light signifying the turmoil within the sky, the flash dissipates as dark and brooding clouds swallow it up in silence, as..." Rezua said with his usual flowery flare before raising his voice in closure, "... the lady, Serrah, steals—my—thunder."

The tinkling merriment of Serrah's laughter drifted back to the young men.

Emanrasu glanced over and met eyes with Rezua, each with a grin planted firmly upon their face.

"It is interesting to know that we get words from them, but if we think about it, it doesn't change the way we do things," Emanrasu said.

Huffing, Rezua responded, "No, not in a direct way. But I, for one, like knowing."

They finished gathering the wood while continuing to discuss the ancient language of the Tubatonona.

The Tubatonona banter petered out, giving way to more practical discussions of travel planning as the night drew on.

As Emanrasu slept each night with his head on the shield and his sword well in hand, his dreams continued. The dreamlike scene of trees and dragons, of the sun and the fiery bird, swirled round and round, each clearer than the previous, but none offered any explanation as to what they meant.

For several days, they traveled, thus training, eating, and sleeping. The invariable awakenings comprised by the twisted mind of Tarlis, who drove home that to sleep heavily was to invite all manner of odd happenings.

Each morning, Tarlis delighted in creative ways for the young man to wake up to, sometimes folded into a pretzel, others with charcoal-painted pictures and words upon his face. Once, the words "Wake me!" were even scrawled across his forehead. There was nothing dangerous about these little jabs, but the intention of lighter sleeping was a clear lesson to be had.

Emanrasu noticed that Rezua was awake each morning, grinning like a madman as Tarlis found creative ways to wake Emanrasu. Rezua would then go off with Serrah, helping her forage and trap. With Serrah leading the return, he even once came back with a deer slew across his shoulders.

The training continued day to day, Tarlis adding steps to the dance and then arm movements as Emanrasu learned to be comfortable in the dance. Adding further complexities to maintain the level of difficulty for the young man, adding a hopping step and a bow, touching his knee to the ground, and righting himself using only his legs, each addition building on the last.

Initially, Emanrasu expected only a month-long journey when he started this trek. However, as they crossed untraveled terrain instead of staying on the well-traveled and worn roads, the journey had been considerably lengthened.

It was a month into their travel when Tarlis deviated from the usual routine. As Serrah disappeared to forage and hunted for the upcoming meals, Emanrasu retrieved his training rocks from the cart, heading out looking for the typical clear area for him to practice. Tarlis stopped him and bade him sit with him on the edge of the cart.

"Emanrasu, you have been an apt student, and I know that you have not always understood the lessons I have been instructing you. You have, however, progressed at an amazing rate, and for someone as untrained as you were, this is a feat in and of itself. Thus, I have grown to rely on your desire to learn and grow without complaint, or at least you continued to strive despite your complaints."

Tarlis continued, "The dance techniques are not well known and are closely structured to create patterns your body will naturally follow. You have taken to them naturally, and I dare say it is better than most of my most apt students ever had. On the morrow, we will start training in shield and sword techniques, and not just the dance."

The Heater and The Hack

"As we delve deeper, we will focus on training your mind as well as your body, to act and react, to consider and reconsider without need for conscious thought," Tarlis explained.

"Put down the rocks, grab your shield and sword, and find an appropriate spot."

Emanrasu, surprised at this change in routine, had no words. Informed, in one fell swoop, he was apt and a good pupil, and it was about to get more challenging and more intense.

He mulled this over as he walked out to an open area a short way away from the camp.

Tarlis followed and, along the way, picked up a branch that was about an arm's thickness and slightly shorter than an arm's length. He tested the strength of the branch and found it acceptable.

Emanrasu stopped, and Tarlis turned to face him.

"We will work on the basics of rhythm, similar to the dance; all fighting has a rhythm if you pay attention. Every fighter has their rhythm, and it is your job to determine what that rhythm is and how best to adjust your own to counter theirs," instructed Tarlis.

Similar to the dance, Tarlis showed Emanrasu how to trade blows with an opponent and what to look for as he did.

"Now, boy, attack me in earnest," requested Tarlis.

Hesitating but a moment and trusting Tarlis knew what he had requested, Emanrasu readied himself and swung a blow to cleave the old man in twain at the neck. The expected destination was unexpectedly air as the sword traveled on its merry little way to nowhere. Emanrasu felt the smack of the cane and the blow to his ribs from the thick branch as the old man deftly sidestepped and ducked. Grinning widely, Tarlis returned the blows for his efforts.

In Dreams and Dance: Chapter Nine

The training continued through the session, always with the same results, and the sting of the cane and the blows from the thick branch became expected until, for once, Emanrasu anticipated the blows and dodged them both. Tarlis stood back and grinned. "That is enough for today. You have shown the ability to learn how to anticipate. Tomorrow, we shall continue, though, without your shield and sword; I would not be appreciative if I were to lose a hand, arm, or head whilst you were training," he chuckled.

Emanrasu allowed himself a weak grin, his body bruised and battered and his muscles tight and weary from the day's instruction. "I thought the dance was exhausting," he thought, almost mumbling it but not quite.

They sorted their gear and sat down to another delicious meal, courtesy of ministrations of Serrah with the help of Rezua.

His head had barely lain on his shield as the dreams returned, the swirling culminating in a leafy branch laid across his face, startling him awake once again.

Only to open his eyes to Tarlis incessantly tapping his face with an entire branch of leaves. He grinned a wide, toothy grin, only to get a mouthful of leaves, causing him to choke and cough wildly.

Emanrasu chuckled lightly to himself as Tarlis rolled in laughter, and he even caught Serrah with an amused grin on her face.

It was the eve of this day when Tarlis became unusually distracted. Though he did not realize it at the time, Emanrasu, too, had felt a building unease.

Several times, Emanrasu caught him gazing back in the direction from which they had traveled.

"I don't know," replied Tarlis when asked about it. "Just a feeling, but I have learned over the mains that feelings and premonitions are just minute details gathered from the things and behaviors you experience. So, I have come to trust my instincts."

Over the next few days, they shortened the resting and training time, opting for pushing forward.

Tarlis stood up on the driver's bench and stared back. His intent gaze was rewarded with a low curse as he dropped back to his seat and snapped the reins to get the ox moving. The snapping became regular as Tarlis garnered as much speed from the beast as he was willing to give.

"I believe your suitor has finally caught on to our ruse." He said, snapping the reins again. "I cannot imagine anyone else would follow our path in such a bold and direct manner. They will be upon before set, I fear."

Looking across the cart at Serrah, her face crestfallen, Emanrasu's anxiety, along with his determination, grew with the jostling of the cart.

"I will not give him the satisfaction, nor her the humiliation, of returning to Erzt like this," Emanrasu thought, drawing his gear closer, steeling his resolve.

"I, for one, will not let you come to harm, Serrah," he vowed, his voice low but firm. "Not while I still have breath in my body."

Rezua threw an arm around Serrah, pulling her close.

"Nor will I," he said, meeting Emanrasu's gaze with a solemn nod.

They pressed onward, silence heavy between them, until at last, Tarlis pulled the cart to a stop.

"There is little to do but face them," he admitted, his expression unreadable. "I... I underestimated their ability to track us. I will stand ready with you, but we must decide how to confront them while we still have time."

With that, the group dismounted and set about making camp, lighting the fire as dusk settled over them. Tarlis laid out his plan, and they debated every detail until all had agreed on the best course of action.

Then, as the steady rhythm of hooves approached, drawing ever closer, they rose to meet their pursuers.

Stones and Struggles: Chapter Ten

"Resilience and adaptability are key to growth; whether facing the weight of challenges or the lightness of unexpected situations, embracing both with a balanced spirit leads to true learning and development."

—RCotD—

The group stood resolutely as the five horsemen approached. As they waited, Emanrasu slung the baldric over his shoulder, tying it securely before settling the shield onto his forearm and tightening the straps. The shield's familiar heft seemed to provide a modicum of comfort as he swung it around experimentally—first alone, then in conjunction with the sword.

Beside him, Rezua lifted a thick limb they'd found—a branch as long as Emanrasu was tall and thicker than his arm. The colossal quill-master adopted his Giant persona with quiet determination.

The two stood side-by-side to meet the approaching men.

Rezua positioned himself closer to the cart with Emanrasu while Tarlis remained slightly behind the others. Glancing at Tarlis, Emanrasu noticed that in the fading light, he had the air of being ancient and frail.

When they had discussed the upcoming confrontation, Serrah insisted they take no risks to save her. She pleaded, explaining that she would find a way out again, one way or the other.

To a man, they all dismissed the notion outright. Thus, they were of a single mind, and in silence, the four waited the last few moments.

"Ho, Serrah!" cried a voice from the approaching men.

Emanrasu glanced at her as she stiffened uncomfortably—no... straightened defiantly—her posture stoic and unyielding.

The Heater and The Hack

"I am not returning with you, Rodick. These men are taking me to Elund, and frankly, I'd go anywhere just to get away from you."

Rodick reached over and, with a chuckle, slapped one of the other men on his leg.

"You hear that, Dialon? They're going to Elund." His voice, light and cheery, somehow grated on Emanrasu's nerves and dripped with unveiled sarcasm and amusement.

He turned back to Serrah. "You're not so bright, woman. They're taking you in the opposite direction from Elund."

"Erald—Erald!" Serrah shouted back at him, her voice cracking in anger and embarrassment. Emanrasu glanced back to see her visibly shaking, face flushed deep red, jaw set firm. "They're taking me to Erald."

Rodick shrugged casually, smiling again—but this time his smile unsettled Emanrasu, though he couldn't pinpoint precisely why.

"In any case," Rodick continued coolly, swinging down from his horse, "you'll be returning with us. Gather your things."

The rest dismounted, fanning out as they approached. The little band stood face-to-face with Rezua and Emanrasu, tension thickening the air between them.

"She said she was not going with you," Emanrasu declared, tightening his grip on his shield. "So, you can remount and ride back alone."

He motioned to Rezua and himself. "Or you can face the alternative."

Throwing back his head, Rodick laughed, and without hesitation, his company joined in. The guard stepped forward and jabbed a finger into Emanrasu's chest for emphasis.

"You, boy, wouldn't be able to face my grandmother, let alone any one of these," Rodick said, waving his arms dismissively toward his companions.

Stones and Struggles: Chapter Ten

Emanrasu felt his heart quicken, and suddenly worried the self-assured guard could hear its pounding. For a heartbeat, uncertainty flickered through him, but determination quickly overtook it. With barely a pause, he stepped forward, coming nose-to-nose with Rodick.

"I will tell you what: you choose which of us you will face, and if you win, you can take Serrah, and we will not stand in your way. Should we win, you and your friends will turn and leave, never to see or bother her again. Agreed?"

"Do it!" one of the men called out from behind Rodick. "And be quick about it!"

The other guards laughed and added their encouragement to accept the offer.

Stepping back from Emanrasu, Rodick studied them in silence before his nostrils flared.

Tarlis coughed—a long, rattling sound that seemed to shake him to his bones.

Rodick's face lit up, a subtle grin flickered, his lips twitching.

"Accepted!" he exclaimed.

"Good, then choose!" Emanrasu demanded.

The smile that had played on Rodick's lips spread into a smirk across his face. "Can I trust you to keep your word, boy?"

"I swear, we will abide by this agreement." Emanrasu turned his gaze to his companions, one at a time. Each, in turn, nodded their acceptance.

Stepping away from Emanrasu, Rodick turned and pointed. "Him—I choose him."

Rodick's fellow guards burst into laughter, and as Emanrasu followed the man's pointing, his heart fell. He had chosen the old man leaning heavily on his cane with his back hunched.

"No!" Emanrasu exclaimed. "Your choices were the two of us, Rezua or me!" Emanrasu argued, tugging at the big man's tunic. "This one here, or me."

Serrah's whispered gasp came softly from behind them. "No…"

Rodick puffed out his chest and grinned once more at his friends.

"But…" Emanrasu started.

"But nothing, boy! You either honor your word, or you do not. Make your choice."

Tarlis placed a shaky hand on Emanrasu and whispered loudly, "It's fine. Mayhap he will take pity on me."

Struggling with his cane, Tarlis approached Rodick. The guard moved back, creating some space.

Stoic but visibly shaking, Tarlis struggled to stand still, leaning heavily on his cane.

Rearing back his hand, Rodick swung at Tarlis's face—and struck nothing.

The twist of the old man's hand on his cane revealed the thin blade concealed within. Before Rodick could retract his blow, Tarlis had slit the man's outfit in five places.

The blade had slid purposefully through the cloth on the underside of the arm Rodick chose to strike with. As he pulled it out, a neat slice in the material appeared. Tarlis's follow-through caught and separated the inside of the tunic on the other arm as well.

Like a harvest festival dancer, the old man slid deftly to the ground, his blade slipping through the pants on the inside of both thighs, cutting into the cloth between the man's legs, then danced back to his feet, sheathing his blade.

In all, the man had an opening on the inside of each of his limbs, and his manhood had a good view of the ground.

Stones and Struggles: Chapter Ten

The laughter from Rodick's friends thundered through the little glade. Not even the dying light could hide the damage this unsuspecting old man could have done.

Rodick's face flushed deep red, his jaw tightened visibly. Quickly drawing back his fist, he furiously advanced on Tarlis as his troop's laughter reverberated around him.

Rezua and Emanrasu stepped forward but halted as a commanding voice came from the back of Rodick's group.

"Rodick!" said the man as he stepped forward.

"Commander?" Rodick froze mid-strike, turning his head over his shoulder.

"You lost, Captain. Accept your losses and move on. Otherwise, you might find the family you wish for impossible to beget," said the Commander, motioning to the knife Tarlis had hovering near Rodick's crotch.

"Gather yourself and mount," he ordered. "We are returning—just as you promised.

"Well played, old man, very well played. You even had me fooled."

The Commander nodded to Tarlis and turned, following Rodick as the guards mounted and slowly rode back in the direction from which they came.

As the dust settled, Emanrasu heaved a sigh of relief.

"I didn't think he'd choose you, Tarlis," Emanrasu admitted. "How did you know?"

"I didn't. But I did know that most city and town guards are full of bullies and brutes. From Serrah's descriptions, he sounded more like a bully. It was easy to conclude that if he were a bully, he would pick on the weakest."

Emanrasu shook his head as he prepared to settle in for the night.

The Heater and The Hack

"Thank you, thank you, thank you all, thank you," said Serrah, reaching out and touching each one in turn.

Tarlis replied stiffly, "You may have seen the last of him, but he may let his pride overrule his prudence." He looked around at each of them. "We must be even more diligent the next few nights."

That night and the following, they kept watch in turns, but Rodick never returned.

The land they traveled remained much the same day after day—fields and woods, the occasional stream, and an isolated farmer growing crops for nearby villages.

As time drew on, Tarlis allowed freedom from training every third evening, to Emanrasu's relief.

During these times, when Rezua was occupied with other tasks or immersed in his studies and writing, Emanrasu would take the time to follow Serrah, noting her skills with the makeshift bow. She was adept at taking down small game and always prepared exceptionally delicious meals, especially considering they were entirely impromptu, based on what she could gather and kill during her jaunts.

*   *   *

One day, while they were out gathering food for their next evening and morning meals, Serrah halted and stood almost impossibly still.

Emanrasu, not wanting to interrupt her, slowly shifted his weight from one foot to another, making a slight creaking noise as he did. She turned to him and motioned for him to be quiet. She pointed ahead of them. Where he had seen nothing before, he at last saw the buck as its head sprang straight up, ears twitching from his slight noise.

Serrah nocked an arrow and drew back, pausing a moment before letting it loose.

The arrow entered the buck's chest, and it dropped like Emanrasu when Tarlis first showed him how to sweep an opponent's feet out from under them.

Stones and Struggles: Chapter Ten

"Looks like we may eat well for the next couple of days," remarked Serrah as she made her way to the fallen buck.

He was not far behind her. She had already begun working on the buck, stringing it up as he arrived.

Tying it off with practiced ease, she smiled at him as he approached.

She explained small details as she worked, recounting the lessons her father once taught her.

"See here, and here," she said, pointing to spots on the legs. "Cut there, and at the throat. That's where the blood drains quickly."

Emanrasu nodded, feeling both respect and a quiet awe for the skill in her hands.

"Had we any need of it, I would be meticulously gathering it, but we are better off leaving the extra weight to soak into the ground," she added.

She efficiently skinned and rolled up the hide, setting it aside for the time being.

"Here, hold this leg out," she instructed him, splaying it out to show him how it should be held. With Emanrasu's help, she made quick work of gutting and butchering the buck, threading a rope through cuts in the meat and stringing it up as if it were fish on a drying line.

She finished and turned to Emanrasu. Their eyes locked, and she stood for a moment regarding him. "So… are you a leg man or a butt man?" she asked without batting an eye.

His heart thundering in his chest, Emanrasu felt his face flush as he stammered, "Yes…"

Realizing that it was not a proper answer, he stammered again, trying to work his way out of the embarrassing line of questioning she had thrown him into.

The Heater and The Hack

She laughed and indicated the legs that had been fastened together and then the shoulders and hindquarters that were strewn together. She asked again, "Leg man or butt man?"

A sly grin snuck in and spread across her face once.

When he finally grasped what she was asking, he grinned and indicated, "I can handle either, but if the butt is bigger, then a butt man I am."

True to his word, Emanrasu hefted the shoulder and butt, along with other miscellaneous cuts, onto his shoulders and waited for her to do the same with the legs.

Serrah grinned and winked at Emanrasu. "If Rezua were here, we would have taken the whole deer…"

Emanrasu gazed at her in mock hurt, and as her expression shifted from humor to concern, his eyes wrinkled at the corners and a grin tugged at his mouth.

"I know," he said. "You forget how long he and I have known each other. He certainly has his useful side when he wants to let it show."

Serrah let out a sigh, then allowed herself to grin once more. Together, they made their way back to the camp, tossing the meat into the cart so she could process it further.

The evening meal was efficiently prepared with Emanrasu and Rezua both assisting wherever they could. "Amazingly delicious," thought Emanrasu as he watched his hulking friend wolfing down his meal. The sun had started to drop below the horizon as the dark overtook the last vestiges of light.

In short order, the four cleaned and packed away the last of the meal until, at last, they snuffed out the fire and bunked down for the night.

Each night, dreams of the Sun, Sky, Tree, Phoenix, and Dragon swirled through his mind, waking him at odd moments—always just as the dream seemed to connect with something in waking life.

Stones and Struggles: Chapter Ten

Each morning, Emanrasu worked on the dance, using large rocks instead of his personal gear at Tarlis's insistence.

Upon recognizing the Dance motif in the dreams, he wondered quietly, "Why am I suddenly having so many dreams of The Dance? I have never been much of a believer, and what does it mean?"

Keeping these dreams and thoughts to himself, he continued to work hard, training and strengthening incessantly as they traveled.

One evening, as they began settling in for the night, Serrah skipped back into the camp talking excitedly.

"You must see this," she said, pulling at each person's arm in turn until the three men acquiesced and followed her.

At the edge of the camp, just beyond the trees, she halted and simply said, "Watch."

They stood there for a moment; the night air was as still as rock. A familiar aroma reached his nose, but Emanrasu could not quite place it.

The breeze picked up a little, and the darkness over the field became suddenly alive with dancing light. The sound of popping and crackling filled the air as the little sparks and flames flitted across the meadow in a dazzling display.

"Isn't it beautiful?" Serrah asked.

"That's the smell," Emanrasu said as he made the connection. "It smells like our chih kit, our girochih and shehchih." They continued to watch as the evening shadows deepened and the wind strengthened.

"That is how the seeds are spread," Tarlis told them.

The crackling of the shehchih and girochih plants rubbing against each other in the wind sent waves of sparks across the field. Random patterns filled the field with light. Twice, there was a burst that sped across the field from one side to the very edge of the other side without stopping.

"Rabbits," Tarlis told them. "The rabbits and some of the other small animals are fast and small enough to dodge through the field, staying under the leaves. They still push the plants by the stems, but they can outrun the sparks and flames." The old man paused as they watched. "Rumor has it that the mixed fields were brought about by the Dragon or Phoenix attacks sometime in the past. I have never seen either, so I am not quite so sure, but I have learned that nothing is discountable."

They watched for quite some time before they turned and made their way back to the camp, satisfied with the majesty of nature.

Many times during the days that followed, the ox was given free rein to pull the cart where it would. Tarlis appeared to trust it to select appropriate trails and otherwise ignored it as long as the ox kept moving in the right general direction.

Tarlis spent the daily travel time discussing techniques and strategies with Emanrasu, using bits of emberchar to draw forms, diagrams, and methods on the seat between them.

Attentive as he was in Tarlis's teachings, he did notice that Rezua and Serrah seemed to be getting along well and spent a significant amount of time each day chatting when the enormous man was not entirely engrossed in his own thoughts.

Each evening, he would practice what had been discussed that day and reinforce past lessons as Tarlis instructed him in the finer points of fighting with a sword.

The days rolled on, and they made good time, that is, considering the route they were traveling.

His training was proceeding well, though Emanrasu always felt he could be doing better. He loved spending time with Serrah but enjoyed training as well.

*   *   *

Stones and Struggles: Chapter Ten

As he grew up toting sacks and barrels for his father, the idea of soldiering never crossed his mind. Even when the occasional guards or assemblagemen passed through on their way to whatever they did, he had never given it a second thought.

"Funny how the task of returning the shield and sword to his ancestral homeland would give him a new purpose, filling him with anticipation," he thought.

Thinking back on the incident weeks prior, when the bandit had attempted to catch him unaware, he marveled at how much luck had played a part. Understanding the elements and tactics that Tarlis had been furiously teaching him gave him a new perspective.

By all rights, he should have felt his life slip away at least twice on this journey: the first time at the camp with the bandit and the second time when he tried to assist Tarlis that first time in the little back street.

"Now, that would have been a sight to behold," Emanrasu grinned silently as he danced with his stones. "If I hadn't stumbled, I'd have been skewered like a pig on a spit. Emanrasu, you've had some luck when you needed it," he mused. "If I believed in that sort of thing—and if the trinket weren't back in Rezua's possession—I'd say the pendant was watching over me."

He moved through the complex motions of the dance, mostly fluid now. Tarlis began regularly swapping out his training stones, each change increasing their size. The stones he used now were the size of his head, but with their natural grips, they were easy to hold.

Tarlis had added arm movements along with the footwork, and at first, the whole movement felt genuinely like a dance. As he advanced and the foot and handwork became more intricate, he realized that he was indeed going through the motions of a battle.

One evening, long after he had come to understand, Emanrasu asked, "The motions you have taught me these past several days feel less like a dance and more like an intricate battle, don't they?"

The Heater and The Hack

"Well, it is about time you started to grasp the concepts. Put the rocks away and sit."

Tarlis sat on the edge of the cart and motioned to the spot beside him. Emanrasu set the rocks in the cart and did as he was bid.

Tarlis's eyes poured over him, and the old man almost imperceptibly shook his head. "My boy, you are by far the most apt pupil I have ever had, and I have trained some excellent soldiers in my time, many good enough to enter the Assemblage's personal guard," he answered in all seriousness.

"Those young men typically train for battle from the moment they are able to walk, and many still will never be worthy of the knowledge I have imparted to you up to this point, let alone the knowledge you still have left to learn.

"You started only within the past, what, two, maybe three moons? According to you, you never lifted more than a table knife to spread your butter."

"Well, it wasn't—that—bad," Emanrasu countered. "I did have the occasional opportunity during the Feast of the Dance to slice off a chunk of the spitted ox. So, I do have a little experience," he grinned. "Just not a lot."

Tarlis shot him a dour look, but the laughter in his twinkling eyes was easy for Emanrasu to spot now. So he replied in mock acquiescence, "I am sorry, master, I should not have interrupted; please continue," he trailed off.

Tarlis sternly continued, his eyes rolling in this playful exchange. "As I was saying,—boy—, you have taken to this like a fat man to a spitted pig, with a fervor and delight I have seen in very few students. I have noticed other things, too. Now might be as good a time as any to relay my thoughts to you."

"Have you ever wondered why you train with rocks and not with your shield and sword?" Tarlis queried.

Stones and Struggles: Chapter Ten

"Well, no, I never really gave it much thought. I guess so that I would not hurt myself if I were to stumble, I suppose, though it is merely a logical guess," Emanrasu replied.

Tarlis grinned, "No, you have more balance than most cats I have seen.

"Have you ever heard of the Black? The Black of the Dance, to put it more formally?"

Without waiting for an answer, Tarlis continued. "No, well, the Black was the keeper of the peace in most of the entire realm. Though he never held a position officially by the Assemblage, he was held in high regard by all that knew him."

Emanrasu shrugged. "Never heard of him."

Tarlis grinned. "I knew that already, or you might have suspected more these past weeks."

"The Black carried a shield and sword, much the same as you do. I had a chance to see it on numerous occasions, and it was a complex representation of the Dance. It was, in essence, subjects of the Dance placed upon a blue and green field, representing the Sky and the Earth. Blue, green, red, gold, and silver. The Sun and Phoenix, the Dragon and the Tree emblazoned exquisitely on his shield," he continued.

Emanrasu perked up as the old man talked about this.

"My dreams seem to follow this same pattern," he thought without interrupting.

"The Black had a son, weak of back and mind if my opinion is to be heard. Though I do not know the full story behind it, the boy stole the shield and sword and disappeared, never to be seen again. Well, at least to my knowledge," Tarlis paused, shaking his head slowly. He looked around as the sun dipped and allowed the darkness to swallow the land.

The Heater and The Hack

"We will continue some other time; we need to get some food in us and get to bed," he said, abruptly hopping off the cart and starting to fuss with various things.

Emanrasu took the hint, and though he suspected Tarlis had nothing pressing to do, he felt the old man was done talking for the night.

"Well, I suppose I will tell him about the dreams at a later time, too!" Emanrasu thought as he slid off the cart. He walked over to the meal that Serrah had prepared, reached in to pluck a morsel of meat, and for his efforts, got a wooden spoon across his knuckles.

"I will let you know when it is ready," she informed him.

She turned to her other tasks, but they both knew he would sneak a piece as soon as she feigned not looking. A routine that had grown into a comfortable interaction, and though it meant nothing, it meant everything.

The group had come to an equilibrium in their complex relationships. Emanrasu, uncomfortable with being the center of attention most of the time, enjoyed the time with each of the others.

Tarlis seemed to enjoy training Emanrasu but was always short and curt with Serrah, never hiding the fact she should not be traveling with them, though he seemed not to mind her being there so much when mealtimes came around.

Rezua's light heart and quick laughter complemented his willingness to help, but he mainly kept to his writing and scribbling. His growing interest in ancient languages seemed to have engrossed him, and now it shared time with his writing. Tarlis once told him, "You should put down that book and quill and learn to defend yourself and others as Emanrasu is doing." Rezua, of course, ignored the comment and never looked up.

Serrah, from the maid to the frightened fugitive to the accomplished gamer, was accepting of Tarlis's dismissive behavior and spent a lot of time with Rezua's help as she hunted, foraged, and prepared the meals. Emanrasu had never seen

Stones and Struggles: Chapter Ten

Rezua put down his scribbles for anyone, so this was an interesting turn. Emanrasu also found she was accepting of his company and allowed him to learn from her the tricks of gaming, as her father had taught her.

Well, at least this was Emanrasu's take on their little family.

He ate and laid down, his head on the shield, the sword close by, and he drifted off.

The Dragon landed heavily in front of him as the Phoenix hovered gracefully above and to the side. The two glanced at each other, and wordlessly, an agreement was made. The Dragon turned and leaned in until Emanrasu and the Dragon were practically touching, nose to nose, the Dragon's breath warm as it exited the Dragon's nostrils. "YOU KNOW!" came the rumbling in his mind. "YOU know."

For once, Emanrasu woke without a start or anxieties. And more, without Tarlis having affected some random chuckle-worthy act on him.

Emanrasu pondered the dream, "I know," he thought, "but know what?"

He mulled the thoughts over and over, and shortly, he heard a shuffling from Tarlis's direction as he realized that it was almost time to rouse.

Emanrasu pretended to sleep, only his breathing making any movement.

As Tarlis stepped across him, and before his foot hit the ground on the other side, he felt Emanrasu's blade lightly poking him between his family makers.

"Ah, you're awake, I see," Tarlis grinned, his foot hanging in the air. "Looks like I have no need to wake you this morn." And with this, he withdrew his foot and retreated to start his morning routine.

Emanrasu smiled, and as the morning progressed, he could not depart with his grin, as it returned each and every time he saw Tarlis.

The Heater and The Hack

Tarlis, in mock indignation, had placed the rocks on the edge of the cart beside his shield and sword. "Select the lighter pair," Tarlis gruffly barked, "today will be an easy day for you in honor of you not sleeping as the dead!"

Emanrasu walked over, hefted first one pair, then the other, then checked again just to be sure. Decided, he settled on his shield and sword. Tarlis raised an eyebrow but said nothing as Emanrasu jaunted off and began his training.

Emanrasu beamed with pride as he performed the motions of the dance.

"I never realized that grinning could hurt so much," Emanrasu thought. The ache in his cheeks more pronounced the more his mouth curled toward his ears.

The thought of his smile needing to be exercised and practiced made him smile all the more, which deepened the pain in his face and caused his grin to increase all the more.

"This smirk shall be the death of me," he mused, as he forced his facial muscles to relax, whereupon he realized the ridiculousness of it.

"Of all things, resting my face..." Emanrasu struggled to keep the widening grin at bay and, after some time, succeeded to some extent.

*   *   *

As the training for strength and footwork of the dance finally came to its typical morning close, Emanrasu allowed his body to relax.

"Put the shield and the sword on the edge of the cart and come here," Tarlis called to him from where the old man had been talking with Serrah.

He placed the weapons on the cart and approached Tarlis as requested. Serrah passed him as she approached the cart, flashing a smile that drew one from him in return.

"How much heavier do you think the stones are than your weapons?" Tarlis asked as Emanrasu arrived.

Stones and Struggles: Chapter Ten

Glancing over to the cart, he saw that Serrah lifted the stones and stowed them successfully, packing them in their typical location. Then she lifted the shield and the sword, awkwardly by the way she slightly struggled, and stored them as well.

"The stones are by far the heavier," Emanrasu told the old man. "I didn't quite understand why we used stones when we started, but I do now. The weapons are not variable and, initially, they were too heavy for me to use repetitively for the lengthy sessions. The stones have gotten heavier and allow us to train with heavier weights than the shield and sword."

He glanced at Tarlis, who was nodding his head in affirmation and grinning. This allowed Emanrasu a modicum of pride to know that he had guessed correctly.

Emanrasu started to ask about the stones, decided against it, and held his tongue.

Emanrasu finished assembling his packs and stowed them on the cart. Tight from this morning's training, he rolled and stretched his shoulders, then leaned against the cart as Serrah stowed her gear. Shortly after that, Rezua and Tarlis loaded their packs as well.

Tarlis stood on the cart's bench and scanned the horizon behind them. He climbed down and finished readying. "With Serrah's suitor no longer a threat, I have been heading toward the road. I still recommend being wary, just in case he comes back without friends," he began. "Traveling on the road will allow us to make much better time and, if needed, the towns can provide a room and a meal, giving Serrah a break.

"So, unless anyone has an objection, we will start following the main road as soon as we get to it."

None of the others had an objection. With that settled, they all climbed into the cart and took their customary places. With a click of his tongue and a quick snap of the reins, they were once again moving toward their destination.

The Heater and The Hack

The following days passed without incident; their routine, now automatic, flowed from day to day. On the third day, as the sun approached its apex, they reached the road.

"So as to not raise any undue concern," Tarlis told them, "I am your uncle taking you to your mother in the Gulf. I doubt we will be queried much beyond that; as for any specifics, when asked, tell them anything that seems reasonable."

"I am not sure I can pass as a sibling of these two," Rezua motioned to Emanrasu and Serrah. "Perhaps I should pretend to be a traveling scribe."

"Or," Tarlis stared directly at Rezua, "maybe I should just tell them you are all a bit daft in the head, and I am taking you to a special place with others like you," he smiled at the thought. "In any case, it should suffice to appease the random overly inquisitive."

As they traveled along the road, Emanrasu found the cart jostled much less, though the road was hardly smooth. He also felt that they had made good time as they traveled and was about to say as much when a shout came from up ahead, followed by a mild thud.

In the distance, they saw a boy getting up from the ground, dusting himself off. He proceeded to a short fence along the road and climbed to the top.

He waited expectantly, and in short order, a cow strolled up to the railing. The cow stood still as the boy climbed aboard, then, once he was settled, the cow carried him a short distance from the fence.

Unexpectedly, the cow started bucking wildly as the boy struggled to hold on, clamping his legs to the cow's sides and hugging its massive neck. It was only moments before the cow sent the boy flying to land heavily with a distinct thud. With her passenger unmounted, the cow began calmly grazing on the grass.

As the cart approached, the boy dusted himself off and proceeded to climb the railing and waited expectantly once again. Amazingly, the cow sauntered over to the fence and waited for the boy to mount again. The result, similar to the last, found the boy picking himself up off the ground as the cow calmly grazed. Twice more, this scene ensued until they pulled up alongside the duo.

Tarlis, obviously curious at this point, called out to the boy, "My boy, what in the name of the Dance are you doing?"

The boy grinned as he climbed the fence once again. "We are amusing ourselves," he stated plainly, his grin never leaving his face. "She enjoys the challenge and attention, and in truth, so do I."

The boy scratched the cow between the ears, then mounted it once again. As they watched, he was once again sent flying to the ground.

He walked to the fence again and grinned at his spectators. "You are free to try your luck if you have a mind," the boy said.

Tarlis responded, "I believe we are good on that matter!"

"Ho, there! Speak for yourself, old man!" Rezua chuckled as he dismounted the cart.

"I will give it a try," Rezua said to the boy as he stepped over the fence.

Rezua sidled up to the cow and threw a leg over the cow as it patiently waited. The cow seemed to understand when Rezua was ready, and the poor thing tried to buck the large man off without luck.

The cow, obviously more intelligent than one would have thought, took a different tactic. She walked up to the fence and leaned heavily against the railing, trapping Rezua's leg.

Rezua winced in pain as the cow scraped him off her back using a fence post. Slipping from the cow's back, he lost his balance and thudded to the ground. The cow looked around, walked out into the field, and began grazing.

Emanrasu could hold back no longer and let out a roaring laugh as Rezua picked himself back up from the ground.

The Heater and The Hack

"Smart cow," Rezua remarked.

"Would you like to try again?" the boy asked with a grin on his face.

"No. No. I think I have been humiliated enough, but thank you for the offer."

The cow came up to the boy as he talked to Rezua and nudged him in the backside. Rezua returned to the cart, shaking his head.

"I am coming," the boy exclaimed gleefully as, once again, he climbed aboard, was thrown clear, and the whole cycle repeated as they watched in obvious amusement.

After a couple more times, they saw the cow nudge the boy again to get his attention, then let him climb aboard, only to buck him off moments later.

Tarlis smiled and shook his head. He clicked, and with a quick flick of the reins they were on their way again. The four companions grinned among themselves as they left the pair behind to repeat the humorous ritual for however long, only the Dance knows.

They chuckled about this for two, almost three, hands after apex, reaching almost half-set before they started seeing other traffic on the road. Two carts had passed them going in the opposite direction, and a man on a horse had sped by going in the same direction as they were. Before night fell, they had reached Bren, which was still a solid ten days away from their destination in the Gulf.

Departure and Derailment: Chapter Eleven

"Within the most unexpected of things and beneath a deceptive surface, a myriad of surprises reside. Stand leery of and never discount nor underestimate that which presents itself without full knowledge and proof."

—*RCotD*—

As the group made their way to the Barein House, the townsfolk eyed them suspiciously and whispered amongst themselves as they scurried away like roaches in torchlight. The tension was almost palpable, and with the night drawing near and dusk entirely upon them, they were ever more grateful to be bedding down in a somewhat comfortable and safe abode.

The inn was cold and stark in the waning light, but the flickering glow from the second-story windows of the well-worn structure offered a brief respite from their long trek.

The wafting aroma of baked goods and roasted meats lingered in the air as they disembarked from the little cart. Tarlis and Rezua departed to secure the cart and the rest of the belongings while Emanrasu and Serrah made their way inside, carrying their packs and the meager belongings that Serrah possessed.

The bustle and murmur of conversation hushed as they entered; many heads turned to them, eyeing them warily.

The innkeep approached, and the quietly anxious atmosphere paused.

"We have no rooms available currently," began the keep. "There is little room and... we..."

The keep trailed off as Emanrasu pulled a silver coin from his pouch. "Are you sure?" Emanrasu asked, glancing around the sparsely populated Great Room. The roaring fire at the opposite end seemed much more inviting than the occupants.

"I...uh..." the keep stammered before turning around and hollering, "Telk! Come here, boy!"

A young lad came scurrying out of the back and presented himself to the keep.

"Sir?" the boy inquired.

The keep leaned over and whispered in the boy's ear, and after a short conversation between them, Telk ran off from whence he had come.

"It appears my first estimation was incorrect. We do still have a room available; however it is our largest room and quite pricey. We generally reserve it for special dignitaries or representatives from the surrounding towns, but since we have seen little in the way of visits from them lately, I would be willing to let you bed there. It is up at the top of the stairs, just a little down the hall. The boy will be making it up as we speak, so it should be ready shortly."

The keep's eyes never seemed to stray far from the silver, and when they did, they seemed to come back as quickly.

"The room will suffice," Emanrasu replied, handing the keep the coin he had been eyeing. "We have two companions that will be joining us as well. See to it that they are shown the room as well."

With the culmination of the transaction, the murmuring slowly resumed, and soon, there was only a furtive occasional glance in their direction.

As the keep led them to a room on the second floor, a man near the stairs was overheard, "... can't continue to stay much longer if something isn't done. The band of ruffians is not only attacking and robbing the good townsfolk, but even the travelers are starting to be accosted."

The woman sitting with him laid a hand on his arm and leaned in close, whispering, "I heard they killed a family and sold the young women into slavery. I am horrified at the thought of... or... it is horrible!" The conversation, now too far away to hear distinctly, caused Emanrasu and Serrah to look at each other.

182

Departure and Derailment: Chapter Eleven

"Perhaps I shall convince the others to stay a while and see if there is anything that we can do," he thought as he returned Serrah's gaze.

Upon entering the room, Emanrasu was disappointed. The room was a sight smaller than the keep had let on, the air filled with a thick, musty smell, though it appeared the bedding was at least fresh. The keeper handed them the key to the room and retreated, closing the door behind him.

Emanrasu glanced around the room; a dresser, two beds, and a bench were all that populated the space.

Emanrasu slid over to the wooden bench and, having already thought it through, decided that Serrah and Rezua would take the beds. Tarlis most likely would take the floor by the window.

"I will have the bench and sleep with it positioned in front of the door. Tarlis will most likely take the floor under the window, so that leaves this bed for you and that one for Rezua. I hope you don't mind too much," said Emanrasu as he sat on the bench.

Serrah let a slight grin sprout on her face, and it grew as she replied to him, "I suppose if I must. I believe I can make do." They both grinned.

"Did you hear about the bandits these poor folk are dealing with? I was tempted to interject in their conversation and offer our assistance," he started. "Should we not try to help?"

Serrah regarded him. "Are you a bit daft, Eman? What can be accomplished? Even if Rezua is of an intimidating size, he is not quite suited for the sort of help they seem to need, which leaves only an old man, a woman, and a wet-behind-the-ears warrior. What could we really do?

"Remember, the townsfolk and local people are grown adults, and I imagine they will handle it just fine," she stated as she sat on the bed opposite him and gazed down at her hands, fidgeting a bit.

The Heater and The Hack

"I, too, feel that maybe we should help in some small way, but there is little that we could do that the whole of the town could not. And I would desire to finish this journey with you 'ere I see my maker, you daft baker's boy," she grinned as she spoke, her eyes sparkling.

Emanrasu knew her jibe was only in jest, and he took it as such, though he replied, "I am deeply hurt, milady, that you would think so little of one with so huge a destiny as mine. How many have you seen undertake such a rigorous task, so fraught with danger at every turn as this? I am the bearer of the rusted shield and the tarnished sword, tasked to deliver them to the secret ones in the caverns under the Gulf." He struggled to keep a straight face as he spun the gigantic Rezua-like tale, one of epic proportions that featured himself as the lead.

Serrah played along and queried about this and that epic piece and the dashing yet fearless warrior that protected the shield and sword.

The door to the room opened suddenly, and out of nowhere, Emanrasu was brandishing the sword. So fast had it appeared, Emanrasu concluded he must have picked it up during one of the more grandiose parts of his little adventure.

Tarlis slipped through the door with Rezua close behind. Rezua closed the door quietly behind him. "We have secured the cart and the ox, and the rest of our belongings are safely guarded, at least for tonight," Rezua reported.

Tarlis summarily interjected, "I suggest we make haste in the morning, as there is talk of robbers on the road to the Gulf, and if we leave at an early enough time, we can slip past while they sleep off the night's drink."

As he quickly glanced around the room, he saw that Serrah had claimed one bed, Emanrasu was already on the bench, and Rezua's gear had been tossed onto the other bed.

"So, I get the spot under the drafty old window, eh?" The grin belied his lamentation as he readied for the night.

Departure and Derailment: Chapter Eleven

"And I was tasked with bedding the ox and stowing the cart while you two did the Dance knows what!"

"As it should be, old man!" came Rezua's grinning retort.

On that, Tarlis and Emanrasu chuckled visibly while Serrah smiled quietly, again looking at her hands.

After a brief discussion, they opted to pass on this evening's meal, and they retired for the night: Tarlis by the drafty window, Emanrasu on the bench after dragging it to cover the edge of the door, and Serrah and Rezua in their assigned beds.

Each, in their own way, was comforted by the small room and the company.

Emanrasu, as had become his habit, lay with the shield beneath his head and sword close at hand.

Above him, the Phoenix and Dragon hovered, facing one another. Their voices carried whispers of destiny and epic deeds yet to come, of life and spirit. They spoke of insurmountable odds that mortals had conquered with their aid, of Tree and Sun, of Sky and Earth—the cosmic eternal balance.

As one, they turned to face him.

Emanrasu opened his eyes to find the first light barely encroaching on the sky. He stood, well-rested, as the others began to stir.

Tarlis was sitting in quiet contemplation, having already packed.

"The rise is about to break, and we must make haste if we are to depart before the bandits rise," Tarlis announced as he scooted the bench from in front of the door.

Tarlis paused briefly and looked back at the others, then quietly slipped out the door to retrieve their cart, ox, and the rest of their belongings.

The Heater and The Hack

As his quiet footfalls disappeared down the balcony, Serrah and Emanrasu continued packing. Soon, they were set and ready to follow Tarlis.

The house was quiet and still in the early morning, save for the aroma of the morning meal. The chopping and rolling of boiling pots were only momentarily distracting as they made their way to the door. As it had been left ajar the night before, they quickly slipped out into the cool morning, eerie in its quietness, and dark as only the time before first light could be.

The soft clucking of a chicken—either up too early or never having slept—broke the silence. The pungent aroma of the cookfires mingled with the smell of roast meats and vegetables.

"Too bad we must make haste," said Rezua.

"Yes, I agree," Emanrasu grinned and winked at Serrah, "I would have loved a meal not slaved over by Serrah."

They hurried down the steps out into the cobbled street and waited.

Some short time later, Tarlis wheeled the cart onto the street. The racket of the wheels on the cobblestones was loud enough to wake the dead.

Tarlis stopped the cart in front of them, and they stowed the gear and climbed aboard, taking their usual places. Emanrasu sat on the driver's bench near Tarlis, with Rezua and Serrah seated in the back, to be bounced around as the Dance saw fit. With a quick click of the tongue and a flick of the reins from Tarlis, the cart was moving, creating a steady staccato in the early silence.

* * *

As cobblestones gave way to dirt, Emanrasu felt relieved to leave behind the stirring sounds of the rise—children's voices, creaking shutters, the first calls of vendors. They'd chosen this time carefully, when bandits were likely sleeping off their night's revelry. The town's familiar mingling of scents—stable hay, smithy smoke, unwashed bodies—gradually yielded to the clean, sharp smell of pine and damp earth from the forest.

Shortly after the sun had fully risen, they spied a group of horsemen at a crossroads, where the northern fork led to the Gulf, and the southern one led to the mountains and, from there, down the seaside to Manesre and beyond.

The group of riders milled about, seemingly waiting for someone or something.

As the cart approached the men, Tarlis hissed under his breath, "Be on your guard."

As the cart pulled up to the ruffians, two had wheeled around and placed their horses in front of the ox, effectively blocking the path.

"Ahoy and greetings, travelers!" called the lead man, his tone mocking. "We are of the Assemblage's highway guard, tasked with collecting tolls for this stretch of road. What have you to pay with?"

Tarlis replied in a meek and almost terror-ridden tone, "We have naught, sire. We are en route to the Gulf to deliver my kin to their home after an extended visit. I have a few coppers if you would, but let us pass…"

The lead man looked at his companions and laughed, "A few coppers, is it? I see a few silver or even a proper gold in that delicious womanhood there.

"Dismount so we may have a closer look, or this will turn unpleasant!"

Knowing the possible danger, Emanrasu had opted to wear his shield and sword. Thanking the Dance, he stepped down from the cart, as did Tarlis, who maintained his guise of feebleness in the face of the poor charade enacted upon them.

The old man fumbled with his cane but at last disembarked with Emanrasu's sturdy hand steadying him until, at last, he was standing beside the young man.

Serrah had climbed down as well, lingering near Rezua, looking ready to bolt.

The Heater and The Hack

The men approached and drew weapons as they did.

Serrah held an arm up as if to fend off the man who approached her and hunched down by the wheel of the cart. Rezua moved subtly to interject himself between her and the approaching men.

The men closed the gap, but as they did, with a twist of his wrist, Tarlis separated his cane, the thin blade already moving. In a single fluid motion, he severed the tendons in the nearest attacker's wrist. Almost without pause and with a visible pang of regret, he hamstrung the horse, sending its rider tumbling to the ground.

He turned to face the other man on foot as he maneuvered his back to the cart.

Emanrasu hastily glanced around, assessing the scene as best he could; an axe man was heading in his direction, accompanied by a young man sliding his sword from the sheath at his side. Three ruffians approached Rezua as he stood between them and Serrah, who cowered by the cart's wheel.

Emanrasu steadied himself in front of the burly axe-wielder, knowing the swordsman was close behind.

"Hold your own, Emanrasu. Use your reactions and your natural instinct as Tarlis has instructed, but do it quickly," thought Emanrasu.

He forced himself to relax, and then Emanrasu allowed his body to act and react, trying not to overthink it.

As the burly one approached Emanrasu, twirling his wicked-looking axe, he traded blows with Emanrasu—forward, back, slide, block, duck, swing. His insurmountable thought was that he must survive long enough to protect Serrah.

Emanrasu exchanged several quick blows before one landed that glided through the man's arm into his chest. Shocked at the ease with which the bone and meat separated, the thought was brief and fleeting.

Departure and Derailment: Chapter Eleven

A little shaken and relieved by his success, Emanrasu had no time to think and, with a fleeting glance toward Tarlis, found him holding his own. He turned and closed the gap between himself and his friends.

Rezua faced three of the imposters and was keeping them at bay by swinging Serrah's bow like a club. As Emanrasu watched, one of the ruffians disengaged from Rezua and moved toward Serrah while the other two moved to block his attempts to protect her.

Emanrasu attempted to engage the man advancing on Serrah. He narrowly dodged the sword of the other forgotten bandit, trading blows as he turned to face the swordsman—a man clearly far better trained than the axe wielder.

His attention and concern, torn between his opponent and Serrah's attacker, shattered him. From the corner of his eye, he saw Serrah—once cowering by the wheel—become a blur of motion, her knife flashing up to slice deep into the inside of the man's thigh.

The attacker crumpled, blood already seeping in cloth-muffled spurts from the savage gash in his leg.

Blood pulsed incessantly, soaking the thin fabric—hope for the would-be attacker drained with each beat.

From whence her knife came, only the Dance knows.

Turning his full attention to his attacker, Emanrasu could almost feel the pattern of the man's attacks—though he misjudged twice.

"No doubt, those will leave scars," he thought briefly.

Emanrasu danced with the skilled swordsman, matching strike and block, unable to find his rhythm—until, at last, his own misstep broke the pattern of his dance. His training said right, but his body went left. His quick recovery found an opening left by the errant counter of his foe. Emanrasu thrust hard up under the man's raised arm, straight into his chest.

The Heater and The Hack

As the man fell, Emanrasu wheeled around to assist Serrah—but there was no need. She drove a final thrust up through the swordsman's throat, under the jaw, and the image of her bleeding the deer several days ago sprang to the front of his mind.

"Her ability to butcher translates disturbingly well to humans," Emanrasu thought fleetingly.

Emanrasu dropped to his knees and spun, every instinct in his body screaming to duck—and as he thrust out his shield, it slammed into the man who had been thrown from the horse.

His sword arced cleanly down into the crook between shoulder and neck, driving deep into the man's torso. The corpse tugged at his blade, but as it crumpled, the sword slid free.

Rezua had swiftly dispatched one attacker, but another had turned toward Serrah. Before Emanrasu could react, his two friends brought down the last of their foes. Serrah collapsed with apparent relief beside the cart's wheel, where she had initially cowered.

Emanrasu scanned the field, catching Tarlis's sharp jerk of the head toward the crossroads. He followed the motion just in time to see the last surviving brigand kicking his horse into full flight. Dust billowed in his wake, already beyond bow range by a tenflight.

Emanrasu turned back to his companions, relief washing over him as he saw Rezua and Serrah still standing. He drew a thankful breath.

The fight was over.

They had survived—alive and mostly whole, a scar or two to show, perhaps, but they were standing.

Departure and Derailment: Chapter Eleven

Before Emanrasu could exhale, Tarlis was already there, slipping past him like a ghost in the wind. He dropped to his knees beside Serrah, his voice low and urgent.

Emanrasu froze.

It wasn't just concern he saw in Tarlis... it was something—something deeper. More profound.

He saw—felt—a raw, unspoken fear that didn't match the man who had stood unfazed before Rodick's guards or lured ruffians into alleys.

That fear—he realized—wasn't for the battle. It was for her.

For Serrah.

They conversed quickly—almost in whispers—too soft for Emanrasu to catch.

He rushed in—but only caught the tail end of Serrah's words.

"...I didn't know, Tarlis. I'm so sorry," Serrah murmured, reaching up to rest a hand on his arm. "You should have told me—I would have understood."

"It is painful, and not something I like to dredge up," came the muted reply. "It was but a moment in time... barely a half day's ride.

"Had I known, I would have wiped them out long before, and it never would have happened."

Tarlis's shoulders dipped as the painful memories returned. He glanced up at Emanrasu.

"I'm sorry for my behavior. I've lived in fear since my wife and daughter... well, mains ago, they were attacked on the road.

"The slavers who took them—I hunted them down..."

He drew in a breath. His eyes welled. His face turned to stone.

The Heater and The Hack

"They were traveling to see me. I was supposed to meet them in Dalridge.

"On the way there, I came across an overturned cart. And when I looked closer, I knew it was theirs. The ox was still bleeding. It had happened recently.

"I followed the trail without hesitation. There were few as skilled as I was—I truly believed I could save them."

His voice faltered.

"I found them. I scouted the camp. I saw where they'd tied my wife and daughter to a stout tree.

"Two men stood near them… touching them…"

He closed his eyes, jaw tight.

"I rushed in. The man I took for the leader didn't expect anyone. He froze. I told them—

'Cut them loose, and I will spare your lives. Loose them not, and I will have you, to a man.'

"The two near the tree looked to the leader. He grinned. He nodded. And they reached out and sliced my family's throats in front of me.

"They laughed—laughed—thinking seven would be too many for one man.

"They laugh no more.

"They'll never be identified—not after what I did in my anger and grief. The last one died crawling to escape.

"When it was over, I dropped to my knees. I couldn't move. Couldn't think.

"I crawled to my lifeless family. I held them through the night."

His voice grew quiet.

Departure and Derailment: Chapter Eleven

"But as rise broke, I knew… if I stayed, I would invite every predator in the forest.

"My soldier's training took over. I searched the slavers, hoping to find something—some sign they were more than just slavers.

"I found nothing.

"Though I gave each lifeless body a final kick or two as I took back the coins and valuables they had no right to.

"I was exhausted. Shattered. All I wanted was to curl up and vanish. But I made myself rise.

"I carried my wife and daughter from that camp, and I buried them. Properly.

"I left the slavers where they fell. Let the wolves have them. I didn't care.

"I've only told a handful of my closest friends about this.

"I would ask you to keep it to yourselves."

He turned back and took Serrah's hands, bringing them to his cheek.

"I never considered—or even imagined—that you would be capable, even adept, at protecting yourself. My past fears clouded my judgment.

"But you've proven yourself—proven you can do what needs to be done. I can't say I won't worry… but maybe I'll worry a little less.

"I've wronged you these past cycles. And for that, I am deeply remorseful."

Serrah replied softly, "There's naught you need to apologize for… well… maybe, if I'd known your reasons, I might've eased your fears a little sooner."

Tarlis looked at her, then turned his gaze to Emanrasu and Rezua.

"You three have become family to me over these past cycles. I've known it for some time… but I haven't acted like it.

That changes today."

He sighed heavily, his eyes wandering—and then halting.

He stared. His jaw dropped open.

Whatever pain had filled him moments before drained away.

His eyes were locked on Emanrasu's shield.

He turned slowly, fully toward him.

Tarlis reached out and took hold of the shield, turning it in his hands.

"I imagined as much," he murmured. "But not in my wildest dreams did I dare to hope."

Emanrasu, puzzled by the sudden shift, slipped the shield from his arm and turned it to face him.

Large portions of the crust and filth that had once encased it had fallen away during the battle. Though still partially obscured, what remained was unmistakable: the sun, the phoenix, the dragon, and the tree were plainly visible in the segments revealed—only the whole remained concealed.

"I suspected..." Tarlis breathed. Then louder—sharper—"But now... Now I—know!"

He looked up, eyes burning.

"You are the heir of the Black!"

"I've seen this shield a half dozen times or more, and there is no mistaking it. Not even in its poorly kept state."

Tarlis reached for Emanrasu's arm and lifted it gently, inspecting the sword. He ran a thumb along the ricasso, and the crust flaked off at his touch.

He drew a deep breath and exhaled slowly.

Departure and Derailment: Chapter Eleven

"There's no doubt," he said quietly. "The shield and sword you carry… they are famous in certain circles—circles I once called my own.

"You, my dear boy, are in possession of the Heater and the Hack.

"These are the shield and sword stolen from the Black… when his son absconded with them."

Emanrasu watched as Tarlis seemed tossed like a ship at sea—lifted high by hope, dashed against the rocks of memory, then rising again.

Fear, regret, remorse, relief, excitement… all churned visibly within him.

Tarlis caught his breath, steadying himself.

"Your natural gifts—and your possession of these relics—lend credence to what I can no longer deny.

"You are the Black's heir.

"And though I know not your destiny, boy… I can say this with certainty: It lies with the Dance."

Evolving Expectations: Chapter Twelve

"The pain is never forgotten, and it is only through renewal and the making of new connections that we can truly temper the pains of the past."

—RCotD—

Tarlis suddenly stood and peered around, "We best not forget what just transpired and what may wait for us, should we dally."

"You have all proven your worth and abilities today; however, there may be more coming. We need to strip the ruffians of what possessions might be useful and then dispose of the corpses. Since the woods are close, that is probably the most appropriate spot. Rezua, gather up all the weapons and anything else you can and stow it in the cart. Emanrasu and Serrah, I know it is distasteful, but we need to search all the bodies for anything that might be of value as well," Tarlis continued.

Rezua stood, gathering weapons and gear while Emanrasu and Serrah stripped the brigands of their ill-gotten wealth—possessions they had no further use for. Tarlis rounded up the horses, having noticed that some were trained well enough to hold in the middle of battle.

Tarlis's shoulders dropped as he reached the horse he had hobbled. Weak from blood loss, it whinnied softly. He stroked its neck, his face tightening—then, with a quiet breath and a steady hand, he sent the poor animal to the Dance.

The sun, less than a hand's breadth from the rise's horizon when attacked, slowly crept up into the sky. The group worked as fast as they could, but searching the bodies was much more time-consuming than Emanrasu had thought it might be.

Tarlis must have sensed this too, and shortly, he told them, "Instead of going through their belongings, just strip them bare and pile the gear into the cart."

197

Emanrasu mulled over the thought for a few seconds—torn between its indignity and the idea that they had attacked what must have appeared to be helpless travelers. And considering they did so with greater numbers, they had no right to claim in death the dignity that they had not given in life.

Having convinced himself, he nodded at Tarlis. "They had no dignity in life. Why should they be granted it in death?" Upon this remark, Emanrasu fell to stripping the bandits, and the others followed suit.

They stripped the horses as well, leaving only the harnesses, which they tied to the back of the cart. As they finished the disrobing and confiscating the gear, Tarlis grabbed the legs of one and dragged him a short way away into the brush toward the woods. "Leave them over here," he told the others. "The woods are farther than I want to haul them, but had it been closer, we would have deposited them there and let the wolves have them at their leisure."

The day grew warm, and the sweat started to bead on Emanrasu's brow.

As they finished, Emanrasu, ever the hopeful, considerate one, paused and turned to the others, "We obviously have no need for these horses, well, perhaps one, and we will definitely not need the bits and bobs of armor. I request that we return to Bren and deliver the goods to the Inn, where all can see that it is possible to fight back against these outlaws. We can divide the spoils and give half to the town if everyone is in agreement."

"We could take it and sell it all in the next town, which might afford us more coin than taking it back to Bren," Rezua commented as he tossed the last of the gear into the cart.

Serrah appeared uncomfortable, "I hate to say it, but Emanrasu is right. The townsfolk need to see that these men can be stopped. If the four of us can take down six of them, imagine how many we could be rid of if a score of townsfolk were to gather up arms and fight."

Evolving Expectations: Chapter Twelve

Tarlis nodded his head in agreement, "I doubt it will really do any good, but I feel I have underestimated enough people already." He focused on Serrah as he said this, managing an acknowledging smile.

"Back to Bren then."

With that settled, they mounted in their usual spots; neither Serrah nor Rezua was quite as comfortable as they usually were, with all of the gear thrown into the cart with them. Serrah smiled in apparent approval as Tarlis coaxed the cart around, horses in tow, and headed back toward Bren.

The group was silent during the jaunt back to Bren. Emanrasu turned over Tarlis's words in his mind. The shield and the sword... the Heater and the Hack... my own father... the son of the Black. He had never once spoken of it, any of it, never let on, never so much as mentioned it in the same breath as his grandfather. Why?

Every night, his father had labored to clean the shield and sword. Emanrasu had thought little of it before, but now... now, it made sense.

Emanrasu flitted over various memories, dwelling on each briefly only to be replaced by another.

"Each memory seems more complete now," he mused. "His father never having time to travel home, his never inviting relatives from back 'home' to visit, or even the skill Father had with horses seems less out of place with the knowledge he was the son of the Black."

Time passed much more rapidly on the way back to Bren, and before he realized it, the houses on the outskirts began to appear.

With the sun now close to apex, the town was alive with activity, and as they made their way back to the Inn, people stared intently at the cart with the five horses trailing behind. They whispered back and forth amongst themselves, and the more curious townsfolk slowly started to follow behind them.

The Heater and The Hack

"I suppose they want to see the culmination of our delivery," Emanrasu thought. "I doubt not that I would be as curious had something of the sort happened in Rintha when I was younger."

What began as murmurs grew into a hum, then a rising din as more and more people trailed behind the cart, drawn by curiosity.

As they arrived at the Inn, the occupants within had already started streaming out onto the porch to see what the noise was about.

The cart drew to a halt in front of the Inn, just outside the yard, and the innkeeper stepped down from the porch and approached.

"By the Dance—what have you done?" the innkeeper exclaimed.

"I recognize those horses, long since stolen from poor Ren before he succumbed to his wounds these three moons past."

Tarlis started to speak, but Emanrasu surprisingly took the lead. "We were ambushed at the fork—six bandits looking to take what wasn't theirs. They even had the gall to claim they'd sell my sister like common wares.

"We were not of a mind to let that happen, and when they made to attack us, we stood our ground and dispatched all but one," Emanrasu explained.

The din turned into an almost roar as the crowd, incredulous of the story, conversed among themselves on the validity of the young man's story.

Emanrasu continued, raising his voice above that of the crowd. "We stripped them bare and left them for the wolves and vultures. We are claiming but a third of the spoils; the rest," he turned to the keep, "the rest we will leave to you to disperse as you see fit and fair."

The jaw of the keep could have been used as a stoop, so low had it dropped hearing Emanrasu say this.

Evolving Expectations: Chapter Twelve

"I am afraid this may not be the end of it; the hoodlums will come looking, and thus far, they have not entered the town to do their ill work, but this may prompt them to retaliate in ways unforeseen," said the keep warily.

Tarlis interjected, "The four of us took out six of these menaces, almost seven, and us with an old man and a woman amongst us. Can you not see that they are naught to fear?

"Gather some stout men and attack them where they sleep. Rid yourselves of this blight on your families and loved ones! You will never live here in peace unless you take action."

The crowd murmured in agreement, though the occasional dissent rang out, and even a scuffle ensued. Tarlis climbed onto the cart, addressing the keep but in a commanding tone to be heard by the crowd.

"If you do not fight, you will never be free of these bandits. They have easy pickings on this road, and they will continue until the travelers dry up upon hearing they must traverse Bren to reach their destination," declared Tarlis. "You will have no news from elsewhere, no coin but your own. Goods will become scarce as the danger to deliver here will become too great to bear the cost of the guards to deliver safely."

Emanrasu watched as the crowd considered those words, even as the keep replied. "We have not the training or weapons to affect the routings that you would have of us..."

"The Dance! You have axes in great abundance for chopping wood, do you not? You have knives to cut your roast and simple wooden clubs if need be. Stand up and have some backbone!" Tarlis projected his voice now, as he spoke not only with the keep but the crowd of townsfolk that had surrounded the cart. The gathering grew in size steadily as townsfolk trickled in.

"Curiosity getting the better of them, I suppose," Emanrasu thought.

The Heater and The Hack

A voice from the back of the crowd cut through the din like a knife through a roast. "And who will lead us?" the voice called out.

"We are not battle-hardened soldiers; we are simple farmers and artisans. We have little knowledge of battles and sword fighting! We would not fare well," another chimed in.

"If you have swung an axe, then you are able," Tarlis retorted.

As Emanrasu peered out over the crowd, he struggled to make out specific words or phrases. His eyes lit on a small girl, and though he could not understand the majority of the crowd, the voice of this one girl pierced everything else—soft but sharp, like the first cry of a wounded fawn. Emanrasu felt the flood of emotions and hope from a single child.

"Mommy... mommy... MOTHER," the small girl said as she pulled at the skirt until the woman looked down at her, her hand moving to hush her.

"Is he going to bring back Daddy and make the bad men go away?" The innocence of the query raked at the last vestiges of callous disregard and solidified his decision.

"I will!"

The voice was steady. Too steady. Emanrasu looked around—only to realize the words had come from his own mouth.

His friends were staring at him.

Serrah had wanted to help the townsfolk from the start, and Tarlis had the experience to plan and lead. Rezua was apt but not really a fighter, though he too, wanted to help.

But the gathered throng was quiet, and no one seemed willing—but someone must.

"I will!"

Evolving Expectations: Chapter Twelve

His angst crept up on him, but the thought solidified. "I do not have the great experience of the old man, but with Tarlis's help... I suppose I can make this a part of my training."

He stepped up to the cart and climbed on, raising his hand as the light breeze danced with the leaves on the ground.

"I WILL!" he shouted to the crowd.

Rezua reached up and jerked his tunic. "What in the Dance are you doing?" he whispered.

Emanrasu ignored him and continued.

"Follow me, and together, we will rid your roads of these bandits!"

He glanced at Tarlis, whose jaw was practically on the floor, as was the keep's moments ago.

Tarlis reached up and grabbed Emanrasu's arm, pulling him down, and whispered to him, "The Dance, you will!"

Tarlis almost hissed, "You can barely survive in a sword battle as is. Planning a full-scale attack on even a group as weak and ill-prepared as they are, you are not ready!"

Emanrasu met Tarlis's gaze and said three words: "Make me ready!"

Tarlis exclaimed, "You shall be the death of me, boy! But... I suppose if we are going to help, they could do worse than you!"

*   *   *

Tarlis let go of Emanrasu and projected his voice once again.

"We... well, HE will lead you against the rabble that worries your roads!" Tarlis shouted to the crowd.

The Heater and The Hack

A voice from the back responded emphatically, "Praise the Dance!" Many chimed in, "Thank the Dance," "We shall be rid of the thieves once and for all!" The murmuring steadily grew as the crowd warmed up to the idea.

Rezua stood there, shaking his head, while Serrah clasped her hands, grinning at the thought of helping this town.

With the warm sun beating down on him, Emanrasu felt good and, after the success in battle, almost undefeatable. "How hard could this be?" he thought. He looked around, surveying the crowd for men or women of fighting worth. As he scanned the crowd, his hope started to wane as the vast majority were either elderly or too young to fight.

Emanrasu leaned into Tarlis. "I do not see a lot of battle-worthy among them," he said quietly.

Tarlis grinned weakly. "Well, it looks like we have our job cut out for us then, doesn't it?" he replied. "We will have to conscript as many as we can and look for help if need be. I can probably round up a handful of worthy fighters, but we will have to make the best of what stock we have."

Emanrasu turned to the keep. "You will be in charge of gathering up what battle-worthy volunteers you can. Tarlis, can we be ready within a fortnight or moon?"

Tarlis joined the conversation. "With the right volunteers, we can. We shall need to use diversions and deceptive tactics—possibly, especially if we do not have the numbers on our side."

The keep peered at the two, then glanced over to Rezua, who shrugged, and finally to Serrah. "Are they really going to attempt this?" he asked.

"This lot has harried us for almost two full turns of the seasons. Ever since the Zerocha was overrun."

Evolving Expectations: Chapter Twelve

The keep shook his head and grinned. "Well, I suppose there are worse ways to meet the Eternal Duo. I used to tell Maridt I would meet the Dance here, but I never expected her to go first, nor for me to go in battle."

The grin fell from his face as he replied, "I will attempt what you ask, though we have many that are out, forming a guard of sorts for the trade goods we sent to Erald, just on the other side of the Gulf."

The keep held out his arm. "My name is Torsun Ramstead, and I vow to assist where able to make this happen. I have had precious few visitors to my Inn since those heathens started harrying the roads, and I had been considering giving up on the Inn and making my way back to Erald, so if we can save my livelihood, I am agreeable."

Emanrasu clasped the outstretched arm. "I am Emanrasu, this is Tarlis, the large one over there is Rezua, and this is Serrah."

"Tarlis, what do you think?" Emanrasu continued.

"We will need two fortnights for any kind of proper preparation. Serrah, if you are willing to stay and help organize, it would be helpful," Tarlis grinned, "and if they find out your skills in a kitchen, we may have to fight the townsfolk ourselves to get you back."

Torsun raised an eyebrow at this but said naught.

Serrah almost immediately replied, "I would be willing and honored to assist in any form that is required." She grinned, "Up to a certain point," she winked at Emanrasu.

Emanrasu was confused for a moment; then her implication became suddenly clear to him. "Oh,—Oh—, certainly that would not be required, and should anyone make undue advances, I shall see that they never do again."

Rezua clapped Emanrasu on the back and grinned at him.

"We shall need a room and meals for the duration," Tarlis said in such a way as to leave little room for debate. "Serrah, take the gear and patch the armor as best you can; get the weapons into the hands of the local smithy so that he might gauge them, and if not ready, make them so."

Tarlis unexpectedly turned out his pouch and counted out sixteen of the twenty-three silver coins stripped from the dead bandits. He handed them to Torsun. "This should cover most of the costs for our stay, the food, as well as the repair of any weapons that might need it."

"Gather those that can meet and fight in front of the inn at a hand before dusk, and I will give them tasks to do while we make haste to Erald and back," Tarlis continued.

"I will select the best horses for us to ride, and you need to pack a small amount of gear," Tarlis said to Emanrasu.

"I will be going as well," Rezua insisted. "And unless you want to give me a beating in front of the whole town, I feel it is settled."

Tarlis stared at Rezua, then shrugged in compliance. "Okay, then, the three of us."

The crowd had begun to disperse as the conversation progressed.

"Find the best among you and have them report to Torsun with all haste—and if the Dance be with us, before the moon has cycled, we shall be rid of this blight on your town." Tarlis bellowed.

A cheer erupted from the crowd, and a few started making their way forward, reporting to Torsun and pledging their assistance.

Tarlis pulled Torsun aside and instructed him on some basic fighting techniques. It was nothing as complex as the dance. It was simple and straightforward enough to be learned in short order. "It will not be enough to stand against a well-trained fighter, but if they work in concert and press the advantage of numbers, it will suffice," he told Torsun.

Tarlis departed to see about the horses, and Emanrasu started digging through the gear to select what he surmised would be needed to make the journey to Erald and back.

Serrah stepped forward, holding out her arm. "Safe travel and journey well," she said, her eyes glistening; the frown and the slight waver in her voice mirrored Emanrasu's own reluctance to part ways, but he was loathe to see these people suffer just for his own personal comfort.

Emanrasu paused and looked at her extended arm. However, in a moment of impulse, he stepped in and hugged her. "I will miss you, and I vow to return as quickly as possible."

Serrah paused, the shock on her face expressing how unexpectedly surprised she was. The shock faded even as she spread a grin and hugged him back tightly. "Please be safe!" she said in almost a whisper.

Not to be left out, Rezua reached out and wrapped them both in a bear hug. "I am going too, you know," he added with a wink.

She loosed an arm and wrapped it around Rezua, well, as much as anyone could wrap an arm around him. She hugged firmly and then pulled away and glided off to assist Torsun in his preparations.

Emanrasu watched her go. "I will return safely," he reasoned. "I can no longer imagine not having Serrah at hand, so much has she just been there in the background these past many moons." His brow knit as he returned to gathering gear for the trip. He felt her absence already—and he hadn't even departed yet.

Rezua clapped him firmly and squeezed his shoulder. He offered his typically sympathetic nod.

The Heater and The Hack

Emanrasu and Rezua, along with a handful of volunteers, hauled the rest of the gear into the Inn for safekeeping. After speaking with Torsun, he turned the cart and ox over to him to get settle in and keep until they returned.

As they readied the cart, Tarlis saddled and prepared the horses.

Emanrasu and Rezua finished offloading the confiscated gear as Tarlis approached. "I've taken a turn with Torsun—showing him some fundamental stances and movements. They won't make warriors of the townsfolk, but they might provide some measure of ability to defend themselves should the need arise.

"There's little left to do in preparing them while we are gone, so I suggest we make haste. It's a long journey to Erald, and if all goes well, it shall be a longer journey back; though, the Dance be willing, we shall have some help."

Torsun approached, leading the most colossal draft horses Emanrasu had ever seen—towering beasts built for endurance and strength.

"I thought you might be needing something a little more substantial," Torsun said, looking at Rezua.

"Wonderful! I was concerned about the poor beast that was going to have to carry me," said Rezua, his eyes sparkling, as his grin brightened his face. He gently clasped the man's shoulder as he took the reins.

"I very much appreciate it," he continued, "and I can be assured that the horses do as well!"

Tarlis, Emanrasu, and Rezua finished saddling the horses and mounted them.

Rezua swung his trunk of a leg over the largest steed, his great size still making the big horse merely seem average. Within moments, the trio was on the road and began the long trip to Erald.

Depth of Decisions: Chapter Thirteen

"In the journey of life, one must understand the weight of responsibility and growth when balanced between strength and morality. Finding an appropriate model and mentor is crucial for growth and balance. Life is precious, and the taking of a life should not be done lightly. One's survival at the cost of a life in self-defense can easily lead us down a path of apathy for life itself. Choose wisely, never defaulting to violence when another path is available."

—RCotD—

The three sped out of town at a full gallop; soon, they were upon and then past the fork in the road where they had been accosted. Within the briskness of the wind and amidst the pounding of hooves, talking was a challenge. However, a thought entered Emanrasu's mind as they approached the location of their recent battle.

He called out to Tarlis, "Should we stop and hide the bodies better?"

Tarlis easily projected his voice, "What? Speak up, my boy!"

Emanrasu repeated himself, hollering at Tarlis, "Should we stop and clean up the area?"

"No! The one that got away undoubtedly informed them of what had happened, and since we were heading in this direction, there would be no reason to suspect we went back to Bren," Tarlis replied.

"Since we were headed in this direction when we were attacked, there is no reason to believe we would turn around and go back."

Emanrasu mulled it over—but Tarlis was right.

The rhythmic clop of hooves wove through the thunderous pounding of the draft horses beneath Rezua, creating a steady beat to the whistling wind. Though

The Heater and The Hack

Rezua looked less than comfortable atop his enormous mount, he managed the ride well enough.

Emanrasu, however, was exhilarated. The motion took him back to his childhood—riding alongside his father, an unexpectedly accomplished horseman. He had often wondered how a baker could be so skilled in the saddle, but his father was never forthcoming, and all such questions had gone unanswered... until today.

The trio rode on, the steady drum of hooves and the wind's sharp whistle cutting through the silence. Emanrasu let his mind wander amidst random thoughts as a snake in the grass, weaving through his father, Rezua, Serrah, and various other fleeting subjects.

Drawn out of his reminiscing, Emanrasu realized Tarlis was motioning them to slow.

Emanrasu slowed and brought his horse to a walk. Rezua followed suit, and soon, they were at a pace that provided Rezua at least what appeared to be comfort.

"There is no reason to wear out the horses so early on," Tarlis said. "It is getting late, and we need to find a place for us to camp and spar. I have much to go through with you; it is time for you to start learning advanced techniques. You have excelled in the basics, and your diligence in your practicing has become near flawless."

"You ride well for a baker's son," Tarlis remarked as they trotted. "How did you come to learn?"

Emanrasu shrugged. Reaching down, he scratched the horse's neck, then patted it.

"Good question. For most of my childhood, I had only the tasks of a baker's boy, but one day, my father took me out on one of the deliveries. We met a man from Tothis, and he had two horses with him. My father had apparently made a sort of trade for either the horses themselves or their extended use... I was never sure which," Emanrasu explained.

"I recall delivering fresh baked goods to the man for mains afterward. My father, as I recall, was an excellent horseman, though he never talked about how he came to be so. Of course, in retrospect, now I can understand why he kept the secrets that he did. I was actually surprised at how well my father could ride, and apparently, he was a fair instructor as well, seeing that I can still ride after all this time," grinned Emanrasu.

As the sun fell toward the horizon, they began to skim their surroundings for a suitable place to camp, eventually locating a small clearing somewhat off the road. They swiftly veered off the road and dismounted. After unsaddling the horses and rubbing them down, they tied them to a tree, giving them plenty of room to graze.

They finished making camp and set about sparring. Tarlis insisted that Emanrasu use his shield and sword during training, trusting in Emanrasu's skill and the influences of the legendary artifacts to spar without getting himself killed. Tarlis used his cane, as he usually would, showing exceptional control and techniques.

Rezua sparred as well, to Emanrasu's surprise. Though the big man was slow and lumbering, he at least seemed to have the balance and motions down.

"How long have you been training, Rezua?"

Rezua grinned, "For many weeks now, though you were always too busy to notice."

The short exchange earned them both a rap with the cane. "Back to work," Tarlis demanded.

They sparred for a while, Rezua focusing on the basics and Emanrasu on more advanced movements. Tarlis worked with each of them in turn as the evening advanced.

The Heater and The Hack

Exhausted, Rezua turned to his writing and drawings, while Emanrasu and Tarlis continued training.

They sparred until the light became dim, Emanrasu's skill growing in leaps and bounds, guided by Tarlis and enhanced by the Heater and the Hack. The precision he felt as he earnestly practiced amazed even himself.

*   *   *

"Hold," Tarlis said, breathing heavily. "I am in excellent physical condition for my age, but I can commonly outlast any young man I am up against.

"You have taxed my endurance and do not show signs of slowing down. On the contrary, you seem to be getting faster and stronger as we continue to spar. So wipe down your equipment and get ready for sleep. Once we have retired for the night, I will tell you what I know."

He did as the old man suggested, cleaned his gear of dust, and carefully sheathed the sword. With each passing day, the tarnish seemed to flake off more quickly.

They stretched out, Tarlis a few feet away—slightly closer than Rezua—the horses beyond, grazing lazily between them and the road.

Tarlis shifted, fidgeting with his cane blade, his eyes drawn unerringly to the Heater.

"The techniques I've been training you in were taught to me by your grandfather—the Black himself. He was my friend and mentor, finding me as a boy and seeing something in me that made him take me under his wing, so to speak…

"I went through the same rigorous training that I've put you through. But what's taken you months—nay, weeks—to master took me several harvestmains."

Tarlis paused as he honed the edge of his hidden blade.

Depth of Decisions: Chapter Thirteen

"Had I not seen it myself, witnessing it firsthand, I'd have called it madness," Tarlis admitted. He motioned to the shield, upon which Emanrasu reclined as usual. "Look at your shield; even during sparring, the filth has been literally sloughing off."

"Yes, I noticed as I was wiping them down," Emanrasu stated.

Tarlis continued talking about the history of the Black, linked intimately with the Dance—a bond linked through lineage and righteousness. "There may be other factors that come into play to link the Heater and the Hack to the cosmic conduit, for lack of a better description," Tarlis said.

"The Black, even though he had the connection, could not explain it much better. He had dreams each night that guided him in decisions of an encompassing nature."

Tarlis closed his eyes and smiled. " I have seen him halt armies—already set on the battlefield, one wrong breath away from war. His abilities were uncanny..."

He looked intently at Emanrasu. "...and he always found the compromise that all could live with, and those that would not compromise out of sheer spite or pigheadedness became intimate with the Heater and the Hack.

"The Black was not an easy man to please. His expectations—where I was concerned—were far beyond what he expected from others he commanded.

"He is definitely a tough man. Well... was."

He ran his thumb slowly alongside the edge of his blade, stopping occasionally and applying the stone. Tarlis paused and glanced up.

"Our journey," Emanrasu said with a wistful shrug, "well... Rezua's and mine, began to meet family in Rinewood Gulf, and now, with my grandfather passed...

"Are you aware of any other family he had? And why— well, I know about your wife and daughter—but why leave the White?" Emanrasu asked as the questions swirled in his head.

"To tell the truth, I rose through the ranks quickly, proving myself, until finally, I was second only to the Black himself. But when my family was murdered, I could no longer bear to be around those familiar haunts. The tragedy took hold of me and buried itself within my heart and soul. It stripped me of everything I thought I was or thought I would be. I left with only the clothes on my back."

"When did you learn about the Black's passing?" Rezua piped up from across the camp, his quill whispering across the page.

"It was several mains later when I heard his son made off with the Heater and the Hack. It was a tragedy, to be sure. However, your grandfather was not the Black 'because' of the Heater and the Hack..." Tarlis said, looking at Emanrasu. The crackling of the fire popped in perfect emphasis of this statement.

"No, he was the Black because he had the brilliance to make hard choices and see the paths forward from impossible situations; these gifts were his own, possibly enhanced by the ancient artifacts, but still his alone."

As always, Rezua listened—but his quill never stopped moving.

"How did he die?" asked Emanrasu.

"I was not around when the Black succumbed, but to hear tell, he was heartbroken by the betrayal of his son, which led to his distractions, and eventually, a knife in his back took his life," Tarlis explained. "Though these are just rumors, and I have not been in contact with anyone that would know for sure in over fifteen cycles."

"Cycles?"

"Harvestmains," Rezua corrected, then held up a finger to his lips before Emanrasu could ask more.

"Your skills are growing at an unprecedented rate; I have never seen someone take as naturally to the concepts of the dance fighting style as I have seen you do. I would swear, during our sparring, you came within a hair's width of killing me over a score of times, only to pull up or alter the path of your sword as it swung past," Tarlis said incredulously.

"Get some rest; we will spar again in the morning before we mount up and continue our journey," Tarlis suggested.

As Emanrasu stretched out, he suddenly realized he did not feel the weakness in his limbs that typically accompanied his initial training sessions.

"I don't feel tired, winded, or sore," he said as he finished stretching and closed his eyes.

"We will have to find ways to advance your training further, then. We can't have you wasting your nighttime on mere sleeping… best to have your body trying to repair the damage of training while you sleep." Tarlis threw an arm over his eyes and grinned.

Across the little camp, Rezua gathered up his journal and quills and settled in. "Good night, Eman; I am glad you have found something you seem to be good at," the big man said with a grin. He rolled over and pulled the blanket in tight.

"I am glad too, my large friend," Emanrasu responded.

Emanrasu glanced over at Tarlis, who was now fast asleep. Laying his head upon the shield, he, too, drifted off to sleep.

The dream solidified and slowly transformed into a familiar scene…

The Phoenix and the Dragon swirled around each other in the blue sky; in perfect balance, they danced. The dance slowed, and together, the pair slowly descended to the ground in front of him.

"Emanrasu, you have taken up the symbols of the Dance; in doing so, you had a choice. Without hesitating, you continue to make choices that right the scales around you. Balance in all!" the Dragon roared.

"In Balance, Brilliance," shrieked the Phoenix.

The Heater and The Hack

Emanrasu, perhaps for the first time, started to understand the interplay of the Dance. He noticed the Sun as it eternally cast forth the life-giving rays, and as the Tree of Life absorbed them, it imparted life to all things in exchange. The Sky and the Earth provided shelter and sustenance for all manner of man and beast, juxtaposing the physical with the ethereal. The Dragon and Phoenix seemed almost an after-effect, providing more definitive activity amongst the entities.

"Emanrasu," the Dragon continued, interrupting his train of thought, "you will keep the balance, and forever are you linked to us. We shall serve to guide you and illuminate the path before you. Stay true to yourself. Awake," the Dragon finished. "NOW!" the Dragon roared.

*   *   *

Involuntarily grabbing the edge of his shield as he woke, he rolled off it, flipping it over on top of himself, briefly musing how anyone, let alone himself, could perform that maneuver. Surprisingly anticipated, the attacker's sword crashed into the Heater with a thunderous clang.

"Balance," the word barely formed in his mind as he shoved the shield upward, cracking his attacker square on the chin. The man dropped, crumpling in a heap. The moonlight glinted off another attacker's knife, and the attacker's hand went limp as the edge of Emanrasu's shield slammed into his wrist, the sound of bones crumpling under the force.

Emanrasu deftly slipped his arm into the straps of the shield as he brought it back up to fend off a sword blow that reverberated through the shield. His leg swept the man in the same fashion that Tarlis had once used on him, and with a satisfying thump, the attacker fell to the ground.

Emanrasu brought the sword around, slamming it into the felled man, cutting deep into his chest.

Depth of Decisions: Chapter Thirteen

Wrenching the sword from the lifeless attacker, he rolled away and assumed a defensive crouch. From this position, he was able to survey the scene around him.

Tarlis was beset by three brigands but seemed to be holding his own.

Rezua, outnumbered four to one, swung his pack like a war club, forcing the bandits to keep their distance. Dashing over to his enormous friend, he barreled into the back of an unsuspecting attacker, forcing him into another and sending them both sprawling.

Emanrasu dispatched the two prone men without thought and turned to help Rezua but found that the meaty quill rider, taking advantage of the provided distraction, had knocked one of the men four strides away using his pack. The man lay motionless, but the remaining bandit pressed in upon Rezua and succeeded in nicking his shoulder before he could recover.

Thrusting the shield between the brigand and Rezua, he forced the man to step back, causing him to stumble, the results of which cost the brigand his life.

Surveying the scene, he saw Tarlis was still keeping his attackers at bay. The dead silence was only broken by the various sounds of battle. The clank and clang of metal on metal echoed eerily through the trees.

As Emanrasu sprinted in the old man's direction, he pointed at his large, winded friend. "...good?" He bellowed the query, using his shield to indicate he was speaking to Rezua as he continued his dash across the small clearing.

"Go!" Rezua shouted as he reached out to calm the skittish horses.

Tarlis, now facing four men, had his back to a tree, and though he was not in a good position, he had thus far kept them at bay by weaving what appeared to be a magnificently executed defense.

Two of the men turned from Tarlis to face him. Emanrasu parried, slamming his shield into the face of one while ducking the other's blade. His own blade sliced deep into the first man's thigh, the blood gushing from the wound as the man fell to the ground.

The brigand scrambled to tie off the leg and stop the bleeding. Emanrasu threw the Heater toward the other, and as the man dodged, the man's sword hand came within range. Emanrasu took advantage by relieving the man of both the sword and the hand.

The brigand watched as his hand and the sword fell to the earth, and as eyes shifted up to look into Emanrasu's face, he lost his head.

Emanrasu dispatched the injured man and turned to Tarlis.

Tarlis, liberated to extol the full extent of his skill, made short work of the two men left.

Emanrasu swung about, his back to Tarlis, trusting the old man to guard him if the need arose. His eyes drifted from his mentor, surveying the scene once again. The carnage wrought was impressive, considering they had been caught unaware.

Though the sound of life slowly returned, there were no detectable movements other than the three of them and the mounts.

A crunch of twigs behind him—Emanrasu spun, sword raised, prepared for the worst.

"Settle, boy! The last one fell to my blade while you watched." Tarlis grinned, his eyes gleaming.

Emanrasu now noticed his heart pounding in his chest, breathed in deeply, and warily stood. He leaned against the tree for support.

"I have never seen the like," Tarlis exclaimed, grinning. "You... lazing around... while Rezua and I are here fighting for our lives... then you proceed to dispatch five... no... six..."

Depth of Decisions: Chapter Thirteen

Tarlis looked over at Rezua, who now held up two meaty hands with seven fingers outstretched. The old man pointed at the fingers of the mountainous man. "Seven… seven?"

Rezua nodded his affirmation.

"Seven of them, and without even asking if we needed help. Practically the alley all over again," Tarlis grinned so broadly that Emanrasu fully expected his face to split in two.

Suddenly serious, Tarlis clapped Emanrasu on the back. "In all honesty, boy! You have proven more than adequate in battle and are surely a match for the Black himself," said Tarlis. "Some of those moves, I never taught you, and one of them, I have never seen done, by anyone—ever!"

Emanrasu saw his gigantic friend had already bound the superficial wound and was dressing again in his tunic.

The trio confirmed that all of the brigands would ply their trade no longer, hurrying along those who had not already succumbed to their wounds.

There was no pleasure in this. "Simply a need to keep them from reporting that only the men on horses were found and the cart, along with the woman, might still be close by," Emanrasu thought as he dispatched the last of them.

"We should probably mount up and leave," Emanrasu said as he gathered up his belongings.

Tarlis waved him off. "No need. If you consider they found us one of two ways, either they happened upon us without looking, or they were sent specifically out to find us."

Tarlis held up a finger. "In the first case, no one would have expected them to find us and thus would not be sending another group until this group is determined to be overdue if they were being expected."

The Heater and The Hack

A second finger joined the first. "In the second case… they outnumbered us three to one, and even had they been victorious, they would not have returned until long after the rise.

"So, in either case, there is no cause for lost sleep. Strip the bodies, drag them off into the woods, and settle in. We will leave at first light."

They stripped the bodies of valuables and dragged them away from the road and deeper into the woods, stashing the brigands' gear some ways away. Tarlis appraised the horses, and they selected the best of them as spares—the rest they staked out strategically around the camp, just in case.

"With the extra horses," Emanrasu spoke as he thought, "pushing harder and faster will be an option. We can rotate them to keep them somewhat fresh, and there will be less of a need to rest…

"It does feel strange, though, the bandits trying to dispatch us and steal what little we had… only served to put more coin in our pouches and pockets. A bizarre turn of events indeed."

Rezua groaned. "Pushing harder will mean no time to write or sketch! Though… I suppose I shall allow it… as it is still all for a good reason. I can catch up later if needed."

The three settled back in, and the night passed quietly, though it was not entirely restful, and in the morning, Tarlis kept glancing at Emanrasu. The amazement on Tarlis's face was still unmistakable even as they broke camp and mounted.

Emanrasu, proud though he was for impressing Tarlis, mulled over the events of the night. "Taking a life—even in defense—had consequences. And those consequences… had a way of manifesting in unexpected ways."

They loosed the unneeded horses and shooed them off to either return to their stables or to embrace their freedom.

Depth of Decisions: Chapter Thirteen

With dawn breaking and fresh horses in tow, the trio rode for Erald—knowing this would not be their last battle.

In Black and White: Chapter Fourteen

"Trust can seem fickle—granted on a whim yet rarely earned. In a realm where life and death often intersect, true trust is never easy to obtain. It demands repeated demonstrations of integrity—multiple proofs that you can be relied upon. To claim such trust, begin by acknowledging both your strengths and your shortcomings. Do not shy away from revealing these vulnerabilities to those who already trust you or to those whose trust you seek. Through this honesty, you forge enduring bonds and discover true companionship."

—RCotD—

The next two days followed the same rhythm—riding hard, switching horses, making camp, training, sparring, and resting—repeated without much deviation.

With the extra coin in their pouches courtesy of the attackers, food was easy to come by. There were enough scattered inns and farmers from which to purchase food, and sometimes, they took a break from the riding to eat, though they mostly ate while they rode.

As they passed through Rinewood Gulf, Emanrasu felt a twinge of regret. This had been his destination once—but now, it was just another place he had to leave behind.

Tarlis pointed toward a distant tree-covered mountain. "Our destination is close to there," he informed Emanrasu and Rezua.

The Gulf was small, taking merely a hand to traverse from one side to the other. While riding through the Gulf, they took the opportunity to walk the horses, even dismounting for a while to stretch their legs.

Emanrasu felt the ache and burn in his legs and back caused by the unaccustomed activity. He glanced over at Tarlis, looking for any sign of discomfort or weakness in the old man, but found none. To his mind, the old man appeared as sturdy as forged steel, especially if he did not feel the ache of the long ride in such a short time. He chuckled softly at the thought of the man actually being forged in fire and coming out shiny and impervious to the "worries of man."

Rezua, on the other hand, opted to walk even when the others rode while walking their horses. His great strides ate up the distance in keeping with the gait of the horses. His lack of comfort riding the horses was apparent, but he had no outward complaint.

"Tarlis, sometimes… it seems like nothing gets to you. Not even this endless riding…" Emanrasu said as he hurried his pace to walk alongside his mentor. "Why are you not sore from all this riding?"

"Boy, you would be surprised how much pain one garners as someone ages. This is just one more pain to ignore. Though I should say I feel the discomfort; however, I just choose to accept it and understand its worth. Without the pain, we do not make as good a time. This leads to not returning quickly enough with help and leaves the fate of Bren lying on the measure. The longer we take, the more likely the measure is one which we do not desire.

"Oh, I feel the pain," Tarlis admitted. "I just choose to ignore it in deference to the task at hand. And… right now… there is a task at hand."

"Tonight, I will teach you a few methods for ignoring the pain. Though they are nothing garnered from the Black, these techniques have served me well over the mains, both in and out of battle," the old man insisted.

As they reached the far side of the Gulf, they mounted once again and rode at a full gallop. Emanrasu gauged they were barely a half day's ride to Erald.

Musing to himself, Emanrasu considered the timeline. "We should be barely half a day's ride from Erald, where we can rest and gather up help from Tarlis's friends, if they are willing, and, with any luck, be back on the road by tomorrow eve at the latest."

In Black and White: Chapter Fourteen

Satisfied with this, he let his thoughts drift off, recalling the dream of the first night out from Bren.

Am I part of this—a cog in the grand scheme of the Cosmic Dance? Why me? What had he done to be blessed or cursed with this?

The incessant clop of the horses had become oddly comforting over the past days. Maybe they were counting down the time until he saw Serrah again.

The thought hit him—unexpected, undeniable.

She would be a fitting companion… wife.

He grinned ear to ear at the idea of Serrah being beholden to anyone. Work with, yes. Barter and trade, absolutely. But devoting herself to one person?

The image almost made him laugh aloud.

As humorous as it was, the fleeting thought refused to leave him.

The more he tried to think of anything else, the more it rooted itself. So, eventually, he let it stay—amusing himself with the idea.

Serrah, cooking and cleaning. Feeding him as she scurried around their—what? Hovel? Castle?

Farm. Yes. Conceivably a farm.

These and other thoughts chased each other around his mind as they made the last leg of the journey to Erald.

The day was getting late when they rode into town, dusty from the road.

Tarlis led the way, weaving through turns and back alleys like a man born to them. Emanrasu was thoroughly lost—but trusted the old man could find his way.

In time, with the sun brandishing its rays full into Emanrasu's eyes, Tarlis pulled up outside a run-down tavern.

The Heater and The Hack

The sign, long since fallen, leaned wearily against the wall beside the door. "Flying Griffon" emblazoned on its face. "A little ironic, if you ask me," thought Emanrasu.

Tarlis stripped the blanket from his horse and handed it to Emanrasu. "Bring the Heater and the Hack, but drape the blanket over the Heater so that none may see. I have not frequented this establishment for longer than I can recall, and things might have changed drastically in that time."

Tarlis nodded to a man on the bench outside and dropped the reins without tying off the horses.

"Are they here?"

"Yes," the man replied. "They are here more oft than not these days."

Tarlis grabbed Emanrasu's arm and firmly guided him inside, with Rezua trailing them.

Once inside, they stepped to the side, out of the walkway, and he released his grip. Their eyes adjusted to the dimmer light inside of the tavern. The Flying Griffon was a run-down tavern with a rough and ready look, similar to the patrons who frequented it.

After a few moments, Tarlis motioned them to an empty table near a rowdy group of rough-looking individuals. Each was wearing weapons or had them placed strategically nearby.

A huge man, a head shorter than Rezua, laughed loudly. He was seated facing the others at the table.

Tarlis, having seated his companions, approached the man from behind, motioning the others at the table to silence. He rapped the big man on the head, and as the big man spun around, Tarlis deftly placed the end of his cane up under the man's chin. He reached up and grabbed the large man's beard, pulled his head down, and whispered something in his ear.

In Black and White: Chapter Fourteen

Emanrasu watched the interaction with some concern, and as the man reached out and grabbed and lifted Tarlis by the front of his tunic, Emanrasu instantly unsheathed his sword, the point of which now touched the big man's throat.

As the table erupted in uncontrollable laughter, Tarlis motioned the young man to stand down. The big man, still hefting Tarlis in the air, brought the man in and hugged him, joining in the laughter.

"How are you, old friend?" the bear of a man rumbled, his deep voice shaking the empty mugs, of which there were exceedingly few.

"And who, pray tell, is your young protector?" the man queried as he peered at Emanrasu. His eyes drifted up to Rezua, who stood at the ready, a chair leg clutched in one of his meaty paws. "Or should I say protectors?"

He grinned and spoke to Rezua, "It is a better club if you actually remove the leg from the chair."

Rezua, looking uncertain, slowly lowered the chair back to the ground as the echoing laughter faded.

The big man set Tarlis down and slapped him on the back.

"Do you know everyone?" the man asked, gesturing around the table.

He waited for an answer to neither of his questions and started going around the table, making introductions as needed.

"Darth, you know, or better remember him quick, as he never shuts his trap about the time the two of you had to fight on the deck of the ship..." the man grinned as he continued.

"Eirikr has a nose for defense.

"Alaric, swordsman extraordinaire... and is the best I have seen outside you, Tarlis.

"Djorn, you know... but I would be remiss if I did not stroke his ego and say he is the best damn gamer I ever met." He grinned all the more when Djorn slammed a fist to his chest in the old greeting of the White.

"Olaf...

"Leif...

"Freydis with the two huge battle axes," he grinned as he held his hands in front of his chest as if testing melons.

"And last but not least, Catlina, who knows how to sail a fallen leaf or blade of grass if you gave her a handkerchief for a sail."

"Catlina, Eirikr, Alaric... this is Tarlis Stormbringer, the last Commander of the White, second only to the Black himself, and the best man I have ever known," he grinned and pointed around the table, "yes, even better than you lot."

Tarlis took the hearty welcome in stride, only stumbling slightly from the jostling by the big man. "Onred, may I introduce Emanrasu, the rightful 'Black of the Dance' sporting the Heater and the Hack, no less."

The table quieted suddenly at this statement, and all eyes turned to Emanrasu, sizing up this young man and staring intently at his shield and sword. Having done as Tarlis had bid him, the shield covered in the blanket, its sigil hidden, even as it still enabled him to wield it should the need be.

Onred swept Tarlis aside, swung a chair around, and straddled it, looking at Emanrasu. "So, you're the Black?"

"And by what right?" queried the large man.

"The last Black died a ten-main ago, with his son having absconded with the very thing that made the Black, and you are claiming to be the rightful Black. Preposterous!"

In Black and White: Chapter Fourteen

He shifted his gaze from the young man back to Tarlis, who said, "He is not claiming the title. He knows little of it. I am the one who recognized him, and we met by chance and luck."

Tarlis motioned to Onred to lean closer and, in a low whisper, said, "Gather those you trust out by the black tree. I can show you what I already know and have the boy prove himself if you still have doubts."

Tarlis dug into his pouch and produced three silver, tossing them onto the table. "For the bill you have most likely incurred and will take a moon to pay," Tarlis said.

"I am not just here about the boy; he has promised, and the White must deliver. Once we have settled the issue of the Black, we can decide if we are White once again!"

"Promised what?" Onred asked with a sidelong glance.

"He has vowed to assist a town under siege from a brigand threat, but details can wait," Tarlis said, laying a hand on Onred's shoulder.

"We shall meet you by the black tree within the hand. We will wait the night through, and, should none show, we will depart and return to our business."

Tarlis clasped arms with Onred and motioned for Emanrasu and Rezua to follow him.

As the trio exited the tavern, the din of conversation from that table was thunderous. Those who knew Tarlis argued to meet him, and those who did not know him were loath to put their faith in someone so old and frail.

Tarlis tossed a silver to the man on the bench, who had tied the horses and even efficiently rubbed them down.

"We will return before long, and should we not return before first light breaks… the horses are yours."

"However, should you keep them through the night and we are able to return, I will toss another silver your way," Tarlis said matter-of-factly.

They traveled briskly on foot in the direction of the tree-covered mountain that towered over the city.

The walk was a welcome relief from the long ride.

As Emanrasu passed the corner of the last building, he paused—then stopped outright.

The tree-covered mountain was not a mountain at all.

It was a single tree, towering to a height Emanrasu had never imagined.

A gigantic oak—massive, multi-trunked, ancient, gnarled with time—rose above a wide arena.

He stared.

He had seen one other like it during a trip to the Tubata Mountains, but where that one bore two trunks and a handful of shoots, this was a forest made of one tree.

Its scale defied language. Even "enormously gigantic" felt too small.

Yet it wasn't just its size.

There was something else.

Something familiar.

Encircling the nearest trunk was a stone-and-marble bench that ran off into the distance, curving around the tree.

Beyond it, eight round tables—also stone and marble—were spaced evenly in a wide ring around the base.

In Black and White: Chapter Fourteen

He gazed intently at the tree, and without watching his path, Emanrasu stepped randomly on the stones leading to the tree.

Tarlis spoke, reminiscing, "I first met the..."

Emanrasu's focus was on the tree, and he barely noticed the tables and bench. He walked up to the tree and reached out... "...something familiar," he thought. At last, it fell into place just as his fingers touched the rough, weathered bark.

This was the tree of his dreams!

"Is this the Tree of Life?" the thoughts raced through Emanrasu's mind in the instant before reality morphed into a dream.

*   *   *

The Ancient Dragon and the Fiery Phoenix were Dancing in the Boundless Sky. The Tree of Life below grasped a hold of Mother Earth as if propping up the universe, with the Eternal Sun's luminescence casting the shadows of doubt away. The Sun, the Sky, the Earth, the Tree, the Dragon, and the Phoenix all spoke in unison. They were not only heard; he felt the words, experienced them, saw them, and even tasted them.

The words spoke to the core of his being. "We are YOU, Emanrasu," they said. "You need not struggle; your path is YOUR path, and though it has always been, and always will be, YOUR path and YOURS alone, it is also OUR path. We have walked this path with you from time immemorial and will walk it for eternity. Welcome back, Emanra Su the Black."

Emanrasu waited... but there was no reaction from the Dance. "This is the part where I wake up," Emanrasu mused. "So why, then, am I not waking?"

The Dragon roared in response, "You are not ready to leave us!"

"Questions you have!" shrieked the Phoenix.

"You seek knowledge," chimed in the Eternal Illuminator and the Life of All.

"We await," came the statement in unison. Emanrasu thought about the past few months.

"Why?" he asked.

"It has always been," came the ubiquitous response. Now, the answers seemed to come from not one but all and none, as if the cosmos itself was answering.

"Ask, and WE shall answer," the infinite ones commanded.

"Then I ask again, why me?" Emanrasu queried. "Why me and not someone like Tarlis, or Serrah, or even Onred?"

"You have the lineage and are of a cosmic origin passed down in your ancestry.

"Mankind struggled to find balance," the cosmos said.

"Emanra Su, In Balance, Brilliance!" The Phoenix's shriek echoed through him and across the ages as if carrying the weight of generations.

"Your ancestors were created to provide guidance and balance the scales," the answer continued. "The war-torn lives were pitiable, the impoverishment that came because of the incessant wars, the ignorance and disrespect between one another, causes us pain. You were created to restore the Balance and ease our pain."

"Me?" asked Emanrasu.

"Your lineage, from back to time immemorial, you were, are, and will always be, a part of us," came the explanation. "You are Balance made human. You are a cosmic part of us, sent to live and guide so that we may not suffer."

"So I am all-powerful?" Emanrasu asked.

"NO!" came the forceful roar of the Dragon. "You are human in all ways save the link to us." Emanrasu furrowed his brow and cocked an eye. "So, my lineage, you say. Then why did my father not say as much?" he asked.

In Black and White: Chapter Fourteen

"Your father…" the cosmos began.

"A thief and a liar," shrieked the Phoenix.

"…your father was not worthy, and your grandfather realized this and refused to give him the objects of his desire. So, he stole them, taking them as a thief in the night, and fled."

"Are you speaking of the shield and sword?" Emanrasu realized and asked.

The cosmic entities responded, "Yes, the Heater and the Hack, as they have come to be known, are part of the link to Balance—to us. When your father took them without earning, without respecting, without honoring, and without deserving, his link to us was severed, and the Heater and the Hack became dormant to lay in wait for the next in line, the next deserving one, the next one—the next with Balance!"

"And what would you have me do then?" he asked, looking at where his feet would be, but nothing but stars greeted his gaze. He suddenly realized that there was nothing but stars and the Dance.

"Live your life!" the Tree responded.

"Seek to understand," quipped the Sun.

"Balance in all," said the Dragon and the Phoenix in unison.

"We have no needs beyond those that you will already accomplish. The Cadre must be formed, and you have already embarked on this task. It was inevitable; live your life in balance, and you will find us and OUR links, our representation in human form.

"This is your only task, though you will achieve this without deviating from your current path. There may come a day, though, unforeseeable to us, when you or your offspring may be needed for a task beyond this.

The Heater and The Hack

The Sky hummed in concert with the Earth, each beat separate but melding together. "The future is not set. There is no fate, but what we make for ourselves. Your choices are your own, as they always have been, and we trust they will always lead you inexorably to us."

"We have seen this and know it, but the time and place, the task and reason, remain even a mystery to US!" the eternal ones admitted.

"Live your life as you would, understand your own motives, and strive for balance. The ripples in the fabric of reality respond to your movements, and as you travel, so does the universe react. Understand, teach, learn, and seek. All things have a scale; seek to balance the scale.

"Without anguish, there can be no joy, since joy without anguish has no understanding qualities. There is no love without heartbreak, no good without evil," the Dance explained.

"Your time with us is at an end; you must return to face your trials. Prove yourself and take your place..." The voices faded around Emanrasu, even as the images faded around him.

"...Black here when I was but a young child," Tarlis's voice filtered back into Emanrasu's consciousness. "I was curious about the tree, and the Black was standing here, just looking at it.

"He never answered my question... just glanced over at me. 'We have faith in you, boy. You will play your part. Would you like to abide with me?' he asked me," Tarlis recalled. "I had no idea who he was and no thoughts at all of the Dance. Since my life to that point was not what you would call a good one, or rather... perhaps I should say, an easy one.

"When this stoic, gentle soldier... yes, I know this feels like a contradiction, but it is true nonetheless. When he seemed to take an interest in me and my life, I was excited about the possibilities and immediately agreed," Tarlis said, a wispy, far-off look in his eye. "That was the beginning of my association with the White and the Black."

*   *   *

The sound of metal on metal became apparent as the former members of the White started filtering into the little garden.

Emanrasu, fully aware of his surroundings now, was no longer compelled and drawn to the Tree.

He glanced around and spied an open area, level and trodden with the feet of men, obviously a battleground or training area, an arena of some sort. It was off to the left as he faced the tree, and slowly, he followed Tarlis, Onred, and the others into it, with Rezua following close behind him.

As the multitude of feet stepped out into the arena, the various pads and clops across the stone were interspersed with the firm tap of Tarlis's cane, which echoed throughout.

Emanrasu, assessing the area, took it all in.

Rows of seating surrounded the arena; whether for spectators or participants, there was no clear indication. Yet the weight of history, forged into and by this massive rink, pressed in upon Emanrasu as the echoes of past combat reverberated in the very wood and stone.

Two strides in front of the main seating were benches; three groupings of six, evenly distanced around the arena, imbued with battles seen and waged, of contests for love or coin; the arena reeked of battles past of all types in a controlled and relatively safe setting.

As Emanrasu took it all in, the thick, musty smell of the forest exuding from the tree, interspersed with the stark, dry air flowing from the fields beyond the arena, somehow reminded Emanrasu of the interplay of children playing tag, much akin to his childhood with Rezua. The large open area of the arena, comprised of stone

235

and inset with a massive depiction of the scene emblazoned upon his shield, evoked a powerful sense of continuity within the history of the Dance.

Opposite the opening where they had entered stood a large podium of sorts, flanked on either side with raised seating. The blazon, also succinctly embedded on the dais, suggested that the arena had seen many battles in days gone by. The limited seating of the arena indicated these were not public affairs, though unimaginably larger than simple contests between friends and comrades.

Tarlis grasped his arm and pulled him close. "Trust my word when I say that to be a part of this group is to be the master of their chosen weapon. These are the trainers of the trainers in the weapons they wield. Do—not—underestimate them."

Onred stepped out into the arena, unslung his pick, and readied his shield; with a wave of his outstretched hand, he motioned to the rest of his mates.

"Choose. Choose the form of your destructors!" Onred exclaimed, waving to his motley band of fighters. He stepped to one side of the arena and motioned Emanrasu to take the center position.

"First blood steps out; do not seek to maim one of us, boy, or you will face the lot of us," Onred exclaimed, pointing his war pick in Emanrasu's direction.

"The boy will not choose; you choose your best or choose them all. I have seen this boy in action, and though he has trained less than two seasons, I trust that each will be nicked and out 'ere he is done," Tarlis stated.

He walked over to one of the observation benches and sat. He leaned back and kicked his feet out in front of himself, looking relaxed and confident in his pupil.

Emanrasu surveyed the warriors… captains, all. Each had earned the title not through birth or lineage but by actions and perseverance.

In Black and White: Chapter Fourteen

"Each in their own right would easily hold their own against a barely trained cub such as I," he mused to himself, "but maybe they do not all fight in concert against a single opponent..."

He studied the group, Olaf assisting Freydis in wrapping her abundant bosoms, "flattening them for better mobility," Emanrasu surmised.

None seemed to be the least worried I could best any one of them, but perhaps..." he thought, "perhaps if they had to be concerned more about harming each other, perhaps then I might have a chance."

He watched for a few moments as each set aside protective gear instead of wearing it, looking confident in the boy not lasting long enough for anyone to be in danger.

He listened to the sounds of these hardened soldiers preparing. He heard the grunt of Freydis, with the tightening of the wrappings, squeezing the air from her lungs as it drew tighter. He could hear the whirling sound of Darth as he spun his blades, primarily for show but always returning them to a fighting position after the visual display of skill.

Each of them prepared in their own unique way, the leather sliding on leather and culminating in the quiet tink as the buckles closed and the soft—shlick—of the blades drawn from the scabbards.

The sun was dropping low in the sky, and soon it would be dark.

"The sun will stream across the arena; hmm, maybe I can use that as an advantage, too," Emanrasu ruminated.

Emanrasu decided and turned back to Onred.

"All," he insisted. "I do not know if it is possible, but the Dance will out—much as does truth—revealing my worth. And should I not prevail, I would not be worthy of your assistance.

The Heater and The Hack

Have at me, and we will see whether Tarlis has trained me well and whether the Dance will guide me. I will not seek to maim or disfigure. However, I ask that one more stipulation be added: should I part even a hair from one of you, you must consider it blooded and step away. Do you agree?"

Onred looked at Emanrasu, his eyes narrowing, but then a grin spread across his face. "You have stones, boy, no sense, but very large stones," he said as he held his hands as if to cup melons waist-high.

Onred glanced around at his companions, who were laughing and chuckling at his humor. Some nodded, and others shrugged or smiled. Turning back to Emanrasu, "Your terms are agreeable, boy."

Rezua, having been a silent spectator up to this point, clasped Emanrasu on the back. "Try not to get killed, Eman. We still have many a glorious and ode-worthy adventure before us, and I would rather you not end this one so quickly!

"Wait, uh, what I meant to say is try not to kill any of them! I would hate to see the pandemonium that would ensue at such an outcome, and I, for one, am just a lowly scribe, you know." Rezua chuckled as he patted Emanrasu's shoulder and quietly stepped away.

Emanrasu watched Rezua, glad his friend had come with them. He knew Rezua would back him up without question and without hesitation should the need arise, as he always had. Rezua walked over, climbed the platform, and sat to watch the ensuing event in safety.

"I could not imagine my life without the little giant," Emanrasu realized, slowly shaking his head at the thought. "I can't believe I never thought that before."

With that, Emanrasu stepped into the middle of the arena, the light breeze shuffling through the leaves of the gigantic tree under which they now gathered. The creaking boughs were a soft backdrop to the metal-on-metal sounds each warrior produced. The smell of well-kept leather and oiled weapons filled the air as his opponents tested their chosen weapons, attacking the air with vigor.

In Black and White: Chapter Fourteen

Emanrasu, too, readied himself, slinging his shield and sword lightly around to feel the heft and bolster his courage. "What have you just done, Emanrasu," he thought quietly as he let his eyes wander around studying the gathering of warriors. Each formidable in their own right, he had chosen to face all nine. "The Dance better have your back, or you will leave empty-handed and bandaged."

He glanced around and evaluated his opponents, "Two battle axes and a ponytail; she will be slower," he decided, and as he made the rounds identifying the speed and reach of each of the warriors and their weapons, he mentally calculated the order based on this.

"Halberd must be first, slower, but longer reach and will be able to push me into the others easily. Take him out and keep one fighter between you and the others so they do not have a clear attack," Emanrasu ran down all of them hurriedly in his mind.

"Halberd, claymore, double-headed axe, dual battle axes, war hammer, pick, cutlass, shortsword, knives," he decided. They circled in much the order in which he thought he should take them out. Onred ahead of him and to the right proper was his first target, Djorn and his halberd.

Emanrasu turned around while he evaluated the lot. He finished his evaluation and turned his back to the halberd, knowing that he would need to take him out first.

"I am ready if you fine folk are," Emanrasu said.

Emanrasu examined them one last time. None were really ready. "Perhaps they think this will be quick, and one of them will blood me quickly," Emanrasu smiled inwardly.

Onred, at the grin spreading on Emanrasu's face, grinned himself before bursting into a flurry of pick and shield, yelling, "Have at him!"

*　　*　　*

The Heater and The Hack

The words did not register in Emanrasu's thoughts so much as he felt Onred's intent as he voiced the words. Thus, as Onred finished the command, he had already anticipated perfectly and promptly dashed to the right, ducking and sliding to nick the halberdier on his ankle, noting the shock on the man's face as he did. He used his momentum to right himself fully before placing Aleric between himself and the rest.

Deftly, he dodged the cumbersome claymore and placed a nick on the man's hand, outing him from the fight. The double-headed axe wielder was on the rear of where he had begun, and immediately, he made his way to him. He darted across, dodging the ill-timed swipe of Darth's blade in his journey to the axe man, but as he passed, he saw the sun blind the knifer and took the opportunity to nick Darth as well.

"That was a bit of luck," he thought, proud that he had eliminated one of the quickest fighters so early.

He could hear the creak of the leather armor, as well as the grating of metal armor, each piece sliding against another, struggling in an attempt to hide and protect vulnerable areas. The sound of feet shuffling on the earth and stone combined with the steady, measured breathing of the remaining warriors hung in the air, just as did the light puffs of dirt that each step kicked up. The little puffs left a light cloud of floating dust as the warriors jockeyed for position.

Emanrasu finally got into position behind Olaf and maneuvered him into Leif, entangling the two, and he efficiently touched them both, one on the arm, the other on the hand. Without conscious thought, he spun and blocked the cutlass with his sword and simultaneously leveled his shield to take the blows from the dual battle axes.

"And very nice ones…" flashed through his thoughts.

He slid to the side, putting Catlina between himself and Freydis, and then rushed Catlina, blocking her cutlass and touching her ankle with the tip of his sword.

In Black and White: Chapter Fourteen

Immediately, he forced himself backward and slid on his backside before nimbly rolling to his knees and from there to his feet.

"Rolling with a shield is impossible, but that is the second time," he grinned silently as he focused.

"Rise!" Catlina bellowed in disgust as she walked away.

Emanrasu visibly relaxed and dropped his guard, allowing Eirikr to advance before dodging the hammer and sliding his shield edge on the side of Eirikr's leg as it slammed into his toe. Eirikr shook his head in surprise and walked away limping, the blood trickling from his big toe.

"I guess sandals were a bad idea today," grinned Emanrasu as he turned to face the last two.

Freydis, with her axes, and Onred's pick and shield, were the only ones left.

As he backed away, not allowing the two to flank him, he said earnestly, "Those—really—are very nice battle axes."

He grinned as Onred let out a laugh that started from his feet and traveled up through his belly and apparently through his shield arm, which dropped a bit.

"There," he thought as he nicked Onred's shoulder. Instinctually sliding to place Onred between himself and Freydis, he readied himself.

"Even with Onred already blooded, he still makes a good barrier," mused Emanrasu as a grin spread across his face. "I have not grinned this much since the time I got the drop on Tarlis and poked him in his family makers as he tried to wake me."

As Onred walked away, shaking his head, Freydis and Emanrasu circled; the nine had now become one, but she had seen all of her companions blooded and seemed to be calculating and measured in her attacks.

The Heater and The Hack

Behind his shield, Emanrasu loosened his strap and, as he dodged to the right, released his shield, sliding it abruptly to the left as Freydis dodged in that direction. Forced to jump over the shield or stumble on it, she leapt over, whirled, and blocked his sword, but not before a full two fingers of her hair drifted toward the dust and dirt.

She grabbed her ponytail and inspected the damage. Freydis roared toward Emanrasu, her axes in full swing. Emanrasu just stood there and allowed her to attack, categorically trusting that he had a destiny to fulfill. One that would not be denied.

Onred himself stepped in to block her battle axes.

"Hold!" Onred commanded her.

She backed off and let the axes lower to her sides, visibly relaxing her facial expression and finally allowing herself to grin. As she let the anger flow out of her, she shifted her axes to one hand and reached out an arm to Emanrasu.

"Well played, Black, well played!" she exclaimed.

Emanrasu reached out and clasped her arm, thin and wiry, feeling the power in her hand and arm as he returned the firm grip.

He swept his eyes around the arena for Rezua, not knowing where he had gone, but as Emanrasu started to turn away, he noticed Rezua as the colossal figure emerged from behind the podium. Rezua's eyes widened, and Rezua's jaw slightly dropped as his gaze lit on Emanrasu. He hurriedly jumped down from the platform and approached the gathering.

"Done, already?" Rezua inquired in relief.

"I imagine you would know were you not hiding behind the podium," winked Emanrasu.

Rezua instantly retorted, "I wasn't hiding, but I can tell you about it later, little man."

In Black and White: Chapter Fourteen

Tarlis had approached, closely on Rezua's heels, and with a grin on his face, queried Onred, "Well? Satisfied?"

"Boy, your stones are of a steel I haven't seen since the Black, and just as you said, the Dance outed you—and you were not found wanting," Onred said, grasping both of Emanrasu's shoulders.

Laughing abruptly, Onred slapped Emanrasu on the shoulder and threw a thick branch of an arm around his shoulders. "A Black, if ever there was one!" he exclaimed.

Onred turned to Tarlis. "You said you've trained him for less than a main?" he asked incredulously. "If you were anyone other than Tarlis, I would call you a liar and beat you soundly for the fib."

Tarlis grinned at Onred, "And now you understand why I found it imperative to seek you out. The White can have a new leader and reform, that is, if you're of a mind to."

"I understand completely. But, alas, a decision of this magnitude is only made over ale and mead," Onred said to Tarlis, grinning like a bard with an unexpected audience. Turning to the motley gathering, he projected his voice as only one forged by mains of command could muster, "To the Flying Griffon!" he shouted.

"The Griffon!" came the group's concerted response. The captains' comradery was plain to all as they grinned, shoved, and clapped each other on the back in anticipation of another round of drinks.

Each acknowledged that they had been outwitted, not necessarily by outstanding skill—although Emanrasu's abilities were recognized by all as better than average. Instead, the cheerful conversation suggested the boy had triumphed over them all with clever tactics—and the sort of stones legends are built on.

Upon hearing the reference, Freydis took mock offense at the mention of stones. Djorn slapped her on the back and laughed, "I suppose axes would not quite work in this context."

The Heater and The Hack

They gathered around Emanrasu, drawing him into their playful antics as though he had been one of them from the onset—never mind that he was young enough to be their offspring.

Emanrasu meekly accepted the ribbing, and the target of ribbing shifted in rounds, sparing none. Not even Rezua was spared as his height was compared to the Tubata mountains and the Tree of Life.

Freydis soon had her arm around the boy's head in a mock stranglehold as Emanrasu struggled to apologize for shortening her hair.

The White gathered their remaining gear and, one by one, made their way to the Griffon. As they filed out in groups of two and three, still discussing the battle, they happily pointed out and compared the little red lines Emanrasu had left them with.

Only Freydis bore no mark—but to hear her tell it, she was the most wounded of all, brandishing her sheared locks as if she had been marred for life and would suffer the shame eternally.

Tarlis glanced over and caught Emanrasu's eye, flicking his head to beckon him over. The others departed, with Rezua, Emanrasu, and Tarlis not far behind.

The trio slowly followed; the dust settled in the arena, accompanied by the soft rustle of leaves jockeying for the last of the sunlight.

Dusk fell upon them as comfortably as a blanket in the middle of winter.

Emanrasu could see from the knit of Tarlis's brow and the furrow in his forehead that he was deep in thought. They walked in silence, Rezua on one side, Tarlis on the other, until the old man reached out and firmly gripped Emanrasu's shoulder.

"Young man," Tarlis began, "I have had the pleasure over the last few moons to train you—a genuinely worthy pupil—in the ways your grandfather taught me.

In Black and White: Chapter Fourteen

You still have so much to learn, but now you are also turning the tables. Just as your grandfather taught me, you are teaching me as well.

"Never have I seen someone come so far and so fast and still remain as compassionate and humble as you. See, that is what I mean," the old man pointed at Emanrasu, whose eyes had lowered and who had slowed his step a bit to keep pace with Tarlis instead of forcing the old man to keep up with him.

Emanrasu looked up at him, and then over at Rezua, who, as always and much as he was wont, was scribbling once again in his book.

"Or maybe he has more than one journal," Emanrasu thought fleetingly. "With as much as he scribbles, he'd need whole stacks of books."

The thought left behind only a grin as he replied to Tarlis, "It's a matter of respect," he stated, "How can one gain respect if one does not give it?"

Tarlis let go of his shoulder and clasped him on the back, the corners of his eyes crinkling as he grinned.

"And that is why you are my family, you, Rezua, there with his incessant penning, and even Serrah. I have come to regard you, all of you, as family," Tarlis stated. "Many others, considerable harvestmains older than the lot of you, do not have that kind of respect, and many do not think they owe respect to anyone."

Tarlis started walking again, and Emanrasu and Rezua followed.

"You have learned much during our time and still have more to learn. The way you handled yourself tonight in the arena," Tarlis slowly shook his head, then shrugged his shoulders.

"I have never seen the like. I would never have thought to challenge them all, but your tactics were chillingly brilliant," the old man grinned.

Chuckling, his eyes widened and wrinkled at the corners, the smile fully encompassing his face. "They never stood a chance; they underestimated you, and that was a fatal flaw. As they struggled not to harm each other, you forced them into one another and took advantage when the opportunity arose. Brilliant, just brilliant.

"You must keep in mind that this was a blood challenge, and such is important, but it is altogether different than a fight to the death. If you can imagine the lot of them fighting in earnest to kill you, you will see a different outcome. I do not want to make light of your accomplishment; only temper it with understanding."

Tarlis laid a hand on the boy's shoulder and halted him, his firm grip squeezing just a bit. "Like I said, you are not done learning, and apparently, neither am I. But the display you showed today, the lessons you have soaked in as we traveled, will serve you for the rest of your life."

Tarlis reached in with his other hand and squared up Emanrasu. Looking him in the eye, he pulled Emanrasu to him and firmly hugged him. "I am proud of you, son!" he whispered.

Upon hearing this, Rezua grinned at his childhood friend and gave him a wink and a nod of approval.

And with that, Tarlis stiffened, straightened his gear, and with a wink to Emanrasu, the three of them hurried to catch up with the others.

Comradery In Motion: Chapter Fifteen

*"Comradery and companionship lift the weary soul and lightens the burden.
Experiences abound no matter the place or time. Cherishing each one and learning
from them feeds the soul in ways that are immeasurable."*

—*RCotD*—

U pon reaching the tavern, Tarlis set a hand on Emanrasu motioning him
and Rezua to wait, then walked over to the old man who was watching
the horses.

Emanrasu waited, shifting from one foot to the other, glancing at the door to the
tavern and then back at Tarlis.

Tarlis spoke with the old man briefly, handed him another coin, clasped arms
with him, and started to turn and walk away. But he paused, turned back to the
old man, and handed him a third coin. The old man said something to Tarlis,
whereupon Tarlis threw back his head, bellowing out a laugh that thundered
through the darkened streets.

Tarlis made his way back to Emanrasu and Rezua, still chuckling. Emanrasu
studied him and raised his eyebrow in a query. Tarlis looked at him and chuckled
again. Without further comment on his exchange with the old man, he headed to
the tavern entrance.

Rezua stood frozen for a moment, half-raising a hand between Tarlis and the old
man like a man watching a game he didn't understand. Emanrasu watched the
futile gesture from his immensely puzzled feather user. He grinned as he
followed Tarlis's lead into the tavern.

Rezua, in disgust, dropped his hand and acquiesced. Slumping his shoulders and
kicking at the dirt, he followed the other two to the tavern.

The Heater and The Hack

The music from the bard's lyre filled the cozy space with cheery notes, which floated around and tickled fancies as it meandered about the dimly lit room.

Emanrasu smiled at the dainty little tune. It sounds like something made just for Serrah... wouldn't be surprised if it followed her around on its own.

"Serrah," he thought, as his pangs of longing to see her took hold, "I have been away but for days. Why does it feel like moons or mains?"

Mulling over his disconnected feeling of time when he thought about Serrah, Emanrasu felt every thought he had regarding the pretty little maid magnified by the distortion in time he felt where she was concerned. "Huh...maid...maid does not even begin to cover how amazing she is," he thought.

Onred's sudden clap on the back shattered his reverie. Emanrasu stumbled but barely had time to right himself before Rezua's meaty hand steadied him.

"Ah, so you are not completely untouchable, Emanrasu! And... where pray tell did you stow your clumsiness when you were in the arena?" Onred bellowed, his eyebrows reaching to the sky and the bellow ending in blazing laughter, quenched only with ale.

"Well, that is quite the roaring blaze of laughter. And quenched only by the ale poured down your gullet, I see... well... mostly down your gullet..." Rezua pointed out, culminating in a laugh of his own, "...by half at least. The other half? Well... it decided to forgo the human host and ran straight to the floor."

Emanrasu chuckled to himself. He smiled and replied, "I am not beset by nine captains of the White, so I am not in need of balance," he quipped.

Upon this statement, those who heard him paused in their merriment and looked at him. He hastily revised his statement: "Pardon, my gentle folk, nimble... I have no need to be nimble... balance is pretty much a requirement these days." The group's levity returned, and Djorn grinned, pointing a meaty finger in his direction and tapping the side of his head.

Comradery In Motion: Chapter Fifteen

"Smart," he mouthed the words that would never be heard above the din now thundering from the table at which the White sat. Onred sat and looked at Djorn sitting beside him; he reached down and grabbed ahold of the nearest chair leg, stealing the seat straight from under the unsuspecting man. The surprise on Djorn's face and the thump with which his backside hit the floor caused another wave of raucous laughter through the group that witnessed the transaction. Reaching down, Onred helped Djorn back to his feet, even as he handed the chair to Tarlis, motioning the old man to have a seat next to him; then, deftly using his feet, while his hands and mouth had quickly found alternatives and were otherwise engaged in guzzling his ale, slid a chair over to Emanrasu. Raising his eyebrows as he continued to drink and nodding slightly, Onred indicated he should sit.

Freydis sidled up, shoving an ale into his hand—and her majestic axes into his shoulder. Throwing an arm around him, she leaned in and whispered, "Would you fancy one?" She winked and sat back, clasping his shoulder in a grip far firmer than most men. As she spoke, Emanrasu flushed red. Seemingly the response she wanted, Freydis threw back her head and laughed, obviously delighted in the young man's confusion.

"The drink, boy, the drink," she said, reaching out and using his chin to guide his eyes away from her axes. Emanrasu turned even redder and stammered an apology, but before he could say a word, her finger pressed to his lips. She leaned in, chuckling, "Just having a bit of fun, boy, no harm in looking!" Then, with a mischievous glint, she leaned back—wiggling just enough for effect.

Freydis suddenly peered past Emanrasu to the hulking Rezua, a grin spreading across her face and her eyes lighting up as she reached out and grabbed his tunic. She led him around the table, where she pushed him onto the bench against the wall and plopped herself in his lap. She reached out and poured Rezua a drink and handed it to him, but not before she measured his hand in hers, marveling at how dainty his made hers look.

The Heater and The Hack

Emanrasu watched as his large friend delightfully allowed the comely woman to lead him. When Rezua winked at him, he knew that Rezua, too, felt comfortable with the group.

"Drink!" Freydis commanded her companions, whereupon, as one, they tipped back their cups and drained them entirely.

Emanrasu was not much of one for ale, and mead was a bit thick and heavy, but as he looked around, even Tarlis was having one, though not at the rate the White were.

Onred finished his ale and slammed the cup down on the table, "So, my friend! Tell us your woes!" he commanded Tarlis.

Tarlis stared at Onred, his eyes fixed directly on Onred's, and without a blink or movement, stared at Onred until he raised his hands in front of himself and sheepishly said, "Okay, okay, I get it... I shall be your captain again, Commander. So, sir," Onred mocked a salute by thumping his chest vigorously. "What be your orders, Commander?" he queried. Tarlis's grin slowly crept across his face until he could hold it back no longer, and he laughed out loud.

In the background, Djorn recounted, "Oh... oh... you fine folks remember the time Freydis was caught dallying with that guy, what was his name, and his bear of a husband came home... oh, what a time that was. Had I not been walking by at the time, I never would have believed it. Freydis, stumbling out the window with the largest hand I have ever seen, reaching out to grab her and pull her back in. Her magnificent axes swinging in the chill breeze, or at least you would have thought it was chill to look at her... ha, ha, ha." Djorn rolled with laughter at the memory. He barely ducked the large flagon thrown at his head, hearing it whiff by, only to shatter against the wall.

"I noticed you didn't mention the night you got your little halberd stuck... oh, that was a time!" Freydis retorted.

Comradery In Motion: Chapter Fifteen

Rezua pulled out his journal and began furiously putting quill to paper until Freydis took notice and snatched them both away, sliding them across the table to Emanrasu.

Somewhere amidst the revelry, Olaf and Aleric were in a test of strength, each trying to push the other's hand down to the table while keeping his own from touching.

The smoke lingered in the air from the pipe between Aleric's teeth, catching the flickering of the fireplace, candles, and the occasional torch.

The bard varied his tunes from the melodramatic to the lovesick to the strums reminiscent of battle, perfectly played and emotional.

As Olaf lifted a cheek, shifting slightly, the rumble shook the table and shocked Aleric so completely that Olaf was able to, with one last effort, slam Aleric's hand down to the table. He leaned back in victory as the berth he was given grew more expansive with the stench. He grinned and inhaled deeply through his nose, letting out a sigh of relief and enjoyment.

The smell of burning oak, the crackle of the fire, and the warmth of the company culminated as Emanrasu let his body meld with the chair. "It seems to be getting more comfortable the longer I sit," he acknowledged to himself. "I am not sure if it is comfortable or if the ale is dulling my senses," he grinned to no one in particular.

Emanrasu looked around and saw that Leif and Darth were involved in a game, a checkered board with miniature statues positioned randomly. Emanrasu watched for a short while until Catlina snuck up on him and, taking his empty mug, shoved another one into his hand, forcing his hand up to his mouth. She grinned as he tried to resist. "You have very nice hair," Emanrasu added as he was looking at her. "A nice auburn, like Serrah's," he said, blinking slowly.

"And there it is!" she shouted. "The boy finally notices me, and it is only in reference to some Serrah girl."

The Heater and The Hack

The group rolled in laughter as Freydis slowly stood, raising her arms victoriously.

Emanrasu took it all in, throwing his head back and bellowing laughter at the stories told. "Would that I grew up around—this—group! I would never have been bored or at a lack of hilarity," he thought as the room wobbled a bit. Onred shoved another mug into his hand, and his great, meaty hand helped Emanrasu to toast as everyone cheerfully knocked together their vessels in honor of whatever it was that they were toasting...

Freydis sidled up to Emanrasu on one side, her arm still firmly hooked through Rezua's as she kept him close. Catlina pushed her way past Onred on the other side, and together, the women teased and warmed the boy, even as the light in his eyes started fading. "The drink..." he mumbled to himself as the women rubbed against him. He smiled as his head began to droop, his hand limp upon the table, still clutching the most recent ale he had barely sipped.

He could hear Rezua's rumbling laughter, and occasionally, his name was called out, whereupon he would grin weakly and try to focus. The dim light grew steadily dimmer in the little tavern until soon he was conscious no more.

The haziness slowly coalesced into the Dance. The Dragon and the Phoenix seemingly chased each other around as they gracefully twisted and turned around each other. The light fragrance of nature slowly swam in and out of his perception.

The sun and the tree stand stoically, knowing that everything revolves around them and they will have their time. The Dragon, still dancing with the Phoenix, roars, "ASK!"

Emanrasu paused for a moment. Though his understanding was growing by leaps and bounds, he realized that they knew his questions far better than he did. He was beginning to understand that they would not offer answers to questions unspoken.

Comradery In Motion: Chapter Fifteen

"The Heater and the Hack," he began. "They are easy to keep; how did my father let them get into such a state of disrepair?"

"He was unworthy," roared the Dragon. "Hiding, hiding, the heater and the hack knew!" shrieked the Phoenix. The Dragon rumbled a clarification, "When the right person bonds with the mystical artifacts, they return to show their true colors. Without a righteous and balanced prospect, they encourage the air around them to build up a tarnish, even as it attracts the dust and dirt in the air."

"They hide when needed to discourage the unbalanced from using them in ways unintended. The tarnish on their surfaces saves them the tarnish of their legend." The Dragon swung around to face Emanrasu.

"Remember, Black, balance, in all things, balance." The Dragon reached out and thumped him heavily in the chest. Then, without warning, he grabbed Emanrasu and rhythmically started pressing on his chest. Trying to move, Emanrasu felt he could not move his arms or legs…

*   *   *

The rough, bristly hair from the horse rubbed against his cheek as he unceremoniously bounced upon the animal's hindquarters.

"Hold!" Emanrasu commanded—or tried to. His stomach had other ideas. Ale surged back up, splattering down the horse's flanks.

The dust and dirt kicked up by the horses obscured his view. "Not that I would be able to see much, tied down to the horse like this," Emanrasu mulled over as his body convulsed in one last attempt to purge itself.

"Ho, ho!" Onred bellowed. "The boy lives!"

"Huzzah!" the group cheered as if they'd just won a great battle.

The sound of a hundred hooves rhythmically hitting the road was palpable. Emanrasu lay there like a sack of beans. He rasped a reply, "And in so being… it would be nice if someone did not continue to treat me as a deer brought back from the hunt!" His throat was raw and gravelly as he spoke, his eyes throbbing in concert with the drums pounding in his head.

There was a flurry of commands, and the horse slowed. The short bristles of hair rubbed Emanrasu's cheek raw as he jostled this way and that.

Finally, after an eternity, the horse stopped, and the rider dismounted. He briefly felt the rope tightening as someone fiddled with what he assumed was the knot on his feet and ankles. His feet were loosened, and a pair of hands lifted his feet to help him off the horse.

As Emanrasu realized what the action entailed, "No!" came his raspy plea. Too late, he could feel the front of his body starting to slide over the horse's haunches, and his feet were flipped rather forcefully up and over. The world did a backflip for him and slammed into his back as the two met.

Amidst the bellowing laughter, he struggled to catch his breath. The world grew darker and darker until suddenly, his greedy lungs drew in the air as if it were the most priceless thing on earth.

"Never have I…" Emanrasu thought, "been a party to such behavior, let alone its target." Rezua walked around the horse and offered a hand.

As Emanrasu struggled to silence the pounding drums in his head, he ignored the proffered hand and rolled slowly over and slid his feet beneath himself. "Not nearly as easy if your hands are tied," he grimaced. Eventually, he was able to get one leg under himself, then the other, and with a great effort, he stood. Swaying unsteadily, Emanrasu glanced around. The light was blinding, making him squint. "Tarlis had said we were coming for help," came the thought, but as he looked around, "Everyone came?" he queried, primarily to Rezua and Tarlis, though he had not yet spied the old man.

"Of course we did!" Freydis's reply came.

His jaw dropped open, and his eyes widened in astonishment, only to close against the unbearable brightness of the overcast morning. "I never would have imagined that all would come. I had hoped for one, two at the most," Emanrasu thought as he cringed from the dull, consistent throbbing somewhere between his eyes and the back of his head. With Rezua holding him steady, he began to struggle with the knot binding his hands, but Darth walked over and, with a whirl of his blade and a lightning-quick thrust, sliced the knot in two.

"We have all found, for one reason or another, that the lives we lead, the lives we led, were taken from us in one way or another as time steadily marched on. Falling back on one another became what we required, then it slowly turned into bonds of friendship, and now... I dare might even say family," he stated as he saw Olaf's grin just in time to dodge the half-eaten fruit-filled pastry.

"You know you love me," insisted Darth vehemently as he swooped in on the pastry and, in one smooth motion, launched it at Olaf, hitting him right in his colossal barrel of a chest.

"Hmmph," came Olaf's reply as he scraped the fruity pastry from his chest. He looked at the mass of fruit and pastry, now stuck to his fingers... looked at Darth, and grinned. Olaf opened his mouth, and slowly, his hand approached his gaping maw.

"Don't!" Darth insisted, almost pleading. And with the pleading command given, Olaf started to drop his hand but thought the better of it and gobbled the dirt and dust-covered pastry.

Darth gagged, pretending to retch—until Emanrasu made it real, doubling over and emptying what was left in his gut. The group howled in laughter even as Darth patted the young man firmly on the back. "There, there..." he said. "We have all been in such dire straits, most of us more than once!"

The rolling laughter swept through the troupe, only to die out moments later as Onred bellowed, "Enough! Let the boy be. We still have hands to go before we make camp, and this foolishness is not getting us any closer to Bren!"

The Heater and The Hack

The heartfelt salutes rounded the group, each almost but not entirely in unison as they thumped their chests with their fists.

"Darth, you and Rezua help the boy to his mount and let us depart, 'ere the sun will drop before we get camp made. And according to the Commander here," nodding in Tarlis's direction, "the boy needs training as much as we can provide," he finished.

Darth acquiesced to his superiors, walked Emanrasu to the horse, and, with Rezua's assistance, helped him mount. Tossing him the reins, Darth gave Emanrasu a half-hearted condolence smile, returned to his horse, and gracefully mounted the steed.

Onred and Tarlis led the group, and the spare horses trailed behind. The group started at a slow gallop.

The jarring ride was almost more than Emanrasu could bear. Fighting the urge to heave, he squeezed his eyes shut to ward off the beating in his head and keep out the incessantly bright morning.

For an eternity, they rode such, stopping only once to switch horses, then returning to the road, the rhythmic pounding of the hooves kicking up dust and clumps of dirt. Soon, the pounding in Emanrasu's head developed a matching rhythm as moons or days passed. Perhaps merely hands as he struggled through the throbbing in his head.

Pointing off to the side of the road, Tarlis spoke to Onred, who turned in his saddle and, as he was wont, bellowed to the group, "There! Make camp there by the open area. Make it in haste, as we will need to start rotations even as we start the boy's training."

The group efficiently dismounted and set up camp, each knowing the drill. After a brief drawing of straws, the guard rotation was set, and they briefly discussed the best order. "Order of what?" queried Emanrasu.

Comradery In Motion: Chapter Fifteen

"Order of your training!" Djorn said, approaching Emanrasu and throwing his arm around him.

"I feel I am in no shape for training," Emanrasu said earnestly.

"And THAT..." Tarlis shouted from across the camp, "is EXACTLY the point!"

"Each one of us, myself included, has been caught in situations where we were not ready, not at our full strength. You can guarantee that someone with ill intent will not sit around waiting for you to sober up before cutting you in two!!" Tarlis continued.

"Now up and strap on your Heater and brandish your Hack!!" he commanded.

Emanrasu's eyebrows dropped to his chin, and a groan crawled out of his gullet as he set about strapping on his gear. His eye caught Rezua across the camp, the frown on his face and the furrow on his brow bearing witness to his compassionate empathy for Emanrasu's plight.

"We will subject him to two a day. Take turns and spend a hand or two with him," Onred said. "Teach him to properly attack and defend against your weapons. If needed, we'll finish the last training on the final night before Bren, giving those training him tonight another chance while he's sober."

The group shuffled purposefully. Djorn and Freydis had the short straws, so they got the first night of training. The others scurried around the camp, coaxing the thick smoke into a crackling fire, taking up positions for the watch, and throwing together a mixture of the provisions they had packed into what could barely be called a stew as it was thin and watery, with half the taste of raw leather.

Bedrolls were placed but not opened to keep out the crawlies; the horses rubbed down and staked nearby to rest and feed.

All of this, Emanrasu noticed in passing as he and the two instructors walked with him to the makeshift training ground. It was nothing more than a flattened area, similar to most that Tarlis had used to train him as they traveled.

The Heater and The Hack

Djorn was up first, and he started explaining the elements of the halberd and the function of each part: the reach, the blade, the pointed end... fluke, langet to protect the haft from strikes, the rondel to protect the hands. He went into length on the different forms the halberd could manifest: blade and hammer, blade, hammer, fluke and spike, blade and spike, and the list went on, and with each new version, Djorn showed him how the motions of each differed. He spoke of the differing strikes and how each had different uses.

As sparring began, Djorn showed him the movements, and Freydis sat back and offered the occasional pointer. Sometimes, he stepped in to show Emanrasu instead of just telling him.

Djorn and Freydis took turns—attack, parry, retreat. Again. And again. They pushed, showing him openings, forcing him to close them. Djorn worked the shield against the halberd. Freydis punished every mistake.

As Emanrasu wielded the Heater and the Hack, the pounding in his head subsided gradually, and his mind focused as the ale's haziness disappeared.

Djorn stepped back, and Freydis took his place. Her axes flashed in the firelight, whirling faster than he thought possible. Emanrasu barely kept up—her speed and control were terrifying. Again, they discussed the different types of battle axes and the methods that could be employed. She showed him how she could use one as a shield by laying it parallel to her forearm to effectively block strikes and quickly flipping it around to bring it into an attack position for a counterstrike.

Djorn pointed out areas that would open up as the two lightly sparred, and Freydis would show how each opening could be closed just as suddenly if Emanrasu was late by the blink of an eye.

Watching them now, Emanrasu felt the weight of what he'd done in the arena. That had been luck. This—this was mastery. There was little chance of him winning a battle of that nature against these two, let alone nine masters of their respective weapons, without a tremendous amount of luck.

Comradery In Motion: Chapter Fifteen

"If I had understood then what I am just beginning to understand now, I would have never had the gall to challenge one, let alone all nine of these weapons masters," Emanrasu thought as he recounted the battle in the arena.

The sun dipping down below the horizon signaled the completion of the lessons, and the trio, with weapons in tow, made for their respective bedrolls.

Emanrasu could not resist one last quip, "Those really are very nice axes," he grinned. Freydis, without a pause or a look back, replied, "I know!" she said, subtly drawing her shoulders back to accentuate her well-developed torso.

After a quick meal of the thin, watery stew, the team turned in, and the guard rotation ensued throughout the night, excluding Emanrasu from the rotation.

Emanrasu, propped on his shield, his sword close at hand, drifted immediately off to sleep, tired from the throbbing of his head and the training he had forced himself to endure.

The dream struggled to become coherent; the Dragon and the Phoenix merely blobs of color against the hazy backdrop of blues and greens. Throughout his night, there was only one recurring thought: "Balance. Balance, in all things, Balance."

A Balance Forged: Chapter Sixteen

"The wisdom of companions produce a leadership that is earned through actions. The strength within one's belief is a key to growth, providing a journey through self-doubt and vulnerability into strength and balance."

—*RCotD*—

Emanrasu woke to the sounds of the camp stirring—boots shifting, murmured voices, the crackle of rekindled flames. Changing shifts for the last watch, the stoking of the fire generated crackling and spitting of sap as it expanded inside the wood until it could be contained no longer. The chill, which permeated the morning, was gradually creeping in with the changing of the season. The fire's heat struggled to push back the insidious coolness. Random leaves fell and settled where they might, emphasizing the closing of the growing season and the swift approach of the new harvest moon, with it, the new harvestmain.

Before Tarlis even stirred, Emanrasu had packed his gear, ready for the day's trek. As he slung the Heater over his arm, he froze. Nearly all the grime—the tarnish it had worn since he plucked it from the pile in Rintha—had fallen away. It gleamed now as if waiting.

For the first time in what felt like forever, Emanrasu really looked at the Heater. It was pristine—impossibly so. It shouldn't be. Not after mains of neglect. Not after how he had found it. He ran a hand over the smooth metal, feeling something just beneath the surface, something unseen but unmistakable. He didn't fully understand it, but… the Dance would find a way.

"Balance," he mumbled softly. "Balance in all things."

Emanrasu mulled over the implications and decided that there must be more to balance than what is on the surface.

A hand on his shoulder caused him to start briefly before realizing who it was.

261

The Heater and The Hack

Tarlis squeezed his shoulder, clapped him lightly on the back, and without a word, went about his morning preparations as the camp broke and readied for departure. Across the camp, the shadowy figure of Rezua sat hunched over his journal, his quill scratching furiously across the page. Firelight flickered across Rezua's face as he glanced up, locking eyes with Emanrasu. He gave a curt nod and a smile, then, with a wink, returned to his writings. Emanrasu returned to his tasks.

Emanrasu felt immensely better today, and his step was brisker and effortless. Even the sounds from the birds and other wildlife echoed the joyfulness of a new day.

From somewhere, the group had brought—or perhaps inherited—a stout and beefy hound, mostly wandering from companion to companion, accepting whatever attention he could get. The hound had short hair and a torn ear, along with the dozen or so scars around its head and neck.

Emanrasu reached down and scratched the hound behind the ears. He grabbed the dog's jowls, looking him in the face before continuing.

"Let's ride," Onred said, projecting his voice without raising it. "We still have a long way to go before we will rest again. And we have no idea what the situation in Bren is."

As Onred's words settled over the group, Emanrasu's thoughts drifted. "Would that Serrah is well," he prayed, frowning a bit and furrowing his eyebrows.

Struggling to dispel the thought of the brigands attacking the town while they were away, he made ready for departure, and in short order, all were mounted and back on the road. The leaves had started to turn from green to a variety of reds and golds, and he knew that, before long, the snows would fall, and ousting the brigands would become a sight more complicated.

A Balance Forged: Chapter Sixteen

The day carried on as the horses kicked up dust. The stray dog darted in and out of the group, occasionally chasing a rabbit, but it always caught up to rejoin the group, only to dart off again moments later.

As the day began to draw to a close, Tarlis found a location for camp. Onred gave the command, and the band of warriors efficiently set up camp, set the rotation, and drew the next set of straws, excluding Freydis and Djorn. Catlina and Aleric were the winners today, whooping their luck to all who bothered to listen.

The camp settled into a routine as Emanrasu worked with the latest pair, Catlina with her cutlass, and Aleric with his claymore. The claymore was not as varied in its typical makeup, but it was wielded in a style similar to that of the halberd. This narrowed the scope of how it was wielded. Like the halberd, there was no shield, and the shorter length allowed for a nimbleness in recovery, which the halberd could not match. Though it was not as long as the halberd, the claymore was very apt in the right hands, and Aleric's hands were immeasurably the right ones. Catlina, as Freydis did the night before, coached him on angles and openings of the claymore, showing him with her cutlass how he could attack the claymore's wielder.

Aleric, in turn, showed openings against Catlina's cutlass. Though the openings were there, the cutlass's speed allowed her to close them swiftly. With each opening, she deftly blocked Emanrasu's sword, only to counterstrike. As she did, her attack would slow, allowing her to demonstrate to Emanrasu the actual opening that she would have as she fought. Her instructions gave Emanrasu a more complete overview of the strategies she employed with her cutlass.

After the instructions, Aleric and Catlina took time to show him how these things would happen in a real battle, and the two of them set to spar. Though each took care not to damage their opponent, they did not pull punches either.

They forced each other back and forth across the small training area, pausing occasionally to admire each other's unexpected methods or skills and to briefly discuss how to defend or bypass the defense of each technique.

The Heater and The Hack

Emanrasu attentively watched the two as they traded blow for blow, the speed and accuracy of each with their chosen weapon again reinforcing the understanding of the incredible amount of luck he had during the arena battle.

When the light dimmed enough that it was no longer easy to see the nuances of the strategies and techniques, the trio paused and reviewed the lessons. Emanrasu, understanding the differences in experience, took the time to compliment the two. "I am starting to understand," he began, "that while the strategy I employed and the luck I enjoyed during the arena bout was sufficient to garner a modicum of respect, the differences in experience shown during training highlight my inexperience."

"Your expertise with the claymore, Aleric, is transcendent. Catlina, your cutlass is absolutely amazing to watch. I hope that you will both honor me again sometime in the future with the opportunity to learn from you," he said in conclusion.

Catlina flashed a grin very briefly, then knitted her eyebrows and scrunched her forehead, a frown appearing on her face.

Emanrasu, confused, asked, "Did I say something wrong?"

She made no reply as they wrapped up the training. As they were all walking back, Catlina paused and peered over her shoulder at Emanrasu. "Don't you like my axes?" Catlina said in mock hurt. From across the camp, Freydis, upon hearing this, fell with laughter while the others joined in the amusement, smiling, chuckling, or laughing at the quip.

Catlina smiled hugely, the wrinkles in the corners of her eyes enhancing their beauty. Still smiling, she turned in for the night without another word.

Emanrasu did likewise, having had quite the laugh himself at the unexpected quip.

As he drifted off, his thoughts went to Serrah.

A Balance Forged: Chapter Sixteen

The Dance was vividly swirling and undulating against the backdrop of stars or nothingness. Although striking in its visual form, the Dance was silent, though Emanrasu sensed that this was no cause for worry.

"Balance, Emanrasu," the final thought came as he woke.

The smell of smoke hung heavier each morning, drifting up and away from the campfire. The sounds of movement seemed to become more urgent with each passing morning, and once again, Emanrasu to stir.

The shifts changed for the last watch of the night, and Emanrasu stepped over and stoked the fire, listening quietly as the crackling and spitting of sap expanded inside the wood until it could no longer be contained.

Rubbing his hands over the heat from the fire slowly dispelled the chill that had sunk to his bones. Random leaves drifted in greater numbers, demanding acknowledgment of the coming Harvestmain.

Emanrasu roused himself and began wrapping up his gear. Once he was ready to travel, he took the time to practice the dance. Tarlis approached him as he was going through the motions with his now-trusty rocks, and Tarlis motioned to him to hold with a wave of his hand.

Emanrasu finished his current sequence and halted, approaching Tarlis with a puzzled look.

Tarlis noticed Emanrasu's questioning look and took steps to reassure him. "Nothing is amiss, young man, though I do want to explain some things as I have come to understand them," Tarlis said with sincerity.

"Almost from the start, and surely as I have watched you grow, I suspected that you were linked to the Black, though I had my doubts early on. Since you were a willing pupil but had no training whatsoever, I dismissed those thoughts. I remember wondering why the Dance would take someone so raw and lift him up," Tarlis admitted. "But I was wrong. What you lack in experience, you make up for in something far rarer: tenacity, dedication, a will that does not bend. You enter into everything in which you are drawn with intensity—one which I have never seen before."

Tarlis reached out and put a hand on Emanrasu's shoulder and squeezed it slightly.

"You are respectful and willing to apply yourself to any task you deem worthy or necessary. I am thankful I was able to meet you in my lifespan," Tarlis continued. "Back when I had you choose between the rocks and the Heater and the Hack and select the heavier of the two, I also had Serrah check which was the heavier pair. Unlike you, she selected the Heater and the Hack," Tarlis recounted. "You, my boy, chose the rocks as the heavier pair, and this confirmed—at least to some extent—my suspicions of your connections to the Black."

"In truth," Tarlis said in amazement, "the rocks are much lighter than the shield and sword—but for you, the Heater and the Hack always appear easier to handle and wield. I had you use the rocks simply because I wanted you to build your strength and develop muscles that would not otherwise be developed. As your grandfather once told me, the Heater and the Hack provide... well... what he called subtle guidance when you use them. They augment your natural abilities, seemingly assuring that luck favors you; a misstep is transformed into sure footing, and a strike that you fail to dodge becomes a narrow miss."

Tarlis continued, "I now believe the best path forward for you is to continue using the Heater and the Hack. So, from this point on, you will train with them. You grow and learn best with them in hand—and by heeding the subtle nudges they may offer you."

Though the revelation of being tied to the Black was not new, and he'd already had more than a fortnight to wrestle with that knowledge, the idea of the Heater and the Hack being lighter—and easier—to wield seemed utterly preposterous.

Scanning the camp, Emanrasu spotted the nearest captain. "Olaf! Settle something for me?"

A Balance Forged: Chapter Sixteen

As Olaf arrived, Emanrasu pointed at the items. "Between the rocks and the shield and sword—pick the lighter pair. Hand it to Tarlis."

Olaf crouched, lifting the shield and sword, then the rocks. He weighed them in each hand. Without hesitation, he handed the rocks to Tarlis.

Emanrasu's jaw was left agape.

"Not sure what that was about," Olaf said, winking at Emanrasu. "But judging by your face, I'm guessing you lost." Olaf grinned and returned to his tasks, readying and packing for breaking camp.

*　　*　　*

Emanrasu stood there, eyes wide and jaw slightly open in surprise. "The Heater and the Hack are lighter?" Emanrasu's voice barely carried. "How is that possible?"

"I always suspected as much when I watched your grandfather wield them, but he never mentioned it, and though I was not one to simply ask randomly insane questions, I finally did ask him," Tarlis remarked.

"When I saw the ease with which you carried them and the difference in your training with and without them, I was convinced I was correct in my assumptions."

Tarlis dropped the rocks, and they landed with a resounding thump. "Your strength has grown exponentially over the time we have been together, and I believe you would be more… or rather, better served by taking up the Heater and the Hack from here on out. Get used to them, feel the weight and heft. Since you deem them lighter, they will yield differently in your hands than the rocks," he explained. "Understanding the weapons you choose is almost as important as understanding the basics. You have the basics down, boy; your dedication to training with the rocks each morning, even though you felt they were heavier, has been commendable!"

The Heater and The Hack

"I decided it was high time for me to tell you what I suspected and have come to believe. This is just further confirmation that you are the Heir of the Black," said Tarlis.

"Use your chosen weapons from this point forward; know them as well as your own crotch, and they will serve you well. Let us break from your training and get ready to depart. We still have many days to go before we get back to Bren, so you will have plenty of time to practice."

With that said, Tarlis turned and headed back to finish packing his gear.

Emanrasu stood for a moment, hefting the Heater and the Hack and looking at them as if he had never held them before. He was at a loss as the questions wandered through his mind, in and out of his thoughts, but constantly slipping away as he came close.

Emanrasu shook his head and shrugged in resignation. Rolling his eyes, he proceeded back to gather the last bits of his gear as well.

The next few days were much the same: sleep, wake, dance in the morning, ride, eat, ride, spar, and train with the captains in the evening. Each day repeated the last, the only difference being who he was sparring and training with.

The training could track the days: Djorn and Freydis, Catlina and Aleric, Darth and Olaf, Tarlis and Onred, Eirikr and Leif. The last two days were spent with the entire group; one would directly spar with Emanrasu, and all the others would chime in on what was done well and what he needed to improve. They all identified weaknesses in each other to be watched and understood.

"You need to understand who you are fighting with and what their weaknesses are," Onred instructed. "You will need to vie to cover those weaknesses even as they will cover yours. This is the difference between fighting alone and fighting with partners or a group. We do not point out weaknesses only to get better. We point out weaknesses because if we are all aware, then we can protect those weak spots, and we are stronger for it. Even as we work to eliminate the weak spots, others will surface. Forever vigilant!"

The group shouted in unison, "Vigilance forever!" Even Tarlis had chimed in.

The dance was not wholly unknown amongst the White, which allowed the dance to gradually grow and amplify, as one weapon style honed another, each becoming more enriched in its layering and interactions.

The final night on the road arrived, and the usual routine ensued, unvaried. On the morrow, he and the White would be in Bren.

Emanrasu was excited, and most of his worry for Serrah had subsided. There had been no signs of the brigands as they got closer to Bren, and Emanrasu decided that this was a good sign and boded well.

He drifted off to sleep; Serrah was his last thought before the night drifted into the dream and the Dance.

The night spent with the Dance was itself becoming comforting to Emanrasu. What once was the cause of restless sleep, in some instances, was becoming a calming influence—the impressions of a greater purpose, of quests, the treasures more valuable than could be imparted.

His first vague impressions of the dreams, which had begun in Rosewood Forest, concluded in more confusion than clarity, though now the transitions were quick and clear, as if stepping through an open door. Each change, less jarring than the last, gaining him focus and clear thought without the need to engage all of his senses, instantly aware of his surroundings without opening his eyes.

With no clear indication of danger present as he woke, Emanrasu rose and gathered his gear. With a nod to Darth, who was currently on watch, Emanrasu stepped away to the training area and, without another word, went through the steps and motions of the dance.

The Heater and The Hack

The realization slowly dawned on him, through each subtle shift or movement... under the weight of steel upon his arm and in his hand... amidst the dance as it had become, not as Tarlis had taught, but his dance... his connection... was now an extension of his nightly dreams, not apart from it.

The dance, as he practiced his training, flowed naturally. Some movements, though, felt awkward and out of place. He closed his eyes and imagined... no, felt... how these movements should flow, and as he retraced his dance with the new movements, Emanrasu paid close attention to what each movement might mean. A parry here, a block or strike there, and with his eyes still closed, he could almost feel the fight as he imagined it. Each step, each block, thrust, and parry seemed to flow logically from an attacker's natural rhythm.

As he concluded his movements, Emanrasu felt the eyes watching him even before he looked up and saw his comrades standing some distance away, watching him intently and whispering to each other.

Emanrasu forced an awkward smile as he observed his audience. The White slowly dispersed, acknowledging him with a nod or a smile as they returned to their duties. Looks of amazement and disbelief hung on their faces like a painting above a hearth.

Rezua sniffed back a non-existent tear and pretended to blow his nose on the corner of his tunic before he, too, turned back to his task of readying for travel.

Tarlis approached him, held out his arm, and Emanrasu locked arms. Tarlis commented, "I have not seen the like in almost twenty mains! Your grandfather used to practice the dance in the same way, lost in his own world, unpredictable, almost beautiful in the way he moved. I asked him once what he was thinking of when he danced. He told me, 'I imagined I was the last man standing after watching my friends go down one by one, and against a hundred different warriors, I was fighting to protect the lives of my fallen men.'

"I thought a lot about his response and vowed that I would work to defend my men as well as he."

A Balance Forged: Chapter Sixteen

"I was not aspiring to such heights," Emanrasu confided. "I was aspiring merely to survive one-on-one against your White, and should I eventually be able to hold my own against even a single one, I will count that as a small victory!"

Tarlis gazed at Emanrasu, a grin spreading across the old man's face. He turned toward the camp, motioning with his arm toward the White as they broke camp. "These are not my White, young man. They are not here because of me. They are here because of you! They believe you will be able to lead them, and once again, the Black will begin to redress wrongs, both great and small."

The group of captains, now well into packing and getting ready to break camp for the last leg of their journey back to Bren, glanced over occasionally, their eyes still displaying amazement.

"Tarlis, I am not sure I am ready, nor am I sure that I have the wherewithal to lead such a skilled group as this. I was able to convince them to join us through arrogance and unadulterated ignorance. I cannot imagine the luck that was with me to best even one of them, let alone each of them one after the other," Emanrasu said, eyes downcast, his foot kicking and digging slightly at the dirt. "They would be following a fraud and charlatan."

"Nonsense!" Tarlis vehemently disagreed. "Your luck notwithstanding, each was bested because they underestimated you, not individually, though that was also done, but as a group. They were cocky and treated the arena sparring as nothing more than a chance to put you in your place.

"No, boy—it was you! You made them believe. Not in the legend, not in the title. In you. And that, with the right leader, no odds are insurmountable."

Tarlis continued, "Had you not proven yourself without a doubt, they would not be here today. To a man, they believe in you, not as the epitome of leadership, but as the possibility of leadership. Each in their own way has acknowledged the spark of something in you that each one of them wants to help nurture from a cinder into a righteous blaze."

"And, with this unintentional display of untapped skill, if they were not convinced before, they certainly are now."

Wrinkles deepened at the corners of Tarlis's eyes as he grinned at the young man—the grin of a madman with a secret only he knew. "You have a destiny, boy. We know not what your destination is, but, be it horse, cart, or ship, we are along for the ride, regardless of where it may lead."

"The White and the Black had a reputation that inspired some and struck terror into others, and we were a part of it then, and we long to be a part of it again. We understand the destination is not the end. Our destination is most likely, and literally, our journey and naught else."

"Now, let us mount and depart for Bren this one last time. I am eager to know how they fared in our absence. The ruse we applied as we departed was thinly veiled and might easily have been seen through. I dare say, if it was, they might have had a rough go of it since we have been on the road," Tarlis finished.

The Leaders and Loafers: Chapter Seventeen

"The need to set aside one's self to assume a role of leadership is not always wanted, but may sometimes be necessary. Ponder briefly and answer decisively, taking into account the information you have garnered. Address what you can and let the rest go."

—RCotD—

T he group was back on the road barely a hand after rise, traveling at a fair pace, wary and watchful. The cool breeze was barely noticeable but always present, and each member of the group pulled their cloaks and tunics just a tad closer.

The road was empty of typical travelers, though one or two large groups caravanning together for safety passed by, keeping a close eye as they passed. Burly guards and hired fighters kept hands on hilts or openly unsheathed their weapons as they passed, ready for the fight should it ensue.

The group stopped and retrieved the stash of goods and gear they had stored away from the attack on their first night of travel, having hidden it away in hopes of retrieving it on their way back to Bren.

The stash was still there, and it was hastily packed onto the spare horses before they continued on their way to Bren.

Seasoned as they were, they kept watch—and soon noticed figures in the distance, observing. The groups seemed to be varied in strength and would idly watch the road from their vantage points. The groups were seemingly unconcerned with the travelers, though they did not approach the road to confront the White.

One group on a hill, perhaps a score strong, watched the group travel the road. They were either brigands reconsidering an attack or locals assessing the situation from a safe distance. Either way, the White traveled unaccosted and at last reached the fork where Emanrasu and the others were first attacked.

The Heater and The Hack

The rest of the journey was brief and uneventful. The chatter among the White was kept to a minimum, with strategic conversation the focus of everyone's attention if any was had. Given the seriousness of the mood, it seemed more prudent to Emanrasu.

As they neared Bren, the overturned wagons strewn across the road were a testament to the continuing harassment of travelers, and any of the valuables long gone. The wagons were the only sign of struggle, and with no indications of bodies, they continued warily on, slowing their pace a bit to keep the horses fresh for a sprint or battle as the need be. Once more, they spied a small group watching, perhaps four or five strong, but they kept their distance. After a quick discussion, Freydis wheeled her horse and galloped in their direction, whereupon the watchers promptly whipped around and made off away from Emanrasu and his gathering of White.

When they arrived at the edge of Bren, it was three or four hands past apex, and the streets were quiet. The group's observations saw indications that there was still life, and those brave enough to peek out from the occasional door or window were cautiously monitoring the White's passage.

The welcome sight of the inn came into view, and a score of men and stout women were training the drills that Tarlis had imparted to the innkeep before they left. The dust kicked up from their shuffling in the courtyard of the inn, drifting away on the breeze as more stirred with each step. They made their way toward the inn and could see the innkeep was busy barking out instructions to this one or that one as he stood slightly elevated on the veranda outside the inn's front door. Serrah, too, was standing beside the innkeep, speaking to him as she pointed out this or that among the group working drills.

Emanrasu's heart raced a little as he saw her, and he struggled not to kick his horse into a full gallop and sweep her up in his arms.

Shocked at his thoughts, he mulled over them.

The Leaders and Loafers: Chapter Seventeen

"Whoa…those were unexpected thoughts," he mumbled quietly, his boyish grin vaporously appearing and disappearing before anyone was the wiser.

Though the thoughts were not wholly unwelcome, he could not recall another time when a woman had caused him such consternation. He shook his head and ran his sweaty palms over his breeches, fighting the urge to grin like a madman with a secret.

The innkeep caught the attention of a young boy and motioned him with a wave of his hand. The boy ran over and took the reins of the horse Emanrasu was riding, and Emanrasu swung his leg over and dismounted. He paused a moment, taking a deep breath and letting it out, holding onto the saddle for a brief moment, trying to temper his excitement at seeing her again.

"Thank you, boy. Can you please make sure my gear makes it to my room? I am unsure which room it is, but I will take that up with the innkeep," Emanrasu queried the boy.

"Telk," the boy corrected, arms crossed, brow raised.

"Um, what?" Emanrasu blinked, caught off guard.

"Telk," the boy said again, with emphasis. "My name is Telk, not—boy!"

"I meant no offense, Telk. Think you can get my gear to my room?" Emanrasu queried again, reaching out and offering Telk a copper.

"Yes, sir!" Telk grinned, pocketing the coin before dashing off—pausing only to scratch the dog behind the ears.

Emanrasu, distracted from his thoughts of Serrah by the unexpected exchange, tempered his excitement a bit. He felt he could now face her without acting like a schoolchild. He thanked Telk and strode toward the veranda. His eyes intently focused on Serrah and the smile she bore.

Smiling, she looked out over the warriors he and Tarlis had gathered, and a sense of pride rushed over Emanrasu, which dissipated almost as suddenly.

The Heater and The Hack

He watched her smile disappear as she scanned the incoming group, replaced with a knitted brow and a frown. She started to turn away—hesitated—then, as if making a sudden decision, darted inside.

Emanrasu slowed, confusion prickling at him. He glanced back at the warriors—joking, at ease. None had noticed Serrah. Or if they had, they weren't concerned. Why was she?

Emanrasu quickened his pace, and as he approached the veranda and climbed the steps, he clasped the outstretched arm of the innkeep. "Torsun," he stated, remembering the name from before his departure. "How is everything progressing?" he questioned.

"Ymanser, welcome back!" Torsun exclaimed, his smile stretching across his face. The relief was apparent, and as the tension seemed to be easing from him, his shoulders relaxed, and his posture not quite as stiff as a moment ago.

"Emanrasu."

"Huh?" came the innkeep's response.

"Ema— Never mind," Emanrasu quickly replied, feeling a bit like Telk. "How goes the training?" he repeated.

The innkeep shrugged slightly and shook his head almost imperceptibly. "Not as good as I had hoped, but better than I had expected," the innkeep stated plainly.

"We do not have an official full-time guard in Bren, and up until recently, we never thought we needed one. So, we don't have a lot of experienced fighters, maybe one or two. The rest are all farmers, merchants, and a few smiths. It seems as though you perhaps—fared better?" Torsun asked.

"Emanrasu," Emanrasu replied, thinking he might as well get it out of the way now.

"Huh?" replied the innkeep as he had before.

The Leaders and Loafers: Chapter Seventeen

"My name is Emanrasu," Emanrasu said again, grinning weakly at the turn of events from a moment ago. His thoughts were not really focused on getting a report from the innkeep, and he could not shake the vision of Serrah turning and darting back into the inn.

"Pardon, Torsun, can you give an update to Tarlis? I must see about another matter," and on that statement, without so much as a goodbye or explanation, he let go of Torsun's arm and made toward the inn door.

*   *   *

He hurriedly entered and scanned the room, which was half-filled with people— some townspeople and others being travelers willing to brave the road from parts unknown to Bren, even with the dangers present.

As Emanrasu scanned the room, his eyes searched out and locked with Serrah's. Her expression drew tight and narrowed, and her brows were knit in concern over something. She leaned in an almost half-turn, looking as if she wanted to run, the other half wanting to stay and face this...this... "What is she concerned about, Emanrasu?" he thought. Even as these thoughts ran through his mind, he strode in her direction. She was standing behind the bar, nervously washing a mug.

Her eyes met his—pleading, uncertain. He had hoped for something warmer, more intimate. "I should not have expected as much since she had never indicated that she was attracted beyond the one day weeks ago," he thought. "I have made up this great scenario in my head, and it is about to come crashing down under the weight of reality." The thought caused the smile to drop from his face, and Serrah no longer smiled either.

"I am sorry, Eman," she said nervously, fiddling with a pendant around her neck that Emanrasu had never seen before. "I had no idea who you'd bring back—or where you even found him. I haven't seen him for almost six mains, and I did not leave in the best way."

The Heater and The Hack

"Slow down," Emanrasu requested as he walked around the bar to face her without the impeding barrier in the way. "Slow down and take a deep breath," he said in a relaxed, concerned tone. "Relax and tell me what you're talking about."

"My father, I am not sure how you found him, but I left abruptly mains ago without so much as a note or a word," she started to explain.

"I don't understand; who is your father?" Emanrasu pried, trying to understand.

"Djorn… Djorn Ironfoot! He's my father!" she repeated. Her voice wavered, and for a moment, Emanrasu thought she might collapse.

Emanrasu reached out to steady her, and she placed her hands on his arms and steadied herself. She took a deep breath and closed her eyes, visibly letting her tension go; her shoulders dropped a bit, and her brow unfurrowed. She took another deep breath and slowly let it out. "Come to the room, I will explain there… please?" she said, almost pleading.

Emanrasu nodded, and Serrah, maintaining her hold on one of his arms, led them toward the stairs and up to the room. They promptly slipped into the room and closed the door. She immediately hugged him and apologized. "I am sorry for behaving this way, and thank you for not making this more difficult than I already feel it is."

She guided him to the bench and let him sit, after which she sat on the bed as she had done many days ago. "Funny how it has only been days, and it feels like weeks, even moons…" Emanrasu's thought trailed off as he scrutinized her face. The tension almost drained from it; she took another deep breath, slowly letting it out and forcing the rest of the tension to leave with it.

"My father…" she began, her voice trembling slightly, "he was a widely known gamer, and though he primarily hunted and trapped for our village, nobles from all around would come to him when they wanted to play at hunting. He would take them out, locate and scare the game in the direction of the nobles, in hopes they were not completely incapable of using a bow or crossbow to take the

The Leaders and Loafers: Chapter Seventeen

animals down. For many mains, as I grew up, he would do this type of thing, and he would leave for an evening, or sometimes a day or two, leaving me with Thura, one of our local matrons. She is the one who taught me to gather spices and herbs and find wild edibles. She was an excellent cook, and when the festivals came around, there was little room at her table." Serrah looked away, and her face tightened slightly as she garnered a far-off look, presumably thinking of her childhood and the happier times.

"As I grew older, my father was called upon more frequently to accompany this group or that, and I spent more and more time with Thura or by myself," Serrah continued. "I was not unhappy, but neither did I feel like I belonged in the life I had been born into. I felt like there was more out there, more that I could, wanted... well... needed to do. My father was recruited by a group calling themselves 'the White.' I don't know exactly what their purpose was, but he started going on trips that would last a week, two weeks, and even longer occasionally."

"I was dissatisfied with my life, and though I still gamed for the village in his absence, I wanted to be anywhere else but there. Thura discussed this with me at length over the span of many months. She took ill, and though the herbs we used had healing properties, they were never enough to cure what ailed her, and she finally passed. We built the pyre and set it ablaze, and with my father gone for almost two full moons, I decided to leave and find my place. I gathered the meager gear that was mine alone, the food that was left in Thura's home, and I left... just up and left."

"There was no ceremony in my leaving, my father absent, the only other one that really knew me was Thura, and with her gone, I was free to leave and find that which I needed. I could find my own way. Which I did, to some extent."

"It seems that I spent a lot of time reinventing myself for one reason or another. I seem to attract bad situations like the one in Ertz, where I needed to leave, many times with only the clothes on my back, a meager coin or two in my pocket, and the pendant that Thura gave me," Serrah continued, frowning at the thought of

Thura. She reached into her tunic and pulled out the pendant that hung around her neck.

He had never seen it before, but then he was not one to stand around staring at people, not even beautiful auburn-haired... Emanrasu caught himself before his thoughts got out of hand.

"What about your father? You did not go back and set things right with him?" Emanrasu asked. He knitted his brow and slowly shook his head from side to side. "You never went back and let him know how you felt and the loneliness of the life while he went off to do whatever?"

Emanrasu looked her squarely in the eyes and saw that she still seemed to be hurt by her father's absence.

"Go and talk to him, Serrah! From the little time I have grown to know him, he seems a man who would understand," Emanrasu suggested. "And if he does not, then at least you tried and would no longer have the unknown weighing on you."

"I thought of him all the time at first," Serrah stated, "but as time went on, I thought of him less and less. The times that I did think of him, I was filled with remorse until eventually, I did go back to the village to speak with him, to try to make him understand. But, by the time I had gone back, it had been mains since anyone had seen him, and though I was saddened by this, I felt it was probably for the best. I would not... well... do not know what to say to him," she said as a lone tear crept down her cheek.

Emanrasu stood and went over to her, sitting beside her, and wrapped an arm around her to comfort her. With this action, Serrah broke down and sobbed quietly as he held her. He could feel her body shake with each sob; the distant smell of lavender from her hair wafted to him as he held her. Her arms chilled to the touch, though the day was not cold. He rubbed them slowly, trying to warm her without distracting her.

The Leaders and Loafers: Chapter Seventeen

"Just try... well just talk to him," he said quietly. "If you don't, you may regret it."

The two of them sat in this manner for some time. Hands in her lap, her head rested on his chest, his arm comforting around her shoulders without being overly oppressive. After a time, she caught hold of herself, and with deep breaths, she was able to cease the tears.

He sat and comforted her, enjoying the closeness, but torn between breaking the contact and encouraging her to go talk to her father and taking her in his arms and telling her how he felt, even though he was not quite sure of the extent of it himself.

Emanrasu opted to just hold her for a bit longer, then slowly withdrew his arm and placed a hand on each shoulder. He squared her up, reached up, and lifted her chin to look at him. She peered up at him, though her head was still slightly down and her eyes still wet from the tears. She managed a weak smile and leaned in and gave him a warm hug, wrapping both arms around him, her face angled slightly up, and her lips pursed as she leaned toward him. Emanrasu's heart thumped like the feet of a rabbit being chased by a hound. She leaned in briefly and snaked around to kiss his cheek, her lips soft, her breath warm on his cheek, and her body pressed soft but firm against his. Serrah whispered, "Thank you, Eman; I feel I needed that, as I do not recall ever missing my father so much as I do now." The two of them stood, and Emanrasu encircled her with his arms. He leaned down slightly and kissed the top of her head, and with one final squeeze, he let her go.

Serrah stood there, composing herself and struggling not to look like she had been doing exactly as she had. She wiped the tears from her face, walked over to the basin, splashed water on her face, and dried it with the cloth nearby.

Emanrasu watched her graceful glide and every movement. "I should have said something," he silently chastised himself, "but not while she is vulnerable," came his self-inspired response. "Wait for a time not fraught with unrelated emotions, or the chances of her response being not fully based on your revelation will introduce unwanted and unneeded complexity."

Simultaneously, Emanrasu mentally kicked himself for missing the opportunity and congratulated himself for not taking advantage of the situation. He went back and forth in his mind several times for good measure before he finally let it go.

*   *   *

The knock on the door startled them both, and they glanced at one another before Emanrasu went to the door and opened it.

Tarlis stood in the doorway. "We are gathering in the Great Room, and your presence is required," he offered.

Onred stood behind Tarlis with a somber look and nodded at Emanrasu as their eyes met. Onred grinned knowingly, "I hope we didn't interrupt… it would have been a shame." He winked at Emanrasu before following Tarlis back down the hallway to the stairs.

Emanrasu noticed Telk standing patiently nearby. "Your gear has been stowed in the next room, sir," Telk told him, indicating the next door down the hall.

"Emanrasu," Emanrasu responded.

Telk immediately understood the game. "Huh?" he said in mock confusion.

"Emanrasu, my name is Emanrasu, Telk, not—sir," Emanrasu said, trying to keep his face stoic and unemotional.

"My apologies, Si… um… Emanrasu," the boy said, grinning, "I meant no disrespect!"

Telk turned, still grinning, and bounced down the hallway, following Onred and Tarlis's lead.

Emanrasu turned to face Serrah once more and saw the tilt of her head and the expression of unspoken questions begging for answers.

The Leaders and Loafers: Chapter Seventeen

"We had this same conversation earlier, but our roles were reversed," he started to explain.

"What conversation?" she asked.

"I will explain later. Go, find your father, do your best to convey how you feel, and let the dice fall where they may. You have no control over others and the way they feel. You can only try to communicate your thoughts and feelings, letting go of the anxieties and sorrow," Emanrasu suggested.

"As you mentioned earlier, your regrets for not letting him know seemed to weigh heavy on you; unburden yourself by making an attempt."

Serrah smiled briefly, hugged him, and headed toward the stairs as Emanrasu reached in and pulled the door shut, following immediately behind her.

The inn's Great Room, hushed and solemn when he was last here, was a bustle of activity and loud conversations. The White, if nothing else, seemed to bring their own entertainment in the form of loud conversation, jibes, and laughter, no matter where they went. The captains were milling around as if awaiting something, though what... Emanrasu had no clue. The tables had been pushed together, forming one long table. Tarlis and Onred stood near the head of the table, and Telk was sitting close by and off to one side. As the boy spied Emanrasu, he stood and inched closer to the head of the table.

Tarlis waved him over, motioning to the head of the table. Emanrasu hesitated, eyes flicking to the seat—the seat of command.

"I would rather not," he told Tarlis and Onred.

The two grizzled warriors looked at him quizzically, prompting him to quickly explain.

"In my mind, I would rather be a part of the group, rather than lead it," Emanrasu said.

"You really have no choice at this point unless you decide to drop everything you have worked toward and leave," Tarlis replied.

"No, I mean, I do not want to put myself above anyone here. I would rather sit in the middle of the side rather than at the head. I would feel less like I am lording over everyone. No matter how others view me, I must still follow my heart and head, and they both seem to tell me that where I sit is a crucial statement of who I am. I am just not the head of the table sort of person, if you understand what I mean," Emanrasu said, trying to explain his thoughts.

Tarlis thought for a moment. "I understand. And rightfully, I should have considered your reaction from the start, as it is obvious now that you would balk at setting yourself in a position above others. I have come to realize that while you might take on the role of leader and even consider yourself a leader, you have never thought of yourself as being above others, which is apparent as I think back on it."

Tarlis motioned toward a spot in the middle of the side and barked some orders to the captains. The benches along that side were parted. A chair was quickly brought over for Emanrasu.

Emanrasu stepped up to the chair, placed his hands on its back, and looked around.

The Great Room was filled with people—townsfolk and White—engaging in various ways, some somber and solemn, others jesting with laughter.

As he gazed around, he saw that Rezua had taken up a table behind Emanrasu's chair and, as was his wont, scribbled and sketched in what appeared to be a new journal.

"I must ask him, sometime, where he hides all of these books of his when he is done filling them," thought Emanrasu, grinning softly.

Telk had moved to a place behind him as well, standing near Rezua. The boy watched Emanrasu intently, and Rezua leaned over and spoke to him. His eyes lit up, and he ran off. Rezua glanced at Emanrasu with a wink and a grin before returning to his writing.

Emanrasu scanned the gathering but saw neither Djorn nor Serrah. He hoped that they were reconciling in constructive ways.

Tarlis rapped his cane on the table—twice. The sound echoed through the room, sharp and deliberate. The din dulled as conversations fell away until only the creak of chairs and the occasional cough filled the space.

"The issue at hand," Tarlis began, "is how to rid this community of the plague that's been sitting just beyond our reach—the brigands who prey on every traveler trying to come or go from this place."

He paused, then pointed his cane toward Emanrasu and spoke directly to the White.

"And since we've all seen the strategy, skill, and stubbornness this one has shown over the last few weeks, I'm turning the floor over to him."

Emanrasu froze. His stomach flipped.

For a second, it felt like that first day all over again—when Tarlis had rapped him on the head for stepping into something he didn't understand. This felt the same. Worse, maybe. Because now, they were all looking at him. Waiting.

"What do I know about any of this?" he thought as he fought to keep down what little was still in his stomach.

He tried to steady his breath, but the weight of it all pressed down hard. He thought of the old man's story—the loss, the pain, the weight he still carried. Understanding had mattered then. And it mattered now.

Deep breath…

He suddenly realized, "I can't know every name or every story in this town—but I can lean on the ones who do."

The Heater and The Hack

He leaned forward, steadying himself on the edge of the table.

"I don't—" he started, as a shrill voice cut him off.

"Why in the Dance should we listen to him?"

A man from the townsfolk—older, loud—pushed forward.

"There are a dozen blooded warriors here. Any one of them has more years than he's been breathing." He motioned toward the White, then jabbed a finger at Emanrasu. "He's barely a boy."

Murmurs stirred. A few heads nodded.

Tarlis appeared ready to speak but stopped when Torsun slammed his fist on the table.

"Enough."

He turned, fixing the man with a cold stare.

"We know your past, Dalen. Know your place—and you might be allowed to keep it."

Dalen went pale. His shoulders slumped, and he drifted back into the crowd.

Torsun looked at Emanrasu and gave a single nod.

"Go on."

Emanrasu took another breath. It didn't help much.

He looked around the table. Faces older than his. Harder. Wiser. All waiting.

"Who am I to speak to any of them?"

"I'd like to tell you I'm ready. That I know what I'm doing. But I'd be lying if I did."

He glanced at Tarlis, then back at the crowd.

The Leaders and Loafers: Chapter Seventeen

"I don't have the experience some of you do. I can't match what the White have seen or done. And I sure as the Dance don't know the lives of everyone in Bren. Not like Torsun does. But I'm not here because I think I can do this alone."

He paused... his mind flailed, searching for the right words. Words that might carry the weight of what he now bore... he found none, continuing anyway.

"I am not... I'm not here because I think I am the most qualified, nor am I the most apt. I am here because I saw a need. No offense to Torsun..." Emanrasu nodded toward him, meeting his eyes.

Torsun nodded back at him and waved a permissive hand.

"...I am here because I saw a need that was being ignored and allowed to fester. Not because no one cared, but because nobody knew what to do without making it worse.

"That is why I am standing here... because I truly believe that if we rely on each other and understand our abilities and motivations, we can fix this... because this is not just me... this is us. We can fix it."

He glanced around the room at the nodding heads as the multitude of eyes gazed back. He gave a short nod, more to himself than anyone else.

"And if you're still willing to follow me and trust the judgment of our experienced leadership—Torsun, Onred, and Tarlis..."

Emanrasu nodded to each in turn as he spoke their names, and each returned the acknowledgment.

He took a breath and finished, "...then maybe... maybe we've got a chance."

*　　　*　　　*

The silence filled the room like a bucket plunged into an icy river. Frigid. Almost no movement.

A cough broke the silence and signaled the conversations to resume.

The Heater and The Hack

Emanrasu waited a moment and held his hand up. The room slowly quieted.

"The truth is, I am half the age of most everyone at this table. So, as I stand here, I ask myself, 'What do I bring to these weathered warriors that others cannot or will not?' My answer is sincerity, meticulousness, steadfastness, and the drive to see something through, no matter the difficulty.

"In order to do this, I must rely on the advice and guidance of each of you. This will provide a path forward through the unknown trail ahead of us." Emanrasu could feel the tension slowly ebbing from his body as he talked. "Our task here is to find a way to put an end to the plague of bandits that are harassing the travelers, and we know it is only a matter of time before they come directly here to have their way and strip what they can."

Emanrasu sighed heavily. "I recommend a cautious, measured path; let us make sure of who they are and their numbers so that we might better prepare."

As Emanrasu looked around the table at the wealth of experience, he knew that herein lay the answer to the problem. There was only the need to draw out the best of the options and put those plans into action.

"In light of this, let us discuss without formalities options for proceeding," Emanrasu concluded.

Emanrasu sat as he came to the end of his impromptu speech and quietly set himself to follow the conversations that erupted around the table. Discussions of this option and that option abounded. The difference in the discussions was striking. The White, each in turn, laid out possibilities as they saw them, methodically working around the group. The conversation between the townsfolk was chaotic and emotional. One or the other banging on the table in emphasis happened more than once.

Looking around, Emanrasu listened to the various suggestions as they were discussed, noting that only Torsun and Tarlis were as silent as he. Both listened intently to the conversations that ensued. The townsfolk, at least the most outspoken of them, were in favor of immediate action. However, many quietly contemplated the suggestions being discussed by the White, intently listening and mulling over the complex actions.

"Now! Now... be damned!" someone barked from the townsfolk, followed by a louder, "You would say that—but we know what happened in—" The rest was swallowed by the crowd as the voices piled over one another in a river of noise. But the more he listened, the more certain he became—the voice was Dalen's. Again.

The White, having had an opportunity to speak, each in turn, were now discussing options. "Verify by..." "Cat and Darth..." "...unknown..." drifted over to Emanrasu as he strained to gather more of the context, without success. The din of the townsfolk smothering the words from the White.

The discussions were allowed to continue for a time, and as the townsfolk's conversation seemed to center around immediate and decisive actions, the White discussed more methodical and exploratory actions.

Emanrasu looked over, and Torsun nodded in his direction, apparently indicating that the townsfolk had discussed enough.

Emanrasu nodded back and reached over and lightly touched Tarlis's arm, garnering his attention. They shared a glance, and Tarlis nodded, grabbing his cane. Firmly, he rapped on the table once more, and the din of both the townsfolk and the White slowly subsided.

Tarlis waved his cane in Emanrasu's direction, and attention shifted from Tarlis to Emanrasu.

Emanrasu took a deep breath and stood once again.

"Torsun, how would you and your people like to see this issue broached? Since you have more stake in this, I would like to hear from you first," Emanrasu stated.

The Heater and The Hack

Torsun stood looking around at the townsfolk, receiving nods and acknowledgment from several of them before he turned back to the table.

"In truth," Torsun started, "we are torn and equally split between taking the time to plan something, which could lead to additional attacks on the road, and immediately attacking the manor in which they currently reside."

"Thus, as the leader of the people of Bren, we have no definitive stance and wish to hear what might be brought to the table from you and your White."

"NO!" came the shout from one of the Bren residents, pushing his way to the front. Dalen, livid in his anger, roared as his fist pounded loudly on the table. "We must act now! No waiting, no scouting—we strike! Damn the consequences!"

Torsun reached out, placed a hand on the man's shoulder, and leaned in, whispering in his ear.

Townsfolk that were close enough to hear stifled grins or openly smiled at the comment as the man's face flushed and reddened.

The man turned away and shuffled his way to the back of the group as Emanrasu watched before turning his attention to Torsun once more.

"As I said, we are split, and we—will—abide by the decision provided by you and your White," Torsun said as he sat.

Emanrasu nodded and turned to Tarlis. "What do we have to offer?" He asked.

Tarlis stood, and his gaze swept the White, each of them nodding in turn.

"We are in agreement; we must have more knowledge of the bandits and their routines. We have no idea of their true numbers, and I, for one, have never seen one of them twice within the groups we have had the opportunity to view. This in and of itself indicates they have a larger complement of men than we might have first thought."

The Leaders and Loafers: Chapter Seventeen

Tarlis continued, "We will need to send someone out to determine these things. Catlina and Darth are the best qualified to go, and keeping the group small will give them the best chance to go unnoticed. Darth's stealth will serve them both well in their task.

"Catlina has a mind for recall and can use her spyglass to view from farther away than we might otherwise need to. This will give us an advantage as we determine what information there is to glean, and upon their return, we can make further plans regarding our actions," Tarlis finished as he sat.

Emanrasu nodded to the old man and turned to the table and the faces that stared back at him.

"From the discussions I have heard go around this table, I believe gathering information and bringing it back is the most prudent action we can take," Emanrasu stated.

"And… with your approval…," he gazed directly at Torsun, "that is the path we shall take." Torsun glanced briefly to his left and then his right, acknowledging the nodding heads, and turned back to Emanrasu.

"We have no better path than the one you offer," Torsun stated plainly. "And without your assistance, we would never have gathered the courage to consider fighting back, and I imagine the town would have suffered for it."

Torson sighed; a weak smile fluttered on his lips. "We agree with your proposal and will do our utmost to play whatever part you would have of us."

A muffled shout came from behind Torsun—followed by a scuffle. A moment later, two stout lads dragged Dalen out, one clamping a firm hand over his mouth.

Torsun's weak smile turned into a grin. "We approve, young man."

Then, from the White, a woman's voice rang out.

'White!'

Upon hearing this command, as one, the White reached for their bowls and tankards, raising them high.

Emanrasu blinked. The White had all raised their tankards—but he had nothing before him. Unprepared, he hesitated, unsure.

A tug at his tunic wrestled the apology from his lips and let it slip away. He turned—Telk stood there with a frown, watching the man being removed. As the boy turned his attention to Emanrasu, he immediately brightened, a smile sliding across his face.

Emanrasu winked, taking the proffered tankard. "You're on the cart, boy—err, Telk."

Turning back to the table, he lifted the tankard, catching Freydis's eye as she nodded in his direction.

"Drink!" came the command.

The White drank, setting their vessels on the table after a single pull.

Upon seeing this, Torsun raised his glass to Emanrasu, who nodded in acknowledgment, then to the White in general.

Prompted in this manner, the townsfolk hurriedly produced their own drinks, and the din of laughter and merriment indicated that, at least for now, they saw and felt hope for the town.

Emanrasu reached into his pouch and fished out a copper. He turned to Telk, who was still at his elbow.

"Thank you, Telk," he said, handing the copper to the grinning boy.

Each Moment of Merriment: Chapter Eighteen

"In life, one must take merriment and enjoyment in spurts and sputters. Oft, situations and moods change in a moment, and if one continuously focuses on only the grim and grime, the quality of one's life deteriorates. Each opportunity to elicit joy from a moment produces a gem that will always be remembered and can be thought back on and considered when one is distressed and contemplative."

—RCotD—

The merriment devolved into pockets of conversation. In ones and twos, the White was beset by groups of townsfolk, withstanding a continuous barrage of questions and clarifications. The White, in turn, explained various concepts and tactics to the groups around them and attempted to impart knowledge to the barely trained faces that gazed back at them.

Emanrasu waved over Catlina and Darth as he approached Torsun and Tarlis.

"Excuse the interruption," he said to the two. "I feel we need to get the plan in motion as quickly as possible, and it is my intent to send Catlina and Darth out before dark, so they can begin gathering any information that might help."

Tarlis grinned at the young man. "We had been discussing that very thing," he said to Emanrasu. Torsun nodded his confirmation as Catlina and Darth joined them.

Emanrasu turned to the two captains. "You will be on your way before the sun has set. You have some hands to make yourselves ready, but I want you to stay and mingle with the townsfolk. The more they know us personally, the better they will trust us."

"Do not discuss anything specific about your plans. We do not know whether any of the residents have sided in one manner or another with the brigands, and I would rather err on the side of caution," Emanrasu informed them. "Use your best judgment and return when you feel you have sufficient information to allow us to plan appropriately."

Emanrasu turned to Tarlis and Torsun. "Is there anything else you would suggest?"

"Patterns," Tarlis said. "Look for patterns and behaviors that seem to repeat or follow a natural schedule. We're searching for weaknesses or laxness that might give us an edge. We may not avoid bloodshed entirely, but if we approach with force and resolve, there's a chance we can resolve this without it."

Catlina and Darth exchanged a glance, and Darth gave a curt nod.

"We've handled things like this before," Catlina said, placing a light hand on Darth's shoulder. She met Emanrasu's gaze. "I know you haven't known me long, but I trust you know Onred wouldn't send the two of us if he had doubts.

"You're growing into this. You read people well. You've shown sound judgment. For that reason, Darth and I will gladly ride out and gather what we can."

Emanrasu nodded, his expression tight with concern. "You are right, in that I have not known you long enough to understand your skills completely. But I trust you; what I do not trust are unforeseen events. The brigands have been bold to set up in this manner—let's make certain that's all there is."

"Do not take unnecessary risks. Whatever you find out—it's only useful if you return. If it comes to a choice between the information and coming back—return safely. We'll find another way."

"Aye," Darth said, brushing off Catlina's hand with a grin. "We'll return. And I agree with 'mother' here. We know the risk. We know what's riding on what we bring back."

Catlina playfully shoved him upon hearing the—mother—comment but grinned as well.

Each Moment of Merriment: Chapter Eighteen

"With your leave, we will return to the general merriment until we can steal away and embark upon our given task," Catlina said, her gaze fixed on Emanrasu expectantly.

Emanrasu nodded, and as the two departed, he noticed the reappearance of Djorn and Serrah.

Emanrasu turned to Tarlis and Torsun. "If I might beg my leave, I have another matter that weighs on my mind and would see it through."

Without waiting for a response other than the beginning of a nod from Tarlis, Emanrasu made his way toward Serrah.

Djorn leaned over, said something to her, and as Emanrasu approached, the man hugged her, scanned the room, and nodded to Emanrasu before swiftly making his way to Onred.

Serrah beamed, her face bright and relaxed as she, too, saw Emanrasu coming toward her. She moved in to greet him, grabbed his hands, and squeezed them gently.

"You were right," she said, the light in her sparkling eyes reinforcing her smile. "He understands, and his only concern was that I was safe and well. He had searched moons for me upon his return when he discovered Thura had gone to the Dance."

"You have no idea... I had been... so... afraid that he would be angry... or disappointed. Thank you for your advice, Eman. I feel I would have never had the courage to approach him without it."

Emanrasu could feel the anxiety and fear drain from him, and in the process, recognized the feelings he had not realized he was harboring. Thinking back... perhaps it colored his earlier interactions.

The grin slipped across his face as the unwanted feelings flowed from him. "I am glad the advice helped," he said. "I, too, was concerned with how he would receive you, but I also knew that confronting the issue gives clarity and, to some extent, I hoped, closure."

Serrah dropped his hands and, grabbing his shoulders, drew him in and gave him a warm embrace, which in Emanrasu's mind did not last nearly as long as he wanted it to.

As she released him from the embrace, she began detailing her interactions and conversation with her father, describing her hesitancy and apprehension in the beginning and how she realized his concern when the tears streamed down the stoic man's face.

Emanrasu listened intently to her words, striving to understand and asking questions to draw her out. He felt more ecstatic the more she talked, and their discussion of her reunion with her father took substantially longer than the interaction itself.

Thus, as the night drew on, the tension in the air from the townsfolk had diminished somewhat with the knowledge that there would be, if not a resolution, at least they were actively seeking to end the informal siege of the brigands on their village and homes.

Emanrasu felt a hand on his shoulder and turned to meet the gaze of Catlina. She nodded to him and, without a word, accompanied Darth out of the room and off to the task at hand.

"Be careful," Emanrasu pleaded silently as he watched them leave.

Shaking off the anxiety and understanding it was out of his hands, Emanrasu turned back to the pleasant conversation with Serrah, which continued well after set had come and gone. The lamps and candles flickered light around the room as the villagers and White alike exchanged ideas, experiences, and stories.

Serrah and Emanrasu slid easily into adjacent chairs and conversed, at first about her father and her past, then about Emanrasu's concerns over being thrust into a leadership position and his inexperience. He talked about his recognition of the support from his friend Rezua, and his appreciation of her, and the mentoring from Tarlis and how invaluable it had been.

They passed many hands in conversation, which wound here and there, covering many experiences and sharing in each other's past misgivings and achievements. Emanrasu reveled in the intimacy. Whether imagined or real, he did not care, as it was comforting regardless of its authenticity.

Emanrasu suddenly realized that he had not heard nor seen Rezua for quite some time, and he laid a gentle hand on Serrah, halting her in mid-sentence.

His eyes darted around the room and spied Rezua leaning back in a chair, snoozing, and relaxing with his journal on his chest under crossed hands. Telk was close by, wielding a long, sturdy stalk of grain, and was intent on lightly touching Rezua's face with it, then pulling it away as the big man's meaty hand swiped at the annoyance.

As Rezua relaxed and returned to his snooze, the grinning Telk would again reach out with his stalk and worry the big man's face until he swiped at the annoyance once more.

Emanrasu looked at Serrah and nodded in Rezua's direction, whereupon she turned, and they watched the boy annoy the big man repeatedly. Once Rezua opened his eyes and sat up, looking around, he spied Emanrasu and Serrah, nodded in acknowledgment, closed his eyes once again, and immediately went back to snoozing and swiping at the imaginary insect.

Grinning all the while, Telk instantly hid the offending stalk of grain behind his back each time Rezua opened his eyes, eyes glued to the floor in feigned boredom.

The night stole away, and people slowly bade each other a good night, and the crowd thinned. A stiff, cloaked man approached Telk, and after a brief, whispered exchange, Telk sighed and followed the man out of the room.

"Must be his father come to get him to bed," Emanrasu mused as he watched them leave.

*   *   *

Overcome by a yawn, Emanrasu realized his time with Serrah had rushed by and suddenly found that it was time for him to turn in as well. The long day had culminated in what had started to feel like an incessant string of critical decisions being made, along with having himself thrust into a position he had anticipated and dreaded. It was topped off with the pride he felt in garnering the trust of the White.

Emanrasu knew that, even though leading would not be easy, he would give it everything he had. With all the lessons learned from Tarlis, and with the support of the White, he was confident in his foundation to make good decisions, and he was willing to accept the consequences of any decision, regardless of the outcome.

He turned to Serrah just in time to catch her yawn. He grinned at her and stood, holding out his hand.

"I feel it is time to turn in," he said. "And you appear to be in similar straits by the look of that yawn."

Serrah took his hand and allowed him to assist her in standing. She squeezed it gently in what he took for appreciation before she let it go.

Together, they climbed the stairs, paused at her door, and bid each other good night.

Emanrasu started to turn away, paused, reconsidered, then decided not to further intrude on her time, turned, and strode purposefully to his own room.

He paused as he opened the door to his room and glanced back to see Serrah still standing outside her room, watching him. He smiled meekly and stepped into his room, cursing himself under his breath for not being more forward and exploring the chaotic feelings that she seemed to cause in him when she was nearby.

Emanrasu paused as he shut the door, hand still on the handle; he sighed heavily.

"Let it go, Emanrasu," he told himself. "There will be time."

He turned around, taking in the cold expansiveness of the room. It was slightly larger than the room they had in the Bucket and Nail in Erzt, with all the same things, but somehow it felt less inviting even with the addition of a fireplace.

The wood was prepared in the fireplace, though it was currently unlit, and the light from the oil lamps cast shadows that danced randomly around the room to the whim of the gentle draft.

He could hear the wind picking up outside and the occasional howling whistle as it zipped through the branches of nearby trees. The sound was soothing in its rhythm, and Emanrasu was glad for the comfort afforded by the inn.

His gear had been placed neatly in the center of one of the beds, and Rezua's gear was tossed onto the other. Telk had been thoughtful in his placement of Emanrasu's pack, giving easy access to the contents.

Rezua's gear, in contrast, had likely been tossed onto the bed, its contents strewn all over the surface, indicating that Rezua had most likely dug through it in search of ink or possibly unadulterated journals, which he seemed to have plenty of.

The room was chilly, though not cold, and Emanrasu decided that the warmth from a fire would chase away the slight chill. He reached into his pack and pulled out his fire kit.

He carefully extracted a pinch of gi and placed it in his fire pot, then sprinkled in a bit of sheh, watching it sparkle as the two plants made contact. Musing over the fields of mingling girochih and shehchih that he and Serrah had witnessed during their journey made him marvel all the more at their interaction.

The Heater and The Hack

Serrah seemed always to be not far from his thoughts, and he sighed in resignation. "There will be time after we are done with helping the people of Bren," he thought, trying to console and convince himself that distancing himself from her, or at least putting his feelings aside for now, was the best course of action.

Emanrasu shrugged and retrieved his grindrod. He ground the plants together, watching the interaction between them increase until the sparkling erupted and emerged as a bright blue flame. He summarily placed the pot under the lay and watched as the tendrils of fire from the pot emboldened, eagerly growing and lapping at the wood above it. The flames successfully took hold and spread methodically to the rest, growing and casting warmth in the face of the chill.

Emanrasu slid onto the edge of the bed and sat, watching the flames lapping at the wood. His thoughts drifted to the task at hand and all of the possible outcomes. His hopes were that the brigand problem would be resolved without conflict, but he knew this was unlikely.

He drifted back to a comment Tarlis had once told him: "Prepare for the worst, hope for the best. The reality will be somewhere in the middle. Things are rarely as good or as bad as you imagine."

These thoughts were still coursing through his mind when he heard movement outside the door, followed by Rezua opening it and entering.

"I tried to rest a bit downstairs, but the damnable insects kept pestering me!" the large man exclaimed. "I think I must have finally got one because they eventually left me alone.

"You should have let me know you were heading up here," Rezua said as he approached the fire and rubbed his hands together in its warmth.

"Sorry, my friend," Emanrasu replied. "The day was busy, and I have had a lot on my mind."

Each Moment of Merriment: Chapter Eighteen

"I am a bit baffled by the trust the White seems to have placed in me," he continued. "I mean... I understand that I impressed them in the arena, but they must know that luck was present during that test. They were lax, and I was determined, but if they had taken it seriously, the outcome would have been much different."

Rezua glanced over at him and raised a single eyebrow questioningly.

"Eman, I... we have known each other since we were children. You have always been harsh in the assessment of yourself and attribute much of your success to the luck of the Dance or good timing."

A smile played about the corners of his mouth.

"Do not think for an instant that I hang around you for your good looks!

"You know... You have always had a good head about you and make good, solid decisions in the midst of chaos.

"Were it not for you, I would have done much more to that man I knocked across the street. It was your calming effect and your ability to clear my head and make me see the reality in the situation that calmed me.

"I think that was when I decided you would be my lifelong friend, whether you wanted to or not!" Rezua paused just long enough.

"Oh?" pressed Emanrasu. "It took you that long to decide to be my friend?"

"Well, the truth of the matter is you were not very adventurous in our youth. You always had to consider everything from the other point of view, and rarely did you spontaneously embark on anything. Methodical and thoughtful was always your approach, and I did not always appreciate that mentality.

"So, yes, it took me that long to see your true value."

Rezua reached out and placed a hand on Emanrasu's shoulder. The massive, meaty paw squeezed with gentle, friendly, and loving pressure. "You have always been there for me, and to my recollections, you have never steered me down a path that we could not easily return from."

He drew Emanrasu up off the bed and hugged him. "I cannot imagine my life without you, and you are stuck with me until the end," the great mountain of a man exclaimed.

Emanrasu hugged him back, and the two broke the embrace.

"I rarely embarked on ventures that I could not justify to myself, and I had tasked myself with trying to keep you out of trouble. This often came with accompanying you on one adventure or another, not because I did not think it would end badly, but because I thought that I might be able to extract you and keep you from getting in too deep into whatever muck and mire of an adventure you were on." Emanrasu smiled as he thought back to many of their adventures.

Emanrasu sat back on the bed, stifling a sudden yawn. Moments later, Rezua mirrored him, seemingly reveling in the soft, deep, guttural staccato grunt of his own yawn, which elicited a genuine grin from Emanrasu as he endeavored to suppress yet another.

"I suppose that I am ready to rest, and by the sound of it, you are as well," stated Emanrasu as he turned to the bed, clearing the gear and organizing it for easy access.

Rezua set about clearing his own bed by gathering the corners of the bed covering and creating a makeshift bag encompassing all of his gear, which he set to the side.

The big man's bulky frame nimbly slid into the bed, and in moments, his soft, deep, resounding snores indicated he had quickly drifted off.

Emanrasu stretched out on the bed, unusually comfortable in light of his normal bedroll-on-the-ground approach over the last few months.

Each Moment of Merriment: Chapter Eighteen

As an afterthought, he swung his legs over and exited the bed. He snuffed out the oil lamps lest something should happen that was unexpected. He smiled broadly at the sudden comparison of his actions to the way Rezua seemed to view him and could not find fault with the little giant's assessment.

Still smiling, he slid back into bed, reveling in the comfort.

*   *   *

Soft, indeterminate colors vibrantly coalesced into a coherent scene. The oft-visited open fields of the Earth, the immense presence of the Tree, the warm embrace of the Sun, set in the expanse of the Sky, comforting in its familiarity. The Dragon and the Phoenix dancing as always in an ever-undulating swirl in the air gave him pause as he admired the beauty of the scene as a whole.

"Your first task is almost complete," came the shriek of the Phoenix. The shriek had become a soothing reminder of the import of his tasks through the multitude of previous encounters with the Phoenix.

"You have surrounded yourself with the Cadre, and though you are not yet knowledgeable in their identities, you can rest assured that your first task is close to completion," boomed the deep, reverberating roar of the Dragon.

Though the voices only emanated from the Dragon and the Phoenix, Emanrasu had come to identify the general feelings of the others; the Tree, the Sun, the Earth, and the Sky were rarely vocal, but the knowledge emanating from them reinforced the vocalizations of the Dragon and Phoenix.

Emanrasu could feel the overwhelming consent in the Cosmic Entities as they concurred with the Dragon.

"Who are they?" Emanrasu asked bluntly, knowing the answer would be cryptic or nonexistent and a direct answer was unlikely.

"They are the ones that will support you in the other tasks you must complete," growled the Dragon in response.

The Heater and The Hack

"Crucial they are to the tasks," added the Phoenix.

The Dragon added in its deep reverberating growl, "Rebirth is only achievable through death, and loss is not always as it seems.

"While we only guide, we are aware of the possible choices and the futures that the choices represent. Your path forward is not easy, and loss will be profound; trust in yourself and your friends. Know that we are watching and observing. Trust that the Tubatonona creations will always subtly affect outcomes for their wielder—but understand: there will be no overt interaction, no magical barrier, no granted ability."

Through the interaction, Emanrasu was left with a sense of the Cadre, a child... three women... and two men, no... three... or two... he was unclear whether the third was a man... perhaps someone that seemed to be overseeing or watching without interaction.

"I still don't quite understand the ultimate goal here," Emanrasu offered.

"I understand that these will be human representatives of the Dance, one for each of you. However, I feel there is something more, and though I am unsure why, the feeling indicates there is another of importance who is also involved."

"What of the other, I sense another...?"

"Your concern it is not," screeched the Phoenix. "know we must, remember we must, and in time, so shall you."

"He has a different path and will walk it when he is ready," came the bouldery voice of the Dragon.

"We know that loss is inevitable, and rebirth is only achievable in death. Loss is not always as it seems.

"Walk your heart, always, Emanra Su, and you shall not falter," said the Dragon. "Time provides understanding."

Each Moment of Merriment: Chapter Eighteen

The conversation ceased, though the dreamlike state and the presence of these powerful entities continued to be felt.

Emanrasu walked through the peaceful fields, running his hand over the fields of grain, feeling the light tickle on his palm as he did. The scene was somehow not just a place, and the feeling that he was accomplishing the task he had been presented with seemed to emanate from the entirety of it.

As Emanrasu relaxed in this environment, he contemplated the task at hand, both his search for the Cadre and the attempt to assist the town.

He analyzed each thought for flaws in his decisions and actions but concluded that there was currently no better path than that which they had already started down.

As this thought came to him, the Dance faded away without further interaction.

The dream was replaced by the darkness of deep and restful repose, and he slept.

It was still dark, the glowing embers of the fire still shedding a dull red glow in the room as Emanrasu stirred.

He stretched his sore muscles, noting silently that the constant practice had lessened the soreness he felt upon waking each morning. As he lay there, he was torn between the reassurance of the bed with the comforting warmth of the blanket and the incessant urge to prepare for the eventualities he knew would come.

"Rezua," he thought, "would smile in understanding and probably make some comical comment." Emanrasu let the grin spread across his face as he swung his legs out from under the blanket and sat up.

He paused briefly, contemplating the events of the day before.

"The brigands seemed to be ever watchful, at least on the road to and from Bren. This will make the task at hand all the more difficult," Emanrasu thought.

Telk, the boy, bright and attentive, seemed to have become resolutely attached to Emanrasu.

"The young lad, with the air of being good in nature and trustworthy in spirit," Emanrasu realized. "He was definitely timely last night with the mead."

"Torsun showed a deep concern for his community and wields a great deal of influence among the townsfolk. He looked willing to accept the help of the White, and he and Tarlis seemed to be friendly with each other."

"Serrah is my downfall, and she is never far from my thoughts. Helping her reconnect with her father and seeing her face afterward was incredibly satisfying," Emanrasu mulled over the thought. "I wish I knew the true depth of my feelings, though I am not sure that would change much. At least maybe I could then express them and understand whether she returned my feelings or not."

Emanrasu knit his brows and frowned slightly as he thought about the task ahead of the White and the town of Bren.

"Unlikely to end well," was his only thought as he stood and made his way to the middle of the room.

The middle of the room was reasonably uncluttered, and Emanrasu, opting to practice in close quarters and without the Heater and the Hack, began his dance.

At first, the room made the dance awkward, but he slowly realized the room was a part of the dance, not the stage for the dance. With this realization, he focused on dancing with the objects in the room, rolling across the table, shuffling the chair here and there. He continued in this manner, feeling the dance flow through him as he incorporated anything within reach.

At one point, he leaned heavily on the edge of the table, tipped it onto two legs, and it slid deftly across his back. The hard top slipped smoothly across, and he set it aright on the other side of him. There was barely a tap as the legs were put down in a controlled release rather than an uncontrolled thump, and if one were not watching, one would not have suspected this had transpired.

The thunderous clapping of giant, meaty hands came to his ears and successfully broke his focus on the dance. Emanrasu paused and glanced toward the large countenance of his friend. Rezua's mouthy grin was so broad that Emanrasu thought at first the corners must be connected to his ears. "Very impressive," the large man said.

"Gently swaying in perfect timing with the battle unfolding within his mind, lithe and catlike in his movements, the grandness of Emanrasu was evident in each perfectly executed move, gliding, sliding, rolling through his complex and varied environment. Without a weapon in his thin, pale hand, he was able to grasp and wield anything within reach of his long, sinewy arms. His hand was lean but had a steel-like grip on the varied implements of his chosen weapons, he..." Rezua recited his imagined narrative, only to be interrupted.

"You think so?" Emanrasu asked, his friend's contagious grin unexpectedly developing on his own face.

Emanrasu turned and rearranged the furniture and items in the room, placing them in their proper places. He grabbed a change of clothing and winked at Rezua before exiting the room in search of the bathing room.

Opening the door, he saw Telk sitting cross-legged just across from the door to Emanrasu's room. Upon seeing the door open, Telk abruptly jumped to his feet, seemingly ready for any task required of him.

"Good morning, Telk," Emanrasu said.

"Have you been sitting outside my door all night, young man?" he queried the boy with a wink.

"Nah, I almost just sat down. I was going to knock, but I know many of our guests sleep until late in the morning and I did not know if you were yet awake. I did not want to wake you," Telk stated, grinning back at Emanrasu.

The Heater and The Hack

"Well, then, show me the way to the bathing room if you will, and then come back and see to it that Rezua, the big giant of a man from last night, does not drift back off to sleep," Emanrasu stated.

This made Telk's smile crinkle his eyes, and he snorted in a stifled chuckle. "Right this way, s… Emanrasu," he said. He led the way down the hall and turned down a short hall on the right, stopped, and opened a door on the left, gesturing with his head that this was the bathing room.

Telk then ducked past Emanrasu, back the way they had come.

Emanrasu glanced in the room and could see the steam rising from both of the tubs; fresh towels and cloths had been laid out for guest use on the bench lining the walls.

Stripping down, he placed his dirty clothes on the floor in front of one of the towels on the bench and his clean clothing on top of the towel, then slid into the tub, the heated water almost too hot to bear; it was a minute or two until his body adjusted and he felt his muscles relax.

Emanrasu scrubbed the dust and dirt from his travels from his skin and hair, working quickly. He could feel the tension drain from him, and as the tension drained, so too did the anxieties brought on by the prior day's events.

"There will be time for Serrah," he thought. "And, as for the bandits, there is little I can do to create a worse situation here in Bren. Moving forward is the only way to eliminate the brigand threat, though it cannot be chaotic, impulsive actions."

Stepping from the bath, Emanrasu dried himself, dressed, and strode down the quiet hallway to his room. As he pushed the door open, the scene within arrested his movement, eliciting a broad smile and a stifled chuckle.

Rezua, a man of mountainous stature, had been driven into a corner—not by force but by the determined advance of Telk, who now stood between the giant and his bed. From somewhere, Rezua had procured a broom, wielding it in a manner both defensive and resigned, as if repelling a great and terrible force rather than a child half his size.

"...told him I would make sure you didn't!" Telk declared triumphantly, addressing Rezua just as Emanrasu entered.

"Alright, alright," Rezua huffed, exasperation evident in the slump of his massive shoulders. With exaggerated care, he set the broom aside, leaning it against the wall as he slowly raised his hands in surrender.

Satisfied, Telk turned to Emanrasu, eyes alight with triumph. "I did as you asked, Emanrasu. I made sure he was up and did not lay back down!"

Rezua's massive finger swung in Emanrasu's direction, though the grin curving his lips betrayed his amusement despite whatever impression he had given Telk.

*   *   *

Still smiling, Emanrasu reached into his pouch, fished out a copper, and tossed it toward the boy.

Telk caught it deftly, his face nearly glowing with pride—until Rezua, with startling agility, lunged for the bed and threw himself onto it, landing stiff and defiant, a great fallen tree refusing to be moved.

The boy's brows knitted together in an instant, his lips curling into a frown as he pivoted back toward Rezua, stepping forward with renewed determination.

"Telk," Emanrasu interjected smoothly before the battle could resume, "you have done as I asked. Rezua is still awake. I believe you can consider your task completed."

Telk halted mid-stride, acknowledging the verdict with a reluctant nod. Still, he jabbed a finger toward Rezua in accusation. Rezua, unfazed, responded in kind, lifting a massive hand to return the gesture. Their narrowed eyes locked, brows furrowed in feigned hostility, though the mirth dancing in their gazes belied the silent challenge exchanged between them.

The Heater and The Hack

It was Rezua who broke first, winking at the boy, dissolving what little remained of the charade.

Telk let his hand drop. He turned to Emanrasu, fingers absently playing with the coin, his joy unmistakable despite the forced neutrality of his expression. He dipped into a slight bow before slipping out the door, the bounce in his step betraying his lingering satisfaction.

"That boy is nothing if not persistent!" Rezua boomed, swinging his tree-trunk legs over the side of the bed and planting them firmly on the floor.

Rezua glared at Emanrasu in mock indignation, complaining, "You could have at least given me advance warning before siccing your little hunting hound on me."

Grinning broadly at Rezua, Emanrasu retorted with a wink, "Oh, as if you did not enjoy the exchange immensely!"

Rezua broke into a smile. "Yes, I suppose I did. The boy has an air about him that exudes merriment and purpose. Quite refreshing from the more mature humor of the White."

The odor of the unwashed grandiose scribe, thick and pungent, drifted toward Emanrasu with an insidious subtlety, growing stronger with each breath. He wrinkled his nose, then reached up and pinched his nostrils shut in exaggerated emphasis.

"There is a bathing room down the hall and around the corner, and I highly recommend you make use of it!" he declared, voice edged with equal parts humor and urgency.

"Pshaw..." came the only reply, followed by the rustling of fabric as Rezua rummaged through the jumbled mass of belongings he had gathered into the blanket the night before.

Each Moment of Merriment: Chapter Eighteen

At last, the mountain of a man extracted a tunic and a pair of pants, sniffed them, and shrugged. Then, as if suddenly struck by curiosity—or caution—he reached down, seized a handful of the clothing he currently wore, and brought the fabric to his nose.

The reaction was immediate. His broad shoulders tensed. His face contorted, shriveling like sun-dried fruit left too long in the heat.

"I suppose I will take your advice," he admitted, his deep voice half a rumble, half a grumble, as he turned and strode toward the door.

Emanrasu watched him go, then exhaled in satisfaction, setting his attention on the untamed chaos left behind. Between the morning's dance with shield and sword and the earlier struggle between child and behemoth, the room bore the unmistakable marks of both combat and mischief.

Without hesitation, he set to the task of restoring order, gathering displaced belongings, and righting what had been upended. Once satisfied, he collected the Heater and the Hack and made his way down the hallway, descending the stairs into the Great Room.

It had already been rearranged, and its purpose shifted once more—tables neatly restored, benches aligned. The space, so recently the stage of the morning's activities, had returned to its proper role as a dining hall, ready once again to receive its guests.

He found a table and sat, leaning the Heater and the Hack against the wall behind him.

"Would you fancy a bit of food this morning to break your fast?" came the question.

Emanrasu grinned knowingly and turned to face the magnificent visage of Serrah, clad in an apron, the light beads of sweat upon her brow a testament to the labors of an already busy morning.

The Heater and The Hack

"I would appreciate a decent meal," he said, composing himself, shifting into the posture of a humble traveler—or at least, his best approximation of one conversing with a tavern wench.

"Then a merely decent meal you shall have, sir," Serrah stated flatly, punctuating the words with a sparkling wink before turning away.

As she departed, Emanrasu allowed his thoughts to settle on the tribulations ahead.

His gaze drifted across the Great Room. For the most part, it remained as he recalled, though now lightly filled with townsfolk, their murmurs carrying the gentle hum of morning routine rather than wary speculation. Unlike the night before, there were no hushed whispers, no furtive glances cast in his direction. The absence of the White was palpable, and with its departure, so too had much of the tension dissipated.

"They, too, needed rest and respite before the tasks at hand take their firm hold," he noted in silence.

Now, where once there had been unease, he found warmth instead—acknowledging each nod and smile as his eyes traveled the length of the room and back.

The air held a coolness that had not been present the night prior, the once-crowded space now lacking the body heat of a packed hall brimming with townsfolk and the entire White. The fireplace, its flames reduced to smoldering embers, offered only a faint warmth, the last wisps of smoke drifting lazily upward into the chimney.

A growl from his stomach reminded him of his current purpose.

He turned just in time to see Serrah exit through a door to the back, a laden platter balanced effortlessly in her hands. The scent struck first—the rich aroma of freshly baked breads mingled with the hearty, pungent essence of roasted meats.

Each Moment of Merriment: Chapter Eighteen

Upon the plates sat greens, roots, tubers, and the bright, enticing colors of berries and edible plants.

Emanrasu exhaled slowly. A merely decent meal, indeed.

She purposefully crossed to his table and transferred the plates to the hard wooden surface of the table. From under her apron, she produced two mugs and three skins.

"Milk, mead, or wine?" she queried him, her eyes sparkling as her enjoyment seemed to mirror his amazement at her skills.

"Uh...milk," he said, finally answering after the thoughts had battled in his head. "It has been many moons since I had any, and I think the mead a bit thicker than I would like and the wine a bit headier."

"Mead, if you please, Serrah," Rezua said as he reached across the table for the item furthest from him before sitting across from Emanrasu.

"A tear of bread found its fate at that moment, torn from its kin like a stump being ripped from the earth. Rezua sent the warm, delicate morsel to meet its maker, so to speak," the flowery prose erupted from Emanrasu, spreading its petals for all to see and hear.

In surprise, his eyes wide, Rezua stopped mid-bite and stared at Emanrasu. Serrah, too, paused and looked questioningly at Emanrasu.

The sudden outburst was as surprising to himself as it was to his friends and caused him to break into a coughing fit, choking on his chuckling laugh. The fit finally passed, and he drew a breath and joined the laughter of his friends.

"I believe I have never heard such prose from you before," Serrah said to Emanrasu. "That is mostly spouted from this one," she waved a wooden serving spoon at Rezua.

"And the next time you inject yourself into a personal conversation, and... mind you the 'and'... reach to the other side of the table for food that could well have been handed to you, you will find this spoon not as much of a conversation piece as a club," she emphasized with a mock smirk, which inevitably dissolved into a genuine grin.

She turned to Emanrasu and curtsied. "Might I join you? I have already informed Torsun that I will be taking a spell to join you, so if you refuse, I will be extremely disappointed." The wink she gave Emanrasu confirmed his suspicion that there was little actual choice in the question.

She glided gracefully into the chair, her gleaming smile reaching out and twisting his emotions and hope.

Emanrasu took a deep breath, smiled back at her, and said, "That was the most awkward action I have ever seen you perform. Beautiful but awkward."

Her eyebrows climbed to her forehead as she gazed at him. "…And to which action do you refer?" she probed, looking as if she was almost daring him to make a verbal misstep.

"The curtsy, m'lady, was wonderful," Emanrasu said, having recovered from his initial misstep. "I was just referring to the typical majesty in your motions, which are not normally merely wonderful, and I thought to bring it to your attention."

Rezua snorted, sending bits and pieces of food across the table. The failed attempt at laughter devolved into a coughing fit as good or better than Emanrasu's most recent fit.

"That was a most deft recovery," Serrah grinned. "What are the plans for today?"

As she spoke, Emanrasu glimpsed Telk as he entered through the main door of the inn.

The boy entered the room and stepped to the side, pausing in the fashion of the White to let his eyes adjust to the indoors. Shortly, his gaze traipsed through the room as a man touched by the moon and escaped under the starry night.

Telk spotted Torsun and started in his direction.

Each Moment of Merriment: Chapter Eighteen

"Boy!" called out Emanrasu in jest, his eyes twinkling in delight. "Have you seen hide or hair of the White or Tarlis this morning?"

Telk stopped in his tracks, turned, and looked at Emanrasu briefly from across the room.

"Old man!" Telk called back, making sure to use the same jesting tone as Emanrasu had employed. "They have gathered across the way since the rise, and truthfully, there was mention of letting you sleep."

"I did not have the heart to tell them you had been up for hands," Telk said, his grin smug, as if pleased with his own cleverness.

Emanrasu tore off a hunk of the still-soft, warm bread and hurled it at Telk.

The boy deftly caught the yeasty morsel, his sly grin never leaving his face. He started backing away in Torsun's direction and raised the morsel of bread in appreciative acknowledgment.

"Anything else?" Telk asked. Without waiting for an answer, he turned and briskly walked toward Torsun, his grin unwavering.

Emanrasu watched Telk retreat, still feeling the lingering spark of his energy. Turning back, he pondered Serrah's question. After a brief pause, he replied, "It appears that the White have already begun assisting with training the townsfolk."

"I should probably wrap this up," he added, gesturing at the food, the conversation, the company. His gaze lingered for a moment before shifting back to Serrah. "At least for my part."

Emanrasu rose from his chair and glanced at Serrah.

"I am sure they are starting to think you lazy and unreliable," she stated flatly, the smile never leaving her face. "You ought to run along and show them you are not quite as lay-about as they might think!"

Her wink made the jest clear. With a slight shove, she sent him on his way.

"Yes," Rezua said. "Maybe you should have gotten an earlier start this morning and not wasted so much time harassing a timid little giant just trying to catch up on sleep!"

"I suppose that is true," Emanrasu said, flinging his response over his shoulder as he made his way to the entrance of the inn. "Then again, I suppose assertive little boys are more than capable of handling one timid little giant, eh?"

"Humph," came the response from Rezua, now unable to speak around the mouthful of bread and meat.

Rezua waved a hand in dismissal of Emanrasu and returned to focusing on the morning feast.

Develop and Persevere: Chapter Nineteen

"One's ability to find pleasure in the day's start and to find meaning and humor can often soften the harsh realities of life. Focusing on learning and growing in all things is a critical aspect of cultivating your life into the full-bodied tree of legacies and legends. The demands of life for effort become more obvious as one ages, though each bit of knowledge adds to your stores and sustains you in times of lean thought."

—RCotD—

Emanrasu exited the inn and felt the cool, crisp morning air wash over him. The scent of bread and meats still lingered in his nostrils as he traversed the short steps and down the path to the road in front of the inn. As he approached the road, he could hear the reverberating—ting, ting, TANG—from the blacksmith down the way.

The air was still, and the billows of black smoke curled lazily from the forge's soot-blackened chimney, pinpointing the source of the reverberating clangs.

Emanrasu scanned the desolate emptiness of the well-worn roadway leading past the inn, noticing the hard-packed earth of the street. It was a testament to the myriads of hooves, feet, and wheels that had traversed it.

The street was unusually devoid of people, Emanrasu realized, shaking his head and pursing his lips slightly in empathy. "The bandit threat must be taking its toll on these people if they opt for the comfort of home and hearth instead of the normal morning tasks."

Emanrasu heard Onred down the lane to his left.

Off in the unseen distance came the guttural roaring command "Gather!" followed by the distinct murmur of the gathering townsfolk, preparing for their first session of training directly under the supervision of the White.

317

The Heater and The Hack

Emanrasu exhaled, pushing his concerns aside. The conflict ahead demanded focus. He stepped out onto the dusty street and strode toward the sound of the big man's voice.

He wove past cottages and shuttered shops, the sound of gathering voices growing louder. In the open field ahead, the White and throngs of townsfolk assembled in anticipation.

The White stood in a ragged line on one side of the impromptu training field, and the scores of the townsfolk gathered to face them. Onred, in the middle of the White, waved the townsfolk in, urging them to pay attention.

Beside Onred, Tarlis leaned on his seemingly innocuous cane—casual, unassuming. Deceptive. The thought brought a grin to Emanrasu as he recalled how deadly accurate and dangerous that old man and cane could be. Emanrasu absent-mindedly rubbed the spot where Tarlis had demonstrated his skill and Emanrasu's ineptitude during their first meeting.

"Pair up! Grab a weapon! We'll be evaluating your skills—so you can not just fight, but survive," Onred bellowed. He motioned toward the stands of various weapons and farm implements.

Emanrasu closed his eyes. It had not even been a full harvestmain since Tarlis had taught him to stand weapons—tips touching, forming a cone. Neat. Orderly.

This kept the weapons organized and made them available for quick access but out of the way, which was especially useful when marching or attacking a location where one expected to be for an extended length.

Emanrasu cocked his head, raised an eyebrow, and shook his head at the recollection.

"The old man taught me more than I realized," he thought, marveling at how Tarlis explained things—never just to be remembered, but to be understood.

"We couldn't have a better commander for the White."

Develop and Persevere: Chapter Nineteen

He paused.

"Or... no. I guess... he's not the commander anymore, is he?"

The realization hit with quiet finality, just as it always does.

He hadn't taken the seat at the head of the table, but they'd placed him in the chair anyway. The fleeting wonder of when he might get used to it came and went.

Shortly thereafter, Emanrasu caught a movement out of the corner of his eye. Turning, he saw the ever-reliable Telk, standing off to one side, scanning the area. Ready to assist with the simplest task or the most complicated, he was ready. "That boy will be wondering how he got in my position too, one day."

He watched as Tarlis and Onred gathered the throng into a semblance of order, pairing everyone off until only one was left. Tarlis looked around to be sure there was no one left for the young man, then caught Emanrasu's eye and gave a subtle nod.

Emanrasu made his way over, snatching up a simple wooden broom handle and setting the Heater and the Hack to the side.

The young man's brow eased visibly at the change in weapon.

"This is Emanrasu," Tarlis said. "He'll be your pair. What's your name, young man?"

"Boldar," came the man's reply.

Emanrasu held out his forearm, and the young man grasped it firmly. "Pleased to meet you, Boldar," he said.

"As am I to meet you," Boldar replied with a nod.

He assessed Boldar, who was half a head shorter than Emanrasu but stouter in girth. The sinews in his forearms were prominent, both to sight as well as in the man's grip.

The Heater and The Hack

Onred walked over and fished out a sword, which was brought over and handed to Boldar. "Do not hold back," he told the young man. "If you can blood him, I will have a silver waiting."

Onred caught Emanrasu's eye and winked. "Let's see how you handle a real test today."

Sixty-one townsfolk were gathered, and sixty were paired off, the last one, Boldar, paired with Emanrasu. Each of the White took charge of three pairs each, as did Tarlis. The experienced warriors were tasked with looking for traits that would indicate a penchant for one or more weapons.

"We will rotate the White amongst the grouped pairs; we need to see what your natural inclinations are so your weapons will follow the White evaluating you," Tarlis's voice projected without bellowing. The old man's commanding presence brought no dissent.

"We shall also rotate the odd man with Onred, and during his tutelage, each one of you will have a chance to win his silver coin as you are pitted against Emanrasu himself."

A soft, low murmur came from the townsfolk.

"The general consensus seems to be one of hope, at the very least, the hope for a silver by the sound of them," Emanrasu remarked to Onred. Onred grinned briefly before his face steeled once more.

"Commence!" Onred bellowed, his echo reverberating off the nearby cottages and shops.

Boldar fought like one possessed. Emanrasu watched as the young man swung the sword, sometimes inconsistent, sometimes with measured acumen.

Emanrasu could see Boldar and anticipated each of the strikes, though sometimes only by a hair's breadth.

Onred called out, "Switch!"

320

Develop and Persevere: Chapter Nineteen

Emanrasu took a moment, gave Boldar pointers, and explained some of his weaknesses.

The White shuffled the pairings within their groups so that the pairs were different with each subsequent change. True to Tarlis's word, the odd man rotated out of Onred's group and paired with Emanrasu.

The townsfolk, by virtue of their training and instruction from the White who led their group, were provided with a slight respite as the attention was directed toward others within their group.

Emanrasu was not given this quarter, and his only respite came during the change of opponents, thus finding himself almost constantly fighting.

The rotation within each group continued until each member had faced all of the other members. The instructions from the White continued with two at a time while the rest looked on. Various techniques were shown and practiced as each of the White identified the most adept for specific weapons and styles.

During his first break, as he started to turn, he stumbled over Telk, barely keeping himself upright. The boy was standing there, a waterskin in his outstretched hand.

Emanrasu recovered his balance swiftly and took the proffered offering. The water was delightfully chilled, and after a couple of draughts, he splashed some on his face and neck. The coolness of the water helped renew his eagerness to learn more, as well as to help train the townsfolk. Emanrasu sighed as he gave the waterskin back to Telk.

"Thank you, Telk," he said.

The thought came to him, "You have managed to fend off the lot of your opponents this morn, and yet, a mere boy sneaks up behind you. Emanrasu," he said silently, "you still have much to learn."

"Reform!"

The Heater and The Hack

Onred's thundering command came sooner than expected to Emanrasu, but as he glanced around, the White were already helping their trainees to pair up again.

The events proceeded much as the earlier ones went, and the rotations continued as the White meticulously evaluated the trainees.

Emanrasu felt the weariness start to seep into his body when Onred eventually called for the meal break.

"Mid-day!" the large captain hollered.

The townsfolk all seemed in good spirits, milling about, discussing this or that movement with one another or with the nearest White.

Emanrasu stretched and let his eyes wander across the scene. He caught sight of Rezua, seated as always off to the side, engrossed in his writing. Nearby, Telk— wineskin in hand—kept his eyes on Emanrasu while attempting to extract his leg from the meaty grip of Rezua.

The huge man, still reading, wore a mischievous grin as if oblivious to the boy's struggle. Finally, just as Telk made a monumental effort to break free, Rezua released him, sending the boy tumbling forward under his own momentum.

He recovered quickly, and with his feet once more under him, he made his way to Emanrasu to deliver the water. Torsun and Serrah crossed the path ahead with a cart laden with food and drink, lightening the mood and lifting the spirits even more. Though Serrah was otherwise occupied feeding the throng of trainees, Emanrasu found comfort simply having her close.

He opted to spend his time resting near Rezua. The two sat quietly, each absorbed in other things, Rezua buried in his Tubatonona language book, mumbling a string of incoherent sounds.

"Words or phrases," Emanrasu thought. "Or the big man's finally lost touch with reality." He studied his friend's colossal face for signs of madness—but saw no more than usual. Just to be sure, he interrupted. "Are you having a fit... or perhaps some fever or other? Shall I fetch a healer?"

Emanrasu shifted slightly as if to find help when Rezua glanced up. "Huh? Oh—no. Some of the words are ridiculously long. Repeating them out loud helps me keep them straight." Without another word, he returned to his book and resumed mumbling.

*   *   *

With that mystery solved, Emanrasu relaxed again and turned his thoughts to the morning's events. This is different from fighting trained warriors, he mused. The untrained are far less predictable. Shifts in weight. A slight rearing of the arm. The tells were obvious—but inconsistent. Reviewing the trainees' movements in his mind, he marveled at how similar they were... and considered how best to counter each one.

Telk, ever attentive, brought over something from the cart for both Rezua and Emanrasu. The young man's diligence did not go unnoticed, and Emanrasu reached in and fished out a copper.

He watched Telk's face light up as if he was the sun itself.

"Now, wouldn't that be a turn of events! Telk turning out to be the representative of the Sun," Emanrasu suddenly realized. "Best to deal with that in the dreams and ask the Dance directly rather than confuse the boy."

It was not long before Onred bellowed again, and the gathering of would-be warriors once more paired off and began evaluations.

The training resumed much like the first two rounds earlier this morning. Emanrasu was more careful now, deliberately choosing to fight defensively. In his mind, this allowed him to better respond to the randomness of the attacks. With this approach, he found he had fewer close calls. The session progressed well, and another break came and went.

The Heater and The Hack

Telk was nearby and always at the ready, Rezua scribbling now in his journal. Emanrasu noticed the White were gathering during the breaks to discuss their observations, pointing to this person or that, sometimes animated. Occasionally, there was a sad shake of the head as one or the other was singled out as particularly unfit or clumsy.

With the break now past, training recommenced, and with each new battle, Emanrasu found little grains of knowledge-laden sand, which he mentally tossed onto the dune that Tarlis had handed him during his initial training.

The sun had traveled several hands past apex when Tarlis finally signaled to Onred that the folk had been drilled sufficiently for the day.

"Let them return to address their daily tasks, and we will pick this up again each day until the time draws on to put this hard work to use," Tarlis told him.

"Gather!" shouted Onred. "We will gather again on the rise and begin at a hand past. Go home and attend to your needs. You have all done well, but none earned a coin of silver this day, so maybe on the morrow, eh?!"

The trainees stacked their weapons in the stands from whence they had been taken and left with smiles and in good spirits.

With help from Rezua, Emanrasu, and the ever-helpful and present Telk, the White finished securing the weapons and made their way back to the inn.

The discussion amongst them focused on tendencies and abilities, as well as deficits and outright faults of the trainees. Emanrasu closed his eyes, visualizing each of the ones he faced, and listed off the things he noticed and how each one was a tad unpredictable.

"Good!" Tarlis exclaimed. "I had truly feared there would be no progress during our journey to recruit the White, but it seems that there is more progress than we have seen in the past."

Emanrasu raised an eyebrow quizzically.

Develop and Persevere: Chapter Nineteen

Onred rumbled a chuckle. "This is not our first time training and assisting a community of this sort with a similar problem. This may not even be our twentieth time."

Emanrasu took his comment in stride and considered the immense amount of experience the White must have accumulated.

From the back came a mock cough. "Cough... twenty-fourth, cough... cough," came the unmistakable voice of Freydis.

"Sorry, I had something in my throat, and it just came out," she cleared her throat and hummed a little, pounded on her chest to loosen the pretend phlegm, motioning to Onred to continue.

"It—may have been our twenty-fourth—but I am sure nobody's keeping track," he said, overtly glaring at Freydis with exaggerated mockery as she, in turn, made a show of appearing humble. Onred, grinning, turned and nodded at Tarlis.

Tarlis paused and looked at Emanrasu expectantly, continuing only after the younger man's nod of acknowledgment.

"We'll continue to build upon the training these townsfolk have already endured. Once Darth and Catlina return, we will be able to make an informed decision as to our best course of action," Tarlis said. "With the luck of the Dance, we'll come through with few losses—but for now, making sure these impromptu fighters are as prepared as possible is our primary concern."

"Get food and some sleep," the old man added. "We have long days ahead and will need to find rest where and when we can."

With that said, Tarlis laid a hand on Emanrasu's shoulder and leaned in. "You continue to show promise as a leader. Keep trusting your head and your heart," Tarlis said, praising him.

The Heater and The Hack

Tarlis patted Emanrasu's shoulder and moved on to talk to Onred. After a quick chat with Onred, Tarlis said his goodnights and made for the stairs and his sleeping quarters beyond.

Emanrasu spent a few moments discussing various techniques for leading training of this sort, realizing once again that the knowledge to be gained from the White was as wide as the Belari Sands and more shrouded than the Gichah Chasm.

He bid his leave from the White and joined Rezua and Serrah at a table where they had already started their meal.

Emanrasu heard Rezua comment as he approached. "...puts up with my absent-mindedness." Rezua paused as he caught sight of Emanrasu. "Though, in truth, he is not much to look at." Rezua's face remained stoic except for the twitching of his cheek muscles, which were obviously struggling to drag a smile out of the mountainous man.

Emanrasu sat in the open chair and proceeded to assuage his hunger.

"It seems that the coming days will be patterned much the same as today. Please understand that I am in no way intentionally ignoring either of you," Emanrasu stated, alternating his gaze between Rezua and Serrah. He struggled not to stare at only Serrah, though that was what he really wanted to do.

Emanrasu turned his gaze toward his plate. "I can already tell that you prepared and most likely cooked the meal."

"I will probably never be able to eat another meal without comparing it to your skill at preparing them," Emanrasu chuckled, as much in acknowledging the truth of it as in the fact his mind was so preoccupied with her during every spare moment.

"The only time I seem to not think of her is when I am actively engaged in something else," Emanrasu silently realized.

Develop and Persevere: Chapter Nineteen

He glanced up at her, and their eyes locked briefly before she hurriedly looked away.

Emanrasu continued the meal with pleasantries and mild teasing of both Rezua and Serrah before he begged his leave of them as he had the White.

He made his way up the stairs and down the hall to his room and, upon entering, found the Heater and the Hack had been brought up and placed against the wall beside his bed.

Emanrasu opted to forego the fire and left a lantern lit for Rezua. He stretched himself out on the bed, pulled the blanket snug around himself, and shortly fell asleep.

The familiar transition from wakefulness to the dream of the Dance was smooth and gradual. Emanrasu welcomed the coalescing of swirling colors into coherent objects and entities. This transformation always prepared him for the more serious revelations the Dance typically brought.

The scene emerged from the swirl. The guttural rumble of the Dragon, as always, came first.

"No," rumbled the Dragon. "He is not a member of the Cadre. However, he will be instrumental in their uncovering."

Emanrasu paused. "Uh... who?" he asked—though he already knew there was only one name in his mind.

"Prepare in earnest!" shrieked the Phoenix as it swooped past. "Maintain your balance!"

"Indeed!" came the Dragon's roar. "Your trials are just beginning. Stand fast in balance and weigh your decisions. Much rides on how you approach your paths in the coming days. In Balance, Brilliance!"

The Heater and The Hack

The discussion with the Dance drifted into the Tubatonona and the creation of the Heater and the Hack—details that Emanrasu forgot almost as soon as they were imparted.

Soon, the Dance faded into blackness, and he slept. Emanrasu swung his feet out of the bed and placed them on the floor, which was cool and brisk on his bare feet.

He stood and hastily dressed, taking the time to revisit his dance of the day before. Within the confines of this room, it seemed that everything was more intimately involved in the dance.

He finished his progressions and, gathering up the Heater and the Hack, made his way to the Great Room.

Serrah was up and serving the few that were about at this time.

"I am starting to wonder if she sleeps at all anymore," he thought.

Catching her attention, he walked over to her. "I am going to be eating a light morning meal and will require something I can take with me to the training grounds. I am going to prepare and be ready when everyone arrives," he told Serrah.

She nodded. "I have just the thing," she remarked as she headed back to the kitchen. She returned a few moments later with a hollowed-out loaf of bread stuffed with meat and some vegetables.

"It makes it easy to handle without the oils and grease getting all over your hands," she explained.

Emanrasu found it was adequate for the purpose she intended. "You are amazing sometimes," he said in earnest.

Serrah giggled softly. "Oh, this was not my idea. I picked this up from a customer at the Bucket and Nail in Erzt. I was amazed that it was not done more often, but people rarely needed to pack their food for immediate consumption.

Develop and Persevere: Chapter Nineteen

"I will see you at the mid-day break. I wish you well today," she said with a smile that brightened the room.

"Thank you, Serrah. Thank you for all that you do," he said. "I will see you at midday."

Emanrasu turned and left the inn, making his way to the empty training ground.

*   *   *

Emanrasu strode out to the middle of the grounds and felt the dance. Each place seemed to have a dance that was best suited for it, but he had to let it find him. He just relaxed, started his dance, and let it take him where it might.

Emanrasu finished his dance and started again slower and with more intent, feeling each movement and each step as he deliberately forced himself to slow down.

He finished this slow dance as the light was breaking rise, and it was only then that he noticed Tarlis sitting off to one side, tucked away against a tree.

As he strode over to Tarlis, Telk arrived, a little winded, water skin in tow. Telk took up a position similar to the one he had the day before. He sat and watched intently.

Emanrasu approached Tarlis, and before he could speak, Tarlis interjected.

"At some point, young man, I will have nothing left to teach you. Your dedication shows in your every action, your every word, even," Tarlis told him.

"The White, as dedicated as they are, have not joined me out here, though I do not expect them to. The deeper the internal need and drive, the earlier one tends to start the day. Even Onred has never started the day with me unless there was a reason," the old man continued. "But you... you've consistently shown not just the desire, but the drive to grow—to be better than you were the day before.

329

The Heater and The Hack

"Only one man I recall ever matching—or exceeding—my drive: your grandfather, the Black himself. I am still unsure the man ever slept at all," Tarlis recalled as his gaze looked off into the past. "And now... you."

His demeanor snapped back to the present. "Look at the boy over there, his name... Telk... is it? I see the same potential in him that I saw in you. No—not the same. Similar. He has a drive and way about him that few can match. I noticed that he has taken a liking to you and Rezua as well, though given the choice, you can see he chooses to be here.

"Anyway, enough of an old man's ruminations. Did you need something? You seemed to be striding over with a purpose."

Emanrasu replied, "I was going to ask if you wanted to spar—however, if you would rather converse..."

"No," Tarlis said as he stood. "There will be plenty of time when this is all said and done."

Emanrasu could feel the wind from the tip of the old man's cane on the tip of his nose as he almost missed blocking the unexpected strike.

Tarlis grinned. "When we first met I practically told you in the manner and actions I was going to strike you, and yet still you had no clue and were unable to stop me... and me going at half speed or slower, too."

"Just now, I gave no indications and took advantage of what I thought was a relaxed and possibly distracted demeanor, and yet, you were still able to recover and successfully parry. I cannot impart how proud I am of your progress, and I would have been proud to have you as a son," the last word lost in the whistling wind and the clank of the wooden cane on the metal as Emanrasu turned yet another strike.

The flurry of blows that followed emphasized why Tarlis was the commander of the White and why he was not only Emanrasu's mentor but his counselor in all things, save personal.

Develop and Persevere: Chapter Nineteen

The two circled, trading blows—drifting toward the center of the field in unspoken agreement.

The dance of the old man was evident to any trained eye—his movements precise and quick. The intricate patterns of the dance allowed for deviations—like the branches of a tree sprouting new shoots through time and practice.

"Your dance is old—ancient—and though intricate, it's becoming less flexible," Emanrasu said, lunging and catching a finger's breadth of the old man's tunic.

The old man caught Emanrasu square on the neck immediately following his success.

"Old and ancient, is it?" Tarlis asked. The question was rhetorical, as evidenced by the welt on Emanrasu's neck.

Emanrasu stepped backward, putting a couple of steps between him and his mentor. He laughed heartily.

"Like the branches of an ancient tree, commander, I didn't mean to suggest it was unuseful or outdated. More that it was a compliment—that the intricacies of your dance are reminiscent of the branching on an ancient tree—numerous and varied."

"In that vein, young man, I see you no longer as a sapling with only a dozen branches. You have grown into a fully mature oak; the complexity of your branches has become intricate, yet you are still growing, and unlike the older, ancient trees, you are still flexible and capable of bending as the wind blows," said the old man as he continued Emanrasu's metaphor.

"Your growth, advancement, and dedication have been astounding. I knew you had potential when we first met, but I can only surmise that the Dance had much to do with our meeting. Your connection to the Dance, your grandfather, and your abilities show that you are destined for this. I am just glad I have been able to mentor and direct your growth."

The Heater and The Hack

Emanrasu reached out an arm to Tarlis, who grasped it firmly.

"Regardless of the outcome of the upcoming conflict, I feel you will make an outstanding Black!" Tarlis exclaimed as he tightened his grip on Emanrasu's forearm.

Together, they walked over to Telk to make him feel included as the White began to arrive, with the townsfolk filtering in after the rise. A random few strode in later and were included in the training, though mental notes were taken as to their reliability.

The day progressed much the same as the last.

Training and evaluations, a break, more training, and more evaluations.

Mid-day was anticipated by Emanrasu as apex approached, and his heart fluttered a bit upon catching sight of Serrah, her smile bringing light from within that only she could accomplish.

The meal was over too shortly, and Emanrasu caught Serrah's gaze and nodded to her. He tussled Telk's hair, gave Rezua a playful kick, and returned to the field.

The training and evaluations continued throughout the day, with only a single break disrupting the flow.

The day ended, the training grounds were put in order, and everyone once again returned to their daily tasks.

That evening, with the evaluation of individuals close to completion, the White discussed separating the trainees into various groups based on the observed tendencies and abilities.

Having spent the last two days immersed in sparring with untrained or, at best, lightly trained fighters, Emanrasu came to an interesting observation.

"I have noticed," he told the White, "that fighting an untrained opponent is much like dancing with someone who does not know how to dance. Their movements are less fluid and more unpredictable, though the movements are normally foreshadowed in subtle tells."

"A trained warrior is less hesitant in his movements, much more fluid. They know the dance," he continued, "and in many cases, they know many dances, and while they are predictable, there is a speed and grace about their fighting style that comes distinctly through."

"When I realized this, I thought of how difficult it might be to face multiple untrained fighters, which, while they are less predictable, still display tendencies that are easier to read," Emanrasu stated.

"But..." offered Onred, with Tarlis nodding his agreement, "if we divide the fighters into smaller groups, say three or four together, even a trained warrior would have more trouble following all of the actions and reading the cues to defend effectively, especially if we can train them to act in concert."

"That is exactly what I was leading to!" Emanrasu said emphatically. "My thought on the matter is to pair the most efficient fighters with the least proficient, and then work our way inward pairing together the moderately trained fighters. We will have more effective help, where the least trained have the assistance of the most proficient fighters."

Tarlis nodded, the corners of his mouth struggling not to smile.

"That is a very astute observation, Emanrasu. In fact," Tarlis continued, "that is the typical method we have used in the past to prepare a community for defending themselves."

Tarlis, at last, could hold it back no more, and the grin snuck swiftly and spread across his face.

"Your grandfather taught me that method, and he, in turn, was taught by his father, and him by his. We are unsure how long this method has been used, but I know it goes back at least five generations," Tarlis explained. "The only stipulation is that this information is never vocalized outside the White. It can be taught but should never be explained. This will keep the method from spreading by word of mouth, thus invalidating it. At least those were your grandfather's reasonings.

"I had no reason to refute his opinion, so this has been adhered to for as long as I can recall."

As Emanrasu listened intently to this revelation, his eyes widened, and his eyebrows lifted upon hearing these were tested and reliable methods.

Emanrasu's face relaxed and grinned. "I never imagined that anyone considered this; it just sort of came to me as I was recognizing the different styles and techniques of the townsfolk; unrefined though they are, I could see how some would complement others if we were able to teach them to work in concert."

The White continued to discuss various training methods and methodologies and what to look for in the trainees to determine which method would work best. Eventually, the discussion ran its course, and the White dispersed to mats and beds.

Emanrasu found Rezua already asleep, the big man sprawled out on his bed, dwarfing it.

Emanrasu grinned, thinking nothing more about it. He settled in, drifting fleetingly off to sleep.

*　　　*　　　*

The dream and the Dance were uneventful, though Emanrasu woke with a feeling that something was imminently approaching.

The White and the training became routine. The trainees were divided and trained by individual White, with the focus on specific methods and styles being paramount.

One morning, Emanrasu queried Tarlis about why the townsfolk were not being trained in the dance.

Develop and Persevere: Chapter Nineteen

Tarlis looked at Emanrasu, seeming to scour the young man's face for signs of jest. Finding the young man seemingly sincere, Tarlis replied, "Unlike you, my boy, the dance does not come naturally to most. Just as in a real dance, one can know the motions, but when a misstep is made, it is likely to disrupt the entire dance as a whole.

"You've unraveled every expectation I held. I've never seen anyone take to the Dance as you have—and to be plain, I didn't think it was possible."

Tarlis leaned on his cane, his eyes following the fluid, clumsy rhythms of the training townsfolk.

"But be mindful—true mastery takes mains to shape. Some train a lifetime and still never reach the place where the Dance becomes a weapon, not just a pattern."

"We pass along what we can in the little time we're given and hope it's enough. Often, it is. But not always. There have been times when we succeeded in battle... but the cost to the community was something no victory could truly repay."

Tarlis frowned, looking at the dirt in front of him. He sighed heavily and then waved a hand in dismissal.

"Let us not dwell on that possibility," he stated. "The training seems to be going better than many we have done, and the preparation Torsun and Serrah put them through while we were gone is a blessing we are normally not afforded."

Emanrasu took the hint and returned to wandering through the trainees and helping when asked. He paid close attention and continued his attempt at learning.

The days passed much the same, with Telk waiting outside the room, a jovial banter between him and Rezua, a morning meal, and then training. The training was always followed by a meeting with the White to discuss progress and the next day's tasks.

The Heater and The Hack

Three days, then five days, then ten days passed. Emanrasu could see the trainees getting better.

"It doesn't seem like we are progressing quickly enough," he thought, furrowing his brow at the thought.

That evening, he was reassured by Tarlis, Onred, and the rest of the White.

"We have done more with less," Onred stated as the discussion concluded.

Emanrasu accepted the answer but still felt uneasy sending unskilled fighters into battle.

Waking the next morning, Emanrasu performed his dance in the room as he had every day since the first. Finishing, he stowed the Heater and the Hack, then opened the door to let Telk in.

To Emanrasu's surprise, the boy was not waiting in the hall. Emanrasu paused, looking up and down the hallway, and waited a few moments before shrugging and continuing with his day.

During the morning meal, Emanrasu queried Serrah about the boy.

Serrah sighed, "His father was outspoken against waiting so long to confront the bandits and has now decided to take Telk and join some others to travel to Erald until the bandits have been dealt with."

She furrowed her brow, "The man, Dalen, I think his name was, never seemed to participate in the preparations but always had a snide comment. I am not sorry he is gone, but I think I will miss Telk and his joyful demeanor."

Emanrasu's long face projected his own feelings, "As will I. The boy was always a bright spot in the day, and I swear the boy never seemed to be far."

A fleeting grin replaced the furrowed brow as Emanrasu reminisced about the boy and his ability to be everywhere seemingly at the same time.

The morning progressed routinely, albeit without the bright spark of Telk.

Develop and Persevere: Chapter Nineteen

Shortly after mid-day, as training resumed, a commotion commenced close to the road, and as Emanrasu looked around, he saw the turmoil drawing in those closest to the area but was quickly spreading outward and attracting more of the training townsfolk.

Torsun stood in the thick of the growing maelstrom, his eyes locking onto Emanrasu. He waved him over—urgently. As Emanrasu hurried over, he was joined by Tarlis and Onred, who had been similarly summoned.

Onred stepped through the growing throng, effortlessly plowing a path to where Torsun stood. Emanrasu followed Onred and Tarlis, taking in the scene when he arrived.

Serrah was kneeling down and hovered over a little girl tending her wounds, even as another woman knelt over a woman doing likewise with the woman's injuries.

"The group that left last night," Torsun said, voice tight. "They were attacked. Arianis and her daughter Kaurin barely made it back—gravely injured. She is unsure if anyone else survived and saw no one else as she struggled back to Bren carrying her daughter."

Torsun hadn't even finished before Onred was already moving, signaling the White to gather.

"I was hoping... I need the White to ride out with me. We have to see what's left." Torsun's voice wavered—anger, grief, and something close to fear.

"We will," Tarlis replied, his voice calm and steady.

Emanrasu looked at the old man, and though Tarlis's voice was calm, he could see the worry in the old man's eyes.

Emanrasu turned and, without waiting, made his way over to where the White were gathering. As he approached, the White dispersed, each singling out one or two of the trainees, commanding them to assemble and follow.

"Onred, I assume we are preparing to help?" Emanrasu asked the big man.

"Yes," Onred replied. "Gather yourself, and we will leave as soon as we are able."

Emanrasu glanced over at the group and watched briefly as Torsun and Tarlis began shouting orders to ready horses and carts. The woman and the girl were gently loaded into the meal cart and slowly transported to the Barein House, where they could be more easily cared for.

Emanrasu hurried toward Serrah and was joined by Rezua as they approached her.

"What is going on?" questioned Rezua.

"The group that left was attacked on the road to Elund," Emanrasu told him.

The big man's brow furrowed, his eyes narrowing. "That was the group that Telk left with, wasn't it?" he asked.

"I am not sure," Emanrasu responded.

Serrah reeled, and Emanrasu caught her elbow. Steadying herself—she met his gaze, eyes burning. "I'm coming with you," she stated flatly. No hesitation. No room for argument.

The three made their way over and helped the group tasked with gathering and preparing horses and carts.

To Emanrasu, it seemed like it was taking forever as he briskly went about the tasks—his thoughts dwelling on Telk, his concern growing moment by moment.

Rushing to make ready, a full thirty men and women gathered to accompany them and evaluate the fate of the rest of the Erald-bound group.

To Honor and Remember: Chapter Twenty

"The measure of a man is never in mains. It is only in the impact of his life on others. One must strive to better themselves and those around them to more completely feel fulfillment and garner respect."

—RCotD—

With preparations finished, the large group rode out, racing out to the point of the attack. The dust being kicked up billowed out behind the riders and caked the nostrils so much that the group, in short order, took to covering their faces with riding clothes to mitigate the dust and dirt somewhat.

Emanrasu, Tarlis, and the White were the first to arrive, sweeping the area and clearing the way for the rest who were traveling with the cart.

Emanrasu scanned the area. The sight that met his eyes was more than he had feared—his chest tightened and his breath hung heavy.

His heart thundered, threatening to burst from his chest; the pulse roared in his ears as everything else dissolved into the image before him.

A pile of bodies lay just beyond the upturned cart, and atop… the boy, knife still clutched in his hand, eerily lying there—still, as if merely resting.

Drawing closer, Emanrasu saw the hilt… embedded in Telk so deep the cross-guard touched his chest.

The last vestiges of hope he had clung to fell from him as he stumbled.

The Heater and the Hack, suddenly leaden with the loss of hope, slipped from his grip.

As his knees gave way, the Hack fell first—its once-familiar weight now dragging, ringing sharp against the earth. The Heater followed with a dull, heavy thud.

The Heater and The Hack

His imminent collapse forestalled by the firm grip closing on his shoulder.

Emanrasu lifted his eyes to Onred, who stood quietly, scanning the scene.

"Stand," Onred said, voice low and steady. "Stand for a moment…"

The silence that followed sat heavy—like thick forest smoke in frost, blanketing Emanrasu.

His grief ebbed—without diminishing—as thoughts of Rezua and Serrah rose—he could already feel the weight of their sorrow and loss.

He felt Onred's pressure on his shoulder and, drawing a breath, slowly resumed his task.

Another breath. He reached up and touched Onred's hand in silent acknowledgment, and he loosed his grip, letting Emanrasu stand once again on his own.

His gaze returned to Telk, and the surge of grief rose—only to be stifled beneath a boot as he resumed his approach.

Telk had died doing what he believed must be done—just as he had that night he stood defiant against Rezua, only because Emanrasu had asked him not to let him rest. "Rezua, the Dance be cursed," Emanrasu thought. "Both Rezua and Serrah are on the cart, making their way here to help."

"We need to put this in better order before the cart gets here. I do not want Rezua, Serrah, or any of the others to come across this as I have," Emanrasu said abruptly as he bent over and retrieved the Hack from the ground. He produced a cloth and swiped at the dust on the ancient weapon, dragging the fabric cursorily across his face to dam the flowing rivers down his cheeks.

Emanrasu sheathed his sword and tucked the cloth back into his tunic. He lifted his head, gathering himself, and took one final deep cleansing breath, then stepped forward.

To Honor and Remember: Chapter Twenty

Walking the final lengths between himself and the bodies, he heard Onred bellow orders to the White, followed by a bustle of activity.

Emanrasu studied Telk's face, taking in every detail—the look on the boy's face frozen in one of defiant resistance. The cuts and nicks on his face and hands, coupled with the slices in his tunic, spoke to Telk's unyielding determination to protect and serve those around him.

The creak of the cart as the White righted it ended in a thunderous thud as it landed on its wheels once more.

Emanrasu looked over his shoulder at the White bustling around, though no one approached him or the bodies before him.

Turning back to Telk, he reached down and carefully pried the knife from the boy's hand, slipping it through a strap on his sheath.

He grabbed the protruding hilt of the sword, tugged, but failed to free Telk from its deep penetration. Several more pulls resulted in no better success.

"The Dance!"

Jaw set tight, he ground his teeth, fighting the urge to get on his horse and exact justice from the first brigand he met.

Intentionally, he stepped back and hung his head, then forced himself to breathe and let the tension drain.

"There must be a way," Emanrasu thought, though loath to place a foot or knee on the boy's body to free it.

"Perhaps… perhaps somewhere deeper," he thought.

"Leverage…" he whispered raspily under his breath.

Emanrasu placed his foot on the body just beneath Telk. Pulling once more, the sword broke free and quickly slipped out from the boy's chest.

The Heater and The Hack

Emanrasu's first instinct was to throw the sword away. His anger wanted to fling it out into the field next to the road. He glanced down at the sword that took the boy's life.

"This sword is a testament..." Emanrasu realized, "... a testament to Telk's bravery and steadfastness. It would be best to have it turned into a proper grave marker for this remarkable boy."

Emanrasu walked to his horse and lashed the sword to the saddle, then sheathed the knife between two layers of leather.

Returning to the bodies, he reached down and gently lifted the young man up, cradling his head gently as if the boy were asleep. Emanrasu made his way to his horse, intending to lay the body across and carry him to the town himself.

"Seems a bit...disrespectful..." Emanrasu realized, mulling over his options. "Better to bring him back in the cart with a bit more dignity."

With this thought, Emanrasu veered toward the cart and laid the boy gently in it. He grabbed a nearby blanket and covered the boy. He wrapped and tucked it as best he could to keep the dust of the road off the lad.

Emanrasu turned back to the pile from which he took Telk. While deep in conversation, Tarlis and Torsun approached the bodies and stood nearby, occasionally gesturing as they continued their discussion.

Studying the bodies as he approached, he noticed for the first time that they were all women and children, save for one man and Telk. The women and children, like Telk, lay facing up as if confronting their attackers, while the man was face down, curled up in a ball, appearing to have been running away or possibly even hiding from the bandits.

"We may never know for sure," Emanrasu thought.

"This was not what I had hoped for," he told Tarlis as he arrived. Emanrasu's voice was barely a whisper as he struggled to hold back his emotions.

To Honor and Remember: Chapter Twenty

"No," Tarlis solemnly replied, "but not wholly unexpected given the circumstances of our notification."

Emanrasu paused as he spoke to Tarlis and found that several of the White had trailed him over, passing him as he hesitated. One by one, they gathered the bodies and took them to the cart.

As Emanrasu turned back toward Tarlis and Torsun, Freydis called out, motioning back toward Bren. Looking in that direction, Emanrasu could see the puffs of dust from the cart and the escorting riders.

Emanrasu sighed heavily, hardening himself against the reactions he expected from his friends.

"At least they won't see the disarray we arrived to find," Emanrasu said. "The sight of Telk was overwhelmingly difficult, and I would not want to put Rezua and Serrah through that. It will be difficult enough for them without also dealing with that sight." Emanrasu's shoulders slumped a little, and he sighed softly.

Tarlis placed a brief hand on Emanrasu's shoulder, then turned to the task at hand. The three proceeded to assist with the rest of the bodies. At the bottom, Onred turned the body of the man over.

Shaking his head, Torsun's curse was barely audible.

"Dalen!" Torsun exclaimed weakly. "The Dance, damn him!" He sighed, "Even though I suspected as much, it is still shocking to find he was this cowardly."

The cart carrying the rest of the townsfolk, along with Rezua and Serrah, at last arrived.

Emanrasu motioned to his friends as he strode over to them. Rezua's face was staunch and flush; his demeanor was one of angst as they waited for Emanrasu.

"I have some bad…" Emanrasu started, only to be interrupted by Rezua.

"Where is Telk?" Rezua yelled. "Why do I not see him?"

The Heater and The Hack

Serrah put a hand on the big man's arm and gently pulled at him. Rezua gazed down at her, and he calmed a little, though the muscles in his face were still drawn and taut.

*   *   *

"We are aware that Telk was among the travelers," Serrah explained. "Rezua and I discussed the probable outcomes of the attack and what it might mean for the boy." She shifted her grip from his arm to Rezua's colossal hand. She held his hand gently, though Rezua seemed to struggle to be gentle in return.

"Telk is among the fallen," Emanrasu replied. He gazed into Rezua's eyes as he said this and watched as hope drained from them.

"He died serving and protecting, just as he was wont."

Emanrasu glanced from the big man to Serrah and back again as their eyes glistened with tears. Serrah outwardly wept, and a lone tear slipped down Rezua's cheek.

Closing the distance to his friends, he reached out, throwing an arm around each. The tears streamed down his face as he mourned the loss of the boy and the sorrow of his friends.

Emanrasu took a deep breath, and when he finally spoke, he was slightly more composed.

"We must finish here and return to Bren. There are decisions to be made in light of this. Also, we need to make sure that no one else attempts to leave until the brigands have been dealt with."

The trio agreed and returned to the cart and the others. Working rapidly to clear the remnants of the battle still remaining strewn about, they shifted bodies between carts to better honor the dead.

Emanrasu climbed up onto the cart with the fallen and lifted Telk's body, handing it over to Rezua, who gently transferred the lad's body to Rezua's cart. He laid the boy gently in it, laying his large hand on the blanket surrounding the body before turning back to the group.

With the clearing and cleanup completed, the townsfolk and the White silently mounted and made their way back to Bren. The only interruption was the two separate sightings of brigands off in the distance. Though the group was ready for a confrontation, there was no move to attempt to follow or intercept them.

Emanrasu, for one, was glad no one insisted on attempting to exact immediate retribution.

He raged inwardly, though outwardly, he maintained a calm demeanor, setting an example for the rest of the people around him.

Emanrasu looked around and located the innkeep, Torsun. The old man appeared weary and almost broken. Emanrasu spurred his horse over to Torsun.

"I do not know your people well, Torsun," he began. "But we will have to break the news to them and impress upon them that we must finish our planning and not do anything rash."

"If any of the others that fell were anything like Telk, I can imagine we will be hard-pressed to calm them," Emanrasu continued. "We must finish the preparations and await the return of Catlina and Darth and the information they have gathered before we are able to retaliate effectively."

"I agree," Torsun said, nodding in agreement.

Tarlis, riding close by, said nothing but nodded.

Emanrasu spun his horse about and returned to the cart that carried his friends and Telk's body. He fell in silently next to the cart, and the rest of the journey back to Bren was spent in silence.

Their return was greeted with the grim faces of the townsfolk. The main road to the inn was lined with those who had heard of the misfortune.

The Heater and The Hack

Making their way to the inn, Torsun called out to various people. He bade them spread out, gathering all still in Bren and bringing them to the inn. The announcement of the events leading to the massacre would be made as the sun reached its apex.

The ominous, thick black smoke darkened the funerary as it billowed out, filling the air—a visually tangible reflection of the grief Emanrasu felt.

Torsun immediately assumed control of the carts, directing them to halt in front of the inn so the bodies could be offloaded onto the veranda.

Sometime before the sun reached apex, Tarlis caught Emanrasu's arm. The young man gazed at his mentor; the weight of his leadership was heavy. The mantle of the leadership was not his alone, and he could see this in Tarlis's eyes, which reflected his own loss and determination.

"Catlina and Darth have returned," he told Emanrasu. "We will have need to meet tonight and finalize our plans."

Emanrasu nodded in understanding, and Tarlis turned and retreated to where Torsun and Onred were ordering directions for this and that in preparation for the announcements.

As the sun reached apex, the mass of people gathered in front of the inn to pay respects to the fallen and to hear what Torsun had to say. The anger and sorrow in the townsfolk thundered in voices and sobs that permeated the courtyard in front of the inn.

The sky was clear save for the billowing smoke, but the air was thick and oppressive with the grief the throng seemed to feel. As best they could, many of the gathered were holding each other for comfort. Cries of sorrow and pain permeated Emanrasu's very core.

The deep black smoke of the funeraries had shifted to a light gray as the fires burned hotter.

To Honor and Remember: Chapter Twenty

Torsun struck a wooden sounding board with a ceremonial rod. The heavy sound reverberated, causing the throng to fall silent as attention gravitated toward him. It had the desired effect of quieting, if not soothing, the gathered townsfolk.

Tosun called out, projecting his voice over the crowd. "Many of you have heard that Dalen's group was attacked as they tried to travel to Erald. Only Arianis and her daughter Kaurin are known to have survived, though we cannot be sure if others escaped since we do not know precisely who had accompanied them on the journey to Erald."

Torsun proceeded to detail the names of those whose bodies were recovered. With each name, the murmuring from the crowd grew until Torsun listed Telk. An immediate hush swept over the gathering, the silence thick with shock, anger, and sorrow as sobs and curses slowly grew.

The dead had been cleaned and prepared, Dalen far at the right end and Telk at the left. The bodies of the fallen had been placed on leather carrying sheets, and to each sheet had been attached twelve ropes, as long as Rezua was tall, six to each side, one for each of the twelve ropesmen, who stood stoically behind their fallen.

These honorary ropesmen were tasked with carrying the unknown, unclaimed, and unwanted—those that had no one willing to stand with them—to the fires. Behind the fallen, Onred, Djorn, Freydis, and Eirikr, with eight townsfolk, stood solemnly.

"As is our custom, we ask for volunteers to carry our fallen; we will start with Dalen at that end," Torsun told the throng, motioning toward Dalen's body. "Dalen was…"

"He was… unafraid… to speak his mind. Regardless of the situation or appropriateness, Dalen was always one to speak his mind. He… was… unconcerned with the right or wrong of his words or thoughts," Torsun said. "Who of you will come forward and accompany Dalen to the fires?"

Dalen's alienation of those he lived with was starkly apparent as no one stepped forward, and Torsun asked again.

"Who among you would disregard your feelings and carry..." Torsun paused briefly, then continued, "Who among you would honor Telk by carrying his father to the fires?"

A murmur ran through the crowd, and a few men stepped forward, standing in a loose line extending out in front of Dalen.

The sigh of relief from Torsun was almost imperceptible, though Emanrasu was watching Torsun intently enough that he understood the anxiety that Torsun felt or would feel if he had to rely on ropesmen to carry Telk's father.

Torsun proceeded to identify the rest of the fallen with a short eulogy about each, which, upon each conclusion, he queried for volunteer ropesmen. Without the hesitancy shown for Dalen, each of the fallen elicited volunteers, who stepped forward and placed an item of remembrance on or tucked under the body they were to carry.

One by one, a line formed in front of each body, the least of which was fourteen strong, aside from Dalen's eight.

At last, Torsun came to Telk.

"Telk, as most of you know, was a boy who seemed to be nowhere unless you had need, and then he always seemed to be at your elbow," Torsun said.

In a softer, wistful tone, Torsun told the throng, "I, for one, will miss the boy and the man he could have been." Raising his voice again, he asked, "Who among you would come forward and accompany Telk to the fires?"

Emanrasu had grown fond of the boy. His intentions were to volunteer as a ropesman, but seeing the streaming crowd that stepped forward for the boy, he realized that these people had known Telk for possibly most of his life, while he could only count in moons from a single hand.

To Honor and Remember: Chapter Twenty

Once the baubles and remembrances had been placed and the line formed in front of Telk, a wave of quiet spread across the gathering. Each individual implored the Dance, Hold, or Surge, as was their leaning.

Emanrasu took a deep breath and closed his eyes, shutting out the whispers of the throng and the sounds of men and animals. Giving his heart and mind leeway to reach out, he implored the Dance on behalf of Telk.

"Never have I interceded on behalf of another, and, in truth, I had never given the Dance much thought. But now, I implore—let Telk be marked for whatever good may exist beyond this life."

"His cycle of life has always been one of service," the Dragon's response, a soft rumble in his mind; Emanrasu, startled, took a step back.

"Never before have you spoken to me from outside my dreams," he said, looking around; his actions and thoughts seemed unnoticed. His thoughts and attention focused inward, waiting for a response.

No further acknowledgment or response was forthcoming. Emanrasu slowly realized that it may have been a response within his own mind, echoing his hopes for the boy.

"May each be carried beyond and guided by the Dance," Torsun nodded to the honorary ropesmen.

The ropesmen stepped from behind the fallen and filled in where needed. The White stepped in line with the eight volunteers for Dalen while the rest of the honorary ropesmen divided themselves among the others.

Making his way to Dalen, Torsun stood for a moment as the crowd quieted.

Reaching down, he touched Dalen's forehead.

"The Crossing of the Ropes," Torsun nodded to the ropesmen.

The Heater and The Hack

The ropesmen ceremoniously stepped forward and took hold of the ropes on their side, then offered them to their mirror on the other side. Each of the ropesmen took their counterpart's rope and loosely draped it over their shoulders before kneeling down and drawing it taut.

"Lift!"

The ropesmen stood, leaning out and away, lifting the bodies off the ground.

"Proceed!"

Torsun nodded to the ropesmen around Dalen, and as a unit, they stepped forward. The crowd of townsfolk parted in front of the procession as each of the fallen followed.

The procession halted at the funerary, where a highly polished plank jutted out from the furnace. One by one, the bodies were placed on the plank, and the plank lifted to allow the body to slide into the fires within.

Telk's body slid down the plank, and as the last eyes to behold the young man's physical body watched on, Emanrasu let his head hang for a few moments.

"...ability and drive... he would have excelled at anything... regardless of the cost," Emanrasu thought, wiping away the tear that stole down his cheek.

He heaved a heavy sigh, his thoughts drifting and meandering.

The throng of townsfolk began dispersing, returning to their daily tasks, and dealing with the losses in their own ways. Emanrasu stood and watched the light gray smoke from the funerary turning a thick black. The acrid smell of burning flesh filled the air.

*   *   *

With the enormous weight of Rezua's hand lightly gripping his shoulder and the warm, soft, firm hand of Serrah slipping into his on the other side, he felt grateful... until he didn't.

350

To Honor and Remember: Chapter Twenty

His world teetered precariously as he realized that it was likely two of the three of them might be here watching one of them fueling the fires of the funerary. His companions steadied him, and he gulped in breaths as he sought to regain his composure.

"One day it will be one or more of us in there. Let us be as Telk and make our last reflect our grit and strength." He squeezed Serrah's hand and patted the giant hand on his shoulder in emphasis.

Removing his hand, Rezua responded in a deep, resonating whisper, "Agreed."

Serrah's only response was to squeeze his hand in return. Emanrasu looked down at her puffy red eyes, realizing for the first time she had spent more time with the boy while they had been off to find the White.

He held her hand firmly as the trio stood mourning, each in their own way.

Emanrasu thought back to the death and funerary of his father, now nearly a main past. They had lifted his father under his arms and legs, swinging him into the funerary pyre—the popping and crackling as his father succumbed to the fire branded on his mind.

"This ceremonial funerary was what Telk deserved," Emanrasu said as he divested himself of thoughts of his father.

The deep rumbling from Rezua's stomach served to lighten the mood, and the friends grinned as Rezua shrugged.

"It is well past the apex meal, and a growing boy needs the sustenance to continue to face the constant need to put pen to paper."

The large man grinned and winked, eliciting a genuine smile from Serrah.

Shaking his head, Emanrasu grinned as well. "Leave it to Rezua to provide needed levity," he admitted silently.

The Heater and The Hack

"We should get back to the rest. With the return of Catlina and Darth, we have much to discuss and decide tonight. You two go ahead back to the inn. I have had a thought and need to speak with the smith and the arborwright. I shall join you at the inn shortly."

Without waiting for an answer, Emanrasu strode off rapidly in search of the smith. He followed the sound of the hammer, effortlessly locating the smithy.

"Ho!" he called as he entered the smithy.

The hammering stopped.

"Ho, yourself."

Emanrasu reached into his pouch and produced two gold coins.

"I have two tasks for you. The first is a remembrance marker for Telk made and devised from the knife with which he defended the others to the last and the sword by which he breathed his last."

He handed the smith the two coins.

"The second will be a collaboration between you and the arborwright which might give us an edge in the ousting of the brigands."

The smith, seemingly already agreeable, perked up at the mention of providing an edge to the Bren in the upcoming conflict.

"I have noticed that the majority of implements used for farming are wooden, and I suspect that the brigands are aware of this," Emanrasu said. "It is my thought to reenforce a substantial number of them, making them deadlier and more useful in the upcoming conflict. The intent is to disguise or hide these changes by maintaining the outward appearance of wooden implements."

The eyes of the smith slowly brightened as they flitted around the smithy.

To Honor and Remember: Chapter Twenty

"I have plenty of material to produce two score of the suggested weapons, but it will be a slow process as I am without apprentices currently, now that Telk has gone to the fires."

Without questioning the smith on how Telk possibly would have found time to apprentice, Emanrasu reached into his pouch and produced four silver coins.

"Find enough willing to help... so that we can have them within two days."

"I will make it so," the smith replied as he moved to set aside his current project.

"Send word on your progress to the inn. Speak to Torsun, Tarlis, or myself only. Keep this project from becoming widely known so that we may have some small advantage when the day comes. I am off to have a word with the arborwright and will suggest that he come collaborate with you on the particulars."

The smith nodded, and without further discussion, Emanrasu exited in search of the arborwright. The woodshop of the arborwright was found easily as it was separated from the smithy only by the tailor's shop.

Emanrasu entered the woodshop and found it empty. The earthy odor of wood, pleasant in contrast to the acrid, pungent air assaulting the senses outside, wafted through the shop.

The woodshop was well stocked with various types of wood, suggesting that there should be no issues with procurement meeting the allotted time frame.

As Emanrasu pondered this, he heard a muffled sound from the rear of the shop. Without hesitation, he made his way in that direction.

Reaching the back of the shop, he approached a door set into the rear wall.

The sound seemed to be coming from beyond it. He palmed the door several times and waited.

Moments later, faint shuffling noises came from within. The door opened, and a man stepped out. Behind him, a cloth draped across the inside of the door hid the room beyond.

"Emanrasu," the man said, offering an arm.

Clasping it, Emanrasu was surprised the man knew who he was.

"I do not know your name, but I assume you are the arborist?"

"I am Lotheir, and yes—I'm the arborwright. Is there something I can do for you? Just name it, and it will be done."

Lotheir directed Emanrasu toward the front of the shop and followed close behind.

*   *   *

"Hope," the arborwright said as they made their way forward, "had been slowly eroding—ever since the ruffians took over the Zerocha. But it returned, at least a little, when you took an interest in us. So… in return…"

He turned to Emanrasu. "What would you have of me?"

Emanrasu reached into his pouch and produced the last of the gold coins and four of the silver coins. He held them out to Lotheir.

"I would have you work with the smith to create weapons that approximate normal farm and ranch implements. I have already spoken with him, though I neglected to get his name as I was more intent on meeting you today as well."

"His name is Bapaksu, but most shorten it to Ba or Bapak." Lotheir grinned broadly as he added, "I tend to use much more colorful names for him, though not all of them are well-deserved."

Lotheir reached out and took the coins, as Emanrasu elaborated.

To Honor and Remember: Chapter Twenty

"The gold is for you," he said. "We are making every effort for a two-day deadline. The silver is for you to hire whomever you feel might help you finish on time. Other than these instructions, I will leave the details to the two of you as I trust that you are more familiar with the work and the available help than I."

"I will finish the seal work in progress..." Lotheir said, motioning to the door from whence he came. "...and meet with Bapak then. I foresee no issues with making your time frame and, should any arise, we will adjust. We shall meet your deadline; this I swear!"

Lotheir offered his arm again, and Emanrasu took it, whereupon Lotheir turned and quickly disappeared through the door in the back, leaving Emanrasu alone once again.

Striding out into the waning sunlight as it started casting longer shadows, Emanrasu marveled at the speed at which the day had passed.

"Now..." he thought. "...to tell Torsun, Tarlis, and the rest of the White. In any case, training must continue on the morrow, if we are to have any chance of success."

Emanrasu quickened his pace back to the inn, searching out any he could find.

"Ho, Onred!" he called as he spied the large captain veering toward him.

"Ho, Black! What would you have of me?"

Emanrasu's thoughts stumbled slightly and slowed at the response.

Onred quietly dismissed the townsfolk he had been talking to.

"This is the first time anyone called him the Black, well, except Tarlis," Emanrasu realized.

"Would you gather Tarlis, Torsun, and the White into my sleeping chambers? I have had thoughts and put them into motion, and I need to make sure I am not veering out of the path we have already been traveling. I will continue to find and inform all that should know, as mentioned, but it needs to be done hurriedly and without stirring up too many questions."

"Within the hand, we shall meet in your quarters," Onred struck his chest in the formal salute of the White and turned to search out the rest.

Emanrasu located Rezua and Serrah and informed them of the meeting, then begged his leave to continue to track down any others he might find.

Returning to his room, he cleared the table to make room for the meeting.

"It will be standing room, but if I am boating downriver with this thought, we should not need much debate."

Emanrasu sighed at the thought and tried to relax.

Serrah and Rezua entered and quietly sat on the edge of Rezua's bed. Though Emanrasu acknowledged them with a nod, he was silent as well.

The time seemingly dragged on, and Emanrasu picked apart every flaw he could think of in his plan. Slowly, the White gathered by ones and twos, nodding to Emanrasu but not disturbing his concentration.

Well before the hand was up, Torsun entered the room, completing the required attendants. Emanrasu stood and addressed his companions.

"Catlina and Darth, I will hear your report shortly, but I wanted to divulge my thoughts so that they might be considered during your report."

"It is my thought to take the townsfolk and meet the brigands openly."

Emanrasu detailed his discussions and agreements with Bapak and Lotheir, as well as his requirements for the two.

As soon as he was finished revealing his plans, he requested Darth and Catlina to report.

To Honor and Remember: Chapter Twenty

The two of them detailed the schedules and patterns that they had meticulously observed, as well as weaknesses in the defense of the brigands.

The plans were, as laid out, reviewed comprehensively and thoroughly, and adjusted as needed to fit the observed timelines and schedules.

As the meeting drew to a close, Emanrasu requested opinions from each of the group present, giving each time to voice any concerns and offer any approval of the path forward.

Each, in turn, approved of the revised plan, and several offered minor adjustments to improve its acceptance and increase the chances of success.

Emanrasu called a close to the meeting. Onred, the first to leave, paused at the door, faced Emanrasu, and struck his chest before exiting.

Each of the White followed suit before leaving, and with each salute, the grin on Tarlis's face grew.

Serrah stood and approached Emanrasu with a smile.

Reaching out, she touched his arm and gazed into his face with what seemed to him to be unwavering confidence.

"You seem never to cease to surprise me. I feel I would never have the courage to join an endeavor such as this, let alone be part of the group planning it. You make me feel like we can accomplish anything."

She squeezed his arm before letting it go.

"I am off to rest. Goodnight, Eman."

Turning to the others, she bade them good night as well and then quietly left.

Rezua stretched out on his bed as Tarlis stepped over to Emanrasu.

"You constantly surprise me as well," he remarked. "I knew that the White would eventually accept you as the Black, but I never imagined it would happen this quickly. You have shown an affinity for leading, and the others undeniably see it as well."

"I second-guess almost every decision, Tarlis. I fear I still have a long way to go before I will be able to live up to expectations."

Tarlis grinned at the young man. "This is the legacy of leadership, my boy. Few things in this world are as cut and dried as to have only one perfect solution. The reason you instill confidence in others is your ability to evaluate a situation, but you actively seek advice and input from those around you."

"You have made me proud, and I am almost sorry for the circumstances surrounding our first meeting." The old man grinned, "almost…"

Emanrasu let a smile sneak onto his face as he rubbed his head. "Well, old man, I can certainly say that I, for one, am definitely sorry for the circumstances. Though I imagine I would repeat my actions no matter how many times I were to relive it."

"I am going to retire to my quarters as well, and our window of opportunity to strike is still six days away, so we have a lot of preparation to do before we transition leadership of the townsfolk to you alone. Making sure that they have complete enough trust in you to follow you even without the White will be crucial as we move forward."

Tarlis stiffened in front of Emanrasu, striking his chest in a salute. He then turned and made his way out into the hallway, shutting the door behind him.

Emanrasu sighed heavily, grinning at the thought of how much more he seemed to sigh than he used to. He glanced around and moved the furniture back to where they started.

Turning down the lamps, he glanced over at Rezua lying on his bed, scribbling in his journal. As Emanrasu walked over to his own bed and began to ready himself, Rezua finished and closed his journal, setting it aside.

To Honor and Remember: Chapter Twenty

"Don't expect me to contribute to that big head of yours. Soon, it will be as big as mine, and if you can imagine someone as little and scrawny as you having a head as large as mine, you will realize how silly you would look."

"I would never presume to get a compliment from you, my gentle giant. I fear you are barely articulate enough to understand how to even form a honeyed word."

As Emanrasu finished his response, he dodged the boot Rezua chucked at him. The crooked grin on Rezua's face was a firm indication that he, too, was surprised and proud of Emanrasu.

"Good sleep to you, Eman."

Emanrasu stretched out on his bed. "Good sleep to you as well, Rezua. Thank you for throwing your lot in with me. It means the world to me knowing you're there."

"You're welcome," came the reply, as Rezua's other boot landed heavily on Emanrasu's chest, eliciting another grin from Emanrasu as he closed his eyes and drifted swiftly off to sleep.

Our Beginnings of Endings: Chapter Twenty-One

"Endings are the inevitable outcome of beginnings, unavoidable and resolute. It is only what happens in between that truly matters and what shapes the future of things."

—*RCotD*—

The colors swirled and coalesced, forming the familiar image of the Dance. The Dragon and Phoenix slowly looped around each other in the Sky while the Earth offered a supportive base for the Tree, which reached upward, touching the life-giving rays provided by the Sun.

"I have questions," Emanrasu started.

"We are aware. Ask, and answers will be provided," came the deep, resonating rumble.

"Why the boy? Why would Telk, of all possibilities, end in this manner?"

"His destiny was fulfilled, his task accomplished. We do not dictate. The Dance guides—nudging, balancing. His youth stole much of his personal agency and left him amidst the whims of others. Thus, many of his choices were made for him."

"But he should not have met his demise in this manner," Emanrasu insisted.

"The boy, Telk, while tragic by your standards, puts him in high regard, not only by mortal standards but in the context of reality and life itself. He was not the only option, but he was the one who ultimately chose his path. Do not mourn him. Rather, rejoice for him and the hearts and minds he reached in his limited mains."

"He shall live again," shrieked the Phoenix. The piercing screech, soothing in its ability to penetrate directly to the core, calmed Emanrasu.

"Yes," rumbled the Dragon. "He will. You should not presume your wants and needs supersede those of each individual. The boy would never choose a path other than the one he chose. Be happy and rejoice in his decisions."

"So, you infer that I can just walk away from what is coming since I can choose?"

"Another, any other, could walk away from their destined path. We sense that you, Emanrasu, through your own agency, could never walk away."

The path he traveled since leaving Rintha seemed inevitable. Emanrasu could not imagine making any other choices along the way, even in hindsight. Except perhaps... Telk... and even then, he would never dishonor the boy by taking his agency from him, so... perhaps... this too was an inevitable choice.

"You are starting to comprehend your role, and this bodes well for balance. Understand, it is never the large sweeping changes that will effect change in the world forever; it is the gradual unnoticed ones that will affect permanent change."

With that, Emanrasu slipped into a deep, restful sleep—something too rare of late.

The cool morning air, crisp and sharp, greeted him upon awakening. The tasks at hand weighed less than before, with a decision now having been made and a plan devised moving forward.

Emanrasu stretched and breathed deeply as he placed his feet flat upon the chill wood of the worn floor.

"The angst..." he thought, trying to force himself to relax with another deep, long breath. "...always seems to be greater than the eventual outcomes should dictate, though I feel the stakes are higher than any before. Just prepare. Do what you can. Project confidence—and trust that faith will follow."

Emanrasu's meandering thoughts slipped through his mind, touching here and there without any final conclusions. He dwelt on the losses already incurred and the ones that might come. The beating of his heart, deafening, he took another deep breath and held it for a moment as the pounding subsided. Standing, he pondered Rezua, marveling at the loyalty the large man had always shown.

"I will need to honor him in some small way," the thought sneaked in. "I will need to set something appropriate in motion…"

The thought drifted away, replaced once again by the upcoming conflict.

Emanrasu closed his eyes for a moment and slowly pushed the imminent events from his mind as he strove to honor Telk without obsessing. Focusing on the next step, he placed one foot in front of the other, strode to the door, and slipped out into the hallway.

The hallway felt hollow—Telk's absence permanent. He paused a moment in silent remembrance before continuing on to the stairs and down to the Great Room.

The room was busier than usual this morning, and Serrah and two other women were bustling around, seeing to the serving and clearing of food and various plates, bowls, and utensils.

Emanrasu approached her, reaching out as she wiped down a table and touched her arm to garner her attention.

Her knitted brow and clenched jaw spoke volumes, but as she looked up and saw him, a smile softened her countenance. He, in turn, felt his anxiety wane and slowly melt in her presence.

"I…" they said in unison. Serrah smiled, eyebrows lifting. Emanrasu returned the smile and motioned for her to speak.

"I have told Torsun that I will help to deal with the morning meal. Thus, I will not be at the training field until closer to apex," she told him.

He nodded. "And I have tasks to tend to as well. The crucial work will happen after apex anyway."

The Heater and The Hack

He let his hand linger a moment longer on her arm before turning and striding to the door, stepping out of the inn into the crisp morning air. The sound of hammers in the distance entwined with the song of the redbirds on the roof of the stables, sometimes drowning them out and other times melding in an odd harmony.

Emanrasu strode out to the street and turned toward the smithy and wright's shops. The slivers of morning sun, shining in various shades of pink and red, struggled to find a path through the clouds gathered on the horizon.

The incessant, rhythmic "tink, tink, clang" echoed through the street as he strode with purpose down the dusty lane, punctuated melodically by the occasional crow of a lone rooster.

Approaching the smithy, he spotted Bapak and Lotheir exiting the arborwright, slowly making their way toward the smithy. So thoroughly engrossed in the parchment Lotheir held, neither noticed Emanrasu until he was almost upon them.

Bapak glanced up and stopped, laying a hand on Lotheir's arm to halt him as well. The arborwright paused, glanced at Bapak, then followed his gaze to Emanrasu, to whom he offered a nod of acknowledgment.

"We believe that we can successfully achieve the deadline. However, we will need an escort to the Dragon Cliffs, or close to there, to procure the necessary supplies," Bapak told him.

Lotheir nodded his head and glanced from Emanrasu to Bapak and back before adding, "We will need to make all haste if we are to finish on time."

Emanrasu nodded. "You have a slight reprieve. We found out late last evening our best time will be better than four days hence."

The smiths exchanged glances, grins spreading across their faces as Bapak clapped the arborwright's back with a hearty thump.

Our Beginnings of Endings: Chapter Twenty-One

"Excellent!" Lotheir exclaimed, wincing under the heavy-handed mauling. "We had taken time to devise several advanced designs, which we thought we would have to forego, but with the extra time, we may be able to fit one or two of the simpler ones into our deadline."

"Anything over and above will help, but our primary concern is upon the basic items, which, as you indicate, have been your priority. If you can provide more, I would be interested in seeing, so do not mistake my focus on priorities as a lack of interest.

"We can spare the White and a score of our recruits as an escort, but they will not be available until after apex. We will also need a variety of unadulterated farm implements brought to the training fields. Would you be able to coordinate those as well?"

"We can and will," Bapak replied after a nod from Lotheir.

Emanrasu turned, heading in the direction of the training field, but paused as Bapak continued.

"With any luck, Lotheir and I will provide the bulk of the requested items by morning on the aftermorrow and the bulk of the remaining items within the allotted four days."

Nodding his understanding, Emanrasu resumed his trek to the training grounds.

Striding toward the training grounds, he could feel the weight of Telk's passing lifting from his shoulders. "Telk, my brave young man, I shall have vengeance, retribution, and justice on your behalf. Your death will not be in vain."

As the sun slipped quietly over the rooftops, through the gently retreating morning mist, the Bren training field exuded purpose—alive with the growing throng of trainees and subtle active intention. Impromptu sparring slowly spread as the townsfolk and White seemingly began to display what he himself felt— the need for action to wash away the residual pain of loss mirrored in those around him.

The Heater and The Hack

His gaze swept over the gathering; he saw it was not just the White training them, but the townsfolk were sparring with one another. Rezua, himself—looking every bit the hairless-bear-of-a-man—was... not merely was, but—was—out among them, training with Darth, Djorn, and several of the Bren.

Emanrasu could see the townsfolk were much more attentive—more focused— today than in days past.

"I hope this level of dedication can carry us through the harrowing task before us," he thought as he approached Onred and Tarlis.

They were engaged in advanced instruction for some of the more promising trainees—imparting complex strategies, distilled into terms simple enough to be remembered once the true battle began.

Emanrasu exchanged nods with them as he passed.

"If only I had the experience of either of them..." he thought, setting himself to the task of assisting the townsfolk still trailing in.

*   *   *

A hand passed, and Onred's deep, resonating voice boomed out across the training area. "Gather!"

Those who were not otherwise engaged halted their training and gathered in front of Onred. Those who were still sparring continued, and soon, as the final clash of weapons left nothing but an echo in its wake, the trainees took their place.

Onred cleared his throat and began.

"We will be transitioning training to Emanrasu, who will continue conducting training each day. The White have been called upon to assist elsewhere..."

The murmur of the townsfolk grew as Onred continued. "We... we White... have provided enough training and are confident you will triumph in your elimination of this oppressive brigandine threat."

Our Beginnings of Endings: Chapter Twenty-One

Emanrasu took his cue and stepped up next to Onred. The captain stepped back and placed Emanrasu at the center of attention.

"We will continue to train each morning and work through the day. This crisis will be decided one way or the other within the fortnight, affording a modicum of justice as we move past.

"With the departure of the White, I have decided to allow you to challenge my worth as both a fighter and a mentor. To this end, I will accept all challenges until apex has been reached, whether singularly or in groups. I will refuse none."

The murmur grew to a low din as the townsfolk turned to one another, discussing the events now unfolding.

"In addition..." Emanrasu said, raising his voice. "I will also allow any challenger to select the weapon for which I must face them."

One of the more advanced and capable fighters smiled, reached down, and plucked a blade of grass. The man held this blade aloft, his voice thundering across friends and neighbors alike.

"Challenge accepted!" he boomed.

Laughter rippled and twittered through the crowd, quickly followed by questions demanding someone relay what had happened that was so funny.

Emanrasu approached the man and accepted the blade of grass.

"Round!" Emanrasu shouted, waving his hand as he turned about. "I want no one to doubt what happens here today."

The gathered trainers and trainees spread out, forming a large circle centered on the field. Emanrasu walked out into the center and turned to face his opponent.

"Choose your weapon."

Looking around the circle, the man seemed to breathe a bit faster, no longer appearing quite as sure of himself.

The Heater and The Hack

"Wooden shield and sword," the man said, projecting his voice for all to hear.

Emanrasu held up a hand and raised his voice. "There will be no training weapons against me this day. There is not a man among you that has not tested against me as I wielded my shield and sword, and today, the offer is no different, and the spoils will go to he who can blood me."

Upon finishing, Emanrasu motioned to Onred, who selected a shield and sword, walking it out to the challenger. Onred conferred with the man in hushed whispers, motioning as if giving last-minute advice and tactical instructions.

Emanrasu waited, relaxed, and without assuming a defensive or offensive stance. He tried to project a man without hope.

He held the blade of grass gingerly in his grasp, his eyes trained on it, giving no sign that he knew or cared about the impending bout.

With Emanrasu thus distracted, the man reached out with the sword and easily touched… empty air.

Emanrasu's movement was slight but quick as he turned his body while stepping away from the tip of the sword.

The man gathered himself, his jaw steeling as he pulled the sword back and thrust it out again, only to find empty space.

Thrice, the man did this, but on the third thrust, instead of pulling back, he swung the sword in Emanrasu's direction.

Emanrasu stepped forward, his hand grabbing the townsman's wrist as he spun his body, rolling up the side of the man's arm before shoving the blade of grass into the man's nose. The invasive piece of grass immediately caused the man's eyes to water, and a sneeze readily built and released as Emanrasu slipped behind him and made an exaggerated motion of snapping his neck.

The silence that followed was more deafening than the sneeze—but not quite as tumultuous as the eruption of approval from the onlookers.

Our Beginnings of Endings: Chapter Twenty-One

The crowd clamored, each vying for a turn at Emanrasu, some in singular combat, apparently trusting that they were more skilled than their unfortunate companion, but each solo encounter came away with Emanrasu's assurance that the result of the first battle was not a fluke.

Some of the trainees organized teams and worked in concert, but Emanrasu could almost feel the paths of the weapons as he stepped into, between, and around them, eliminating each team member in turn.

Emanrasu moved from one engagement to the next, and each subsequent group grew more massive than the last—until Tarlis rapped his cane against a shield to get everyone's attention.

Slowly, all heads turned and at last faced him. He looked out over the trainees.

"I have one last demonstration to ask. Emanrasu, when you first met the White, they tested your mettle. Would you again be willing to be tested by the White?"

Emanrasu wiped the sweat from his forehead. He thought back to that day so long ago—and to all the days since.

He considered the training he had received from each of the Captains, and he mulled over the realization that his initial challenge to face them all had been foolish, but that its brazenness—and their underestimation of him—had played a crucial role in his win.

Looking at Tarlis, he realized there would be no such underestimation this time. Each of the Captains of the White would be ready for him.

Emanrasu sighed.

"I will accept. I do, however, have stipulations. We will use only the farm implements provided by Lotheir and Bapak," he said, nodding to where the two stood next to the cart piled high with various tools.

"Upon each of the White being touched, they will step away as before. But I am opening it up to everyone. Should..."

The Heater and The Hack

Emanrasu let a sly grin slip across his face.

He pointed at Onred in recognition of the large man's leadership of the White—and signaled his intent to challenge that leadership. He emphasized the intent in his words:

"When… the last White falls, then I shall be fair game for any and all. The White will keep close watch and track my opponents, for the one who bloods me shall walk away with the coin that Onred has kept safe since the beginning."

"Should… or rather, when the White are defeated, any and all may strive to earn the coin.

As each one of you is touched, you will step over to the White, touch the Heater, and then return to the fray. In this manner, we will continue until such time as I lose—or until everyone is too tired to continue."

"Accepted!" bellowed Onred.

Without delay, the rest of the Captains of the White nodded their agreement—some grinning, others chuckling or shaking their heads in amused disbelief.

"Trainees!"

The roar echoed, reverberating throughout the surrounding buildings.

"Form!"

Emanrasu, surprised by the command projected in his own voice, let his eyes follow as the White closed in around him. The trainees gathered beyond them—two or three strides—as the last vestiges of sound dissolved into a hush of reverent whispers.

The White took their places in the familiar circle, reminiscent of the Arena battle so many weeks ago.

With a curt nod to Tarlis, the old man gave the signal to commence. The White attacked in earnest, seeking, as did the others, to test Emanrasu's skill.

Our Beginnings of Endings: Chapter Twenty-One

The captains of the White had watched him, trained him, and sparred with him daily. Emanrasu watched as they closed in, though this time he let his mind relax, and unlike the last time, he had no strategy. As the captains approached, he saw and felt the patterns each was using, attacking in concert, not just two or three at a time, but four and five.

*　　*　　*

Emanrasu smiled.

"Like trying to run through pouring rain without getting wet," He thought as he slipped and slid through the narrowest of misses.

His gaze flitted amongst the White, and he was able to anticipate each action and deftly dodge their attacks. The captains were wary and wise this time, intimately familiar with their hubris when they last faced Emanrasu.

Their complex tapestry of assists and assaults was truly a marvel to behold, weaving weapons together, blanketing the young man in complex patterns.

This time, Emanrasu danced, feeling the shifting of the attacks and the subtle sweeps of defense, and today, there was no luck involved in his style. He relied on his natural speed and the skills taught him by the very ones he faced. One by one, the White were touched and ousted from the contest, and each with a smile stepped away.

A quick touch behind the knee and Eirikr, the last of the White, acquiesced and limped away.

He grinned, shrugging to his companions who were already sitting on the side.

Grinning in turn, Emanrasu knew the touch had been little more than a scratch, and his eyes followed the captain as he walked away.

A flash off to the side forced his attention back to the field. He narrowly dodged the strike that would have ended his challenge.

The Heater and The Hack

The confusion caused by the throng of trainees who suddenly rushed him was a little disorienting at first, and several times, he shifted his body enough to avoid being touched by a hare's hair.

Emanrasu settled into a rhythm of twisting and turning, his gaze roved around him, drawn by sound and movement, and perhaps... something more.

"I understand, now, why everyone spoke so highly of my grandfather's ability," Emanrasu thought. "I can anticipate everyone easily, but I won't be able to continue to fight indefinitely."

Emanrasu had begun to notice most of the fighters he was avoiding now—he had touched more than thrice already. Each resting before returning to the fray. The steady stream of bodies offered him no rest.

His pounding heart grew louder and more incessant, the pressure of blood in his eyes caused his vision to shift into a subtle soft pink. His tongue felt thick and dry.

The toll of these effects progressively hampered his senses.

He could feel and see his body slowing as the combatants became a mere blur. His reflexes struggled to react to every new opponent until, at last, he felt the graze slip along the side of his cheek.

Boldar's face burst into a radiant smile as he dropped heavily to one knee, leaning on the pitchfork with which he had just bested Emanrasu.

The thundering voice of Onred cut through the training field, "Blooded!"

"Blooded by Boldar!"

The roar of the trainees was deafening and not readily quieted.

Emanrasu trudged slowly through the throng over to the seating on the side of the training field. Mired in congratulatory opponents, he did not care if everyone knew he was exhausted, since now he could barely focus on those grabbing his forearm and pounding his back in merriment.

With the task now behind him, the energy within him slipped quietly away, and more than once, he was propped up by the townsfolk surrounding him. As he approached the edge of the training field, he was steadied by the massive grip of Rezua's hand, which dwarfed his shoulder. The throng dissipated, retreating into the training areas and starting impromptu sparring matches or training amongst themselves.

A waterskin was thrust into his hand. Looking up and struggling through the haze of exhaustion, Serrah's comfortingly beautiful visage met his gaze. Managing a weak smile, he lifted the skin and drank. The cold liquid devoured the ravages of thirst as it flowed in great gulps down his throat, and helped to moderate and slow the heavy beating of his heart.

With a cloth, Serrah reached up and wiped the beading streams of sweat several times before giving up and letting the rivers of salty liquid flow undisturbed. The shades of pink deepened to reds and browns as the sun silently slipped further past the horizon. The battle had lasted the entire evening, almost up to set.

Emanrasu took a deep breath and looked about. Lotheir and Bapak were still on the field conversing with Tarlis and Onred. Emanrasu touched Serrah's arm and, garnering her attention, nodded her to follow him.

Looking for Rezua, he found the meaty man standing behind him, as always, scribbling away at the parchment he had never parted from. Emanrasu lightly kicked the gargantuan shin, whereupon Rezua immediately let out an insincere yelp and threw himself to a knee.

"Help gather the White," Emanrasu told him, trying to stifle the grin as he reached out and placed a hand on Rezua's shoulder.

The Heater and The Hack

"Thank you, my friend, I needed that," he told the big monstrosity, then pushed him sharply just enough to force him off balance and sprawl upon the ground as Rezua's grin spread in the perfect mirror of Emanrasu's.

"Now pick yourself up, my large noggin-headed friend, and stop struggling to lessen the seriousness of the mood… at least for the next hand or half," Emanrasu told him as he stretched out his hand. "It is time."

Turning, he walked over to Tarlis, Onred, and the smiths. An unease formed, flushing through his veins. The chilling thought of leading without the counsel of the White left his mind covered in thick, pillowy layers of goose down. He stood before the older men, took a deep cleansing breath, letting it push unevenness up and out through his lips, where the words bolstered his resolve.

He gazed up at the sky, then looked at the smiths. "My apologies, Masters, I never expected this to draw out as long as it did, and it puts us further behind…"

"Nonsense," Bapak interrupted, exchanging a glance with Lotheir. "We have already discussed it and decided that we would rather have witnessed the display of skill we saw this day than shave off even two days of work."

Lotheir chimed in, "In my fifty-two mains, I have never seen the like. Master Emanra, we were honored to be present and to watch. You won out against sixty-three opponents, facing each fighter multiple times."

"Emanrasu, Lotheir. My name is Emanrasu," he told the arborwright.

"Yes, I know, and Bapak was given the name Bapaksu at birth. However, holding to the old Tubatonona language, Su is a title of honor. Thus, your name would literally mean Master Emanra. But I suppose that the study of languages is a tangent for another time."

Emanrasu felt the expected nudge from behind as his mountainous friend prodded him gently with the back of his hand, making faces and eye motions. As he glanced up at Rezua, he could tell his mountainous friend was impressed with Lotheir and seemed to expect Emanrasu to be similarly impressed.

Our Beginnings of Endings: Chapter Twenty-One

"I am sorry my knowledge is lacking in that vein," he replied to Lotheir.

"But I think Rezua might quite enjoy that conversation. However, we need to get onto business."

Turning to Tarlis and Onred, he lined out the request for materials the smiths had made, and of which he had committed the White to accompany them for protection.

"Yes, we are aware," Tarlis said. Onred only nodded, the muscles in his face twitching in the effort before they loosened, allowing a smile to sneak out. "We will leave tonight, and making haste, we should see the supplies and materials safely back to Bren before apex and four."

"This will still give you plenty of time to execute your weapons," Onred added, placing a hand on Lotheir's shoulder.

Onred's eyes shifted to Emanrasu, "My Black, with the commander's approval, I turn the training and responsibilities over to you."

He thumped his fist to his chest in a salute, the grin returning as he let his hand wave toward the townsfolk still out on the field. He leaned into Emanrasu, his lips close to his ear.

"Be proud, young man! Tarlis's unwavering faith in your abilities has once again been proven to be well-founded. You have mastered, in weeks, what most of us have been striving for moons and mains to master!"

Emanrasu nodded a short acknowledgment of Onred's words, but as he had none of his own in reply, he opted to shift the focus to the task at hand.

Striding over to the location where Onred first organized and subsequently orchestrated the town's training, Tarlis took a place on one side of him and Onred on the other.

"BREN!" Emanrasu's voice projected over the din of fighting.

The effect was almost immediate as sparring and conversations ceased, all eyes turning to Emanrasu.

"Gather!"

Once the inhabitants of Bren had gathered, Emanrasu continued, "The White have done their part. They have prepared us for the fight ahead. I say 'us' because, even though we…"—he waved a hand at Rezua and Serrah—"…have not lived in Bren long, we have developed a strong affinity for it—and for you, its people."

"I say this because the White have been called elsewhere. I want to say how proud Rezua, Serrah, and I are to be a part of this community."

"With their departure, I take up the role of leading your training. You have my thanks—and my trust. Are there any who object?"

Emanrasu paused while the people of Bren who were currently present glanced around in silence. He let the thought sink in for many moments, but there was only a single cough within the throng gathered.

"With that being said, and unchallenged, we are done for today. Bren! Dismissed!"

* * *

As the crowd dissipated, Emanrasu found himself approached by various residents who, clasping his arm, expressed their faith and dedication to seeing this through.

The training field was now almost empty, and Boldar approached, holding out his arm.

Emanrasu produced a smile, clasping the man's forearm with his. Boldar smiled back.

"It seems that I have had the honor of bookending your training in Bren!"

Our Beginnings of Endings: Chapter Twenty-One

"I can say for certain you bookended the formal portion of it, my good man. But I, for one, seem to always be learning. And if you study something with a critical eye," — he reached up and touched his cheek where Boldar had won his due — "you'll find that there are lessons in everything."

"Indeed," Boldar said, offering a slight bow as he turned and departed.

Emanrasu said his goodbyes to his mentors, Tarlis and Onred, and all of the White in turn. The comradery of the White extended not only to Emanrasu but also to the inclusion of Rezua and Serrah.

Emanrasu trailed behind the White as they left, walking with his friends — Serrah on his left, Rezua on his right.

He slowly halted, and after a step or two, his companions did likewise. Glancing at each other, then turning to look at Emanrasu, they waited.

"I need both of you to know that neither of you are ever far from my mind. Though I have been inundated with tasks concerning the welfare of Bren, and constantly training to become what we must have for the good of these people… I want you to understand that I would not—could not—do this, nor would I want to, without you both."

Emanrasu's heartfelt words brought a trickle of tears to Serrah's eyes, and as she wiped them away, Rezua's emphatic, overzealous reaction made her smile.

"I—knew—it!" Rezua verily shouted to the sky.

His grin crinkled the corners of his eyes. "You really can't live without me!"

Emanrasu shoved the big pile of walking muscle without moving him even a hair, finding, as always, the act was not the action. Ceasing his attempt to emphasize his appreciation, and as he turned back to Serrah, Rezua suddenly took several steps back and landed heavily on the ground.

After his feigned defeat, Rezua laughed, and in a mockingly friendly tone, said, "You really are a master!" With a wink and his smile emphasizing his banter,

The Heater and The Hack

Rezua climbed to his feet. Emanrasu and Serrah simply shook their heads as the three made their way back to the inn, chatting and discussing the events of the day.

As the trio entered the inn and made their way to the stairs, they found the Great Room busier than usual — abuzz with the events of the day.

Emanrasu's stamina and skill took center stage in the majority of the conversations. With animated gestures, the townsfolk continued to show their appreciation and approval, even after Emanrasu started climbing the stairs with his friends.

As they approached Emanrasu and Rezua's room, Serrah reached out and grabbed Emanrasu's hand. "Tomorrow will be... different, without Tarlis and the White here, almost reminiscent of the time you were off to Erald, looking for help. But I am glad you are staying here this time..." she trailed off and squeezed his hand before letting it go.

"Good night, Black," she said, pausing in her tracks.

"Well, how does it feel, using my grandfather's title on me?"

"I am not sure yet, but I suppose we shall get used to it," she said, eyes sparkling as she turned away and slipped quietly down the hallway. His eyes followed her down the hall, and he saw her briefly glance up at him just before she stepped into her room. He could hear Rezua returning from down the hallway.

He glimpsed what might have been a smile on her face just before her door closed, but... it could have been the play of light from the lanterns in the hall. Emanrasu paused briefly at his door, just before Rezua's large shovel-like hand pushed him aside.

Without comment, the big man stepped through the doorway and into their room, quickly closing the door until only a narrow crack remained. As he slowed the closing of the door, Emanrasu saw him staring intently from behind the door. Just before the door shut completely, Rezua batted his eyes rapidly several times, smiled sweetly, and produced a grin that only he seemed to be able to make. He pushed the door shut with a loud, emphatic thud that echoed down the hallway. Rezua's muffled laughter rang out from behind the door.

Emanrasu shook his head and breathed in deeply but stifled his inevitable sigh with a grin. He opened the door and closed it behind him with a thud. "Rezua, my love, I am home!"

The corner of the pillow grazed the side of his head as he sidestepped it. He reached down, picked the pillow up, and looked at Rezua. "Why, thank you! I was in need of a second pillow upon which to support my enlarged head tonight."

Rezua's face went blank for a moment before he broke into a rolling fit of laughter.

"If only I could be privy to his thoughts right now," Emanrasu mused as he flipped the pillow back to Rezua.

He sat on the edge of his bed and suddenly felt the remnants of energy drain from him as his body begged him for rest. The aches he had ignored for a significant portion of the day were magnified with the loss of energy and pulled at him. From his sitting position, he leaned slowly to his side, letting his head settle on the pillow...

The pains of the day dissipated as the colors coalesced. Almost immediately, the scene formed into the familiar field of green Earth with the Tree and the Sun in the Sky. The Dragon and Phoenix, seemingly in the perpetual swirling dance, projected satisfaction without the why.

"I feel that I have made strides today. My destiny, or the end goal of my choices, be it either or neither, seems closer now than this morning," Emanrasu declared in a clear dream-laden whisper.

The Dragon rumbled back, "You are closer than you know, Black. The Cadre is near-at-hand, and though Telk's transition has placed another in his stead, our representatives are—now—all within your grasp. Your recognition of them is crucial, though you should not struggle with it needlessly. What will be—is already, and what is already—will be as always."

"Place your focus on rest and recover your strength as the culmination of your first trial is close upon you."

"Yes," Emanrasu said. "The brigand threat shall be handled within days, and the people of Bren can rest easier with them gone."

"No," the Sky and the Earth whispered in unison, breaking their usual silence.

The Earth shuddered. "Your trial will not be so easy, but do not despair. What things are—are not always what they appear."

"Preparations made—transform possibilities," said the Sky. "Your diligent preparation bodes well for your possibilities."

"Sometimes, I long for the simple rest I used to have, where dreams were only dreams," Emanrasu said with a mental sigh.

The Phoenix broke into an unsettling high, high-pitched shrieking laughter. "For you, it was never! Emanrasu, your path always!"

The Dragon finished with grumbling vibrations. "Your choices led you always to dream of us; it has never been—not so. Our influences through the Heater and the Hack, and through your growing connections to us, allow you to focus, understand, and remember. Your acceptance helps your focus."

"As for your rest…" The harmonious response resounded in a way Emanrasu had never felt. This was not a simple heard response… The Dance responded in every way Emanrasu could perceive—sight, sound, touch, taste—as well as sensations he could not begin to describe.

As the response faded, the darkness swarmed over Emanrasu with a soft, warm blanket of encompassing nothingness as dreamless sleep took him.

To Leading with Reason: Chapter Twenty-Two

"The need and want for leadership is engrained in each of us. The want to be protected and the need to protect is a constant that drives us all. Beyond this, the remembrances and considerations of those who provide lessons of life fill our lives with joy and sorrow. Prepare yourself and honor the fallen in the same manner as the life they led."

—RCotD—

The aches permeated his sleep, dragging him back to wakefulness. Every muscle he had in his body seemed to be screaming for relief—from the muscle on the outside of his smallest toe to the one that rode up his inner thigh—twisted in tight little balls. Even his eyelids ached in protest. Emanrasu lingered in bed, not relishing the pain—but accepting it.

As he swung his feet to the cold, hard, unforgiving wood floor, his mind steeled enough to attempt the start of the day.

Emanrasu heard a sound and turned his head as the creaking and stretching of the webbing on Rezua's bed threatened to leave him on the floor.

As he watched, Rezua groaned, swung his feet to the floor, and stood. Then, without a word, he turned up the wick on a lantern and scurried back under the blankets.

"Why?" Emanrasu asked, raising a tired eyebrow. Then he sighed. "Never mind. I'm too exhausted to even try to understand you today."

He drew a deep breath, lungs tight with ache. Even the air felt thick and heavy today, weighing on him like a score of blankets.

Standing, he raised his arms above his head, elongating himself in a stretch that tugged at every muscle from his feet to the tips of his fingers.

Savoring one last breath, drawn and exhaled quietly, he heard Rezua's soft snoring, signifying he had slipped back to sleep.

The Heater and The Hack

Shoving the pains and aches from his mind, he picked up the Heater and the Hack and started his morning ritualistic dance. However, instead of the deliberate ritualized movements, he allowed himself to move with a chaotic irregular flow. He could feel his body slip naturally into positions of strength, and without pain, his body glided through motions he could not remember practicing.

The movements felt right, and he paid attention to the positions and the ability to attack and defend from each of them. They were not all the best positions, but they were solid stances and pain-free. Mostly, they felt natural.

As Emanrasu brought his little morning ritualistic exercises to an end, the pain in his muscles returned. He found himself leaning into positions that did not cause undue pain.

He scratched his head and stretched his arms, now holding the sword and the shield high above his head. Somehow, he was starting to enjoy the aches. He grinned at the thought, and after dressing, slipped quietly out into the hallway.

As the door closed behind him, he heard the scribbling of quill on parchment. Emanrasu only shook his head and let his feet make their way to the stairs as they had done so many times before.

As he placed his foot on the first step, he made a vow to himself.

"Keep up the appearance. If they are to have hope, they must have something to believe in."

"Good morning, Black!" came the enthusiastic greeting from Boldar.

His greeting was immediately mirrored by the table full of folk and half a dozen sprinkled throughout the Great Room.

Emanrasu glanced up, subtly struggling to stand straighter and project a sense of well-being he did not feel. "Good morning, Boldar! I trust you shall save some coin for later?" He grinned at what he hoped was a well-placed tease.

To Leading with Reason: Chapter Twenty-Two

"Yes, sir, I would not spend it all on this lot," his hand indicated the companions seated with him, whereupon there was a flurry of pushing and pulling as they all had a go at Boldar, comradery reminiscent of the White and their gentle teasing and banter back at the Griffon.

Boldar smiled all the while, and as the ruckus settled, Emanrasu spoke once more.

"I am trusting that you will—all—be at training today. We have a lot of new things to go through, and—we—need to make sure we are as prepared as possible."

"Yes, sir," came the slightly out-of-sync flurry of replies from nearly everyone there.

Emanrasu felt flush with joy as he thought back to the distrusting attitude they had shown on that first night. The resilience of the townsfolk was a joy for him to behold. Knowing that, regardless of the outcome of the upcoming conflict, these people would continue to foster a sense of protectiveness gave him the strength to shrug off the aches. He nodded to them and turned, almost tripping over a little girl.

The sudden, unexpected twisting to avoid her reinforced his struggle for composure as the path of pain raced from his left knee up through his neck. He winced with a grunt he was unable to stifle.

The little girl was ushered back by a woman—bandaged heavily throughout her torso. Serrah, too, was motioning the girl back while helping to keep the woman steady and upright.

"Serrah," Emanrasu said, his composure returning somewhat.

Serrah promptly replied, "Black, this is Arianis and her daughter Kaurin; they are…"

"...the only survivors. Yes, to my knowledge, they are, but we still hold out hope, as there are at least two others unaccounted for," Emanrasu replied in a tone that was unexpectedly curt.

Serrah's expression never wavered despite his curtness. His heart and eyes silently pleaded with her for forgiveness that he felt his new role as leader wouldn't allow him to express openly.

"Yes... hope," Serrah confirmed. "Arianis insisted on thanking you personally for your attention to the aftermath of the attack."

Arianis struggled clumsily in an uncooperative curtsy until she gave up and offered her arm, which Emanrasu took.

As he grasped her arm, his other hand reached out and grasped her elbow, providing her additional support as she wavered.

Serrah moved to help the woman steady herself but found it almost impossible with the numerous wounds upon her back and sides. She gave in and stepped around to help steady her as Emanrasu had.

The woman, Arianis, looked up at Emanrasu. "Thank you for your attention and help..."

"...I really didn't..." Emanrasu interrupted, but was cut short by the woman's dismissive hand as she waved it to curtail his words.

"Thank you for your attention and help in protecting the people of Bren and your consideration while retrieving the fallen in the aftermath of the attack.

"We have suffered under the brigand threats for mains, with no one stepping up to address it. Until you, that is." Arianis squeezed Emanrasu's arm in emphasis as she finished.

"I just want you to know that we..." she glanced around and reached out for the girl's hand, bringing her closer, though she stayed half behind her mother's skirt.

To Leading with Reason: Chapter Twenty-Two

"…are grateful, and she wanted you to have this."

She ushered the girl forward, almost pushing her toward Emanrasu.

"Go on," she told the girl.

Emanrasu let go of Arianis's arm, relinquishing his support to Serrah. He turned and faced the girl, kneeling to put her more at ease, though he instantly regretted it as the deep, lingering aches wrenched at his every muscle. His eye twitched slightly, but his gesture of kneeling seemed to bolster the girl's courage, and gingerly, she stepped forward, holding out her hand. In her hand, she held a pendant, which was no more than a small rectangular tile of wood on a string.

Kaurin hesitated and started to turn back to her mother.

"Tell him, Kaurin," Arianis urged the girl, nudging her slightly from behind.

Eyes on the floor, she turned to face Emanrasu. Frowning, Kaurin faltered, then began with a whisper, "Telk…"

The girl took a deep breath and blurted out, "Telk gave me this before we left on the trip.

"He said it was for good luck and that if we had it with us we would be safe and then we got attacked which I thought was bad but then momma was able to get us home and that was good but Telk died because he gave it to me and I want you to be safe…" the tears welled up in the young girl's eyes as she spouted the river of words, holding out the pendant.

He accepted it from her, and a smile shone across her face. Her mother, Arianis, visibly relaxed and smiled as well. It appeared the gifting was a fulfillment of some kind for the two of them.

His gaze shifted from the little girl to the pendant. His eyes opened wide, jaw slackening, as he noted a subtle likeness between this pendant and Rezua's.

The Heater and The Hack

Tentatively, he turned the pendant over in his hand, fingers brushing across the familiar carvings. Tubatonona symbols encircled an engraved shield and sword, reminiscent of—if not identical to—the ones on Rezua's.

The pendant was small yet intricately crafted—polished oak, smoothed with care. It felt almost exactly like Rezua's in the hand. The same surprising weight. The same quiet pull.

But where Rezua's was plain, this one bore a blue stone set into the upper half. It caught the light with a subtle shimmer, glowing faintly as though lit from within. The lower portion... that soft green tinge again—like moss caught in wood grain.

His fingers continued flipping it, slowly, unconsciously, as his thoughts began to churn.

*　　*　　*

This pendant, like Rezua's, embodied the Dance.

But...

Blue for the Sky. Green for the Earth.

If that were true, then the Sun, Phoenix, Dragon, and Tree would be...

He paused. The thought hovered—too large to finish.

"This blue stone," he murmured, not quite sure if he meant to say it aloud, "it must represent the Sky. Does that mean..."

"That means... Rezua's pendant..." Each thought drifted—just beyond reach— floating away when he got close. He had to let it go, but he knew that he would have to look into this deeper. For now, the day stretched before him, and his duties would not wait for the depth of investigation needed.

He looked the young Kaurin in her eyes, and despite her initial shyness, her gaze did not waver.

"Telk gave it to you to keep you safe. I think he knew that it would do him no good since he was willing to give his life to protect as many people as he could. I think... I think he wanted—you—to have this special protection. So that even if he was unable to succeed, he knew you would be safe. What do you think?"

"Well... but..." Her eyes welled up once more as they spoke of Telk and his protection of her.

"And..." Emanrasu reached out and took Arianis's hand, pulling her closer to her daughter. "And... you—know—it helped to keep your mother safe, too. Even though she got hurt, she is still here by your side."

Her face brightened at the suggestion her pendant kept her mother safe, too. She peered up at her mother with a smile and slipped her little petite hand into her mother's.

"I think you're right; I should keep it."

Emanrasu reached out, looping the string around her neck and gently settling it against her chest.

"I am going to have my very large friend find you and take a look at it. Do you mind?"

She seemed to perk up at the question.

"You mean the man with the book? Telk's friend?"

"Why, yes, I believe that would be the one."

Kaurin reached out with both hands, placing one on each of Emanrasu's cheeks. She steadied her gaze and took a breath.

"That would be nice; Telk liked him and talked about him a lot," she blushed a little and added, "he talked about you a lot, too... he liked you and the big man a lot."

The Heater and The Hack

Emanrasu blinked back the tears welling in his eyes as he continued to struggle with the magnitude of Telk's true sacrifice.

In light of the revelation of this new pendant, everything seemed in flux.

He took a deep breath, reached up, and gently took her little hands in his. He looked at her steadily, and still, her gaze never wavered.

"I think we shall become good friends," he told her. "Maybe we will have adventures together sometime; wouldn't that be fun?"

The profound emotional tone of Kaurin's reply seemed to soften amidst thoughts of the adventures awaiting.

"I would like that, and I think Telk would be happy if I adventured, too."

"Mother..." her tone shifted to a more serious one as she turned to her mother. "...when you feel better, we shall go on an adventure with 'manrasu."

Arianis gazed down at her daughter without speaking.

Kaurin softened her tone, "It would be all right for us to have an adventure, wouldn't it? Maybe we could pretend to take Telk, too. He always talked about adventuring and saving the world."

Her eyes welled up yet again, and she swiped at the tears with the back of her wrist. Emanrasu broke, and to maintain his composure, he glanced around, taking in the scene that had unfolded without his knowledge. Serrah and Arianis seemed to be holding back tears, but the men in the Great Room had fallen silent.

Some of the men had let their heads drop, while others were stoic, though tears welled in many and streamed down more than one cheek.

Boldar, in particular, sat stiff in his chair, his face and jaw set in stone as the little salt-laden tears snuck down his face.

Emanrasu pulled her to him and hugged her briefly before letting her go and standing. He laid his hand on her head, looking at Arianis.

To Leading with Reason: Chapter Twenty-Two

"We will plan something in the future if you are willing and of a mind. After the rest of this..." Emanrasu said as he waved an inclusive hand, "...has been dealt with."

Arianis leaned in, wrapped her arms around him, and hugged Emanrasu unexpectedly. She reached up, placing a hand on his shoulder, pulling him down slightly. As she reached up, she whispered in his ear, "Thank you... thank you, thank you, thank you!"

She let him go and pushed him away slightly. She reached down, snagged up Kaurin's hand, and headed toward her recovering room. Serrah paused briefly and caught his eye, mouthing a silent thank you before following Arianis.

Emanrasu's mind was a flurry of thought as he made his way outside and stepped onto the path leading out to the road.

The words of the Dance invariably left their marks embedded permanently in his mind: "...Telk, while tragic by your standards... in the context of reality and life itself... was not the only option, but he was the one who ultimately chose his path... rejoice for him and the hearts and minds he reached."

"If Telk was an option for the Cadre, and he made his choice..." Emanrasu stopped short and closed his eyes as the convoluted path that led to finding that pendant in Kaurin's possession refused his every attempt to focus.

"If Kaurin is Sky, it would fit the cryptic words of the Dance, as Telk not being the only option..." he thought as he fought through the confusing turn of events.

The slight morning breeze, cool against his face, along with the incessant pounding from the smith, only served to exacerbate his inability to focus on the dance.

He took a deep cleansing breath and slowly started walking again, the crunch of the dust and dirt underfoot oddly annoying today.

The Heater and The Hack

"If... if Kaurin, by virtue of the pendant, is the Sky, and the pendant is... then Rezua... what is Rezua?" The scream of frustration built up from his toes, gathering speed as it rose. "Come on, Eman, you should know this; it is, or it isn't, but it should not be this hard to figure out." He raised his fist slightly and opened his mouth but stifled the response before it exploded.

He quickened his pace toward the training grounds. He could hear the men from the inn starting to trail out, no doubt heading this way.

"Let it go, let it go... Eman," he thought as he shrugged away an icy shudder. "Speak with Rezua later. He is more familiar with the Tubatonona language, so he might know if there is an actual connection."

Emanrasu's tightened shoulders and taut face loosened and settled intentionally as he continued his rapid stride.

"If Rezua does not know, garnering cryptic answers from the Dance might be a struggle."

Emanrasu, though not fully relaxed, could feel himself letting go of the anxiety around Telk and the pendant.

Stepping onto the training field, Emanrasu made his way to the instructor's box.

"Not quite a box," he thought as he made his way to it. "...more of a little raised bump in the ground." He shook his head at how ridiculous it sounded and smiled. "...a box..." he muttered softly.

Making his way across the field, he was peppered with a barrage of greetings acknowledging him as "Black," others a simple "good morning" or a nod of their head.

As he reached the instruction box, he turned and watched the gathering trainees. Almost all of them took it upon themselves to practice, while others instructed or offered help.

To Leading with Reason: Chapter Twenty-Two

Emanrasu made a mental note of the ones mentoring or helping others, adding it to a growing list in his mind.

The trainees began snuffing out the torches as the sun softened the darkness of the early morning sky while stragglers scurried to beat the rise.

Rezua and Serrah finally arrived, pausing a couple of times on their approach as Serrah's hand flitted in quick, subtle gestures to something she held in her palm. Once finished, she handed the item to Rezua, which he placed around his neck, and the two resumed progress toward Emanrasu.

"Rezua, there is another pendant," said Emanrasu as his friend drew closer. He raised an eyebrow. "Can you take a look?"

"Serrah mentioned that it looks like mine?"

"I believe so. Let me see yours," Emanrasu said.

Rezua took the pendant from around his neck and handed it to him.

Emanrasu examined the front, then flipped it over. "It's different—the stone is bright blue, where yours is only tinted," he said, pointing to the top half of the wooden tile.

"And… the text on the back looks similar. I believe it's Tubatonona, like yours," he said, looking at the back.

As the first sliver of sunlight pierced the fading darkness, Emanrasu returned the pendant to Rezua.

"Let me know what you find," Emanrasu said as he shoved the pendant into Rezua's hand and turned away to face the gathering throng.

"BREN! HEED!" His command echoed across the field. A hush fell over the trainees, followed by the soft shuffling as they began to organize.

The Heater and The Hack

The weight of his first words as their leader pressed upon him. Deserved or not, for the first time, his voice was not just his own but theirs, and he realized there was no turning back, at least not for him.

The trainees gathered, and the immediate quiet was striking against the low, subtle din of the trainees' practice.

At the forefront, Boldar stood as the trainees flowed together—no longer just a loose gathering but a rank and file that marked a genuine fighting force. As the Bren settled, Boldar seemed satisfied with the organization of his fighters and turned to face Emanrasu.

*   *   *

Boldar saluted, indicating they were ready.

Emanrasu inhaled deeply.

"Bren!" He shouted to focus their attention on him.

The stillness shattered as the response "BLACK!" thundered across the field as three-score fighters struck their chests in unison.

Emanrasu's breath caught. His jaw tensed, his chest tightening as the moment hit. He could see and hear—even more than that—he could feel they weren't just following orders. They believed. Noting that almost every face looking back at him mirrored the comrades around them, each carried a smile, though their eyes were disciplined and to the front. Boldar's face beamed as the last echo stilled.

Emanrasu hastily wiped the look of confusion and surprise from his face as he turned to glance at Serrah. Her grin mirrored those of the trainees, yet her stance was as staunch as any—rigid, immobile, immovable. She did not return his questioning gaze, standing as still as stone, her eyes fixed forward; yet, in that very stillness, the respect and admiration virtually exuded from her as if her statuesque presence itself spoke the acknowledgment of his transition to leader.

To Leading with Reason: Chapter Twenty-Two

As the weight of Tarlis, Onred, and the White's final instructions settled over him, he paused—letting it sink in.

A grin crept, slow and unstoppable, across his face, stretching to the very tips of his ears. He took a deep breath, holding it for a moment as anticipation surged through him—the command forming not only for them but for himself, a literal and figurative order to steady and prepare.

"BREATHE!" he commanded.

His voice rang through the training field, a sharp, forceful break in the silence, echoing from wall to wall. The trainees started, then grinned—relaxing as instructed—but were caught in the moment as the sound of his voice settled around them.

"Each of you!" Emanrasu projected to the gathered fighters, who were no longer stiff and staunch. "You have spent many weeks training for the culmination of the confrontation with the brigands. That moment for which we have all anticipated and dreaded is fast approaching."

His outstretched finger swept from side to side as it followed his gaze. A cough in the distance was swiftly muffled, followed by a whisper, then silence.

"I spent the last few days struggling with what to say today. There are many things we protect as we begin the end of this reign of indignation and terror."

Squaring himself on the Bren fighters in front of him, he slowly raised and opened his arms to indicate his inclusion of all, from the far left to the far right.

"All of you have made a sacrifice for your community." Murmurs of agreement slowly spread in hushed whispers before the quiet again took hold.

"One of our own stood in defense of those who could not stand for themselves!" Again, the hushed murmurs and the return to quiet.

The Heater and The Hack

"We train now, not for ourselves, but for the fallen, for the respected, and for those that hold our hearts!" The murmur spread louder, shortly followed by another hush.

"Those that know, understand! Those who do not know will!

"FROM THIS DAY—until the brigands fall…" Emanrasu's eyes locked with Boldar's; the glossy shine in both men's eyes spoke to the understanding of what was to come next.

"…until they fall and fall for good—WE FIGHT FOR TELK!"

The roar of affirmation sent a shiver down his spine, like the unexpected touch of a lost lover. This exuberance, only tempered by the image of Telk's smile and the unrelenting vision of the boy's broken body on the pile he had fought so desperately to protect, flashed through Emanrasu's mind.

Turning his head to his friends, he included both Rezua and Serrah in his declaration. "As the tears we shed fall, and the days move on, we must move on! Though we must never forget, we must also never dwell! We must honor, but not lose ourselves in grief!"

Emanrasu let tears escape and slip down his cheeks for all to see.

He gave pause, allowing the fighters to grieve or stew in anger.

But as the emotion subsided, Emanrasu spoke once again, "HOY! BREN!"

"BLACK!" came the response, the sound reverberating through the compound as if one.

"I will work with Boldar to finalize our internal leadership; we shall reform after the apex meal.

"DISMISSED!"

The collective sigh was palpable as the fighters relaxed and broke into various tasks, duties, and relaxations.

To Leading with Reason: Chapter Twenty-Two

Emanrasu approached Boldar and, in a whispering discussion, agreed upon the men and women who would round out the command. The focus was on those who consistently and openly offered others assistance or instruction.

"These will be the captains of our Bren fighters. Gather them and come to me."

Boldar nodded in response and rapidly went about gathering the Bren captains. Once the prospective captains had been gathered, and at Boldar's signal, Emanrasu stepped down and stood beside Boldar. He gazed at their faces, let his gaze fall to the ground… these are the ones that will form the core of Bren's defenses from this moment forward. He inhaled and looked up, letting out the breath.

Standing in front of the Bren leadership, he addressed them. "I have seen ability in all of you, but—more than that—I have seen the willingness to provide those in need with guidance and direly needed assistance."

His gaze swept across his captains, "From this moment forward, I consider you lot the captains of the Bren. If any of you would like to bow out of the duties that come with this step forward."

The captains, almost in unison, stepped out from in front of a man of slight build. Urged by the others, the man stepped forward. His steady and sure stride hid the man's poor health. "I am not much good in a fight," he said, punctuating the statement with the blood from a coughing fit. Somewhere in the distance, a dog barked, giving rise to a cascade of barking that caused a momentary pause.

As the cacophony died out, Emanrasu continued. "What is your name?"

"Galin, Black," he responded as he stifled yet another coughing fit.

"I am excluding you from our actual confrontation, but unless any of my other captains take issue with it, I am going to place you in charge of any dedicated one-to-one instruction for those that show promise but need direct attention, as well as those whose lack of ability would be detrimental to our efforts on the battlefield," he told Galin.

The Heater and The Hack

Looking around at his captains, "Do any object?" His question was punctuated by the sounds of scuffling and sparring that surged in the background as light clouds of dust drifted past.

His gaze touched and was returned by each captain with a shake of their head, and without hesitation, each indicated no objection, even offering a glance, a touch, or a nod of support to Galin.

"Then it will be so."

"Boldar will be the Bren Commander," Emanrasu informed them, "...this is not up for debate. The position is his to keep or lose as to his abilities." Emanrasu nodded to Boldar, who nodded back in acknowledgment.

"We will pick up again after apex, which is when I will make the announcements. Do any of you foresee resistance from the fighters we intend to field?"

Again, he settled his gaze on each in turn, and again, his gaze garnered a shake of the head.

"Then return by apex and form a line in front of the box facing the rank-and-file," he told them, "I will make the announcement, and we will break up the fighters by style and ability. Tonight, you will all meet in the inn at sundown, and I will go over our final plans so that we may train specifically on these components as we prepare to finally face these bandits and push them out of Bren, forever."

"Dismissed."

The captains departed and spread out as each was wont while Emanrasu turned and strode back to the box where Serrah stood conversing quietly with Rezua.

"I feel as if I have been speeding through mountainous terrain with as many ups and downs as I had today. I will be glad when we finally conclude this unsavory business with the bandits."

"We will have to make sure that they understand the cost of taking and holding the land around Bren."

To Leading with Reason: Chapter Twenty-Two

Emanrasu, Rezua, and Serrah stood in the box, watching the Bren as they went about addressing their morning routines. Since they were released until apex, some were left to handle needed tasks at home or elsewhere. Others, intent on mastering a skill or just understanding one, stayed on the training grounds, working with those who could help.

Emanrasu started to feel somewhat at ease, knowing Rezua would handle the pendant investigation. Just having Serrah nearby was also a comfort.

"She gives me more comfort than I am willing to acknowledge," he admitted quietly. His thoughts drifted back through all of the events with this woman they had met in the Bucket and Nail so many moons ago.

He looked around, letting his gaze settle casually on her as his thoughts drifted by. She suddenly glanced his way, locking eyes with him as the warm, welcoming smile grew across her face. He returned the smile.

"She knows how uncomfortable I am," he thought, his heart thumping heavier in his chest and quickening like a stampeding horse. His heart seemed freed and imprisoned all at the same time. His face turned red, though the air still held the bite of the morning chill.

Emanrasu heard Rezua cough, though it seemed forced, and he watched Serrah's eyes dart from him to the annoying mound of interruption. Her face, eyes crinkled with the intimately warm smile she had offered him, broke into a toothy expanse of enjoyment.

He glanced over at Rezua just in time to catch his eyes darting away and upward, following a non-existent cloud or bird in the sky as he rocked back and forth, heel to toe, his hands locked behind him, holding his quill and parchment journal.

"Black?" Boldar queried him. "We are almost ready, and apex is nearing. Do you want us to begin, or should we wait?"

Ripped from his thoughts of random secrets between his friends and focusing on Boldar's words, "...apex..."

The Heater and The Hack

The question came into focus, and Emanrasu studied Boldar, then let his gaze scan slowly over the training field. There were still a substantial number of the Bren absent, though, by the looks of the fighters streaming in from the street, this would soon be rectified.

As the gathering swelled, so did the muted din of voices. The drifting scent of someone's impromptu dinner sent a grumble through Emanrasu's midsection.

"You may wait," he said. "I believe I said after apex, and even if I didn't, giving a few extra moments seems prudent."

"Aye, Black," Boldar answered with a curt salute before returning to the captains to relay the message. They exchanged a few brief words among themselves and quickly settled on something—apparently without feeling the need to consult Emanrasu. As much as he wanted to guide and oversee every fighter, he knew he had to trust his subordinates to act in his stead. Leadership wasn't about control; it was about confidence in those beneath him.

The incessant tinking of the smith, striking in rhythm with the low grumble in his stomach, brought a grin to his face.

"And now… nobody wants to just come out and speak to me directly. At least now that I'm officially regarded as the Black," he mused, shaking his head. The grin, however, never wavered.

He exhaled sharply, amusement flickering in his gaze. "I suppose if I wanted to control everything, I should have had the smiths make me some toy soldiers. Not sure the bandits would take us seriously, though."

His imagination took hold. He pictured himself standing before the brigands' stalwart stone gates, an army at his back—a thousand strong, each soldier a masterpiece of exquisitely crafted ironwoods and precious metals.

"Hoy there!" he called out in his mind, adopting the booming authority of a battle-hardened commander. "If you just leave, we will allow you to go in peace; however…."

To Leading with Reason: Chapter Twenty-Two

Emanrasu's grin promptly faded as he shook off the random thought and refocused on the task at hand.

Watching the fighters as they flowed back onto the training field and merged with the rest of the Bren that had remained on the field, he realized how much Tarlis had taught him. Thinking back to that first lump on his head when Emanrasu had stepped into that dark, oppressive alley to save the stooped old man with the gray-white hair from the trio of unsuspecting street thugs. The lessons from that day to this had culminated in his leading a town of new fighters to reclaim their dignity, autonomy, and pride.

*　　*　　*

The flow of fighters slowed to a trickle and then quickly to a drip. Boldar, who had also been monitoring the incoming Bren, turned and looked at Emanrasu, who nodded. He turned to the captains, and together, they all positioned themselves as requested in front of the box.

"Bren!"

"Black!" came the surging reply from the field as the fighters formed rank and file.

Once the fighters were gathered, Emanrasu addressed them.

"As you all know, we have a seemingly monumental task ahead of us. The bandits have made themselves at home, and your livelihoods… your families… and the very ground beneath your feet now depend on your actions in the coming days!" His voice projected out across the field of Bren fighters as they returned his gaze.

"We will take back what is rightfully yours… and we—will—dissuade any who would think to stand against Bren in the future!"

The Heater and The Hack

Emanrasu paused to let his words sink in as the Bren fighters shifted uncomfortably at his words. Whether he was worried about the outcome or something unknown, he did not know, but this is what had to happen.

"To this end, we have trained… trained to be ready! On the morrow, we will focus more specifically on tasks… tasks that we will use to regain direct control of the roads around Bren!"

Emanrasu noticed Torsun had stepped onto the field and was headed to the box, skirting around the fighters currently assembled.

"Torsun is your chosen representative… as has been demonstrated numerous times! However… he has acknowledged a need… a need to provide more for this town than he has the capacity to give!"

Emanrasu motioned to Torsun to join him, and as he approached, it suddenly struck him that the tinking of the smiths was quiet. A lone dog and the birds in a nearby rustling tree were the only sounds other than his voice. The smell of the leather and dirt hung thick in the air.

He waited until Torsun stepped up next to him. "Torsun has allowed me to provide the spark."

"Bren! This… I swear to you! Should you follow me, we will be done, and you will be back to your normal lives within six days. But… we still have work… and Boldar," Emanrasu pointed to Boldar, "and the captains I have selected… will be instrumental in carrying out my wishes."

The uncomfortable demeanor of the Bren erupted in a volcanic release of affirmations. The "yesses" and "yeahs" melded with the "ayes," and various other indicators of approval rang out over the formation like a wave.

Boldar glanced at Emanrasu and made as if to quell the outburst, but Emanrasu signaled to let them release their pent-up frustration.

To Leading with Reason: Chapter Twenty-Two

Emanrasu let the men and women vent for a few moments before he held up his hand.

The gathered Bren quieted as if the collective had breathed in and was now holding its breath to see what came next. The change in the direction of the breeze brought the acrid smell of the forges.

Emanrasu turned to Boldar. "Boldar! As the Black, and by virtue of the test by battle, and appointment by Torsun, I hereby appoint you as my commander, and the men behind you as your captains. Each position is one of honor and merit, which may be lost as quickly as it was won."

Emanrasu stepped down and offered an arm to Boldar, who instead slammed his fist to his chest in a salute. "Black!"

At this point, he reached out and grasped Emanrasu's arm, looked him in the eye, and nodded.

Emanrasu returned to the box, turned around, and faced Bren's fighters once more.

"Ultimately, it all falls to me, but I need to drive home..." he thought briefly before he addressed the Bren.

"Boldar is my representative," Emanrasu impressed upon the captains as they looked up at him. "His word is—my—word and should be treated as such!"

Only nods greeted him after this, and not one of them moved a hair otherwise. Staunch and invariably immobile to the main, these captains were.

Looking out over the fighters, "These captains... these captains are representative of Boldar, and by extension,—me. They will be treated as such!" he called out to the field.

"You..." he projected his voice as he reached out both hands to include everyone there. "You and your families are what we fight to protect! Let your families... let them be the shehchih to your girochih... let them be the spark... the spark

401

needed to set a flame amongst us all... a flame that will raze the brigands from this land, ONCE and for ALL!"

The roar from the fighters was deafening, and the thumping of chests in acknowledgment of this course was thunderous.

Emanrasu held out his hands, palms down, to quiet the fighters, but still, it was a few moments before the order returned, and all eyes were again facing him.

"Boldar, with your captains, work to divide the Bren into companies of men of one mind. As I step aside, take the box. I will assist, or guide as needed, but for now, you are in charge!"

Emanrasu thumped his fist on his own chest to acknowledge Boldar, and a lone voice, somewhere in the back of the rank-and-file, rejoiced in Boldar's appointment. "Way to go, Boldar!"

Boldar grinned, returned the salute, and stepped to the box.

Emanrasu, Rezua, and Serrah followed Torsun down from the box and to the edge of the field, where Bapak and Lotheir stood.

"Masters, what news have you?" he asked the smiths.

"We have procured the needed supplies, and we can guarantee the weapons within five days at most. And that is only if Lotheir and I must attend them all by ourselves," Bapak replied, a grin sprouting and instantly withering across his face. His eyes were darkened with circles, indicating that they had most likely ridden throughout the night.

A glance at Lotheir revealed the same gaunt look of Bapak, but both men's eyes were alight, crinkling and reinforcing the wrinkles at the corners.

"They appear to be satisfied and confident," Emanrasu thought.

"If we have the time, rest well and oversee the weapons directly. They do not need to be convincing from any direction but the ones we present to the brigands."

"We will, Master Emanra," Lotheir offered. "You might consider the advice yourself. Running a small army on little—or no—sleep is begging for defeat." The smith shrugged as a yawn took him, and he scrunched his eyes, his mouth gaping wide. Bapak suddenly turned away, though the reflection of Lotheir's yawn was evident in his vocalization.

Bapak shuddered upon finishing his yawn and turned back to the group with a grin.

Bapak admitted, still grinning, "I was going to deny our tiredness, but I feel I would be dismissed as untruthful now."

Emanrasu grinned, and the two smiths turned and retreated back to their smithies. He turned to his companions. "Do I really look in need of rest?" he asked.

"You do seem to be a bit less energetic," Serrah said as Torsun nodded in agreement.

Rezua nodded in agreement as well, but in typical fashion, he could not remain silent. "You look much like a lone mother with seven newborns standing in a closet with no place to lay." The slow wink of Rezua punctuated the implication of Emanrasu's perception of time, which might have worked if everyone else around them had followed suit.

"Your attempt at hilarity notwithstanding, I am starting to lose steam, however..." Emanrasu flexed his arms a little and stretched his back and neck. "I seem to have worked out most of the aches from yesterday, though I may stiffen up as they return through the inactivity of sleep."

Together, the four made for the stables, verifying the carts, horses, and oxen needed in the coming days. Though there were quite a few, thinking this might be just barely enough, Emanrasu tasked Torsun with gathering half again as many.

"Better too many than too few," he said to Torsun as the two parted, Torsun to take care of the provisioning, and Emanrasu, with Rezua and Serrah, off to the inn for a meal and the meeting with the Bren command.

Without a word, Serrah veered off, slipping toward the kitchens and the recovery room.

The Great Room was quiet, save for the fire's gentle crackle, spitting and popping its slow, steady song.

Emanrasu sat down at one of the tables and stifled a yawn of his own, then stood and stretched to try and stave off his exhaustion long enough to meet with the Bren commander and his captain.

Rezua grabbed the chair from the other side of the table and took it to the side of the room, trading it for the more monstrous Rezua-sized chair that someone had set there.

The mountain of man grinned as he brought back the forest's worth of wood that must have gone into making his chair.

He set it next to the table but found that the chair's bulk did not allow him to put his legs under the table.

"I suppose I must talk to someone about a decent-sized table," he said with a grin. "Are you able to meet with your commanders tonight? I could go and inform them if you need to rest."

" Captains. Well... In truth... Tarlis is the only—never mind. No need to put it off. We need to make sure everyone has as much time to prepare as possible, since our time is quickly coming upon us."

Rezua looked at the sunlight on the floor of the Great Room as it streamed through the window.

To Leading with Reason: Chapter Twenty-Two

"Then, I suppose if you allow me to, I will head back and prompt them to finish up quickly as you are eager to speak with them on the logistics surrounding the confrontation with the bandits," he gazed at Emanrasu with a sidelong glance and a raised eyebrow.

"Yes, I suppose that would not be the worst idea you have ever had.

"That honor goes to you for thinking you could ride the cow that young boy had."

"That was no ordinary cow," complained Rezua, "I swear it was smarter than any man."

"…certainly smarter than you," Emanrasu said, winking at the large man.

Rezua stood, "Surely you do not jest! I swear the cow whispered in Tubatonona as it scraped me off using the fence post!

"In any case, I am sure it could come up with a better strategic plan, were we to properly consult it!" Rezua exclaimed over his shoulder as he slipped out of the inn.

"Stay the course, Emanra Su, your first trial and the gathering are near at hand."

The warmth of the words surrounded Emanrasu like a blanket, the subtle soft tone of the Earth gentle and supportive…

Emanrasu started as a hand took hold and shook his shoulder. Jerking his head off the table, he looked around to gather his bearings.

Serrah, it was only Serrah…

"Are you alright?"

Emanrasu cleared his throat a bit, "Yes, I am a bit tired and will be glad when I can finally stretch out and rest properly."

"Where is Rezua?" she asked as she set the food upon the table.

The Heater and The Hack

The exquisite aroma of the delectable dishes reached down deep, and the rumbling in his midsection returned with a vengeance as his eyes roamed over the feast.

"He, too, thinks I need to sleep sooner rather than later. So he was off to gather Boldar and the captains, pressing them to finish quickly in order that they might meet me sooner."

"Well, then, eat while you can. We can be certain you do not want to get your hands in the way of Rezua's maw and meat shovels!" she said with a wink and a grin.

The food quenched the rumble in his gut, providing sustenance that he—only now—realized he had none of today. His focus on preparations had taken precedence over his need for food, but now it felt as though he had never eaten in his life.

The rest of the evening rapidly passed, and with Rezua's return, the banter during the meal provided a well-needed break. It seemed to last forever, but for a moment, as they waited for Boldar and the captains.

The expansion and contraction of Emanrasu's perception of time made it hard to track the actual expenditure of time.

The commander and his captains arrived, and Emanrasu broke down the concepts of the plan to present themselves as unorganized townsfolk with inadequate weapons and indecisive dedication to the confrontation itself.

His plan accounted for nearly everyone in the town—anyone who could walk and lift a hoe or pitchfork had a place in it. But beyond sheer numbers, he knew the sight of them moving as one would be unforgettable—shaping the young, instilling a strength that would echo through the community for mains to come.

The Bren Command, the agreed title of the group, concurred with his intricate plan, and though discussion of small details tweaked the overall implementation, they seemed to revel in the idea.

The evening finished, and once the Bren Command had departed, Serrah's soft hand ushered him to his room.

He tried to brush her off, but she insisted on accompanying him until he was stretched out on his bed. Her soft, warm lips on his forehead made him smile as he drifted off, imagining her lips touching his.

Entwining Hope in Despair: Chapter Twenty-Three

"In the weight of leadership, it is crucial to understand the price of your actions and inactions. The risks weighed upon the greater good, whether community or cosmic, are never easy in light of one's personal costs. Regardless of the losses incurred, it is critical to understand the underlying lessons. Understanding that losses can provide the drive to keep moving, cherish each loss, and make it your own."

–RCotD–

T he exhaustion clung to him, permeating his body. Emanrasu opened his eyes, lying still, weighing the cost of movement. Unsure how late it was when he turned in, he assumed it was much earlier than usual.

The light from the night lantern danced, playing in the shadows around the room. The biting cold shored up his breath as it hung in the air, reinforcing the need to resolve the siege from the brigands as fast as possible.

Rezua's rhythmic breathing and the occasional light thuds from someone trudging the hallway were the only sounds that broke the silence. The mild, acrid odor of burnt wood mixed with the pungent smell of the chih that had been used to light it.

Emanrasu sat up and swung his legs over the side of the bed. He shuddered at the chill of the icy floor.

Gathering his clothes, which had been hung neatly over one of the chairs at the table, he quickly dressed.

The harvestmain will soon be upon us, and with all of Bren diverted into preparing defenses, the harvest will pass undone—lest we swiftly handle this threat. It will be moons—or seasons—before another chance arises, and most likely, all harvests until then will be forfeited to the brigands.

The Heater and The Hack

Emanrasu shook his head, "Bren will not hold out for long should the bandits decide to force the issue first."

He stretched, muscles still tender from the leadership trials but easing more this morning. As he moved through his morning dance, the odd discomfort of yesterday faded away.

The realization came upon him that he seemed to have noticeably fewer pains since he awoke. It was almost as if his body was subtly using other muscle combinations to compensate and bypass the aches.

Upon finishing his dance, he retrieved a clean set of clothes, setting them aside for his bath.

He stretched again, feeling his muscles extend smoothly without pain.

Upon finishing his dance, he retrieved a clean set of clothes, setting them aside for his bath. He stretched again, feeling his muscles extend smoothly without pain.

Rezua took a sudden breath—then exploded with a sneeze that rattled the lantern glass.

Emanrasu closed his eyes and smiled. Without turning around, he acknowledged the no longer slumbering mass-of-bone-and-muscle. "Good morning, my very large friend."

"You should turn up the lantern, stoke the fire, and let me sleep until the sun lightens the sky."

"I had thought of doing just that, briefly, very, very briefly…"

Emanrasu had steeled himself for the inevitable pillow or shoe that never came. Looking around, he saw Rezua sitting on the edge of his bed, gently touching the floor with his toes as one would test the waters before jumping in.

"It's still cold, my large, overly pampered, hairless, bear of a man."

Entwining Hope in Despair: Chapter Twenty-Three

"I can see that, or more to the point, I can succinctly feel it," Rezua said.

"Succinctly?" Emanrasu grinned teasing. "Is that a Tubatonona word drawn from the sheath of your book to brandish me with?"

Rezua perked up. "Well, now that you mention it…"

He stood and reached over, drawing something from his pouch. Emanrasu watched the big man shudder like a dog fresh from the lake throwing off water.

"Looks like the cold caught you unaware despite your gentle attempts to ready yourself for it."

Rezua's shudder passed, and without responding, he turned and faced Emanrasu, his eyes bright and sparkling, his mouth drawn back at the corners of his face like a loaded crossbow.

He held in one hand the two books he had acquired in Erzt and, in the other, dangled three pendants.

"Sit, my mousy little man without meat or muscle, and I will bury you in a volley of words as would bury a man without such a magnificent title as the Black!"

"I, my skinny little lord, am here to amaze you with delights beyond your comprehension in such a manner as to leave you reeling, but staunchly eager for more."

"The magnificent object to which I am now provid—"

Emanrasu interjected, "Oh, you drown me in words without saying a thing, Brute! What are you on about?"

Though his eyes still danced, Rezua's grin slipped from his face as he looked over.

"Sit, you must see this," said the big man, setting the books and pendants on the table.

The Heater and The Hack

He then stepped over to the lantern, turned it up, and brought it back.

Emanrasu sat down and picked up one of the pendants. The blue stone immediately suggested that this was Kaurin's pendant, the one that Telk had given her.

"This is Kaurin's?"

"Yes, she allowed me to take it on the condition that I only show you. She said Telk had told her to keep it secret, revealing it only to the very big man and the Black."

Rezua's voice quickened. "She didn't know what the Black was—until she heard them call you that. She wouldn't stop pestering Arianis to meet you."

Rezua grinned and took a deep breath, forcing himself to slow down.

Emanrasu pored over Kaurin's pendant with its bright blue stone. Rezua reached over and slid the next one in front of him.

"This is mine," he said. "What do you see?"

Emanrasu gazed at Rezua's pendant and flipped it over and back. "Nothing is striking about it, nothing that sets it apart. Not like Kaurin's."

Emanrasu felt a little disappointed, and his shoulder sank a little as the frown grew on his face. "I had hoped that there was more of a connection amongst the pendants," he told his large companion.

"As did I, but with the plainness of mine, the blue stone is out of place, though it could have been done to give it a bit more jeweler's look to it. Until…" Rezua reached over and turned the third pendant so that it was face up on the table and slid it over next to Rezua's.

Lightning surged up Emanrasu's spine and his jaw slackened in concert. "The… Their… This can't be a mere coincidence! Where did you get this?" Emanrasu stuttered, trying to force the words before his comprehension could fully envelop the meaning of the pendants.

He stared down at the new pendant and its bright green stone inset in the bottom half of the pendant.

Rezua moved with sudden purpose, retrieving the Heater and laying it sigil-side up on the table. "Look at the colors," Rezua said, poking at the shield.

Emanrasu looked at the colors of the shield, glanced at the pendants, and back at the shield. "They are..." He took Kaurin's, placed it on the blue field of the emblem, and the new pendant, positioning it on the field of green. "They are, they seem... perfectly matched..."

"Exactly," whistled Rezua, his voice cracking like a young boy getting the first hairs of mainhood. "You asked where I got it, and you will never guess in a hundred lifetimes. Kaurin's—mother—Arianis!"

Emanrasu glanced up at Rezua to determine if this was in jest. Excited, the big man was throwing hands and arms alike in all directions as he emphasized his words. Emanrasu had learned over the mains that this was a sign of absolute honesty from the big man.

"Her mother?"

"Yes!" Rezua exclaimed, "She said it has been in her family for... well... since it was given to her grandmother!"

Rezua grabbed Emanrasu's shoulder. "Can you even comprehend how unlikely this would be?"

The puffs of air from Rezua's gesturing, danced with the lantern flame, flitting it back and forth, gently, as if in rhythm with his excitement.

"But that is not all! Turn them over..." he said, his hand hovering, as though tempted to flip them himself. "Go ahead and turn them over."

The Heater and The Hack

Emanrasu took a deep breath and picked up the pendants. The heavy beating of his heart mirrored the weight of the Dance. All of his dreams pressed in as he hesitated, then placed them both on the table.

His mind and emotions spun in undulating waves while the dancing colors of his dream had swirled before materializing in the familiar Dragon, Phoenix, and the others.

He closed his eyes and felt the heft and texture of the Tree mixing somehow with the burning oil of the lamp and flipped them over.

He opened his eyes and focused on the two pendants before him, feeling the palpable connection of this little wooden tile to the Tree of Life pulling his focus into the center of the pendants.

*   *   *   *

The same exquisitely detailed shield and sword adorned both, and though they were uncolored, both were unmistakably the Heater and the Hack. Around the Heater and the Hack image were Tubatonona symbols encircling the shield and sword. On each, they were distinctly different.

The green stoned pendant inscribed with symbols in repeating patterns.

The blue glyphs were shorter in length, but with different repeated patterns.

"Tell me you translated these…"

Rezua slowed and stopped; his eyes fell to the floor, and if there were dirt on the floor, Emanrasu felt the big man would have kicked at it.

Emanrasu's heart skipped.

Entwining Hope in Despair: Chapter Twenty-Three

"Alas, the words were not listed in any of my books…" Rezua said, his shoulders drooping as Emanrasu's hopes drifted away.

Rezua sighed and buried his hand into his pouch. He pulled out a piece of parchment, grinned at Emanrasu, and slammed the paper down on the table, causing the pendants to jump.

"But!" Rezua grinned and returned to his galloping flow of words. "I am sure you don't just keep me around because I can find words in books!"

"I was able to find some, but others I had to piece together, but I believe it is clear enough to indicate that I am on the right track if not spot on."

Rezua pointed at the green stoned pendant, "ru vu dokzevi par… which roughly translates to… The breadth of life, sustained and protected."

He grabbed the piece of parchment and pulled it close with a meaty finger. He glanced at it, running his finger down through the scribbles on the page.

"There… all right, the blue one, its… um… nadok nʌ dokmak… which means…

Only bound by the edge of the earth, or maybe it means something more like horizon."

Blinking, Emanrasu stared at his wonderfully oversized friend and his understated, subtly indispensable intellect, "So the breadth and life sustained and defended, that must be earth, well not earth, The Earth. Only the Sky is bounded by the horizon, as nothing else spreads the expanse other than the sky."

Emanrasu's mind swirled as Rezua bowed, then his hands raised in victory. He sat there for many moments, watching Rezua until the big man slowed to a slightly unstable stop.

Rezua placed a hand on the table, steadying himself, "I suppose in retrospect, I should have expected to make myself dizzy."

The Heater and The Hack

"The Dance... they hinted that I was close to having the Cadre... gathered," Emanrasu said, tripping through the words as he stumbled through his thoughts. "This is my first real indication of a tangible connection to the Cadre."

He closed his eyes, trying to remember the exacting words the Dance had imparted to him without success.

"Master Scholar," Emanrasu said, standing and scooping up the pendants.

He grinned, holding the pendants out to Rezua. "Rezua-Su," he said, letting the concepts settle onto their collective ears. "You, my good man, are most deserving of such a title. I was merely born with it."

Rezua gathered up the pendants and, selecting his, placed his around his neck. It dangled just higher than halfway down his chest.

"At the level of his heart," Emanrasu mulled over the thought as Rezua put the other two pendants into his pouch, tucking his into his tunic.

"I am speechless..."

A thought came to him. "What if... and hear me out... what if the pendants..." he stopped abruptly, shaking his head as he looked down at the Heater still lying on the table under the light of the lantern.

"I don't know..." He peered at Rezua, "We need to keep this to ourselves for now, or at least until I can get some sort of clarification from the Dance."

"Have you told anyone else about this?"

"No," replied the exceptionally large, meaty voice. "I worked and puzzled over this until late into the night, and, when I thought I was done, I laid down. In truth, though, I could not sleep and found myself relieved when you—finally—woke and rose."

Entwining Hope in Despair: Chapter Twenty-Three

Suddenly, Emanrasu stepped over and threw his arms around Rezua and squeezed his appreciation. Not quite reaching around the immense bulk of his friend, he hugged the man as best he could.

Dwelling on the pendants, the morning galloped by in a blur, every action, every word, every event seemingly having a deeper meaning that was just beyond the surface.

The two broke fast and then parted ways.

Rezua to return the pendants to Kaurin and Arianis and then to settle in to write and try to get some sleep.

Emanrasu checked on the weapons' progress with the smiths, then headed to the training field, leading the Bren in tactics with the simplistic rural tools.

He explained and demonstrated how the tools would be reinforced.

Specifically, having them practice in groups of twos and threes, he showed them how they could use the pitchforks to successfully capture and control an opponent's arms or legs, leaving them vulnerable.

"While this is not deadly in itself," Emanrasu told them, "we will use it to control our enemy only long enough to dispatch them."

Emanrasu took care to make sure that his Bren command understood the plans and practiced them with the Bren fighters.

The groups divided into twos and threes, always including someone proven in combat or conflict. Someone who could steel themselves enough to make the fatal blow to each of the brigands encountered.

The day passed in a blur, and even the subtle interactions with Serrah seemed filled with truths just beneath the surface, undetectable.

She gifted him with a package but made him swear to open it only on the day of the confrontation with the brigands.

The Heater and The Hack

The day came to an end, and now, as the meeting with the Bren command was behind him, he felt filled with a modicum of hope. As his head touched the pillow, he closed his eyes, and his thoughts drifted to questions about the Dance.

"What are the pendants? Do they indicate who is in each role? What lies beyond the confrontation with the bandits..." Emanrasu's mind delved into the answers as he silently lay, hoping for sleep and to dream.

Upon awakening, he felt disappointed as his sleep had been simple darkness interspersed with dreams that reeked of the mundane with no coherent rhyme or reason. The cool morning hung in the air, immobile and staunchly unforgiving.

To offset the frigidly bitter disappointment, Emanrasu struggled through the day, focusing on each task to the best of his ability. His days progressed, but as filled with precision and activity as they were, the constant nagging of something missing ate at him. Life continued in repetition with a mix of hope and disappointment, followed by sleep. Thus passed the days leading up to the eve of the confrontation.

The frustration of questions without answers was disheartening, as the incessant drills and lessons of both self-reliance and taking agency in all situations ingrained in him by Tarlis were always close at hand. The eerie silence of the Dance felt ominous and, in his mind, magnified his shortcomings.

He knew the Bren would distinguish themselves well, but felt answers would illuminate crucial flaws or enhance alternatives. The dangers presented to the Bren, as well as his friends, Rezua and Serrah, made him feel as if he had missed something... something of import. Whatever was missing, if he did not understand what it was, he could not anticipate its effect.

"I cannot fail...," he thought.

He worked hard to help these people, developing feelings and friendships. Some of them were destroyed despite his efforts. His mood darkened with the memories of Telk and the others who fell in the attack.

Entwining Hope in Despair: Chapter Twenty-Three

"Much like the bakery..." Emanrasu gritted his teeth as he recalled the costly error

He had flipped uncountable bags of flour, checking for grainflies. With untold bags inspected, he had found nothing, and yet, it had only taken one time to learn the lesson. Leaving one bag unturned had ruined the entire store of flour and burned the sickly sweet, acrid odor of a grainfly infestation indelibly into his mind.

Just one more bag, one more revelation... just one... and though it may reveal another or even illuminate an infestation of flaws with our plans, it starts with just this one bag of questions.

Emanrasu gritted his teeth in frustration—just one.

"Rise!" he exclaimed as he stood in the box on the training grounds. He shook his head and silently implored the Dance, "Just talk to me!"

Desperately, he sifted through his options, evaluating each from every angle before setting it aside with the others.

Sighing in resignation and having found nothing with which to assist in clarifying, he took a deep, cleansing breath. The imagined oversight grew more significant in his mind as it hid within his unturned thoughts.

His thoughts drifted back through his conversations with the Dance.

The revelations when he touched the tree in Erald's arena stood out; his shock and awe of the first daytime dream had been unexpected.

"But, even before that..." Emanrasu chewed on the thought. "On the trip to Erald, the night we left Bren... Had I not been sleeping on the Heater and able to successfully roll off it and deflect that first blow..."

Emanrasu shuddered as he recalled his naivety, which was not so long ago... not even a main ago. He struggled to think of others...

The Heater and The Hack

"On the journey from Erzt... it felt like the Dance visited almost nightly during their travels that led them to Bren. Or maybe it was the training Tarlis put him through. It was... after all... literally called the dance."

His mind swirled with the possibilities. Swirled with the thoughts of dance and the Dance, much like the first coalescing of the Dance from the swirling colors.

"Swirling colors... Swirling colors..." Emanrasu thought as his mind struggled to dredge up his long-buried thoughts.

He struggled to uncover the earliest memories of the same swirling colors but could not recall them being present any further back than the bandit's attack in the Rosewood Forest when he had unwrapped the Heater and the Hack.

He stood with a blank stare. "To think, the very act of unwrapping the Heater and the Hack, even without the knowledge I have now, saved my life, and possibly Rezua's as well."

Emanrasu struggled to recall any earlier instances but had none before the battle in the Rosewood Forest.

*   *   *

After his near demise at the hands of the brigand, he took to keeping the Heater and the Hack near at hand, and his lack of training notwithstanding, it still had given him great comfort to have them nearby.

"Nearby..." The word skipped through his thoughts as he realized how much that word was not the whole truth of it.

He smiled at the diminishing of the word in the context of his actions. "More aligned with incessantly nearby."

He had constantly worn or carried them, occasionally letting them stand in odd corners, but never were they out of reach, especially in the early days of their journey.

Entwining Hope in Despair: Chapter Twenty-Three

"Never out of contact... for fear of being without protection, especially during their escape from Erzt. Contact... always... even as far as to sleep on them." He smiled as he recalled using them almost nightly.

It was during this trip that the Dance seemed to get stronger.

Emanrasu froze. "What if... what if... it was the direct contact with the Heater and the Hack that enhanced, or initiated...

"The Dragon said something about them facilitating contact... I am almost sure of it."

His decision was simple and might bear out the underlying reason for the Heater and the Hack. He would have them close at hand enough to have direct contact.

"If it was to supplement or enhance the connection between the Conduit and the Dance... then it makes sense it could break through the silence.

"Slow down, Emanrasu... Think it through logically... You carried the sword and the shield into the Rosewood Forest, but they were hung on your pack."

"Unpacked and unfurled them from their coverings..." He recalled being somehow more anxious or eager to strap them on.

"I successfully defeated the brigand... But that was luck... or..."

"I felt better the next day... even outpaced Rezua... outpaced Rezua... outpaced..." He returned to the thought time and again, "When before that had I ever strode faster and harder than Rezua? Never...?"

"And in Erzt, when I met Tarlis... the old man easily put me down... so, maybe it was not the Heater and the Hack that helped me against the brigand; likely it was always just luck."

Emanrasu grinned and opened his eyes. Sitting up, he mulled over the thought that should have been his first. "If touching or being in contact with them helps..."

The Heater and The Hack

He walked over to where they were pedestaled and retrieved them. Bringing them back to the bed, he slid them beneath his covers and summarily slid in with them, laying on the Heater with the Hack beside him.

"Well, if they help… this is as best a chance as I can give them…"

His head slowly turned from one side to the other, and he relaxed slightly, realizing that just the act of doing—something—was oddly comforting and had driven the bulk of his angst away.

"Maybe it helps… maybe it doesn't… but it does feel good to take action."

He closed his eyes and was eventually able to drift off to sleep.

There was something amiss, something not quite right, and angst flooded his thoughts. Unlike previous dreams of the Dance, there was now a hidden unknown, and the bright clarity of the emerging scene was not present.

Thick, slow, undulating colors struggled to twist and turn about themselves in his dream.

Emanrasu concentrated on the swirling Dance, forcing his will upon the colors. The colors slowly coalesced into vague semblances of the familiar entities.

"We are in dire need of the Cadre," the Dragon's hesitant rumble came. "We are survived, but just…"

"We have little strength to illuminate as once we did; the Cadre will help us… help us… regain strength and bolster our presence," the Sun said, struggling to force its muted rays through the thick, almost dust storm-like haze.

The childlike optimism of the Sky assisted the Sun, "We have lost the Phoenix, but the Cadre can help… you are close."

"Yes, close," beamed the Sun, finally without struggle.

"The Phoenix will rise, but we fear for the timing…" the Tree offered.

Entwining Hope in Despair: Chapter Twenty-Three

"…which ties to life itself," continued the Earth, bolstering the Tree.

"But the Phoenix is most powerful in defeat, a paradox that even we do not fully understand," continued the Tree, stronger and more coherent with the help of the Earth.

The thick, hazy mist suddenly vanished, and Emanrasu could perceive the Dance clearly, except, as alluded, without the Phoenix.

"Yes, the Pendants help to channel, much as the Heater and the Hack assist you, the pendants facilitate connections with the others. We already feel the added strength of the Earth and the Sky—you must find the others." The Dragon rumbled clearly.

"You are close, but you must recognize each and every representative. You are the Conduit," the warmth of the Sun's words gave Emanrasu more hope than he knew in many days.

"We must rest. You must return." The Sun's warmth faded. The Dance withdrew into the void, leaving only hope… and doubt.

The chill of the morning was harsh as Emanrasu put foot to floor.

He wiggled his toes as they slid along the hard surface, smooth save for the hints of the wood grain structures worn within the grain of the long floorboards.

The incessant dull throb in his head and the tightness in his chest, only now realized because of their absence, had seemed to disappear in the night.

Emanrasu bounced to his feet, and retrieving the Heater and the Hack found his morning dance progressed quickly in a now familiar form, his hand both instigating actions and following the paths of thought as Emanrasu tried to imagine the conflict this day would engender.

As he flowed through the smooth actions of his morning dance, he felt a sudden sense of impending interruption and crouched in a defensive position just as the door to his room flew open.

The Heater and The Hack

It took him a fleeting moment to take in the scene before relaxing, and Rezua's great body had frozen at the door.

As Emanrasu recovered from the unexpectedness of his action, Rezua let out a long breath and grinned.

"Your magnificently prepared and battle-ready stances shall provide cause for my rhythmically beating heart to finally acquiesce and refuse to start again one of these magnificent mornings!" The impressively large scribe exclaimed, airing his complaints to no one in particular.

"Good morning, Black! If I knew not what the day held in store, I would swear this day feels downright festive!"

Rezua stepped in and closed the door behind him as Emanrasu recovered from his defensive position, removing the Heater and sheathing the Hack. He leaned them against one of the table chairs and retrieved the package Serrah had given him several days prior.

Rezua retreated to his bed and laid out a great expanse of clothing, which, in truth, was merely a tunic and trousers, accompanied by a thick protective gambeson and tabard of sorts. His garb, obviously new, as Emanrasu had never seen it before, was fittingly a muted creamy yellow, reminiscent of parchment, and bordered in black.

The massive expanse of towering man was draped in parchment-like fabric, which fit his personality as naturally as a leather sleeve fit his journals.

"I must remember to find someone who can make him sleeves for his journals..." Emanrasu sighed at his own inattention to his closest friend's needs. His constant focus on Bren had pushed them to the back of his mind.

"Just something—anything—to remind them that they are never far from my thoughts."

Entwining Hope in Despair: Chapter Twenty-Three

Shaking off the thought, he turned his attention back to the package from Serrah. He untied the bindings, peeled back the folds, and found himself staring at a set of pants and a tunic—his own.

A sigh, a twinge of guilt. Another reminder of how often he had neglected those closest to him.

The fabric was black—blacker than anything he had ever seen outside one of Rezua's inkwells. He rubbed his thumb against the cloth, half-expecting it to come away stained. When it didn't, he pulled back, studying his unmarked skin. The fastness of the color was a testament to its quality.

"Once this is behind us, I must do something for my friends. Journal sleeves for Rezua... and perhaps a skirt or blouse—something smooth and silky—for Serrah."

A grin broke across his face, sudden and undeniable.

"More like a durable leather outfit and a fine pair of exceptionally made knives for that one."

Emanrasu buried himself in the enormity of her gift as he unfolded the trousers and slipped them on. Fastening them around his waist and looping the suspenders over his shoulders, he squatted several times and assumed various stances to get a feel for them. The fit was appropriate, and they were neither too loose nor too tight.

*   *   *

Trying to minimize his hope for something more, Emanrasu shifted the narrative from his hopes to one more solid and feasible.

"She is an attentive one," he mused, "... though no more than she would do for any friend. Like Rezua... she does things for him, and with him, too..."

A sudden thought occurred to him.

425

The Heater and The Hack

He looked at Rezua, letting the words float—soft, easy—the question folded quietly beneath them:

"She chose a fitting color for you, my very large friend. I think you would step into a library and immediately disappear amongst the parchments," he grinned.

Rezua mirrored his grin at the imagined scenario.

"No, I think Serrah had that made for you, but me..." Rezua smirked. "She left me to my own devices, so I had one of the seamstresses put this together, and in truth, the color was the only remnant she had large enough to cover my muscularly expansive physique."

"I think Serrah had one made for herself as well," he continued, "... but I have not seen it, if she did."

His joy was tempered as the confirmation unfolded. His discomfort grew, and the weight of it settled—Rezua left to his own devices.

His gaze returned to Serrah's gift, and as he unfolded the tunic, his jaw dropped open as his eyes took in the scene he had just unfolded. The powerful twinge of guilt deepened as he stared at the smooth black fabric.

He stared down at the tunic. The realization of the amount of consideration and thought that she had put into the gift tugged at his heart and brought him to the edge of tears. His callous disregard of his friends stood in full splendor, highlighting his overwhelming desire to help them.

As he stared down at the emblem, the exquisitely embroidered sigil from the Heater stared back at his inattentiveness in blinkless accusations. The small patch of intricately woven threads provided just a hint of color amidst the deep, shadowy black of the cloth.

Emanrasu reached down and fingered the smooth cloth, solidifying his vow to address his lack of attention once this day was over.

Entwining Hope in Despair: Chapter Twenty-Three

A scuffle from Rezua caused Emanrasu to look up to see Rezua leaning awkwardly against the wall with one hand, one leg in his new trousers, the other leg stuck somewhere in-between. His free hand was held up, palm toward Emanrasu, signaling he was fine.

Emanrasu grinned, welcoming the brief levity and humorous interlude that only Rezua could provide to break him out of his spiraling self-abasement.

Emanrasu reached down and started dressing himself in the black tunic, trying not to think hard about what it represented for his inattentiveness. Instead, he focused on the intentions of the giver, realizing that Serrah was only showing her appreciation.

Glancing over at Rezua, the large man, leaning his great bulk against the wall, had successfully extracted and reinserted his leg into his pants and was pulling them up and fastening them in place.

"I see you finally learned to put your pants on," Emanrasu commented with a wink.

Rezua grunted in response but otherwise ignored the comment.

The sleek black attire of Emanrasu contrasted starkly with the bulky protective gear worn by Rezua.

Emanrasu paused after he finished readying and even walked over and helped him to finish securing his protective gambeson and tabard.

Finished dressing and preparing for the day, Emanrasu gathered up the Heater and the Hack, whereupon he and Rezua exited the room, entering the thick, solemn atmosphere without.

They made their way down and out of the inn, passing the thick aroma of food. Emanrasu was too anxious for food, and Rezua simply followed silently behind without complaint.

427

The Heater and The Hack

The throngs gathering in the training area spilled out into the street, as it seemed the whole of Bren had turned out as requested. The multitude should present quite a sight as they marched upon the brigands.

The way parted for Emanrasu and the larger Rezua as they headed to the box.

Serrah was already present; yellows and whites highlighted the bright reds and golds of her outfit. Reminiscent of a flickering fire, she needed only to add a splash of blue, and she could represent the intense heat of the forge.

Kaurin and her mother, Arianis, stood by the box, waiting.

The vast sea of bodies gathered in the training grounds was impressive, and Bapak, along with Lotheir, had already distributed the mock farm implements, then joined the masses of fighters, taking their place in the defense of the town.

Emanrasu made an intentional detour to thank the two for their diligence and work in preparation for today. In return, they thanked him for his leadership and guidance, regardless of the eventual outcome.

Emanrasu rejoined the others and looked out over the gathering, where many were wearing small squares or masks about their noses and mouths, including all of the Bren command.

Baldar stepped out of the crowd and saluted Emanrasu as the latter entered the box.

"Commander," Emanrasu said, saluting Boldar. "Approach."

He waved the commander forward.

"Black," Boldar said.

"How are the fighters, and do you feel we are prepared?" Emanrasu asked in a softer and more casual tone.

"As you have said, we will not know for sure until we are done, but I believe we have prepared as best we can," Boldar replied.

Entwining Hope in Despair: Chapter Twenty-Three

"Have you selected the escorts for Arianis and Kaurin?"

"Yes," the commander responded as he pointed out a small group of fighters off to the side of the mass of bodies.

Emanrasu waved to the group to come forward, turned around, and acknowledged Kaurin and Arianis. Grasping Arianis's arm, he placed a hand upon her shoulder.

"I know you are not fully healed, and if I thought you were not of import, I would not ask this of you. I intend for you to stay out of harm's way, and the bulk of attention will be on us." Emanrasu waved his hand, indicating the gathering. "But we are providing you with additional protection to get you to the designated meeting spot and..."

Arianis held up a hand. "I am feeling well enough," she insisted. "And though I do not know how Kaurin and I can help, maybe you can explain it better someday."

"Thank you, Arianis. I look forward to that day."

Emanrasu knelt down and looked at Kaurin, "Keep your mother and yourself safe, okay?"

"I will. I am the sky!" she said exuberantly. "I think Telk will be with us, too!" Her hand closed around her pendant as she said this last.

Emanrasu hugged her, and she hugged him back. He stood and gingerly placed an arm around Arianis and gave her a squeeze as well. "Try to stay safe, and at the first signs of problems, you need to leave. The two of you are paramount going forward, and though I feel the need for your presence today, your survival is vastly more important."

"I will do my best to extract ourselves at the first sign of trouble," Arianis said as she hugged him back. She reached down, took Kaurin's hand, and led her over to their guard.

The Heater and The Hack

Emanrasu watched as they made their way out of the crowd and progressed as he had requested.

Emanrasu turned to Boldar. "I see that you and your captains are appropriately masked, as are many others in the crowd."

"Do your captains understand the why of it?"

"They have been informed that you are to be the only recognizable one giving orders, and that this will hide the recognition of the ones that relay and repeat your orders to make it harder to target the command."

"Good. This will allow them freer reign to assist where needed and provide better protection to groups that may struggle."

"Have you selected the fighters that will accompany the rest of the residents back to town?"

"I have, Black. They are already amidst and amongst, and the word has been spread."

"We will not travel at a fast pace, not only to allow those who cannot keep up a chance to maintain, but also to make sure that our troops are not overly taxed when we arrive."

"We are as prepared as we can be, and I wish I were confident in the outcome, but it is our job, Boldar, to present confidence where we may have little. Keep that in mind. You are the Bren commander, and as such, you will hear my doubts and concerns more than most, and yours should only be expressed to me," Emanrasu impressed upon Boldar.

"Yes, Black, you have made it clear, and I understand and concur. Though, today, I have no concerns," Boldar stood straight and thumped his chest in a salute.

The salute was returned, and Emanrasu held out his arm in respect.

Entwining Hope in Despair: Chapter Twenty-Three

Boldar took his arm and held it for a brief moment before letting go and turning to face the crowd.

*   *   *

"BREN!" the commander shouted.

"BLACK!" came the thunderous rolling reply as everyone, non-combatants included, responded as one.

"Present!"

The thunderously continuous roar of the crowd as they brandished the makeshift weapons held by the women and children alongside the more deadly mock makeshift ones carried by the trained defenders of Bren.

Emanrasu held up a hand, and the crowd noise slowed and stopped.

"Today, we will do what we have been preparing to do," he projected his voice out over the entire crowd, which was now hushed.

"Our preparations give us the ability to defend Bren and to exact justice for those who have already fallen!"

"Doing no less than our youngest defenders have done as they fell in the face of this plague, WE WILL FIGHT!"

"Today, we will be rid of this plight on the people of Bren!"

"Today, as one, we will take back that dignity and pride which rightly belongs to Bren!"

"Today, we move and act as one! WE ARE BREN!"

The roar of "BREN!" in acknowledgment, agreement, and relief dwarfed the roar of "Black!" and caused the ground itself to tremble as the thundering crash of a falling tree dwarfs the sound of the timberman's axe. The roar, palpable and resounding to the core of one's being, shook the buildings and houses.

The Heater and The Hack

Emanrasu's gaze rode the wave of humanity in front of him… from one side to the other and back, the earth-shaking force emanating from these people a savory feast of hope.

"We are ready," thought Emanrasu. The reverberating cacophony of the response forced out his last vestige of doubt, and a smile spread across his face at last, letting himself fully believe in his own ability to lead.

The morning was still cold and dark as they placed the first foot on the road to Zerocha Manor. The quiet padding of feet as the multitude traveled accompanied the sound of the carts bouncing over the uneven, rutted road, broken only by the score of horse hooves and the hushed whispers.

The multitudes rotated in and out of the carts as they traveled slowly to the final confrontation. The last rotation of riders, as Emanrasu had mandated, was the actual fighters that would be participating in the battle directly.

"This will give the last bit of rest afforded by the carts to those that will need it the most," Emanrasu had told the Bren command during one of the meetings.

As the mass of bodies made the final approach to the manor, there was a quiet flurry of activity, and the sunlight began casting shards over the distant trees and hills. Without stopping, fighters unmounted the carts while others lifted children and women up into them, making ready for the flurry of departures that would shortly ensue.

Together, they readied for the false bravado and presented incompetence and weakness, which Emanrasu hoped would invoke a sense of superiority in the brigands. He had reviewed his intended plans with the White extensively before they departed, and Emanrasu hoped to engender a sense of nonchalance in the bandits, bolstering their beliefs of easily defeating the farmers, ranchers, and townsfolk that presented themselves.

Emanrasu led the ragged-looking array of townsfolk, distancing himself out front to gain better insight before the Bren fighters came abreast.

Entwining Hope in Despair: Chapter Twenty-Three

He watched the brigands start to gather along the short walls surrounding the manor, as well as filling the balconies and accessible rooftops. Many of them turned to one another and enjoyed a good chuckle. Emanrasu was too far away to hear the exchanges, though their body language was dismissive.

Emanrasu slowed down, allowing the townsfolk to catch up, and by the time the townspeople were within an arrow flight of Zerocha, they had come even with him. Swinging his gaze from left to right and back, he found the Bren were in line with him, fanning out to either side, keeping pace with him.

They were five hundred strong, including women and children, compared to what appeared to be perhaps one hundred bandits. The breath hung in the air, a mist weaving amidst the throng hid some of the details of their masses, but children and women were intentionally funneled forward to present women and children at the fore.

Twenty-three mounted fighters, including Emanrasu. All of the horsemen, expert riders to a man, had trained for several hands over the last couple of days to look intentionally uncomfortable and unsteady in the saddle. Each excelled in the task and appeared every bit the part of riders without training as they approached.

From this distance, the laughter and insults could be heard. Emanrasu dismounted his horse, handing the reins to one of his horsemen.

"Make them believe," he whispered to the man as he accepted the reins. "...our very lives may depend on you."

The man performed amazingly as he urged the horse forward with the wrong foot in the stirrup, which forced him to hop on the other foot awkwardly. Finally, dislodging his foot, he launched himself up and over the saddle, falling heavily on the other side as he tried to mount.

Were the circumstances different, this would have been more entertaining, but even as it was, many of the children had to be hushed or muted to keep them from laughing out loud as they enjoyed the antics of the horseman.

Emanrasu was impressed with the man's skill, though his heart was still in his throat. "If we are all this competent, we shall win out easily," he thought, "and I have to trust our training and our plan!"

He performed a few other mishaps before he righted himself and sat securely in the saddle but made a spectacle out of bringing the horse in line with the others.

And as if on cue, the horses on either side moved uncertainly with expertly guided hands.

By this time, the full force of the brigands had been summoned out front to view and face the townsfolk.

Emanrasu shouted, "Bren!"

The word echoed around, bouncing off the walls of the manor. The reply was muted and half-hearted, almost unintelligible and overlapping: "black…Black!"

The army of Bren shuffled around uncomfortably.

"Present!" Emanrasu shouted the command for everyone to hear.

The farm implements were raised unsteadily, and the isolated shouts and roars intended to encourage felt lacking and without substance. The subtle shifting of weapons went undetected as they were readied for the horsemen, but the deafening roar of the training grounds faltered and failed.

Rezua and Serrah glanced at each other, then at Emanrasu, who, upon seeing their knitted brows and questioning eyes, merely shrugged his shoulders, trying to present his own apparent confusion.

The disarray of hoes, rakes, pitchforks, and the occasional scythe set the stage for the ill-equipped and unprepared townsfolk.

"BREN!" The high-pitched mocking command came from the bandits. This was followed by several other bandits mockingly echoing Emanrasu and his attempt at instilling hope and courage.

Entwining Hope in Despair: Chapter Twenty-Three

Two score bandits, mounted, trotted up from behind the gathered brigands. This show of force prompted Emanrasu to start sending people home, which he initiated by holding up one hand.

With this signal, the backmost rows and a few from within the ranks themselves began moving toward the carts. These individuals briskly moved to the carts, and as each cart filled, they spun around and started retreating.

For a few moments, Emanrasu feigned ignorance, lowering his hand as he walked out in front of the throng of townsfolk.

But as the sound of carts and running feet grew, he was prompted to look behind him and noticed the desertion of his army. Serrah and Rezua seemed almost in a panic as more and more deserted the show of force that had been so powerful back on the training grounds.

Lowering his hand, in turn, signaled even more to retreat until it seemed the brigands had routed the townsfolk with merely a show of force. The abandonment appeared to leave only the incompetent men and ill-trained horsemen to face the overwhelming force of the brigands.

Eighty poorly trained townsfolk against a hundred bandits without compunction to give quarter or grace.

As many of the horsemen flitted their eyes around uncertainly, the Bren army decreased once again, as the exaggerated fear on the face of the horsemen provided a fair reason for departure. The riders kicked their mounts, spun them around, and galloped to the closest hills in the direction of Bren.

Sixty-seven fighters remained after the desertion of the riders, and only six mounted remained, accompanied by the sixty-one on foot, including Rezua and Serrah.

*   *   *   *

The Heater and The Hack

The staccato drumming of hooves on the hard-packed earth thundered as the bandits were spurred into motion. The joy and delight the brigands expressed as they bore down on the much weaker forces of Bren was a manifestation of their ill temperament.

Dark shadows upon the conflict were ushered away, escorted by the sun's rays as they glinted off various shiny baubles on the clothing of the opposing forces.

The thick clouds of hastily cooled breath hung in the air, drifting slowly and playfully dancing with the dirt and dust in the morning light.

As he felt the earth beneath him tremble under the charge of the bandits, Emanrasu felt the morning breeze dance in tandem with the sunlight on his face as if it were guests at a royal wedding.

Catching the eyes of Rezua and Serrah, he grinned at his friends, urging them to follow his lead and retreat several steps away from the charging bandits.

With the recognition of the charge, the remaining Bren horsemen split and galloped off to each side. The whole of the middle ranks were left open and defended only by the apparently inept townsfolk of Bren.

The front row of Bren fighters swiftly knelt and gripped the sturdy horsebreaker. In unison, they lifted it until the supports swung back and into place, settling the heavily reinforced trip bar just above the knee level of the horses.

As the Bren dodged and rolled, jumping back and out of the way, the first of the leading wave of mounted slammed into the horsebreaker. Unable to stop, the warrior-bearing horses crashed into it and threw their riders in a mass of grunting, whinnies, and chaos.

The subsequent waves were caught by one or both of the horizontal ropes as they jumped over. The horses tumbled forward with their bandits, their legs entangled either on the ropes or downed men and mounts of the preceding horsemen.

Entwining Hope in Despair: Chapter Twenty-Three

The last two horses, having had enough time to see the tumultuous floundering in front of them, skidded to a sudden, unexpected halt. The force of the stop sent their riders flying heels over head into the chaos of which the other bandits and mounts were now swimming.

The underlying crisp, clean smell of the coming harvest permeated the morning and contrasted with the more overt, pungently metallic odor of blood.

He paused briefly and looked around, finding his friends embroiled in a battle they all would have preferred to avoid. The look on his friends' faces was a mixture of sorrow and determination as they set about the ugly business before them.

The fighters of Bren worked in haste to dispatch the fallen bandits. Using the teamwork and techniques impressed upon them, they worked in concert to immobilize and eliminate each of the stunned and confused brigand horsemen. The ground lapped up the warm red droplets from each devastating blow.

Emanrasu shuddered as the Bren fighters went about the unsavory work of dispatching their enemy. Though the tactic worked almost perfectly as rehearsed, the shrieking of the horses placed a punctuating exclamation upon the scene that he had neither expected nor would ever forget. The sound penetrated deep into his soul as the steeds had plummeted forward, and riders flew to the ground in great resounding thumps.

Emanrasu wiped the bandit blood from his cheek and glanced around, taking stock and numbers. His heart was heavy with the actions he knew he was responsible for initiating. His absolute certainty of their necessity gave him little solace.

A full twenty bandits were dispatched within moments of reaching the Bren, and their mounts, which were largely unharmed, milled about behind the Bren, still jumpy and skittish.

The Heater and The Hack

A confused shout from the brigands on foot signaled that the attack of the retreated Bren horsemen had begun, joined by the mounted fighters who had stayed behind. The groups converged on the ill-fated bandits from both sides.

While the reserve fighters from Bren had begun the dispatching of the unseated bandits, the bulk of the Bren fighters closed on foot to engage the now confused bandits in hand-to-hand and melee battle.

Emanrasu, Serrah, and Rezua accompanied the charge to the bandits on foot. The brigands, now fully embroiled in the fight with the Bren mounted, did not ignore the incoming fighters, and with calls and orders made, two bandits rushed to separate buildings, throwing open the doors and calling desperately within.

The flood of fighters from these buildings caused Emanrasu's heart to drop. The untold numbers now streaming from the buildings, combined with the White still not having made an appearance, bode poorly for the Bren. Emanrasu saw that the incoming reinforcements were not bandits or brigands.

Even at this distance, Emanrasu could see the weapons were militant rather than brigandine and well cared for. The shine of polished steel combined with the variety shifting to polearms and curved swords reinforced his evaluation. The precision in the way they drew their weapons and paused to scan the battle before entering the fray screamed warriors of an unexpected magnitude.

Their dress was not familiar, and the flowing styles and the multitude of colors in their clothing seemed chaotic as though subtly hinting at... something... more.

"Recognize the effort and see us through," came his silent plea to the Dance.

With the influx of reinforcements, Emanrasu saw Bren riders unmounted, and horses fall as the new wall of brigands slammed into the beleaguered Bren fighters. The Bren accounted well and stood fast against the bandits and even held their own against the new threat. Slowly, though, the Bren were losing ground and being pushed back.

Entwining Hope in Despair: Chapter Twenty-Three

The intensity of the battle continued to increase as the Bren, once on the offensive, were now fighting for their lives, faced with overwhelming numbers.

Emanrasu lost track of Serrah in the fray but possessed no time to search, as he was himself pressed on all sides. As he focused on the task at hand, he could feel the subtle stretching of time; every motion was deliberate, every step precise. Even as he quickly danced through the brigands, he struggled to keep up with the sheer numbers while protecting those within his reach.

A sudden flash of steel followed the twang of a crossbow.

His gaze fixed as he watched the crossbow bolt bury itself deep into Rezua's chest at heart level. The large man's thick tree-limb-sized club, freed of Rezua's control and now limp hand, landed heavily on the bandit who would become the recipient of Rezua's final blow. The impact of the bolt lifted the small giant nearly from his feet while the momentum of his club carried him in an awkward twist.

His body landed heavily as it was flung backward by the force.

Emanrasu's thoughts juxtaposed this gentle giant and his ink-laden weapon of choice with this protective mass of furious man, both now gone, leaving nothing but a cloud of emotion as his disbelief and sorrow ground him to a halt.

He involuntarily flashed to their last interaction as they approached the Zerocha Manor, riding beside his large companion as he deftly guided his cart; the stench that exploded from around the large man as he had lifted his cheek from the driver's bench was a source of hilarity for them both.

His only true childhood friend had fallen while he watched. The large scribe twisting with the power behind the bolt, spinning into the instant when the world, for one breath, forgot to move.

Then the knife found his cheek, and thoughts of Rezua were cut short; his focus was once again on the battle. Emanrasu's anger exploded in a flurry of strikes and parries as he felled one after the other.

The Heater and The Hack

"Serrah!" his mind shouted as his eyes scanned the field at each opportunity. More desperately now, he fought through one after the other as he struggled to catch sight of her. "I cannot lose her, too. Not after Rezua... I just..."

He took a deep, crisp breath of air, refocusing on his dance. Time seemed to slow, and he could see the intentions of over a dozen brigands. The paths of weapons and twitching of their muscles spaed their strikes and defenses. Emanrasu unabashedly used this to mount a devastating flurried attack, pushing his way into the new fighters, but each fallen bandit had another behind him waiting in the wings to take his place.

Forcing himself out in front of the Bren, and as the bandits gave way to these new warriors, he could see that eyes would follow him.

"If I could just... get them to focus on me..." he thought as he parried and sliced deep through the throat of a new warrior.

Pushing deeper into the colorful warriors, he knew that their skill eclipsed the Bren. Some of them sported strange and unique weapons that Emanrasu had never seen. An unusual pattern of hooked polearms and double-bladed staffs seemed popular.

Others wielded familiar weapons, such as swords and knives, but in ways that were unfamiliar and, though similar and as fluid as the dance, were not quite the same.

Finally, deep amidst them, he was faced only with these new warriors. He could feel that they had not expected to face a skilled fighter. This knowledge seemed to bring more attention to Emanrasu, drawing the fighters back to him and away from the others.

"Hopefully... their attention to me..." Emanrasu ducked and sliced the tendon in his opponent's ankle, "draws it from Serrah... and the rest of the Bren." he thought as he fought.

He was being approached singly, as though each was testing their skill against his. The others waiting their turn seemed to have forgotten or dismissed the Bren as inconsequential. Emanrasu saw that the Bren were no longer beset by this superior threat and turned his focus to them.

Taking a deep breath, he pressed the issue, successfully dispatching the man against him, and instantly threw himself against the men encircling him, dispatching three more before the circle once again formed, and he was forced once again to face only one.

"Odd," Emanrasu thought as he noticed that, despite the bandit's overwhelming advantage in numbers, they were beginning to retreat.

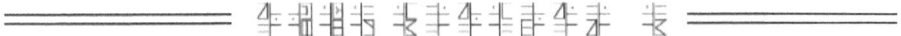

Love, Loss, and Zerocha: Chapter Twenty-Four

"Within the unknown are hidden truths within truths, each a layer protecting the last. Strip what you need in order to find a level at which you can live. Some are content on the surface of life, while some must strip away each layer to the core. Be wary of those that cannot find contentment, for they will encounter the core of the cosmos."

—RCotD—

He steadied his breath as the warriors in colored garb argued—hands slicing the air, bodies leaning in and pulling back. It looked heated.

They struggled to reach a consensus, seemingly, though he could not be sure. The words, strange to his ears, still carried the unmistakable pulse of emotion beneath them. Phrases punctuated by emphatic gestures—rage flared unchecked. Words of honor rose—proud, inflated—while lower voices pushed back with steady control. Every movement hit the air with conviction.

Their expressions and postures felt oddly familiar—much like his own when excitement and passion crept in.

Perhaps they were deciding the order in which they would face him.

He wiped the sweat from his brow and stepped toward them with purpose.

As he advanced, the whole circle on that side shifted backward—but not in fear; it seemed they were still locked in fevered debate. Arms flashed, shoulders turned, disagreement still thick in the air.

For the moment, he could not engage any of them. But they were watching him. That much, at least, was certain—and it kept their focus away from the Bren.

"Where are the White?" he muttered, gritting his teeth.

A glance told him the Bren had seized the moment. They had begun to pull back, sensing space. But the bandits and brigands, reading the same shift, surged after them with renewed force.

It was a mercy there hadn't been more archers and crossbowmen. The Bren had dropped their larger shields for speed and greater mobility.

Then the thought hit him again—crossbow... bolt... Rezua.

He threw himself into the warriors, forcing them to engage, making their indecision irrelevant. Rezua.

Emanrasu's chest tightened as the weight of Rezua's fall began to bury itself in his heart. His breath hitched. The sense of loss pressed down on him as though half of himself had been torn away.

His arm, however, moved of its own accord—the Hack slicing through the air, blocking, parrying, and striking with the precision of long-practiced instinct. His body, conditioned by endless repetition, knew the steps of the fight better than his mind did. Even as his thoughts threatened to overwhelm him, his muscles acted, dancing through the fight.

Balance. The word came unbidden, as if carried on the rhythm of his movements. In all things, the Dance finds its way. Even now.

"Rezua," he muttered under his breath. "As far back as I can remember... he was always there. Perhaps even more so than Father..."

He tried to push the thought away, knowing there was nothing he could do to change it. Focus.

With monumental effort, he poured his grief—his fury—into the arc of his blade, weaving it among the colorful warriors, forcing them to turn their attention once again to him.

The Bren fought with the desperate zeal of those defending home and family—hardened by weeks of training but still raw against seasoned killers. But the brigands moved with the efficiency of those who lived by the blade, veterans of ambushes and skirmishes.

Love, Loss, and Zerocha: Chapter Twenty-Four

The colorfully garbed warriors were something else entirely—seemingly honed by war and unburdened by fear. Their unfamiliar weapons and distinct fighting style elevated them above the brigands. And yet, to Emanrasu's thoughts, even amidst their deadly prowess, none—not one of them—moved with the grace or mastery of the White. Emanrasu knew this from experience.

The sudden slide of boots across the dirt brought his mind back. An opponent aimed a kick at his face, but Emanrasu easily avoided it, and the now toe-less boot swung wide.

The clash of his internal grief and the demands of the fight tugged at him, forcing a furrow deep into his brow, dragging down the corners of his mouth. Focus, he reminded himself, fighting the wave of disheartening thoughts.

Rezua was the other half of me. His mind roared, Well... until Serrah. The image of Serrah surged into his mind, pushing all else aside. Serrah! The Dance! Serrah!

His heart thumped heavily. His breath caught, and for a moment, he felt as if he couldn't draw in enough air. His mind swirled, overwhelmed, and cold droplets appeared on his brow. He swiped them away with the back of his hand, but the thoughts lingered.

Metal clanged against metal. The breeze of the enemy's blade brushed his hair as he parried the strike.

Emanrasu tore his mind away from his spiraling thoughts, forcing his focus back to the fight.

His chest tightened again, but this time, he used it—burying thoughts of Serrah deep within the rhythmic movements of the dance. With every swing of his blade, every block and parry, he vented his emotions, dropping two more foes in quick succession.

The remaining enemies circled him—casual now, almost like the Bren during training, not men in battle. They dragged their fallen comrades from the circle without hesitation or concern, their colorful garb a stark contrast to their callousness.

The language they spoke felt foreign, too—more like the mysterious Tubatonona, a language Rezua had continuously poked and prodded, trying to decipher its meaning.

Rezua... The name echoed again in his mind, a constant companion to his every movement.

Emanrasu dropped another of the brightly garbed warriors, his arms weaving a tireless defense.

*   *   *   *

"The language, the unfamiliar weapons, the garb..."

Who are these people?

He parried and swept the legs of his foe, adding a thin red line across the attacker's throat as he tumbled. The next attacker came from behind, but Emanrasu had already heard the footfalls—padding, scuffling—creeping up from behind.

The blade glanced off the Heater, and Emanrasu thrust his hilt into the attacker's chin. The warrior crumpled. For an instant, Emanrasu was weaponless as the man fell away.

He snatched up the curved sword of the multicolored fighter. Its weight was uncomfortable and unbalanced.

He blocked with the shield and awkwardly used the curved sword to eliminate the next opponent.

Then he threw the blade at the oncoming foe, using the instant it bought to plant a foot against the fallen warrior's chin and yank the Hack free—just in time to parry.

Love, Loss, and Zerocha: Chapter Twenty-Four

As this man fell, Emanrasu noticed the bodies were no longer being removed with the same precision. His opponents, too, had thinned—and were no longer coming one after the other.

In the brief pause between clashes, Emanrasu caught a subtle shift: a growing number of bandits and the colorfully garbed warriors were drifting toward the courtyard beyond the buildings from whence they'd come.

As they moved, the urgency in their pace increased—until Emanrasu finally heard it: the faint clang of steel on steel.

But this was different.

The rhythm was more deliberate, more purposeful. The beats struck with calm intent. The Bren fights rang more hesitantly, irregular in tempo.

"The White!" Emanrasu shouted in joy. "The White have arrived!"

His voice rippled through the battlefield. The shouts and din of the Bren swelled into a flurry of noise. Encouraged, they surged forward with renewed strength, even as the brigands, bandits, and multicolored strangers peeled off to face this new threat.

Word of the White spread through the enemy ranks like sparks before a stiff breeze—fast and unmistakable.

Emanrasu's own opponents fell back, and one by one, they dwindled—until, at last, he dropped the final warrior.

Seizing the lull, he scanned the battlefield for Serrah—or Boldar, for that matter, whom he hadn't seen in quite some time.

As he labored to soothe the growing pressure in his chest, he stopped one of the Bren.

"Have you seen Serrah or Boldar?" he asked the young man.

The Heater and The Hack

"They had pushed ahead early in the fight," the man said, motioning toward the courtyard where the clank and clang of metal echoed faintly to their ears.

Emanrasu's breath hung in the chill air like his heart hung in his chest. A fleeting thought of Rezua was guiltily replaced by concern for Serrah, and the abject terror grew from his ignorance.

Glancing over to where Rezua had fallen, he saw only the blood and the brigand.

"I suppose Rezua's body has already been returned to Bren for preparations," he thought, stifling the pain of guilt and regret as he returned to help the man with the unsavory task of permanently preventing any of the previous combatants from rising behind them.

One by one, they dispatched each body. Whether it was already a corpse made no difference, as they inflicted wounds from which none could recover.

The clashing and clanging from the courtyard grew more and more infrequent, while the reverberating shouts of direction grew clearer.

A small group of Bren had joined Emanrasu and the young man—Rennard. Together, they made short work of the rest of the fallen brigands and the multicolored ones.

Emanrasu and the others strode purposefully to the courtyard, where the last of the dwindling pockets of enemy fighters still fought on.

The acrid smell of burning flesh filled the air near one of the pockets—one of the bandits had died falling into the fire pit. The growing fear on the faces of the remaining bandits and warriors bloomed steadily as their numbers waned.

Unfortunately, the stench remained. There was only the choice to leave him until the battle finished and it became safe enough to lift him out.

As Emanrasu approached, the last of the brigands fell, and the sound of battle subsided into an eerie, muted silence broken only by the wiping of weapons and the crackling of fire.

Love, Loss, and Zerocha: Chapter Twenty-Four

Emanrasu shouted to the Bren, "If you are wounded—even a scratch—go back to the carts and have yourself tended."

The pride in his heart matched the effort of the town on this day.

He resumed his search for Serrah, and his eyes found her across the courtyard—conversing with another Bren, calmly cleaning her daggers.

He did not know when he had ever felt such relief. The horrid thoughts that had tickled at him since he last saw her—clawing at the edges of his mind—were at last buried beneath the sight of her alive.

"I should have known she can take care of herself," he muttered to no one in particular.

His heart freed, and once again, he turned his attention to the aftermath. Bodies of the brigands and bandits were strewn across the compound, many slumped against walls or draped over broken structures—still enough to give the illusion they might yet rise.

A voice behind him—Boldar. Emanrasu spun and quickly spotted him. He approached the firepit at the center of the courtyard and motioned for Boldar to join him.

Together, they lifted the still-smoldering man from the flames. The pungent, acrimonious odor clawed up in feeble, writhing tendrils of smoke, stabbing at Emanrasu's eyes like needles. His stomach turned as the man's flesh shifted unnaturally beneath the scorched tunic—almost causing him to lose his grip.

They tossed the body unceremoniously to the side.

Emanrasu found a discarded cloak from one of the other bandits and draped it over the remains.

"There. At least he will not continue to taint the air with his stench more than is necessary."

The Heater and The Hack

He glanced at Boldar, who—much like himself—was speckled in minute dots and splashes of red. A neatly stitched cut ran just under the commander's jaw.

The sound of wooden wheels echoed in staccato beats across the cobblestones as Emanrasu watched men gathering the dead for transport to the pile just outside the compound.

"How did the Bren fare, Commander?" Emanrasu asked, still scanning the courtyard. "I feel we did well... but what are our losses?"

Boldar stepped up to him and gripped Emanrasu's upper arms, his gaze locked steady with his own.

The commander let a grin slowly spread across his face before answering.

"To my knowledge, Black, we had no losses. Not even one."

Emanrasu smiled back, his brow unknitting, the knot in his back slowly unraveling.

"That is great news," he said. "I hadn't expected the Bren to come through unscathed. Even though that's what we trained for, I still feel it's an unexpected boon."

Boldar's eyes shifted—drawn to something behind Emanrasu.

He let go. "I'll get a more detailed account for you and report back later," he said as he moved past.

Emanrasu patted his shoulder as he passed.

"The unexpected appearance of the strange warriors could have thrown the battle into complete disarray," he mused. His relief at the Bren's success was only tempered by the thought of Rezua.

"I suppose it's still understandable we're considered outsiders," Emanrasu thought, dropping his hand. "Though I will make sure Rezua is honored by Bren for his contribution."

Love, Loss, and Zerocha: Chapter Twenty-Four

He let his eyes journey back and forth across the courtyard, searching for the White.

He spotted Catlina and Freydis standing outside one of the main buildings, pointing at something on the blackened wall. Wondering how the White had fared, he strode toward them.

Nearing, he caught part of their conversation.

"See, here—and here," Catlina said, pointing. "We'll need to have Tarlis confirm it, if he can, but I swear this is it."

"Greetings," Emanrasu said. "How fared the White?"

Catlina glanced over at him. "Eirikr fell and breathed his last. Djorn is also fallen but still breathing—last I heard. How did the Bren fare?"

"As of now, the Bren has not suffered any losses." He hesitated. "Though Rezua... Rezua fell. Bolt to the chest."

*   *   *

Just saying the words deepened the furrow in his brow and the frown on his face.

The brows of the two White mirrored his expression.

Emanrasu glanced toward Serrah. Grateful for her safety, he softened his face and took a deep breath.

She was across the courtyard, helping to move bodies and directing the Bren, calmly pointing out this or that as she issued instructions.

"We think this might be of interest to you," Freydis said, pointing at the wall. "Though we'll need to confirm with Tarlis—or at least get his opinion—but look at this."

She walked over and ran her fingers across a series of methodical indentations— lines and curves that looked like a carving hastily covered or defaced.

The Heater and The Hack

"Does this not look like a tree? ...and here... I feel this could be a sun..."

She pointed to other sections. "Dragon... phoenix..."

She glanced at Emanrasu and shrugged. "Maybe I'm reading into it too much, but to me... it looks like it might once have been a symbol of the Dance."

Emanrasu contemplated the wall.

"...maybe," he thought.

Above the images, peeking through the paint, he could just make out some symbols—shapes similar in form to the script on the pendants Rezua had shown him.

Tubatonona, perchance?

"Maybe... it's tough to make out—it's covered in black, much like the rest of the buildings," he said, looking around.

That was when he noticed.

All the structures were painted or dyed in a deep, uniform black.

"Were they trying to cover something up?" Emanrasu mused.

"In any case..." he said, shifting his tone, "the unexpected appearance of the multicolored warriors had me concerned at first. We were slowly losing ground until your arrival. Do we know where they came from?"

"They were followers of Chaos, to my thinking," Tarlis called out as he approached.

Love, Loss, and Zerocha: Chapter Twenty-Four

"Your grandfather spoke of them. He described them as colorful in dress—distinct from the brigands. He also noted subtle differences in the weapons they wielded."

The light glinted off the small, finely forged plates of Tarlis's armor as he approached, their scaled effect shimmering with each deliberate step. The surety in his movement magnified the pattern—each stride casting a ripple across the gleaming surface.

"Their style of fighting was definitely not something I've seen before," Tarlis continued. "I'm unsure from whence they came..."

The air was still thick with a sharp, noxious smell of burning flesh. A stifled cough drew their attention, and they turned.

"Pardon the interruption," Catlina said, nodding to the men. "Djorn and I saw no sign of them when we scouted—so either they knew of our presence and were already lying in wait, or—more likely, they slipped in after we had left."

"It turned in our favor in the end," Tarlis said, his eyes roaming the ground in front of him as one foot idly traced a pattern in the dirt. "To lose only one... it's almost as unexpected as their arrival was."

"Rezua was felled as well," Emanrasu said, his head drifting downward, matching the motion of Tarlis's own. "A crossbow bolt to the chest—dropped him where he stood. Though his final blow accounted for the foe before him... it was his last."

He kicked at the ground, sending a plume of dust curling through the air, followed quickly by a second.

A firm hand settled on his shoulder, grounding him. Tarlis gave it a gentle squeeze.

"He is a great loss," the old warrior said. "We count him among the fallen White."

The Heater and The Hack

Emanrasu's fists clenched at the thought of the friend he would never again walk beside. He closed his eyes tightly, willing back the tears he could feel building.

He drew a slow breath.

"Thank you, Tarlis," he said. "That means a lot to me… possibly more than you'll ever know."

His thoughts drifted back to his large friend's raucous laughter, always able to lighten the mood, even in the wake of embarrassment.

He remembered the thunder of Rezua's voice echoing through the bathing room in Erzt when he'd been mortified by Serrah.

A small smile tugged at his lips. He glanced across the courtyard and saw Serrah still assisting with cleanup, helping the Bren lift bodies into carts for disposal.

"What happened to Arianis and Kaurin?" he asked, suddenly remembering they were to meet with the White.

"We're unsure whether their presence helped," Tarlis replied, "but as you requested, they remained until the last opponent fell. After that, we sent them back to town under Djorn's supervision, and to ease your mind, he was not so battered as to interfere with their safety."

"I've become quite attached to the White," Emanrasu said, casting a sidelong glance at Tarlis. "I consider you all family, you know. I never much felt at home… even with my father at the bakery."

Behind Tarlis, Boldar approached.

"I think I'll make Bren my home," Emanrasu continued. "Now, knowing the shield and the sword have no one else but me—and truly feeling I may be the rightful heir—it seems only fitting to settle here, especially in light of..."

"I think Torsun would agree," Boldar said, stepping up beside them. "Making your home here would be a good thing."

Love, Loss, and Zerocha: Chapter Twenty-Four

Freydis caught Tarlis's attention and motioned to one of the buildings. "What do you make of this?" she asked.

"… in light of this. Perfect timing," Emanrasu told her.

Tarlis stared at it for a moment, then stepped forward and scraped at the black covering. Drawing a knife, he poked and prodded several spots in the wall's surface before turning to Emanrasu.

He held out his hand. "Hand me the Heater," he said.

Emanrasu unstrapped the shield from his arm and handed it over.

Tarlis stepped back, putting distance between himself and the wall, then raised the Heater in front of him—comparing shield to stone. He glanced between the two, his eyes narrowing, his brow furrowing.

Slowly, the crease in his forehead eased, and he shrugged.

"I've never seen the like," he said, returning the shield to Emanrasu. "Fate or destiny—maybe both—seem to follow you around, boy."

He tapped his temple, then pointed toward the wall. "I remember your grandfather speaking of a place—the one the Black and his White built and held. He never could name it, let alone find it."

Tarlis jabbed a bony finger at Emanrasu. "And you… you stumble into truths that should not be found so easily. I believe this is the place he was searching for. And when this wall is fully uncovered, I believe its symbols will match the emblem upon your shield."

Freydis bumped Catlina with the back of her hand. "Told you…"

She grinned and nudged her again. And again.

"Yes, yes, you did…" Catlina muttered, smiling despite herself.

The Heater and The Hack

"Excuse me," Boldar said, veering toward the edge of the courtyard. Someone was calling his name.

"I'll probably have to wait to give a full report back in Bren," he added over his shoulder with a grin, then disappeared into the rising voices beyond."

"I suppose we should all get back to the tasks at hand," Tarlis said, his gaze resting on Freydis and Catlina.

Emanrasu got the distinct feeling they'd been sidetracked from something more important—confirmed by the sheepish looks on their faces and the speed at which they departed.

"I, too, have things to address," Tarlis added, turning back to Emanrasu and offering his arm.

Emanrasu clasped it.

The firm, poignant grip was a welcome punctuation mark to the old man's quiet mentorship—a silent acknowledgment of everything he had offered without fanfare.

"I am certainly glad to have met you, Commander," Emanrasu said.

"Likewise," Tarlis replied, his grin brief as he turned and walked away.

*　　*　　*

Emanrasu leaned against the wall, his eyes skimming across the carnage wrought.

Bodies strewn about in odd angles, left where they fell amidst the chaos of the battle. The Bren, once milling about, stirred to life as Boldar's orders cut through the morning air.

The acrid, pungent bite of burning flesh lingered, thick in the air, oppressive as a weight pressing down on him, and the shards of light from the rising sun matched the starkness of the cold, crisp morning. The clanking of metal on metal, and the

Love, Loss, and Zerocha: Chapter Twenty-Four

creaking of leather against leather became a constant backdrop as the Bren gathered up the fallen brigands, bandits, and colorfully garbed warriors.

As planned, the bodies were stripped and separated from their weapons and the other equipment left strewn about in the aftermath—the equipment—destined for the smiths and artisans for repurposing, the bodies for the wolves and carrion.

Emanrasu's sweat-drenched tunic invited the cold to come and lay against his skin. Shuddering from the chill, he drew a breath and, upon releasing it, steeled himself once more against the briskness of the morning. The exertion spent leading up to this moment, entwined with an emotional fatigue that tugged at him as if walking through a deep bog, left him exhausted and hollow.

As Tarlis turned and departed, Emanrasu searched for something to keep himself occupied. The buildings on the compound needed to be investigated and cataloged, but that was for another time. The weight of their victory settled over him—not as crushing as this morning's reality but profound in its own quiet gravity.

The little group, which had started this journey from Erzt, had, with the help of the White, successfully rallied the town, bolstering its spirits, providing hope, and giving them back their pride.

Looking across the courtyard, he gazed at Serrah, dressed in the bright yellow and red tunic and trousers she had decided upon for her battle dress. The relief at finding her unscathed was immeasurable, and he still felt the remnants of his fear sneaking around the corners of his mind.

The journey from Erzt had endeared her to him, and when he struggled with her possible loss, especially on the heels of Rezua's fall, it was almost more than he could bear.

With abilities that far exceeded her appearance back in Erzt, he grew more and more impressed with her as each day passed.

"Erzt..." The thought flitted, unfocused, shifting like sand.

The Heater and The Hack

"...the embarrassment in the bathing room seemed such a long time ago..." A smile crept across his face, which only grew broader as he recalled the stench of her disguise.

Closing his eyes, he imagined her standing next to him as girochih and shehchih danced in waves ahead of the breeze as the night deepened. Vowing to reveal his feelings before this day was out, he scanned the courtyard and stepped over to a group of the Bren as they went about hefting bodies and equipment into carts.

Wandering around, he helped where he could, loading carts with the bodies of the brigands and bandits, along with the occasional body of the colorfully garbed warriors.

The crushing loss of Rezua bore down on him again, forcing his shoulders to sag. The vision returned, over and over, ceaseless. Again, the bolt struck—again, the giant scribe fell. The memory slammed into him, vivid and merciless. Grief twisted in his gut, sharp and unrelenting.

"Grappling with the large man's loss..." he thought as he gathered the weapons close by. "...will never pass."

The safety of Serrah and the ultimate success against the occupants of the Zerocha Manor served to soften his grief but not his regret. Trading one for the other felt like an unwinnable choice.

The black buildings held an ominous and unnerving air as he let his sight scan across the courtyard.

The fighters from Bren, or simply the Bren, as Emanrasu came to think of them, were being directed by Boldar as they dispatched the foes still moving and gathered up the dead.

Emanrasu's first command and his guidance of Boldar as his second had turned out well—if success could be measured in survival rather than cost. Rezua's unexpected demise, Eirikr's loss, the blood that had seeped into the dirt beneath them—none of it felt like a price paid, only a debt incurred.

Love, Loss, and Zerocha: Chapter Twenty-Four

The trading of the town's safety for his friend's life settled like iron in his gut, too steep a cost, too bitter a choice. In the rush of battle, in the frantic press of strategy and instinct, the decision had been made before he even realized he was making it. But now, in the quiet that followed, its weight gnawed at him.

He had always counted the risk in terms of his own life and had imagined death in battle as a solitary fate—his, not theirs. That comfort had been stripped away. Would he have chosen differently if he had known? The answer lay just out of reach, refusing to solidify into anything he could accept.

The town stood. Rezua did not. Eirikr did not.

And in the end, he could not say if the trade had been worth it.

The incessant barking of dogs in the distance brought him from his depressing revelry, only now impressing itself upon his ears, only to be drowned by the gathering crows and other scavenging birds.

He peered across the courtyard opposite Boldar and spied Tarlis working with Darth and Olaf. Further and beyond them, Freydis and Catlina were intent on tasks Tarlis called out to them.

Serrah helped the Bren lift and pile the bodies into the cart, his eyes following her as the conversation ensued.

She stood up and stretched, and catching his eyes, she smiled broadly, reaching down to lift the next body.

As she reached down, a hand shot up from the prone body of a warrior. Grabbing a fistful of her tunic, the warrior dragged her close, plunging the dagger blade in and out of her chest and torso several times at an almost blinding speed.

For a breath, the world stopped.

Serrah—her body convulsing, blood spilling.

Then Emanrasu was running, the roar ripping from his throat.

The Heater and The Hack

SERRAH!

Thundering across the courtyard, he tore off the Heater and the Hack, flinging them to the ground as he ran to her. He barreled toward her, his gaze afixt as she seized the tunic of the multicolored warrior and pulled him close.

Her blade materialized swiftly in her hand, and she plunged it deep into the warrior's skull through the man's soft throat. She twisted the blade violently, and as the warrior shuddered and stopped moving, she slumped over, pulling the now motionless warrior atop her.

Tarlis, the first to reach her, grabbed the back of the multicolored tunic with one hand. In one motion, he lifted the warrior from Serrah, and the sound of cloth tearing ripped through the still silence that followed his roar.

Tarlis effortlessly threw the man's body more than four horse-lengths away, where it crumpled lifeless against the side of a building.

Emanrasu reached Serrah, throwing himself to his knees and frantically working through her tunic to evaluate her wounds. Her hands clenched, one around her dagger, the other still clinging to the remnants of the multicolored cloth her hand had ripped from her attacker.

His heart seized.

Rezua. Now Serrah.

The weight of it crushed him—unbearable.

He struggled to staunch the bleeding as others arrived. The gathering of Bren townsfolk and fighters provided for whatever he asked. The silence of the gathering, to him, spoke volumes of their respect, not only for Emanrasu but for the magnitude of support shown to and provided by this remarkable woman over the last moons.

Love, Loss, and Zerocha: Chapter Twenty-Four

Knowing it was ultimately insufficient, he bound her wounds as best he could; tears filled his eyes, blurring his vision before a swipe of his forearm cleared them once more.

Tarlis placed a hand on Emanrasu's shoulder. As he knelt, his armor glinted in the sunlight, accompanied by the whisper of metal on metal as the scales rippled with each motion.

Serrah's gaze turned to Tarlis, and she managed a weak smile that disappeared into a bloody cough.

"You did well, girl," Tarlis said, his stoic figure belied by the quiver in his voice. Emanrasu knew Tarlis, too, had grown to love this young woman, gradually filling his heart as the daughter he once lost; she had become family.

She coughed, and the tepid spray of blood spattered Emanrasu's face, mixing with the warm tears he struggled to hold back.

"I should have told her!" Shouting in silent anger and desperation, his mind struggled.

Reaching down, he pulled her to him, lifting her to bind her untenable wounds. His hands and body were almost automatic in their actions as he looked up into the eyes of friends and acquaintances, then back down at the beautiful face of Serrah.

"I am sorry... I should have..."

"Don't..." she whispered as she struggled to form words.

Her raspy, gurgling breath tore at Emanrasu's heart, leaving him empty and filled with guilt and rage.

Shoving the guilt and rage deep into himself, he peered into her face. Her eyes focused on him, her face relaxed a bit, her fists clenched tightly by the pain that seemed to dominate her.

The Heater and The Hack

Serrah raised her arm weakly, her grip unrelenting as her fingers still clamped tight around the ragged piece of cloth. She gently coaxed him closer into a hug, the hug he had so desperately wanted before all of this. He held her close, her shallow breathing getting weaker by the moment. He could only say the one thing he had struggled not to say.

"I love you," came the whispered admission. "I don't know why, but from the moment we met in the inn—me, a wandering idiot with a silly quest, and you, working beneath your skills as a maid—since that very day, you have always been in my heart."

She coughed again, the warm spray spattering his face once more.

Her mouth opened, but the gurgling refused to form words.

As she struggled to focus on him, her eyes streamed tears steadily down her face. "I know," she mouthed. Her body relaxed, her eyes ceased to focus as the last breath seeped from her, and she grew still.

Her eyes, once glassy orbs of exquisite beauty, turned dull, now unmoving. Emanrasu stared, unable to look away from the fixed, unblinking gaze of the only love he had ever known. Regret tightened in his chest as he reached up, sliding his fingers over her eyelids, closing them for the last time. He held her body gently in his lap, cupping her head in his hands.

Shrugging off a hand that touched his shoulder, he buried his head into her shoulder, pressing his cheek to hers. Her last rasping breath crept out of her and finally stopped. First Rezua… now her… the pain continued to grow unattended.

People started moving away to leave him to grieve, each offering a light touch on his shoulder, back, or head in support as they did. The chill in the air, once brisk and refreshing, now crushed him, almost callously oppressive. As through a thick pane of frosted glass, his conscious acknowledgment of the people leaving was barely noticeable and without consequence.

Love, Loss, and Zerocha: Chapter Twenty-Four

"Rezua... and now Serrah..." thoughts swam in uncertain random circles. The exquisitely horrid reek of her transformation into the old hag was now a memory he struggled to hold onto.

He held her, waiting for the chill to take her as he struggled to understand the depths of grief. His wait fully encompassed him as the snow blankets every part of the field. Thick, soft, oppressive cold drained the warmth of his feelings away, leaving behind a cold, barren, lifeless mass of sorrow.

Holding her, his body provided continual contact, keeping her body warm. This kept his mind full of hope with the illusion that she, somehow, had not fallen and fed his hope unreasonably. His fingertips against her throat confirmed there was no pulse.

Leaning over, he kissed her forehead, then picked her up and gently slid her off his lap, back down onto the dirt that so eagerly lapped at her life's blood.

He brushed back a wisp of hair from her face and knelt beside her for a fleeting eternity.

A hand gripped his shoulder, and he looked up. Tarlis nodded as he gazed down at him, whispering, "It is time."

Emanrasu's heart sank.

Her life had ebbed away from him, much the way each wave of sparks and flames ebbed and flowed across the fire fields. Closing his eyes, his thoughts drifted to the fields of girochih and shehchih she had shown him and the spectacular waves of sparks.

Tarlis helped him to his feet. He shifted unsteadily under the weight of the loss of his friends, his thoughts buried in clouds of grief. He stood for a moment, a hand on Tarlis to steady himself.

Tarlis, after a time, took a deep breath.

"What...?" he whispered, dropping to his knee as he reached out to Serrah.

463

Her skin continued to redden, the color deepening with each heartbeat. Tarlis reached out—tentative, deliberate—and the instant his fingers brushed her shoulder, his fingertips sizzled and hissed. He snatched back his hand, tendrils of smoke trailing behind it.

"She's burning up," he muttered, half in disbelief, holding out his singed fingers. "Her body... I've never seen the like."

He stared at Emanrasu, jaw slack, eyes wide—sharp and glinting with questions that had no answer. For a breath, time hung suspended between them, held in place by Emanrasu's sorrow and dread.

"What in the Da—"

The explosion tore through the air.

The world convulsed. Emanrasu and Tarlis were hurled across the courtyard like discarded dolls. The earth rose to meet them—and everything went black.

The swirling images of the Dance rushed in and filled the void of his consciousness with the promise of answers but dissolved just as suddenly, returning him to the harsh, biting, crisp cold of the morning.

The cosmic representation of balance to which he was tied provided no relief and served only to engender more resentment in his losses.

Emanrasu opened his eyes and struggled to his feet, taking in the scene and aftermath. The deep thundering boom had sent nearby horses into a frenzy—some rearing, others sprinting away as handlers scrambled to catch them.

The incomprehensible force provided nothing to which he could tie it, and the magnitude of it was similar to the full force of a horse's charge.

He briefly hesitated, filling his lungs with the crisp, cool air, clear but tinged with the acrid and pungent odors of burnt flesh wafting about them.

Moments ago, there had been hope. But now—now only he and Tarlis remained.

Love, Loss, and Zerocha: Chapter Twenty-Four

Of the small group who had departed from Erzt, seeking to protect Serrah from the abuses heaped upon her. Just the two...

The bonds that had formed during the journey, now tattered and torn, seemed to die in the wake of Rezua and Serrah's fall.

*   *   *   *

The handlers of horses and drivers of carts struggled to gain and maintain control of the spooked beasts.

Emanrasu glanced over at Tarlis and, seeing that the old man was moving and not apparently harmed, shifted his gaze to Serrah's body.

The tendrils of smoke indicated intense heat, and Emanrasu hurried over to her, quickly followed by Tarlis. As he drew closer, he could see the charred patches burnt through her tunic and trousers, which produced wisps of smoke.

Then—Serrah breathed.

A deep, shuddering gasp.

Emanrasu dropped, knees hitting the dirt.

Impossible.

He stared and then turned his gaze to Tarlis, who rushed over and, upon reaching her, waved him over.

"Come! Now!" Tarlis exclaimed. He turned to the courtyard and roared, "I NEED A CART, NOW!"

The commander's voice produced instantaneous flurries of action.

Emanrasu, his eyes glued to Serrah as he approached, watched her eyes open as she again gulped in the air her lungs should never have again.

Her eyes opened wide, her hands no longer locked in a grip around her dagger and the piece of cloth. As the dagger and cloth fell to the ground, she ran her hands frantically across her torso where the warrior had repeatedly buried his dagger. She gazed up at Emanrasu, her eyebrows knit, the furrows in her forehead deepening just before her eyes closed, and her body relaxed once more, though now her chest was rising and falling rhythmically.

Tarlis reached down and tentatively touched her. The sizzling flesh from his previous attempt was absent this time, and Emanrasu watched as he reached out and placed his fingertips against her throat.

He gaped back at Emanrasu, and the look on his face was indescribable, his jaw slightly slack. He motioned again to Emanrasu. "Help me!" he shouted insistently.

As a cart pulled near, the two lifted the now-breathing body of Serrah into the cart. "Get her to Torsun, Now! With all speed!" Tarlis told the driver. "You," he said, pointing, "and you, too! Get in and make sure that nothing happens to her along the way."

The two young men remained silent and climbed into the cart. The driver snapped the reins, and the cart lurched forward.

Emanrasu closed his eyes, his chest tight as he struggled to even out his ragged, breathless wheeze, pulling at the frigid air, sharp and biting. It did nothing to cut through the mottled, twisted thoughts churning inside him. His knee buckled, and he lurched, dropping awkwardly to one knee where Serrah had lain.

The ground was hard beneath him, cold and unforgiving. He braced himself with one hand, his breath becoming uneven and ragged as his eyes fixed on the dirt. His thoughts slowed, stumbling and clawing for understanding. She had been here, lifeless. Only moments ago.

Reaching out, he slipped his fingers around her dagger, looked at it without comprehension, then tucked it into his belt and reached out for the fluttering scrap of cloth she had still clenched in her grasp while life had drained from her. As he brought it up, something slipped from the fabric.

Love, Loss, and Zerocha: Chapter Twenty-Four

A soft thud against the dirt.

Emanrasu froze.

His eyes automatically followed the sound.

His consciousness shattered in a burst, swirling as his eyes struggled to focus. Unable to comprehend, his thoughts fractured into incoherent fragments. He stared, his mind grasping, reaching, found no purchase. A wooden pendant lay in the dirt, half-hidden in the cloth torn from the multicolored warrior's garb.

The Phoenix—unmistakable. Exquisite.

Not just... not just a pendant... one of —the— pendants...

His fingers shook as he reached out.

His mind reeled.

The Dance swirled at the edges of his vision, teasing truths just out of reach.

The silky wood was polished warm as breath, and he saw the familiar shield and sword surrounded by Tubatonona script. Flipping it over slowly, he scrutinized the other side.

It was as nondescript as Rezua's, each image simple and basic, except the Phoenix—the intricate details of this one little image, constructed with exquisite craftsmanship, adorned with inset gems.

Such was his anticipated surprise that the pendant slipped from his fingers and landed once again with a dull thump in the dirt.

"What is this?" Tarlis posed the question. He reached down and laid a hand on Emanrasu's back as the latter struggled to gulp in the air around him.

As the world around him struggled back through the abject darkness, he felt the hard, dusty ground beneath him. He opened his eyes to find that he was seated

467

with his legs out in front of him, leaning over with his head almost touching the ground between his knees.

He breathed in, feeling the incredible coolness of consciousness return with a rush. The warm hand on his back shifted.

"Never... never... in all my mains..." Tarlis struggled with his words. "Never have I seen one of your level of conditioning drop so suddenly unconscious..."

"Not like that, in any case or cause."

Emanrasu sucked in the frigid air—sharp, biting—reeling as his mind struggled to understand the thoughts and actions that led him here.

"There was... There was a pendant," Emanrasu stuttered.

The complex thoughts spun once more but more controlled as Emanrasu started to understand the implications of what he saw.

"This one," Tarlis responded, holding out the pendant for Emanrasu.

Taking the pendant, he studied it once more, confirming his earlier observations.

"The Phoenix... it... It is the Phoenix," he stammered in a flat, unemotional tone as his eyes shifted from it to Tarlis.

"Yes, I noticed," said the old man. "Are you going to stay conscious?" he questioned, his piercing eyes digging for an answer.

Drawing a deep breath, Emanrasu felt more controlled and comforted, less confused and out of control.

"Yes, I was... startled... and Serrah... Serrah! I need to see her... I need..." he said as he stumbled through his thoughts.

"I need to know if she is alright..." he trailed off.

"There will be time for that," Tarlis's flat response lifted him from thoughts of Serrah and brought him back into the present.

Love, Loss, and Zerocha: Chapter Twenty-Four

"I need to show you something. If you can control yourself, I have something that may give you pause. I know it did me."

"I will survive, old man. Though I am glad you were the one by my side when I lost consciousness."

Or blacked out, he silently thought. The thought of the Black blacking out brought a smile to his face as he stared up at his mentor.

Tarlis reached beneath his scaled armor.

Fished for something.

Emanrasu's breath caught in his chest as the old man pulled free a pendant— another pendant.

Connections abounded through Emanrasu as he anticipated what the old man was talking about.

The vision of Tarlis, in one fell swoop, grabbing the tunic of Serrah's attacker slipped through his thoughts. Unobtrusive as it was at the time, this old man, this timeless dispenser of wise adages, had sent the man a full four horse-lengths into a wall.

"You... you are the Dragon," Emanrasu stated in one final realization as he stared up at his mentor.

"The strength, the wisdom..." he let it sink in as the sunlight glinted off the scales of Tarlis's armor. "Scales, scaled armor..."

Shaking his head in disbelief, he continued to stare at the old man.

"I would not say that I am the Dragon," Tarlis chuckled as he removed his pendant and held it out to Emanrasu. "...but your grandfather gave this to me many harvest mains ago. He was convinced he was close to fulfilling the tasks of the Dance, but his loss of the Heater and the Hack severed much of the conduit between him and the Dance, according to Onred."

The Heater and The Hack

"I left well before the sword and the shield went missing, so I am taking his word for events that befell the White and the Black after I departed."

Emanrasu turned the pendant over and over in his hand, finding the smooth surface was typical of these pendants. The intricacy of the dragon in Tarlis's pendant matched the exquisite quality of the Phoenix in the one Serrah clutched so desperately.

He closed his eyes to give the concepts time to lumber through his mind in search of a home. Eventually, they came to rest and live beside the immeasurable worth of the Heater and the Hack and his ability to battle master swordsmen and earn their respect.

"We still have many things to discuss, but it would be best to gather the White together to get a full picture," Tarlis recommended. "We are delving into things that I do not understand, and even the White may not all fully be aware."

"Return to Bren and rest. I will return later, and we will make plans then." Tarlis laid his hand on Emanrasu's shoulder, then held out his arm.

"Speak with Boldar and have him set up a large garrison for the next few days. There may be stragglers, and I want to make sure that we do not lose anyone because of laxity."

"I will speak with him. Go, get rest, and check on Serrah," the old man said.

Knitting his brow, he stared at Emanrasu, "And boy… you need to have a long conversation with her…"

Emanrasu tried to smile but lacked the emotions. Instead, he just steadied himself and took Tarlis's arm, gripping it firmly and grabbing the old man's shoulder with his free hand.

Handing Tarlis's pendant back to him, Emanrasu turned and scanned the courtyard for the Heater and the Hack he had so unceremoniously thrown off as he ran to Serrah.

Someone had leaned them against the hearth of the firepit.

He nodded to Tarlis, retrieved the Heater and the Hack, and made his way back to Bren.

His thoughts on the way back swirled and were lost on the road, each visited then left behind for another.

In this manner, the trip to Bren was both an instant and an eternity as he finally dismounted, handed over the reins, and climbed the steps of the inn.

Knowledge of Chaos: Chapter Twenty-Five

"In every life there is that which is unknown, unforeseen, and untold. Our journey is to tell the tales untold, to effectively see the unforeseen, and seek to know the unknown. As one continues down the path of life, do not despair. A heart has room enough for all those who have passed beyond."

—RCotD—

Every story has an ending, and as Emanrasu approached the entrance to the inn, he pondered his.

"Rezua..." Emanrasu shuddered. "I am going to have to tell Serrah about his fall." He dropped his head a little and tried to shake the thought off for now.

In the distance, the howling of dogs married well with the melodic voice of an unknown song. Both echoed and reverberated in a strange, almost foreign language.

"Familiar, but not quite..." thought Emanrasu as he reached for the door.

The door burst open, and Telk stepped out, trailing a line of children behind him.

"Sir," the boy said as he barreled past.

Emanrasu froze; the chill of the air had softened, but the shiver that now ran up his spine ripped through him. His eyes followed the boy...

"...not Telk..." Emanrasu finally muttered. "...similar mannerisms, similar voice... but this boy was smaller, and the hair was the wrong..."

Bit by bit, he picked out the features—his chest tightened, joining the lump in his throat and the weight on his shoulders—hesitantly, he turned back to the door.

A shadow, a reflection, but not the same... never the same.

Telk is gone.

The Heater and The Hack

And now... Rezua is gone, too.

Rezua, who had always been there.

Rezua, who could not—should not—be gone.

Serrah almost joined him. Almost.

Emanrasu took a deep breath to thaw his angst and confusion. He stepped through the open door and was immediately greeted by happy faces and enthusiastic voices.

"Black!" "Bren!" were the most common cries throughout the Great Room. Townsfolk surrounded him, both those who participated in the initial display and those who had taken part in the battle.

Everyone patted his shoulders—or made the attempt—as he gazed around at the sea of smiling faces and shining eyes.

"They seem grateful..." he thought as he clasped arms with many. Still others, he just touched on a shoulder or arm to make them feel included.

"...grateful almost to a fault," he finished the thought as he struggled to move past without ignoring anyone. He lifted his eyes and scanned the Great Room. It was packed full, even more so than he had ever seen it, and the eyes of a great majority were focused on him. As his gaze moved across the room, those who caught his eye lifted a drink or nodded their appreciation. He returned the acknowledgment to each as best he could.

The throng pressed in on him, the inner circle of people changing as he touched and acknowledged each, letting them depart through their friends, only to make room for others. His eyes now flitted from the people around him to the people in the room. He acknowledged them with words and touches, scanning the room, doling out smiles, and returning nods.

"ENOUGH!" a booming voice pierced the din. "Give the man some space!"

Knowledge of Chaos: Chapter Twenty-Five

The throng dispersed, though Emanrasu continued to touch and acknowledge some as they turned away.

"Thank you for that," he said with a weary smile. "I wasn't quite expecting a reception like that."

Torsun smiled at him and nodded in the direction of the bar. "She is back there," the innkeep said with sparkling eyes and grinning lips.

Emanrasu grinned back at him, assuming he could only mean Serrah. He hurried to the door behind the bar and stepped through, slipping past servers and cooks, staring intently at each of them as he passed, trying to recall names or even if he had ever met them.

*   *   *

Shrugging his shoulders and shaking his head, he entered the hall beyond the cooking area.

"Mommy, mommy, it's the black man..." Kaurin screamed to her mother, her growing grin and squinting eyes never looking away from Emanrasu as she edged slowly back toward the door, where she hesitated.

"Hello, black man," she said as she curtsied awkwardly. "How are you today?"

Emanrasu smiled, and though he really wanted to see Serrah, he couldn't resist.

"I am doing wonderfully, little Sky," he said as he bowed.

Kaurin giggled, turned around, and ran back through the door to the room.

"Mommy, he remembered! He called me Sky!" she exclaimed, the elation bright in her voice.

Emanrasu drew a deep breath, briefly soaking in the joy of the moment. As he came even with the doorway, he glanced in and caught Arianis's eye. He waved to her but continued past to the next door.

The Heater and The Hack

The door was closed.

Emanrasu paused, still basking in the laughter of Kaurin and Arianis as the aroma from the scullery wafted throughout, growing progressively harder to ignore.

The floor creaked as he shifted his weight back and forth as he turned to the door.

He raised his hand and knocked.

"Yes?" came the query from within.

"May I come in?"

A flurry of activity from inside produced no answer—until the door flung open and Serrah launched herself at Emanrasu, accosting him with an overzealous embrace. The force of her hug drove him backward, and only then did he catch sight of Kaurin, who had silently snuck up behind him.

Twisting to avoid stepping on the girl, he tried to redirect Serrah's momentum—but overcompensated and lost his balance. Her force, unabated, sent them both sprawling. Emanrasu narrowly missed Kaurin as he and Serrah tumbled into a heap.

A delighted shriek from Kaurin—and the thump of hurried footsteps—brought Arianis rushing into the hallway.

Serrah, now face-up beneath Emanrasu, wasted no time. She hugged him close, stunned him with a quick kiss on the lips, and then promptly pushed him off and sprang to her feet.

She coughed, turned away, and only then saw Arianis standing nearby, grinning ear to ear.

Serrah buried her face in her hand and let her hair fall forward, but the flush in her cheeks was not so easily hidden.

"Um..." Emanrasu said from the floor. "I think you've just made my first twenty questions completely redundant."

Knowledge of Chaos: Chapter Twenty-Five

His heart, buoyed by her actions, floated on a sea of resplendent relief. He reached up to her, and she took his hand, helping him to his feet.

Kaurin tugged on Arianis's sleeve, and as she leaned down, the child cupped a hand and whispered, "She kissed him!"

Arianis placed a gentle hand on Kaurin's head and guided her back toward their room, though Kaurin struggled to glance sideways at Emanrasu the whole way.

"But Mommy…"

The soft click of the door closed the scene and left Serrah and Emanrasu alone in the hall.

Serrah glanced down the corridor, then turned and—more gently this time—wrapped her arms around him and squeezed.

Emanrasu held her, and he made no move to let go.

At last, she released him and took his hand, leading him inside. The simple tunic she wore was typical of the ones he had seen in the past, and the colorful red and yellow one lay on her bed, spread out with needle and thread nearby.

"Are you…" Emanrasu started.

"Fixing my tunic? Yes…"

"No, are you…"

"Hungry? Tired? Glad to see you?" she riddled him with responses, followed by answers. "Yes, a bit. I thought you would get the hint in the hall, but yes."

"No, are you…" He paused, waiting for her interruption.

Serrah stared at him.

"Are you well?" he finished. "The last time I saw you, well… before that… you were not doing very well."

"I am doing fine; I feel very well."

She quickly gathered the sewing and, rolling it, placed it to the side on top of a small dresser. Sitting down, she patted the bed a little way away.

Emanrasu reached into his tunic as he sat down, pulling out the Phoenix pendant and holding it out to her.

Staring at it, she reached out tentatively and lifted it from his hand. She shifted her location to position the pendant under the sunlight streaming in through the window.

She studied it for a long while, eventually wrapping the string around it and holding it out to Emanrasu.

"I saw that man wearing this, and I felt as if you would want it," she said. "It seemed somehow connected with the Dance. I know that you have an intimate connection within it."

"Do you understand what happened to you?"

"Yes, the man struck me several times, knocking the wind from me. But I managed to dispatch him with one of my knives," she said, her gaze flitting around the room. Her eyes settled, and she reached over, retrieving a knife from beneath the tunic on the dresser.

Emanrasu reached into his tunic and, as she continued, he pulled out her other knife. "I am not sure where... Oh—thank the Dance..." she said.

"They were a matched pair from my father," she held them up side by side, showing the similarities.

"Thank you for returning them. I was afraid I would never get it back." She said softly.

Knowledge of Chaos: Chapter Twenty-Five

"After I managed to take care of the man who attacked me, well... I know that before I passed out—you were... crying... I think, and Tarlis kneeled next to you. He said something about being family, which made me feel good."

"Anything else?"

"Well," she said, a grin playing on her face, "maybe... I think you said something, but I could not quite make it out."

"Oh," Emanrasu said, his head and heart sinking.

Serrah scooted closer to him and took his hand. She pried it open and gently placed the pendant in it.

"Why, was there something else I should have heard?"

"Um, well..." he took a deep breath, his eyes darting to her face and then away.

"I... I love you."

His unfocused eyes gazed at the pendant as he spoke, "I think from the moment I saw you at the inn.

"You captured me from the first day." Glancing up, he took her hand. "Every day since has just served to tighten your grip on my heart."

He placed the pendant in the palm of her hand, his eyes welling up as he recalled the worst moment of his life.

"You were dead, Serrah. Your blood... the man did not hit you; he stabbed you, repeatedly... over and over..."

A tear escaped and slipped down his cheek, followed by another and then a third.

"I could not stop him, Serrah..." He looked at her, locking eyes.

"I could not save you," he grimaced, then swiped at his tears. "But you... you saved yourself. Your instincts told you to get the pendant. I believe that is why... that is what..."

He paused and took a deep breath. "I believe that it was intended for you all along. The Dance... they have human representatives, people that embody the essence of each aspect of the Dance.

"Telk must have been the Sky... but he passed it on to Kaurin, knowing his actions from that point would result in his death. He passed the Sky to Kaurin, and her mother... she—already—had the Earth! She already—was—the Earth."

Serrah sat, listening intently. They held hands as he continued.

"You were gone. Your breathing stopped, and the wounds quit spouting blood. Tarlis confirmed this as well. And then...

"...and then there was some sort of explosion, as if life itself had burst, and...

"...you breathed again. The Dance be praised, you breathed again.

"We practically threw you into a cart and sent you back to Torsun."

"That is when I found the pendant you had been clutching... it had been hidden within the cloth that was torn from the warrior's tunic when Tarlis..." he shifted slightly, "Tarlis threw him: with one hand, he lifted the man and threw him three or four horse-lengths into a wall—into a wall!

"Serrah, Tarlis... he is the Dragon—The—Dragon. He has the Dragon pendant! How could I have not seen it?"

Emanrasu shook his head as he recalled.

"All this while... Tarlis..."

Emanrasu patted her hand, which was still wrapped around the pendant.

"You are the Phoenix, Serrah. Just as I missed the signs for Tarlis, I missed the signs for you. Every time you left and had to restart your life, every time you chose to transform into something different, something better.

480

Knowledge of Chaos: Chapter Twenty-Five

"It was always you: it was your choices that molded your destiny, just as mine have molded mine."

"I believe you," Serrah said. "…but I couldn't have been dead. I had the wind knocked out of me… anyway, I was very groggy and disoriented when I got back, and it was then that Rezua visited me, all in bright white garb, mind you. I guess his new tunic was soiled or something. He stood there just in front of the window."

She motioned to the window, which overlooked clotheslines upon which hung linens and clothing.

"He told me that I would be okay… that choices have been made, but the choices are our own. He didn't stay long, and he said, 'I have to go now, Serrah. You shall have your time with Eman once he returns. I know his heart and soul have been rended and returned to him, so just remember me to him and know that I will forever watch over you both.'

"I closed my eyes; I was so tired, and when I opened them, he was gone."

Emanrasu's heart sank as the emotional extremes of this day kept ripping him apart.

"Rezua… Serrah—I am sorry… Rezua is dead. I watched him drop from a crossbowman's bolt, deep in his chest. He fell, lying still and lifeless as the battle raged around him.

"I went back to find his body later, but he had already been gathered amongst the dead and transported back with the wounded, even before you were attacked."

Serrah stared back at Emanrasu, her eyes blank and her face expressionless as she locked eyes with him.

"…but he was here. All in white…" She paused, then slowly continued as tears welled up in her eyes. "I remember… I even joked about it not fitting him."

The Heater and The Hack

They sat together, holding hands without talking for a long while, each in their own thoughts.

"I mean... he was glowing in a way... I don't know..."

Dropping her head to her chest, Serrah quietly sobbed.

Emanrasu let go of her hand, reached out, and pulled her to him, encircling her with his arms. Her heartbreak reached into him and once again squeezed out tears he thought had been exhausted.

After a long while, Serrah stopped weeping, and they just held each other until Serrah gently pushed him away.

"I am tired and want to rest," she said.

With a hesitant sidelong glance, she continued, smiling. "...and you need a bath."

She held a finger up under her nose, making her words painfully clear. She snorted a chuckle, and they both broke into laughter, which helped release the last vestiges of abject sorrow from Emanrasu.

"He is best remembered as he was and how he died," he told her. "He was a great friend, a scholar of untold proportions, and immensely helpful in every way."

Grinning at his description of the large man, he added, "and hugely protective; falling in defense of Bren is a way he would have chosen."

Emanrasu stood, gave her a final tentative hug, and made his way back to the Great Room, where, once again, it took Torsun's firm words to unpack the swarm, allowing him to mount the stairs to his room.

*   *   *

Emanrasu paused at the door, took a deep breath, and entered the room that he and Rezua had shared.

Knowledge of Chaos: Chapter Twenty-Five

Someone had laid Rezua's battle-stained garb over one of the chairs, with his pendant and journals stacked reverently on the table.

"I miss you already..." Emanrasu whispered, picking up the pendant and feeling the smooth surface and the intricate design. "...why?"

His finger traced the writing on the surface of the journal as he sounded out the unusual word written there, "Recoated, rehcotted, reckouted... Tubatonona... I will miss him," he thought as his finger ran over the smooth surface.

A single tear broke free and stealthily snuck down his face. Emanrasu placed the pendant on the table and picked up the journal.

As large as it was to him, he imagined it was small to his bear of a friend. He thumbed through the pages, looking at the writing, but the watering in his eyes blurred the pages.

Within, he let his hand slide over the smooth parchment of the first page. Through his tears, he could make out the first part.

> Peering intently down the street, the sun well overhead at apex, Emanrasu smiled.
>
> His overly large friend, Rezua, squatted...

He took a deep breath, wiped his eyes clear, and flipped to the back of the journal.

Confusion sprouted as he read the last entry of the book.

> Serrah raised her arm weakly, her grip unrelenting as her fingers still clamped tight around the ragged piece of cloth. She gently coaxed him closer into a hug, the hug he had so desperately wanted before all of this. He held her close, her shallow breathing getting weaker by the moment. He could only say the one thing he had struggled not to say.
>
> "I love you," came the whispered admission. "I don't know why, but from the moment we met in the inn—me, a wandering idiot with a silly quest,

and you, working beneath your skills as a maid—since that very day, you have always been in my heart."

As he read, his confusion grew. Someone had written about his intimate interaction with Serrah.

"Perhaps as a last acknowledgment of the… his… important, yet understated role in the group," he thought. It was almost irreverent but perhaps unintentionally so.

He read on.

> As she struggled to focus on him, her eyes streamed tears steadily down her face. "I know," she mouthed. Her body relaxed, her eyes ceased to focus as the last breath seeped from her, and she grew still.
>
> Her eyes, once glassy orbs of exquisite beauty…

Emanrasu's eyes grew wide, and his mouth gaped slightly. His mind raced wildly at this last description. This image, burned into his mind at the loss of Serrah, could have been seen by no one else.

"There is… it is…" he said aloud, stuttering half to himself. "…it is impossible… she…"

His mind struggled to comprehend how this could have been possible when he heard a scuffle out in the hall. The door burst open just as his sword, snatched from the sheath, came level with a bare chest. A prominent bruise located above the man's heart trailed a neatly sewn slice that made its way across his chest and above the nipple on the other side.

Throwing up his arms and showing his palms, the massive tent-sized towel dropped to the floor while twig-and-berries still indecently swung from the recent movement.

Emanrasu followed the impossible expanse up to the face, just as…

Knowledge of Chaos: Chapter Twenty-Five

"Sorry I startled you. I stumbled outside as I was opening the door…" Rezua said, looking down at the blade.

Glancing back into Emanrasu's face, his visage drew taut, and his brow knit.

"Were you weeping? What is wrong? Did something else happen? Were you reading my journal? Can I pick up my towel? Is the sword really necessary?"

The barrage of questions continued until the sword clattered to the floor, and Emanrasu reached out and, throwing his arms around the immense expanse of nakedness, hugged his friend.

His loss of words that caught in his throat was only matched by his feelings for Serrah and the realization that she would be the Phoenix.

Rezua pushed him away and retrieved the towel from the floor.

"I know you must have thought I was dead, Eman, but I had no way of letting you know the truth of it. By the time I came to my senses, I was being jostled about in one of the carts as they ran a needle in and out of my chest," Rezua said as he ran his sausage-sized fingers over the thin line across his chest.

"I went and saw Serrah; she seems extraordinarily well, all things considered."

"But is this your writing? How?" Emanrasu stumbled on each question, falling into the next as he struggled to understand. "Why would you…

"You couldn't have known; you were dead! Well… I thought you were dead, but in any case, you were not… there…"

Emanrasu stood dumbfounded, his eyes fixed on the big man.

Rezua raised a finger. "Give me a moment…"

Rezua slowly struggled to dress but succeeded in slipping on trousers and a tunic. He retrieved a couple more journals from his pack and returned to the table, sitting in the large chair.

The Heater and The Hack

Motioning Emanrasu to sit, he opened up a journal and read the first passage.

> The sky, a bright blue that faded into purples, reds, and yellows, peeked through only in patches amidst the foliage while sunlight struggled to stream through the leaves of the canopy created by the forest.

He glanced toward Emanrasu. "Do you recall when I wrote this?"

> …silently illuminating the road; sparsely it lay, here and there, the bulk of the road hidden in a ragged cloak of blackest shade. The forlorn trees murmured quietly in the whispering wind as they stretched their boughs eagerly across the furrowed…

Rezua brushed something off the page and continued.

> The dirt, rutted and gouged unevenly, filled with gashes from the wheels of many a cart and wagon. The stark and stoic road, soft as freshly kneaded dough from the recent soft sprinkling of rain, had the musty earthen aroma…

He finished and peered at Emanrasu. "I told you I was documenting the journey." He flipped a couple pages.

> …faithful scribe entered the clearing, scanning it deliberately. His eyes fell upon Emanrasu, sleeping soundly in his roll. His weapons were close at hand, as always, the steel and tinctures glinting in the gathering dusk.

"After I wrote this, you told me to quit being so epic. So, I struggled, but I think I have become a decent writer over the last few moons."

The big man grinned and turned a page.

> "I am not sure we want that version to become known. We both know that is not the way it happened.

Knowledge of Chaos: Chapter Twenty-Five

"You saw... had I not had luck on my side that night, we might both be lying on the blood-soaked ground," Emanrasu said, correcting the tall tree-with-a-quill.

"It's called poetic privilege, Eman, you know that—at least..."

"After that, I tried to stick to more straightforward and less complicated prose, but every now and again, it seems to slip back in.

"I always thought I made most of it up, just taking poetic privilege. But this morning..."

Rezua waved his journal around, gesturing animatedly as he spoke, pausing only to emphasize a point or when he stumbled upon something revealing. Then, with a sharp motion, he slammed the journal down on the table. He winced, sucking in a breath, then rolled his shoulder, stretching his bruised muscles with a grimace.

"...this morning, I visited Serrah, and she told me some of what happened. It all fit what I had written. I asked her about being stabbed and dying, but she didn't seem to recall any of it. So, I did not press her..."

Rezua slowly closed the journal, his hands lingering on the worn cover before he lifted his gaze to Emanrasu, his expression shifting from disbelief to something far more confident and certain.

"She's the Phoenix, and Tarlis is the Dragon..." His breath hitched. His fingers pressed firmly against the leather of the journal, as if grounding himself. Then, with a sharp exhale, he looked directly at Emanrasu.

"I see these things... Eman, I... I —see— these things!"

"I see your dreams of the Dance. I thought... I thought it was just me... filling in random things, but this morning... I knew she died and came back, even if she didn't. How is that even possible?"

Emanrasu stared at the enormous, foreboding enigma.

The Heater and The Hack

"Eman, today, I thought I was a dead man. The last moment of watching the bolt hit my chest," he reached up and ran his fingers over the thin red line and the stitches holding it together.

"I had a dream of my own, just like what I had been imagining yours were like."

"The swirling colors coalescing into the Dance." Rezua shook his head in a slow, even motion.

"I will not bore you with the entire conversation, since almost all of it is already documented from your dreams, but there is one thing I never realized."

"Wait," Emanrasu said, his brow growing even more crinkled than previously. "You can see the future?"

Rezua reached up and lifted the pendant off his neck, slipping it out of his tunic. He held it out, showing Emanrasu the back.

"Inscribe the past... understand the future... It isn't about seeing into the future or about foreshadowing events... it's about knowing what must be done because we have documented the struggles we had to go through! It is about hindsight, not foresight!"

"This is the only thing on my pendant that is different. I studied it in excruciating detail after my dream. The writing on the back doesn't match the simpler writing on Kaurin's or Arianis's. The writing on my pendant is ornate and exquisitely crafted, and somewhat out of place against the simplicity of the rest of the pendants. Well... the pendants we have seen so far, anyway."

"This confirmed what the Dance told me." He set the pendant down in front of Emanrasu.

After a short pause, Rezua told him, "I am the Chronicler."

He reached over and closed the journal Emanrasu had opened when he first came in, and Rezua poked a sizably meaty finger at the writing on the outside.

Knowledge of Chaos: Chapter Twenty-Five

"RCotD…"

"I wrote that upon all of my journals after getting back."

With typical Rezua flair, he stood, struck an imposing stance, and exclaimed, "I am Rezua, Chronicler of the Dance."

He grinned, and his eyes lit up like the spark of the fire plants. He reached out and grabbed Emanrasu's shoulders.

"Do you know what this means?" He shook Emanrasu, punctuating each phrase. "Eman, I am connected intimately to your journey! And I thought I was just a guy in the corner of your epic journey!"

Rezua let go and dropped back into his chair.

Emanrasu, his mind suddenly buried in the silt of unbelief, stared at his exceptionally large friend. His fingers tightened around the edge of the table, steadying himself against the onslaught of unrelenting realizations.

The thought… Rezua alive…

The thought ripped through him. "Rezua and Serrah are both alive!"

Serrah and… Serrah!

"The Dance! I told Serrah you were dead."

The words fell from his lips like stones, each heavier than the last. The weight of them settled in his chest, pressing, suffocating. He had told her Rezua was dead. He had held her as she grieved him. And now—

Rezua was standing right in front of him.

He exhaled sharply, rubbing his face with both hands, trying to force his mind into order. This changed everything. And Serrah—

"I have to tell her…" he breathed, barely above a whisper. Then, louder, more certain—

The Heater and The Hack

He looked up into the face of his gentle giant. "Rezua, we... I have to tell her.

"... and this conversation is not over," he pointed at his huge friend. "There isn't... I mean... I have... I have too many questions, and things have... I don't know... snuck up on me or something. I feel that things are moving too fast to understand coherently."

Emanrasu stood.

"Come with me, she will need... well, she is going to need to see you herself."

Rezua stood and sauntered over to his bed. He reached down and folded a great expanse of bright white cloth.

Emanrasu pointed to him, then to the cloth, then back to him. "Were you... earlier, were..."

"Yes," Rezua said, "for some reason they stripped me down when they stitched my gash. Instead of trying to help me put my tunic back on, they just threw this over me. I wore it until I got up here to take a bath."

Rezua scrunched his nose as he finished, "which is probably something you should consider sometime soon."

Emanrasu shook his head. "I am almost afraid to go anywhere or say anything... or even look at anything... nothing is as it seemed yesterday. Or even this morning."

"I feel like I might go down and have a conversation with Boldar, and he turns out to be my grandfather, the Black. Or the horses in the barn are just masquerading as unicorns or some such.

"Or... or even see Telk come slipping up behind us." Emanrasu sighed. "I miss the boy..."

"Yeah, I know... so do I," Rezua admitted.

"Rezua, Chronicler of the Dance," Emanrasu repeated, the words feeling both strange and familiar on his tongue. He stared down at the journal, his finger tracing the letters once more.

"It's funny," he said softly. "When I first saw it, I thought it was... something else. A word I didn't understand."

Rezua smiled, an unmistakable glint of mischief in his eyes. "Maybe it was, Eman. Or it could be that you just weren't ready to see it yet."

Emanrasu opened the door and glared at Rezua. "I don't want to cheapen the... but I really do need to know... do you see me all the time... I mean... when I duck behind bushes and relieve myself? Do you see everything?"

Rezua grinned with a wink as he walked by, his silence speaking nothing and volumes simultaneously.

"Well?" Emanrasu asked as Rezua slipped past him and out the door.

Pulling the door, Emanrasu continued, "I really think you need to..."

The simple wooden door latched with quiet finality. The firm thunk, deep and resonant, echoed with lingering defiance, like the last note of an ancient song swelling through the fabric of time. Chaos and Order—forces that once raged endlessly against each other—now struggle, bound beneath the edicts of the Dance's eternal Balance.

Epilogue

Emanrasu watched as Rezua sat down and pulled out his writing utensils. He broke out a journal, worn and ragged, and opened it. The journal bore no external markings, just as with his documentation of the Dance.

As Emanrasu continued to follow his friend's every move, Rezua looked up. Their eyes locked, and Rezua grinned.

"I write about other things, too! It is much like having things you love to do, but in a way, you find you're also doing it as a part of your job. Like a blacksmith that makes exquisitely detailed swords and armor all day long... but at night he just wants to make a few horseshoes."

He opened his journal, and as Emanrasu watched over his shoulder, Rezua began to write.

"The constricted confines of this illustrious journalistic endeavor have made it clear that the magnitude of this mythical adventure cannot be contained within the gentle, cradled bindings of a single manuscript. The historical writings I am penning must continue across one, or possibly two, more volumes, striving to illuminate the cosmic forces that tear at the fabric of the world, demanding sides be taken. So, with the gathering of the Cadre, I sense the defense of Balance begins in earnest.

The Black and the White, tasked with recovering the relics of the Tubatonona, face an unrelenting challenge as the Surge of Chaos rises. Clad in their vibrant and defiant colors, the warriors of the Surge vie for these relics, seeking to fracture the Balance of the Dance.

Ahead lies the inevitable confrontation: the Surge of Chaos and the Order of the Hold, each striving to unravel the intricately woven tapestry of Balance and claim dominion over its scattered threads."

—RCotD—

The Heater and The Hack

Rezua sighed and looked up again.

"With this journal filled, and the journey to the Zerocha house complete, I probably should write something about why I wrote the journals. What do you think, Eman?"

"You probably need to make sure the ones who read it understand the limitations… and probably the fact it is kind of a historic document. But let's face it… you are much better at this than I." Emanrasu grinned and poked his friend.

Emanrasu watched as Rezua, once again, put pen to paper and began writing.

"The Heater and The Hack – Chronicles of the Dance -:- RCotD Tome I

Prelude:
As I set ink to parchment, I carve into the annals of existence the historic context of what has unfolded within this tome—a record, immutable and unyielding, for all to see and know. In dreams, I am as a bird upon the wing or a cloud adrift, an observer …"

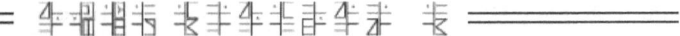

About the Author

Les Waggoner's journey into writing wasn't a straight path—it was a winding road paved with history, philosophy, and a lifelong love of storytelling. Inspired by classic authors like Roger Zelazny, Stephen R. Donaldson, and J.R.R. Tolkien, he spent years (mains) exploring ideas and narratives, never expecting they would coalesce into a novel.

A veteran of the U.S. Armed Forces, his time stationed abroad sparked an enduring fascination with duality—the tension between opposing forces, the interplay of chaos and order—concepts that would later form the foundation of his writing. A passion for heraldry, history, and symbolism further enriched his worldbuilding, culminating in his debut novel, The Heater and The Hack.

At 58, he finally put pen to paper, transforming decades of ideas into a living, breathing story. Now, he writes not just to entertain but to challenge perspectives, expand minds, and invite readers into a world where balance and brilliance intertwine.

May the Dance guide your journey.

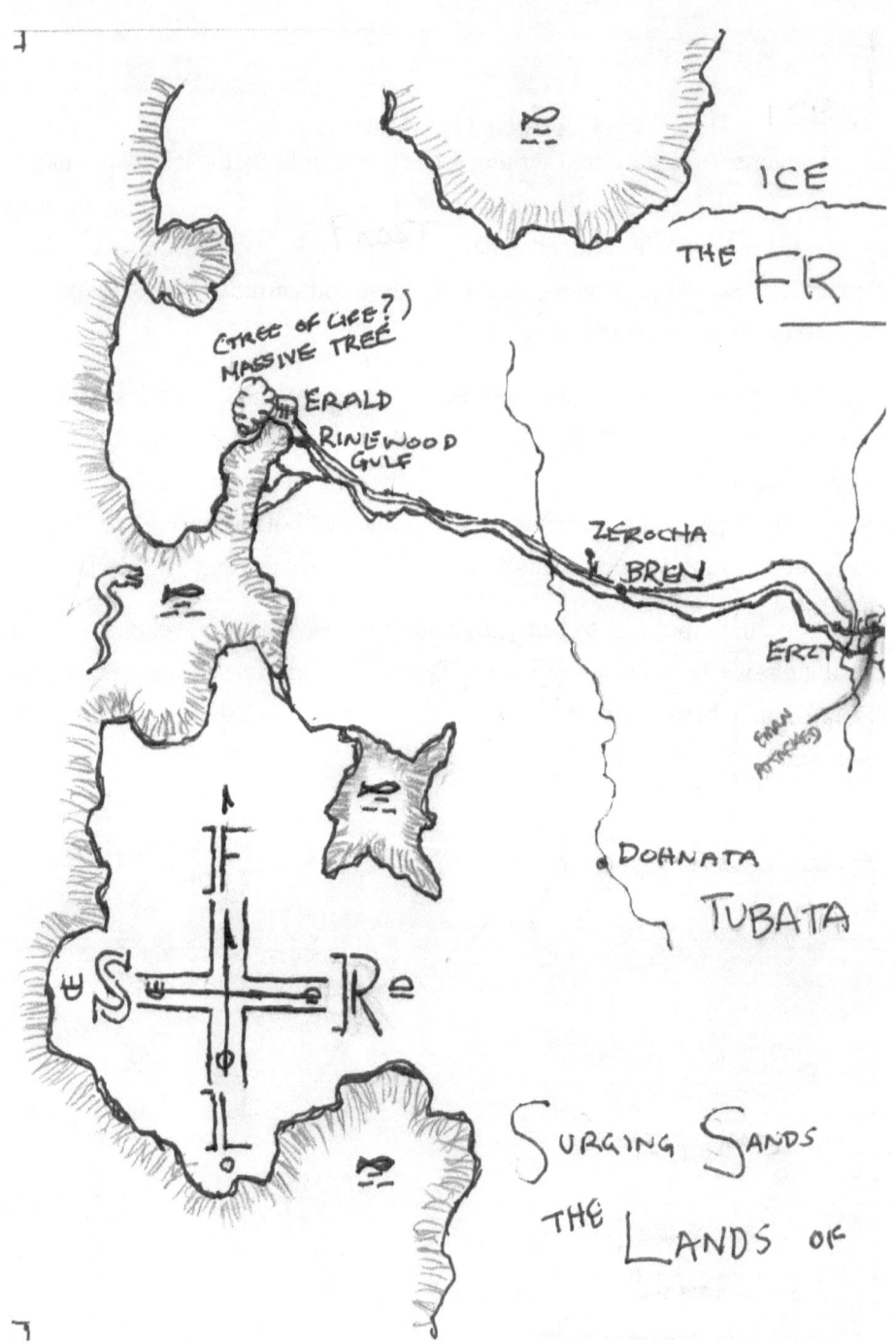

ICE

THE FR

(TREE OF LIFE?)
MASSIVE TREE

ERALD

RINEWOOD
GULF

ZEROCHA

BREN

ERZT

(FARM
ATTACHED)

DOHNATA

TUBATA

SURGING SANDS

THE LANDS OF

ICE SPIRE

FROST RIDGE

OST

TOTHIS

RINTHA

ROSEWOOD FOREST

ARIS

ELLND

MOUNTAINS

KRELISH

W RINTH – ROSEWOOD 12d
R.?? ROSEWOOD – ERZT 1d
C ERZT RISE TO CROSS 4h
C CROSS FROST TO FIELD 2h
C SET TO POND 1-2F
C TO CAMP ON FARSIDE 1F
    OF POND
C POND TO BREN 2M
    CROSS BROKEN LAND
H BREN TO ERALD 3d
W ERALD TO BREN 7d 2h
F BREN TO ERALD AND
    BACK HERE DONE
    WITH EXTENDED TRAVEL
    USING SPARE HORSES
    (TO SPELL PRIMARIES)

FLIGHT: 100 STRIDES
TEFLIGHT: 10 FLIGHTS
TWEFLIGHT: 2 TEFLIGHTS

WALKING: 7-8 TF PER HAND
RUN: 14-20 TF PER HAND
HORSE WALK: 7-9 TF PER H
HORSE RUN: 50-60 TF·H
HORSE TROT/WAGON: 30-45 TF
OX CART ON ROAD: 3-4 TF
OX CART OVER BROKEN LAND: 5F-2TF

MAP IS INACCURATE
BUT GIVES A GENERAL FEEL
LIGHT IF YOU CAN DO BETTER: DO
WE NEED A TRUE CARTOGRAPHER

The Heater & The Hack Reader Contest

Official Essay Contest Rules & Terms

1. Overview & Purpose This contest is designed to encourage thoughtful reader engagement, deep analysis, and inspire deep engagement with The Heater and The Hack.

We're looking for essays that explore the novel's themes, characters, structure, and emotional resonance—whether it moved you, challenged you, or left you asking questions.

If you can prove me wrong or show me something I missed—you're already a contender.

2. Eligibility

- Open to all **readers who purchase a physical copy** of *The Heater and The Hack.*
- **eBook readers may participate but are not eligible to win prizes beyond Honorable Mention** unless proof of purchase for a physical book is provided.
- **Public reaction post:** Entrants must post a note, reaction, or review on a **publicly accessible platform** where it can be viewed by others (e.g., Amazon, Goodreads, a blog, Reddit, social media, or a forum).
- Entrants must be **18 years or older** or have **parental/guardian consent**.
- **Family members, close friends, or individuals affiliated with the author are NOT eligible** for the general contest but will be eligible for the friends and family contest.
- **One entry per person is allowed.** If an entrant wishes to submit a **revision**, they may submit **one revised entry** that **explicitly states** it supersedes the original submission. Any entrant submitting more than one entry without a revision statement will have all entries disqualified.
- Entries must be **original work. AI-generated content or plagiarism will result in immediate disqualification.**

3. Submission Requirements

- **Legal Name**
- **The name you prefer we use for publication** (e.g., instead of Leslie R. Waggoner III, you may prefer L.W., L. Waggoner, or Feldon Carter).
- **Shipping Address**
- **Deadline:** June 1, 2026.
- **Word Count:** 750–2,000 words.

- **Accepted Formats:** PDF, Word document, or within the body of an email.
- **Proof of Purchase Required for Prize Eligibility:** A photo of the physical book with a digital order confirmation or a store receipt.
- **Screenshot or picture of a note, reaction, or review:**
    - The review or reaction must be posted on a **publicly accessible platform** (review site, blog, forum, or social media) and must include a **visible URL** in the screenshot.
    - *The post must remain accessible through the end of the contest.* If the original post is removed before the contest deadline, **entrants must notify heaterhackcontest@leswaggoner.com with a new post and updated screenshot** to maintain eligibility.
- **Submission Email:** heaterhackcontest@leswaggoner.com.
- **Subject Line Format:** "HH Novel Essay Contest Entry" or "HH Novel Friends and Family Contest Entry"

4. Judging Criteria Essays will be evaluated based on:
- **Engagement & Depth** – The extent to which the essay engages with the novel's themes, characters, and underlying messages.
- **Emotional, Intellectual, or Spiritual Impact** – The ability to convey how the book resonated with the reader.
- **Reader Impact & Reflection** – The essay's ability to provoke thought and discussion.
- **Originality of Thought** – Unique perspectives, insights, or analysis.
- **Writing Quality** – Clarity of ideas (polished prose is not required but strongly encouraged).

5. Excluded Criteria: Essays will NOT be evaluated on the following criteria.
- **Positivity or Negativity** – Entries will not be judged based on whether they express a positive or negative opinion of the book.
- Praise and critique are equally valid.
- A thoughtful criticism may rank higher than uncritical praise.

6. Prizes
- **Grand Prize:** $200.
- **Second Prize:** $100.
- **Third Prize:** $50.
- **Runners-Up (2–5 selections):** No cash prize but may receive signed books or special mention.
- **Honorable Mentions:** Recognition for essays demonstrating strong engagement but not placing.
- **Chronicler's Choice / Author's Pick:**
    - Winner earns the right to **collaborate with the author** on a **piece of lore** for a future book.

- o OR may **write a short story** to be included in the author's book of short stories.

7. Legal Considerations

- **VOID WHERE PROHIBITED.**
- **Entrants are responsible for ensuring participation is legal in their country, state, province, or locality.**
- The author is **not responsible** for any legal restrictions that prevent participation.
- If an entry is **disqualified due to legal restrictions,** the entrant **forfeits eligibility.**
- No purchase refunds will be issued under any circumstances.

8. Intellectual Property & Rights

- **Entrants retain ownership** of their essays and are **encouraged to publish them elsewhere.**
- By submitting, entrants **grant the author a perpetual, non-exclusive license** to publish their essay **with full credit.**
- If essays are included in a **future published collection,** entrants will **not receive monetary compensation.**

9. AI & Plagiarism Policy

- **AI-assisted writing is strictly prohibited.**
- Suspected AI-generated content may require **additional verification or rewriting** before being considered.
- **Plagiarism will result in immediate disqualification.**

10. Winner Announcement & Prize Distribution

- **Winners will be announced by July 1, 2026,** on leswaggoner.com.
- **Winners will be contacted via email.** If a winner does not respond within **10 days,** an alternate winner may be selected.
- **Monetary prizes will be paid via PayPal, check, or another mutually agreed-upon method.**
- **Physical prizes (e.g., signed books) will be shipped free within the U.S.**
- If an **international winner** is selected, alternative prizes may be offered due to shipping restrictions.

11. Discretion Clause

- If **no entries meet the judging standard,** the contest **may be extended or adjusted** at the author's discretion.
- The author reserves the right to **modify or cancel the contest** if unforeseen circumstances arise.
- All changes will be **published on the author's website,** www.leswaggoner.com.

12. Privacy & Data Handling

- **Personal information will only be used for contest purposes.**
- The author **will not share or sell personal information** to any entity **without express, personal written consent**.
- Entrants' emails and mailing addresses will only be retained for **contest-related communications and prize distribution**.

13. **Judging Process**
   - **The contest will be judged primarily by the author.**
   - The author **may, at their discretion, include additional judges to assist in evaluating entries**.
   - The **final decision** remains **solely with the author**.

Final Notes & Encouragement This contest is designed to encourage **real engagement** with *The Heater and The Hack*. Whether the novel resonated with you, challenged you, or left you with lingering thoughts, this is your opportunity to explore and articulate your experience.

Depth matters more than praise. If you noticed something in the novel that others might miss, your insights could be especially valuable.

Any additional clarification required will be done by the author and displayed online at https://leswaggoner.com/the-heater-and-the-hack-essay-contest/

I look forward to reading your entries.
Leslie R. Waggoner III–www.leswaggoner.com | heaterhackcontest@leswaggoner.com

This contest is subject to all applicable federal, state, and local laws and regulations. It is **void where prohibited by law**. If any jurisdiction prohibits contests of this nature, residents of that jurisdiction are **not eligible** to participate. It is the entrant's responsibility to ensure participation is legal in their place of residence. The author and affiliated parties are **not liable** for entries disqualified due to legal restrictions.

If any provision of this contest is found to be unenforceable or invalid, the remainder of the contest rules will still apply in full force. This contest is **not affiliated with, sponsored by, or endorsed by any retailer, platform, or publishing entity**.